FANGS & FINS

BLOOD, BLOOM, & WATER BOOK ONE

AMY MCNULTY

CHAPTER ONE

EMBER

Someone must have invented sweat-resistant business suits.

Because I had no other explanation for why these movers were all dressed like they were about to hold an 8 A.M. conference in a boardroom overlooking Manhattan.

"How can they see where they're going?" asked Ivy across the kitchen table, her slightly husky voice low. She held a torn-off chunk of bagel halfway to her mouth, her jaw hanging open as she stared at them.

There was that, too. All of them wore sunglasses. Sunglasses and suits. I supposed they looked more like bodyguards than businessmen. Which made even less sense.

"Don't stare," said Ivy, averting her eyes as one guy—he seemed younger than many of the others, but who could tell behind those shades?—breezed past her and deposited a big brown box with "Kitchen" scrawled across the side atop the already-cluttered counter.

"Oh! Sorry," I said, jumping up and running to grab the assortment of half-used dish towels, dirty dishes, and junk mail covering the counter. "I guess we should have cleaned this stuff up." I locked eyes with him—or I think we did, as his sunglasses turned my way anyway—and something like fire shot up my body.

I couldn't even see all of his face, but somehow, deep down in my bones, I could tell he was hot. I had a knack for that. I'd yet to translate said talent into anything resembling a boyfriend or even a date past that third grade social Mom had forced our then-neighbor's son to accompany me to. But I sure could pick them. In my head.

I broke off our stare first when Ivy cut between us and pulled open a cupboard. "Since you had, like, zero notice before three people moved into your house, I think you get a pass." She frowned, shutting it and opening the next one.

"A glass?" I asked, moving around her to pull open the proper cupboard. The hot mover guy stepped aside and headed back toward the hallway leading to the propped-open front door, but he did linger slightly, his head turned over his shoulder. I wished I could see his eyes. My instinct was telling me they were sexy and vibrantly colored—whatever color they may have been.

"Thanks," said Ivy, but there was a smirk on her face when I turned back to face her. I realized I was holding the glass I'd taken out for her in the wrong direction. It was a hair's breadth from clinking against the window over the sink overlooking our backyard and the line of trees that led to the woods behind our property. That was what I got for staring after Mr. Sunglasses Mover instead of watching what I was doing.

"Sorry," I said, handing the glass over. Ivy approached our fridge and made herself at home, pulling out the orange juice her dad had put in there the night before. Apparently, she and Autumn liked the pulpy kind, which meant we'd now be stocking two types of OJ in our already-crammed shelves.

It took me a moment to remind myself that she was making herself at home *because* this was her home now. Her dad was going to be here all the time, and she and her sister were going to live here half the week. *Her* sister. My sister. My step-sister anyway. Ivy Sheppard, one of the most popular Union High students, was now my step-sister.

True, it hadn't happened until I was eighteen and a senior in high school, but at least I could say I'd finally had my wish granted and gotten a sister. There was Daryl, Dad's son from his first wife, but since Dad was mostly out of the picture, Daryl was no more than a distant blip. He'd friended me on Facebook a few years ago, but we commented on each other's posts so infrequently, Facebook had long ago decided not to bother showing us each other's posts unless we somehow managed to get enough likes to make the algorithm blow up. And since my life had practically zero "blow up" moments to it so far, well...

"If I never have to move again, it'll be too soon," muttered Ivy as she pulled the glass of orange juice away from her lips. A blur of white in my peripheral vision caught my attention. My black-spotted white cat—*our* cat, now, I supposed—had braved coming out from the basement despite all the activity to pick at his breakfast. "Did my dad mention that my mom just moved over the summer?" Ivy asked, crouching to pet Arty—short for "Artemis"—on the head. He stiffened but allowed himself to be pet as he chewed and she stood again, shuddering before downing the rest of her glass, making it look like she'd had to steel herself before ingesting the drink. That was how I would have felt if I'd been drinking pulpy OJ. "I know college is right around the corner, but man, am I done with packing up two sets of everything. Whatever I can't fit into an overnight bag isn't coming to college with me."

"Do you know where you're going?" I asked. "To college, that is?" I took the glass from her and flipped it over to place it in the top rack of the dishwasher. While I was at it, I did my belated daughterly duty and started loading the rest of the dishes waiting to be put inside, too.

"No," said Ivy, her full, bright red lips frowning. "Though not for my parents' lack of nagging." Her eyebrows scrunched together as she crossed her arms and glared at me. "Do me a favor and never bring up college around my dad, okay? It seems to engage his 'get child to get serious about applications' protocol."

I laughed. "Sure."

Ivy watched me a moment more and then picked up a dirty

plate. *Ivy Sheppard* was helping *me* with chores. "And you?" she asked. "Thought I better ask before Dad walks in and gets reminded I'm less than a year away from adulthood and still none the wiser about my plans post-Union High."

"Bradview," I said, referring to the small liberal arts college about ninety minutes away. "I'm already accepted."

"Ah," said Ivy, a flittering smile appearing on her face. "That's right. Dad said Noelle's 'kid' was bright. Full scholarship, right?"

"Well, a good scholarship," I admitted. "It covers most of tuition, minus room and board and all that."

"Lightyears better than I could do." She wiped her hands on a towel, and I took note of the chips in her dark blue nail polish. "I think even Bradview is out of my reach."

I bristled somewhat at "even Bradview," but I didn't say anything. So it wasn't as prestigious as an Ivy League or as fun as a state college. The campus was cute. And it had courses that interested me. It boasted a ninety-two percent job placement rate. It was more than good enough, right? My best friend, Journey, refused to believe my choice had had anything to do with something other than how close it was to home. My mom would be lonely without me... At least that was what Journey had said before Mom's whirlwind romance. Now she had three daughters and a second husband. Her world no longer began and ended with me.

"I'm sure that's not true," I said, not letting my drifting thoughts stop me from responding.

Ivy laughed wryly. "Next time we get report cards, I'll show you."

"Oh, you don't have—"

"Where did you find these guys?" boomed Easton—Ivy and Autumn's dad, my step-dad—as he entered the room. The cat shrieked at his sudden entrance and bolted back down the basement stairs. Easton stared at my poor, overwhelmed furball with a curious expression, but he didn't say anything. He had on a dress shirt and finely pressed slacks, but his tie hung loosely on either side of his neck and his sleeves were rolled up. "The Secret Service?"

He watched two of the moving men as they passed through the hallway, a curio cabinet balanced almost completely levelly between them.

"I let my secretary handle the arrangements," said Mom as she scooched around the movers, her purse held high above her head, to join us in the kitchen. She had on her weekday face—makeup that was subtle but flattering—and the ashen blonde hair she shared with me was arranged into bun perfection behind her head.

"Morning," she said, and before I could reply, she pecked her lips to Easton's.

Right. Morning to him *first...*

"Morning, sweetheart," she said, tapping her fingers to my back lightly before she reached around me to grab her stained coffee mug. "Morning, Ivy. Where's your sister?"

"Probably still in bed."

"She better not be," said Easton. He squeezed my mom's shoulders and went to head toward the stairway, almost smacking head-on with one of the movers clutching another box marked "Kitchen."

"Whoa, buddy," said Easton, spinning to try to avoid him and tripping over his own two feet.

Before Mom could do more than gasp, the mover had let go of the box, wrapped an arm around Easton's waist to pull him upright, and then caught the box before it had dropped more than two inches.

Oh. Mr. Seems-Younger-Hot-Stuff is back. And he has got some moves.

"Well," said Easton, clearly a bit flustered. He reminded me of a teenage girl for a second. "Thanks, bud. Quite a set of hands on you there."

The snort that Ivy let out was enough to draw everyone's attention, even the sunglass-donning mover.

"Here, let me," said Mom, pushing forward to take the box from the mover. But he held tight.

"No, ma'am," he said, and his deep voice sent a jolt to my legs. They went wobbly like JELL-O. "Policy is the customer doesn't handle it until we've put it down safely. I don't want the boss saying I wasn't cooking with gas."

Mom looked at him like he had a screw loose—he probably did, given his choice of attire while performing physical labor—but pointed to a free spot on the table. Easton disappeared down the hallway, calling Autumn's name up the stairs.

"That's quite a uniform you all wear," said Mom, always eager to fill any prolonged gaps of silence. "Doesn't your dry cleaning bill get a bit out of hand?"

"*I'm* surprised none of you pass out," added Ivy as she crossed the room to grab her purse off the table before the mover could squish it with the box. "Or bump into something."

The mover's lips turned up slightly in a smile. "They're for protection," he said, tapping one of the temples of his glasses before digging both hands into his pants pockets. "I don't go anywhere without my cheaters. UV rays are bad for the eyes." He jutted his chin toward the hallway, which was filled with light from the propped-open front door.

No one could argue with that. Unless it was to ask what "cheaters" even were. I supposed the context made it obvious: sunglasses. And why did none of them take the sunglasses off once they got inside? Then again, they had their hands full.

I was making excuses for a moving company's bizarre attire choices.

Easton came back in, Autumn stomping her feet behind him.

"Thank you for choosing our company," said the mover. "I'm heading off shift, but Leopold will finish the kitchen." He looked over his shoulder. "I think we're almost finished."

"I don't want to go to school unless I find my hair tie," whined Autumn as she crossed in front of him, plopping herself down at the table.

Ivy sprang into action, standing behind her sister and gathering her long, dark brown hair into a ponytail. It was clear they were sisters. Autumn was like a mini-Ivy without all the makeup. The only difference was the color of their irises: Ivy's were deep blue, whereas Autumn's were pale brown.

"Didn't I tell you to put your most important things in your tote bag?" asked Ivy, leaning forward to look Autumn in the eye, her own brown ponytail whipping her face.

"I *did*," said Autumn, huffing. "Dad *lost* the tote bag."

"I did not lose the tote bag," said Easton as Mom stepped forward to tie his tie for him.

"Thank you," said Mom to the mover, who nodded curtly before making his exit. I hadn't moved from my post against the kitchen sink as this had all unfolded. I couldn't take my eyes off him, and I thought—for at least half a minute—maybe he was keeping an eye on me, too. But I couldn't say for sure with those dark lenses.

The minute he turned the corner, I spun around to face the window over the sink. It was hard to make out my reflection, but I saw enough to know my hair was still a mess. That was what I got for coming down for breakfast before I swapped my flannel pants and baby tee for something resembling out-of-the-house attire.

"I told you to put it in your car," said Autumn from behind me.

"I did," said Easton. "Ivy, honey, are you ready for school yet? Ember..."

I spun around, not used to my name on my new step-dad's lips yet. Not used to this whole father-daughter thing at all, really. Though I supposed I was too old now to get much of it. "Yes?"

He looked me over quickly and grimaced. "Are you... ready for school?"

In my pjs?

Mom laughed as she patted his chest, his tie tight around his neck and his sleeves halfway rolled down. He was coming together as a proper office worker, though he had nothing on the sleek attire of the movers. "Ember, go get ready for school," said Mom. "You're going to be late."

"Right," I said, squeezing my palms together. I'd lost track of time in all the bustle. I was used to a quieter home. A *much* quieter home. Not that I was complaining necessarily. It was just different.

"Ember, please don't be late," reiterated Mom. "Ivy's counting on you."

I scooched by without comment, avoiding the boxes starting to spill into the kitchen from the hallway. Supposedly, Easton, Ivy, and Autumn had downsized their things in preparation for moving in with Mom and me in our slightly bigger home, just like we'd done a few Goodwill runs to prepare for it. If they actually had downsized, I'd have hated to see how much they used to have.

"It's no big deal if she needs a few more minutes," said Ivy, no sense of bitterness to her voice. She undid her hair and slid her own ponytail holder around Autumn's hair. "Here, nut. You can use mine."

"I want *mine*," said Autumn.

"This is the same thing," said Ivy. She leaned down and whispered into her ear and Autumn nodded.

I felt like I was intruding, so I headed toward the stairs, squishing against the banister to let more of the besuited, bespectacled men past. I didn't think I imagined their heads turning my way as I did. I *was* wearing my pjs, but considering they were the ones in suits lifting a dresser, I'd have to say I reserved the right to be flabbergasted they'd care.

I whispered "excuse me" and decided to ignore the stares.

"*Christopher Columbus*," said one of the men quietly—so quiet, it was almost like he hadn't intended for me to hear. "Where's Dean?"

"He's heading off," said the other as I reached the third stair. "He took note of them."

I froze. *Took note of what?* It went quiet then and I realized that these guys weren't even breathing hard, like the dresser held aloft between them was nothing more than a bag of groceries.

"Miss?" said one, speaking loudly. "We need to get past."

"Right," I said, putting my feet into action. When I got to the landing, I stepped aside and watched as they breezed up the stairs and into my old playroom, which Mom and I had cleared out for Autumn.

Nope. They didn't even break a sweat. No wonder they didn't dress pragmatically.

"Ember!" shouted Mom from downstairs.

I ran into my room and shut the door, pulling out black leggings, a striped skirt, and a navy blue sweater. I changed quickly —I usually showered at night—and ran a brush through my hair. No makeup. The few times I'd tried it, for dances and such, it had itched. And no one had even noticed the difference. So all that was left was a stop at the bathroom to brush my teeth. It was going to be hard getting used to sharing the bathroom with two new sisters —it already was, thus the fact that it was so nearly time to leave and I still wasn't ready—but they were already downstairs, so it was finally my turn. My bladder uttered a "hallelujah."

"We're leaving!" shouted Mom up the stairs after I'd finished in the bathroom. "Have a nice day, honey!"

Easton was taking Autumn to school and Mom was off to work herself. That meant the movers would finish up the job with no one in the house, but apparently, Mom's assistant had already arranged for them to lock up and drop by the office with the house key.

It all felt a bit dodgy, but that was what happened when your parents got married on a whim a few months after they'd started dating and your new step-dad's house sold in two seconds flat. They'd thrown together a small courthouse ceremony on Saturday and had spent all last week getting ready for the move.

I went back to my room to grab my backpack where it hung off the back of my desk chair. I was about to turn to go when I froze. One of those suited movers was in the backyard—walking into the little woods back there that belonged to our neighbor.

"What the heck...?"

The movers had no business in the backyard. And certainly not on the neighbor's property.

I blinked. Maybe I'd just seen things. Or maybe this crazy moving company just happened to employ some really nosy, inappropriately dressed young gentlemen.

"Ember, we going?"

I took a deep breath. *Right.* Off to school with one of the coolest girls I knew.

"Coming!"

When I saw what might have been a flash of green light from the woods out of the corner of my eye, I brushed it off as an eye floater.

Maybe if I hadn't, I would have been better prepared for how my life was about to turn upside down and sideways round.

CHAPTER TWO

IVY

My new step-sister was slower than a grandma on these back roads. It was unclear why she'd chosen the back route when we were running a tad late, but she was the model student, not me. I couldn't care less if I was late for Mrs. Marton's European history class. She was so used to me sleeping through it that she might not have even noticed if I wasn't there with my head on the desk in the back row.

"Sorry," said Ember, biting her lip. She hunched forward over the steering wheel, her hands clutched rigidly at three and nine. All she was missing were the buckets of sweat. "I don't usually leave so late."

"It's been a hectic few weeks," I said, drumming my fingertips against the passenger side window. "Dad and Noelle should have let us make a long weekend of it. Though I could see Mom making a fuss about that."

"That must be hard," said Ember, inevitably getting to that topic of conversation everyone gets to when they find out you're a fifty-fifty kid. "Spending half the week in one home and half the week in another."

"And don't forget the rotating Wednesdays and holidays," I added, knowing that if I didn't, she'd probably bring it up next. I shrugged. "Once in a while, I miss something I left at the other house or get annoyed at how much longer it takes to get to school from Mom's, but it's fine. Autumn's my constant. And I have both parents in my life."

"Right," said Ember, her voice going soft. *Oh.* Here I was getting annoyed at the divorce topic, when she didn't even have a weekend dad.

I thought better than to ask, but she told me anyway.

"I only see my dad once a year or so," she said. "Sometimes he comes into town on a whim and calls me from a motel."

"That sounds..." I heard my phone buzz from my purse, but I thought it impolite to check it just then. First ride to school with the new step-sister and all. "Hard," I finished. "If someone called me out of the blue like that, I don't even know if I'd be free to go see him. I'd be like, 'Uh, thanks, but I have plans. With people I actually see on a regular basis.'"

"Well, I... I'm not always so busy." Just then, Ember braked a little too hard as a light turned yellow, and I could see in the side-view mirror that we came dangerously close to getting rear-ended.

"Whoa," I said, my hands instinctively spreading out toward the dashboard. "Sometimes it's safer to go through yellows, you know? The car behind us planned to go."

"Sorry," said Ember, shirking. She adjusted the rearview mirror as if she needed to see traffic behind her more clearly. Clearing her throat, she tapped the steering wheel as the traffic crossed the intersection in front of us.

"No, I'm sorry," I said. "I don't mean to sound like your driver's ed instructor."

"I'm the one who... Do you have your license?" she asked.

"Yeah," I admitted. "Just no car." And no car insurance and mechanic bills and yeah, it was a pain, but I wasn't about to get a car to get to the job I'd need to get the car and have significantly less time with all my friends.

"You can drive mine sometimes," she said. "Why don't we switch? Like you can drive us on the way home today."

"Oh," I said, twirling a strand of hair around my finger as the light turned green and we were off. "Thanks, but I'm probably getting a ride home with friends. We usually hang out after school."

"Right. Of course." Ember chewed on her bottom lip. "I should have known."

"I don't mind switching driving duties with you in the morning," I said, "but that's only if you're sure you're comfortable with it. It's your car."

"It's Mom's car, actually," she said. "She paid for it. And pays for the insurance and everything."

Ah. That explains why no one's said anything about Ember having a job. I knew Noelle was kind of a big shot in our nowhereville small town—Dad met her at one business meeting or another—but her house, while lovely, wasn't quite a McMansion. It was a little old, even—though layers of remodels were evident in expansions like the modern bathrooms juxtaposed against the vintage, scratched staircase railing. I supposed it couldn't have been cheap to own all that land, though. "We'll ask her, then."

"She won't mind," said Ember, smiling but focusing entirely on the road. "Now that you're her daughter too."

I winced instinctively as I tried to ignore the vibrating of my phone. I couldn't help but notice that Ember's, tucked into the console, had only buzzed once since we'd left.

"Are you going to Homecoming?" asked Ember, though I could hardly see the segue. As she executed a turn, she seemed tense. It reminded me of how aunts and uncles without kids talked to you, like they were searching for something to say.

"Yeah," I said, "probably. Though I haven't gotten a dress or anything." With the whirlwind of Dad putting his house on the market and the marriage and moving, I'd skipped more than one shopping trip with my friends that would have afforded me the opportunity.

"Who are you going with?" asked Ember.

"Just friends," I said. "A few guys asked, but I've been there, done that." I shrugged. "Dates kind of take the fun out of it if you're not that into the guy." We were nearing school now. This wasn't the route I was used to taking, but I could see the clearing of the football field a few blocks down the road. "How about you?" I thought to ask finally. "You going?"

"I wasn't going to," said Ember. There she was, talking like a nun in a library again, her voice just barely above a whisper.

"Why not?" I asked, genuinely curious.

"No one to go with."

I didn't know if she meant no date in particular or no friends. I wondered what mine would think if I added her to our party. It wasn't like she was a pariah or anything. I just didn't think anyone thought much of her either way. When Dad had told me Noelle's daughter's name and that she went to Union, too, I'd had to really think hard to picture her. And then I'd realized we'd had some classes together throughout the years and I ought to have known who she was right away. She did well in school, apparently, but she wasn't even the know-it-all talkative type who dominated class debates and discussions. She was pretty quiet during class.

"What about your friends?" I asked.

"I might go with Journey," she said, and it clicked after half a minute that she must have meant Journey Slowe, a cute but nerdy and bubbly girl who kind of overpowered any conversation she inserted herself into. Now that I thought harder on it, there was always this pale blonde wisp of a specter-white girl hovering a few paces behind Journey. From gorgeous braids to an eclectic fashion sense that always complemented the deep brown of her skin tone, Journey simply overwhelmed Ember at every turn.

"Are you and Journey close?" I asked.

"She's my best friend," said Ember. "Our moms were roomies in college and now her mom is head of marketing at Mom's company and her dad and grandma's restaurant is one of Mom's biggest customers. You know, that old-fashioned diner off Park Road?"

I nodded, thinking of the desolate strip of the occasional store and the one diner on the outskirts of town. *That* was Noelle's best customer? One of these days, I'd have to ask what it was Noelle did exactly, besides employ half the town and dip a toe in the rest of all the business going on here.

We pulled into the school parking lot then and immediately got caught up in a traffic jam caused mostly by teenagers who were embarrassingly slow to pick up their feet. I couldn't blame them since school was what awaited them once they quit the lot, but we'd gotten enough lectures about immediately exiting our vehicles after parking to constitute a course itself. I got my phone out then, finally thinking it less rude to get in touch with everyone. I waved at Grey and Paisley as we passed them. They were sitting on Grey's trunk, their arms woven around each other's waists.

"After you're done hanging out... wherever," said Ember as we pulled into a spot, "why don't you ask your friends over to our place? We have a roomy backyard and sometimes, when I think Mom's not looking, Journey and I go for a short walk in the woods. They belong to one of our neighbors, really, but it's not like their house is in sight of the entire line of trees."

Ember's idea of a good time was sneaking into a woods an acre or so behind the safety of her nice, big house. I laughed. "Sure, maybe sometime," I said. "But we should probably get everything unpacked first before I have company. And Dad isn't keen on friends at the house on a school night if we're not doing schoolwork."

"So we'll say we're doing schoolwork," said Ember, turning off the car and dropping the keys into the front pocket of her backpack. "That's what I tell Mom whenever Journey comes over. It's half-true anyway."

"Well, I don't know about today," I admitted. "But thanks for the invite." Opening the door, I grabbed my purse and tote bag with my books, notebooks, and tablet. "See ya," I said, and before I could hear her response, Lyric appeared out of nowhere, draping an arm around my shoulder.

"So how'd it go?" she asked, her voice lowering as she leaned into my ear. We kept walking, putting plenty of space between me and my step-sister. "Your new family driving you crazy yet?"

"Not anymore than the family I already had," I said. Her arm dropped as we stepped up beside Grey and Paisley.

"Congrats," said Paisley.

"On what?"

"Your dad getting married." She leaped down off the car. "And moving and all that."

"Thanks," I said, not sure if "congrats" was the right word, but whatever.

Grey jumped down beside his girlfriend. "Yeah, congrats." He sounded *so* enthused. Before I could acknowledge him, he jogged over toward Ashton's car, which was just pulling into the lot.

"Hell-o," said Lyric, and I immediately knew that tone.

"What happened to you and Raelynn now?" I asked, well aware that Raelynn wouldn't stand for Lyric "cheating with her eyes," as Rae called it.

Lyric snorted. "Nothing. Girl's already inside, though, so no one's going to know, so long as neither of you tell her." Her eyes widened pointedly at Paisley and me in turn.

"Scout's honor," said Paisley, doing the Vulcan salute. Paisley got things like that mixed up sometimes.

I laughed and noticed Lyric staring off over my shoulder— whoever it was who'd caught her eye, they had to be pretty hot. She was nuts for Raelynn—they'd been dating for almost a year— even if she still liked "window shopping."

A man in a suit. And sunglasses. A young man, I supposed. Surely not a student? What was with that "bodyguard" look today? He had a couple of books dangling from a strap he gripped tightly in one fist, but he sure didn't look old enough to be a father to a teenager, either.

He stared in our direction as he passed. I thought he was going to do the "lower the shades and check out the ladies" thing, but he didn't. He just stared pointedly, his head clearly turned in our direction.

"Lyric gets all the interest," muttered Paisley.

"Grey's probably happy with it that way," I said, nudging Paisley with my arm. She was short, so my elbow practically smacked into her shoulder.

"I don't think he's checking *me* out," said Lyric. "Ivy...?"

"*Yeah right*," I said, but I could feel my face flushing. "Why would he be...?"

But he headed inside the school then, his sunglasses pointed at us until the last minute, oblivious to the whispers and stares of all the people around him.

"Is he blind?" asked Paisley, and she meant the question genuinely. He didn't have a dog or a cane with him, but he hadn't taken his sunglasses off before stepping inside.

Then it hit me. "I think that's his work uniform," I explained, the strangeness of it all hitting me harder than it had that morning. "He's a mover."

That brought up a lot of questions I didn't have any answers to.

CHAPTER THREE

EMBER

"Em! Tell me you had time to watch *Riverdale* this weekend." Journey had begun two school days last week asking me if I'd gotten around to watching it and I'd had to remind her that no, Mom had sucked up all my free time with clearing out the playroom and guest room so my new sisters could have their own spaces. Then there were the texts on Saturday and Sunday—Journey's parents had taken her on a short weekend trip to Chicago for a food services conference her dad had needed to go to. The wedding had been so last minute, even Journey and her parents hadn't shown. It had just been us girls and our parents at the courthouse. Mom was holding a celebration in the backyard later in the year once everything was settled. But in any case, I was days behind with my DVRed shows and had little hope of catching up until things had settled.

"No," I said, shutting my locker and leaning back against the cold metal. "I'm going to have two episodes to watch at this rate."

Journey bounced in place, clutching her tablet tightly against her chest. "Oh my god, you don't know how hard it is to keep from spoiling you." Her eyebrows furrowed. "How on Earth have you kept from being spoiled?"

"I haven't been online much." It was true. Between the wedding and all the getting-to-know-each-other b.s. from the day before, the most time I'd had to myself had been in the bathroom. And even that had seemed more rushed when an eight-year-old was pounding on the door to let her in.

Journey took a timeout from hyperventilating at the prospect of not being able to discuss one of our shows with me to cooly and calmly say "hey" to Dante and Avon, her cousin and ex respectively, as they nodded curtly her way. They loved her—everyone who knew her did—but they were doing their best to seem cool these days and they strolled though the hallways with slow, measured steps and their heads held high, their shoulders thrown back, like they had all the time in the world.

Journey let out a sigh of impatience as we headed off to class, and for a second, I thought she was reacting to the boys' brush-off, but no, it was back to TV. "I just... wish you'd managed to watch it. You won't *believe* what happened."

"Mom made Ivy and Autumn and me hang out all weekend," I said, hoping that would be the end of it. I *was* dying to know what happened, but it would just have to wait until I got some peace and quiet. My new step-sisters spent half the week with their mom, although I couldn't remember whether or not she had them this Wednesday. I knew she was supposed to have them all of Saturday, but she'd dropped them off—her mouth in a thin line, her workout clothes at odds with Ivy's and Autumn's dresses—at the courthouse and they'd spent the afternoon and evening with us to celebrate our parents' impromptu wedding.

"So how did that go?" asked Journey. She'd already solicited my opinion on the nuptials by text and her mom and mine had had a long conversation Sunday morning via phone all about it, so it made sense that she would care more about my take on the new relations than on the lackluster wedding itself.

"Fine," I said, and I meant it. "It's been hard adjusting to all the noise and having so many people around, but I bet things will settle down nicely once everything's unpacked."

I froze. Coming down the hall from the administration office was a man in a suit and sunglasses carrying a small pile of books by a leather strap.

Everyone was staring at him—overtly or less obviously, heads turned, glances tossed over shoulders.

Journey had gotten a few steps ahead of me before she, too, jerked to a halt. "What the...?"

She'd voiced what I'd been thinking, but the thing was, there was more to it than the oddity of his appearance. I knew this man. This heart-fluttering rush of heat coming up from my toes. This was the hot guy from this morning. Who'd put in an hour shift moving boxes and furniture in a suit and sunglasses and then hopped on over to Union High for a day of school. Because that made sense.

I opened my mouth when I swore I caught him staring in my direction, but he moved quickly and my line of sight was soon blocked by a small crowd of students who crossed the hallway.

"Hey, Journey!" said one, a girl I was pretty sure was named Lyric, who walked sandwiched between a girl whose name I forgot and Ivy. Ivy quickly smiled as she caught my eye and nodded, and I felt a jolt at being acknowledged by her, even if for a second. I hadn't really paid *too* much attention to her until Mom had told me the name of the daughter of her boyfriend-turned-one-week-fiancé. But I mean, I knew of her. Everyone knew about her. And Lyric and the girl whose name I forgot and the whole baseball team that acted as their entourage.

"Hey, guys," said Journey, her attention immediately drawn away from Secret Service student wandering the halls. I didn't stop thinking about him, though—but I couldn't find him with all the people milling about. First period was due to start in just a few minutes. "Paisley, you do okay on that assignment?" Somehow, despite having a calendar booked through next decade, Journey often managed to be a tutor. "Tell your mom I *loved* that Homecoming dress she made for you!"

The girl whose name I forgot nodded and waved as the group passed, her boyfriend's arm never moving from around her waist.

"Speaking of," said Journey, "please tell me you've decided to come."

"I don't see the point," I said, keeping my eyes peeled for suit boy but resigning myself to the fact that he was gone. "No one will go with me."

"*I'll* go with you," said Journey, not for the first time. "I've been so busy with tutoring and Model U.N. and volunteering, I haven't had time to ask anyone."

"What about Avon?"

She snorted. "*No.*"

I hadn't meant because she was nuts over him or anything—I knew she was crushing on Devam Kapoor these days—but because it hadn't been a bad breakup. Maybe they could go as friends.

I'd say then maybe she could ask Dante to take me as a favor, but there was no way he didn't have a date by now. It was less than two weeks away.

"Besides, even if I wanted his puffed-up behind on my arm, he's going with Misa."

"Misa Caperton?"

"What other Misa is there?"

I shrugged. I didn't exactly keep track of all of the thousand or so kids who went to Union High. Although Journey probably actually did.

"So *anyway*," said Journey, "that means I won't leave you high and dry like you always seem to think I do."

"I've never said such a thing—"

"You've never said it, but you certainly project it." She stopped to take a sip of water from the water fountain, saying *hi* to yet more students I barely knew. "You know, if you talked to people a little more, you wouldn't go to every dance stag," she said, wiping her mouth. "Dante told me that lots of guys think you're hot, but you're also kind of..." She didn't explain what I was "kind of." Blushing at the thought of Dante thinking I was hot, I didn't feel up to asking.

Dante had danced with me before. Only at Journey's behest. And he'd seemed bored the whole time, eager for the song to end. So I doubted very much he thought I was hot.

I was just tired of getting all dressed up, taking lots of pretty pictures, carefully eating food while avoiding staining the uncomfortable, slinky gowns, and then literally sitting on the sidelines of the dances, waiting for Journey to stop by and drag me onto the dance floor for the fast songs.

It wasn't that I *needed* a boyfriend, but if I did have one, I wouldn't feel so dumb sitting every slow song out.

"Fine," I said, tired of both Journey and Mom nagging me about it.

"Fine what?" asked Journey.

"Fine, I'll go to the dance..." I knew that even without a date, Journey wouldn't be sitting out many dances, but even so. Maybe Ivy would want to go dress shopping with Mom and me or something. It'd be dumb to go dress shopping and not have a reason to buy a dress.

"Yay!" said Journey, and she threaded her arm through mine just as the first bell rang overhead. "We're going to have so much—"

She might have said "fun," but my brain rattled around my skull just then, so it came out kind of blurry.

I felt Journey's arm swapped for strong hands on my shoulders. They gripped me tightly, practically keeping me from falling over.

"I'm so sorry," said a deep voice. "Are you okay?"

Some guy was holding me up. He had on a letter jacket, jeans, and a gray T-shirt. His short, blond hair looked to be comprised of wet, solid spikes.

"Ember, cripes, do you have a concussion? Are you made of stone, Calder?"

Things were starting to come back into focus for me and I noticed Journey gazing at the guy's face and then his chest. There were some rock-solid abs there, as my forehead could now attest. Literally rock-solid.

He gingerly pushed aside some of my hair, his fingers grazing my forehead as he stared down at me then like I was some sort of specimen. "I'll walk her to the nurse's office."

"I'm fine," I said, trying to twist out of his grip. He let me go, but the second I wavered just a bit, he swooped in to steady me.

"I'll go," said Journey. "I mean, it can't be serious, but—"

"What happened?" I felt like I was missing something.

"We turned the corner and you slammed straight into Calder Poole," Journey explained.

I had no idea who she was talking about. Other than this guy, obviously, but who *was* this guy?

Journey filled in the details I didn't even ask. "Junior. Swimming team?"

Nope. Not swimming a bell. I giggled a little. Not *ringing* a bell.

But with his green irises, all full of concern, staring me down, he was ringing my hot-guy sensor. I might have been the slightest bit loopy, but *that* was certainly intact.

"I can do it," he said. "It's my fault. It was almost time for class and I wasn't watching where I was going."

The bell rang overhead. *Oops.* I'd never had a tardy.

Journey growled and stared upward, like she could pinpoint where the bell was and snarl at it for not caring that I was about to faint from slamming my forehead into a young hunk's pecs.

"Go," said Calder. "And explain what happened to Ember to the teacher."

Ooo, he knew who I was?

"What about your class?" she asked.

"I'll deal with it later." He put a strong arm around my shoulder and started guiding me back toward the direction of the administration office, where the nurse's office was. I tried to avoid ever going there. Viruses and bacteria and blood and all that.

Journey bit her lip but then nodded. "I'll go tell her, but I'll see if she'll let me meet you there."

"I'm *fine*," I said, my head already getting clearer. "It's just a bump. Go to class." She did as asked. I ran a hand over my forehead as I watched her go and flinched. Even if it was a small bump, there was clearly a bruise there. Right after I'd decided to go to Homecoming after all. Perfect.

"I'm sorry," said cute-but-too-young-for-me Calder as we made our way to the realm of colds and flu and communicable diseases just waiting to happen. The hallways were so different between classes, so empty.

"It's fine," I said for the millionth time. "I'm fine. I'm sorry."

We walked in silence for a few minutes, though I was so close to the tall underclassman that I swore I could hear his rapid heartbeat.

"Ember, do you...? That is, are you...?"

Whatever he had to say, it just wouldn't spill out. I felt my palms getting sweaty then. Was he asking me to the dance? He knew my name. Maybe he'd watched me from afar for ages just out of the range of my hot-guy-sensor and I hadn't even seen him in the shadows. Maybe this morning's little round-the-corner "accident" hadn't been an accident after all, but an excuse to get me alone. Sure, just bruise and concuss the girl you have a crush on to get her all to yourself, then ask her out. Super romantic.

But dang it, I just might take him up on the offer if he can ever get it out of his mouth. I couldn't let him know he was the first to ever ask me, either. *Play it cool, Ember.*

"Do you have passes?" asked a woman as we got nearer to the nurse's office.

"I'm just taking her to the—"

Calder grew tense and his feet stopped moving so quickly, I nearly toppled over. Almost as an afterthought, Calder thought to grab hold of me tighter and bring me back to standing.

My head swimming, I noticed the woman in front of us at last. Pale, voluptuous, her bright red hair pulled tight into a bun at the back of her neck. She had on a dark navy business suit and criminally-high heels and... She was wearing cats-eye sunglasses.

Rather than finish his sentence, Calder let go of me then and *ran* down the hallway in the other direction. Ran like the woman was chasing him instead of simply staring stiffly in our direction, a clipboard in hand.

So much for my secret admirer escort.

CHAPTER FOUR

IVY

"Grey, *stop*. That's gross." Paisley scrunched her nose up as she stared at Grey beside her. He was trying to make the guys laugh by dangling strands of spaghetti in the air above his head and slurping them down one by one.

Naturally, it *was* making the guys laugh. Because even junior and senior boys had the mentality of kindergartners.

Instead of kowtowing to her sense of reason, Grey brought his latest sloppy red strand closer to his girlfriend's face and made a point of ingesting it as disgustingly as possible, his jaw opening wider, revealing the mess of food inside his mouth as he chewed.

Paisley shrieked and I had to look down at my phone, about to gag. This was why I had no interest in a boyfriend. What did my friends see in each other is what I wanted to know. Besides the sex, I supposed.

That was all they really saw in each other, wasn't it?

"So how do you like your new mom?" asked Raelynn, pointedly covering the side of her face and staring right at me so she wouldn't have to get a look at what Grey was doing.

"She's all right, I guess," I answered. I wasn't that close to Raelynn, so she probably didn't *really* care, but what else did you talk about with someone whose dad on a whim sold his house and got married and forced two new family members on you in a matter of weeks?

"She has a new sister, too," added Lyric as she wove an arm around Rae's shoulder. Lyric ate like a bird, picking at her salads and greens like she was grazing. I supposed that made her more like a goat. But her vegan diet and track team exercise paid off in her tall, lean, muscly frame. Not that there was anything wrong with curves, mind you, but I'd almost be willing to give up grilled cheese if I knew I could feel as fit as she did. Almost.

"Oh?" asked Raelynn. "How old?"

Lyric snorted and I scanned the cafeteria to search for signs of said sister. Part of me was worried she'd sit with me and make things awkward for all of us, but the other part of me knew that was bitchy and was determined to let her if she asked. Fortunately, she hadn't.

"Eighteen, I think," I said, finding her next to Journey Slowe and nodding toward her. "Ember Goodwin."

Raelynn glanced over her shoulder to get a good look. "Journey's quiet friend?"

"That's the one." Sufficiently distracted from whatever antics were still going on at the other end of the table, I'd regained my appetite and tore off a piece of my grilled cheese to dunk it in my tomato soup. The soup tasted like SpaghettiOs without the pasta, but after what Grey was doing with his pasta today, I might not have been able to stomach noodles for the foreseeable future regardless.

"She's a total geek, right?" said Lyric. It was more a statement than a question.

"I guess." I dabbed my lips with my napkin and took a sip of my milk. The little container didn't hold much and my straw was echoing out already. "We haven't spent much time together without the whole family."

"There's nothing wrong with being good at school," said Raelynn, and she was clearly miffed, like Lyric had insulted her. She *was* better than most of us at school and I think she was in Model U.N. or Debate Club or something.

"Yeah, yeah, you little geek." Lyric ruffled her hair, which made Raelynn blanch as she quickly moved to try to smooth it again. Lyric kissed Rae's cheek. "But you're *my* geek."

Now Raelynn's pale brown cheek flushed. It was probably her Irish dad's blood in her.

Raelynn cleared her throat. "Did you get a dress yet for Homecoming, Ivy?"

She knew better than to ask Lyric. She and Paisley were getting their own creations crafted by Paisley's mom. Paisley had half-heartedly asked me if I'd wanted one, too, but I'd had no desire to overburden the poor woman and besides, I could throw on an old dress. Wear what I wore for Dad's makeshift wedding. Whatever. Wear something with confidence and you'll always look good. It wasn't like any guys remembered what you wore from one day to the next. "I might just wear my winter formal dress," I said, trying again to get a sip of milk and forgetting that my carton was going to ring hollow.

"Oh, *no*, you're not," said Paisley, suddenly sliding closer to us girls and ignoring the laughs and incomprehensible grunts coming every few moments from the boys beside us. "We'll go shopping with you."

Raelynn studied Lyric up and down. "I don't want her to see what I'm wearing until the dance."

Lyric pretended to wipe away a tear. "It'll be like our wedding day," she said, her voice wavering. That made Raelynn clam up again, but I didn't even think she picked up on the fact that Lyric was just teasing her. Which I thought was awful of Lyric. See? Again, what did people see in my friends? As dating partners anyway.

"And you two already have dresses," I said, but I knew those puppy dog eyes Paisley was sending me meant she couldn't care less. She wanted to go window shopping at the very least. I wouldn't be surprised if she found something and then made her poor mom put aside her work for the past couple of weeks just on a whim.

Cradling the empty milk carton, I stared over at Ember and

Journey. Ember didn't look quite like the somewhat talkative girl I'd rode with this morning. She looked sad—or sick maybe? Part of me wondered if I should have gone over there and found out. If Autumn and I had gone to the same school, I wouldn't have even thought about it. I'd be there, at her side, feeling her forehead.

"Yeah, but I'm an expert at helping people pick out what to wear," said Paisley, snapping me back to the moment. "Raelynn, Ivy, and I could go shopping without Lyric."

"Thanks," Lyric said dryly.

"Or you could come and just hang out somewhere else while we try things on," said Paisley, trying to compromise. Anything to get her and someone else clothes shopping.

"Sure," I said, feeling like a dog owner giving in to a spoiled pup. "You guys just figure out a good time and I'll come." I stood before we could bother discussing it further. Paisley liked to make meticulous plans and sometimes it drove me kind of crazy. Shaking the empty milk carton as if that said it all, I stood and grabbed my purse, aiming to get another beverage. My feet started carrying me toward Ember and her friend, but I was hit with a sudden slam of awkwardness as I got halfway there, so I made a sharp turn and cut through a couple of tables of rowdy sophomores. I'd forgotten just how much more immature boys could be at that age. Suddenly, spaghetti shows didn't seem so bad after all.

"Ivy!" called one, cupping his mouth with his hands. "Looking fine!"

"Ivy!" said another, like it was a song.

I didn't fail to notice the glares of the girls peppered throughout the boys as I passed, but I just nodded, jangling that milk carton again like it was my excuse not to stop and talk.

"Nice sweater," said one of the girls in that tone where you're ninety percent sure the person means it sarcastically, but you might look like a jerk if you call her out on it in case she's genuine.

I glanced down at my sweater—off-the-shoulder, deep purple, some well-placed holes throughout to give it some punk rock flair. That and my black jeans with a few tears in them made it look like I'd been mauled by a bear or a very large cat, but that was kind of the point. "Thanks," I said, pushing between their chairs to go faster. "I got it at—"

Before I could finish telling her—as if she really wanted to know—I stumbled, bouncing on one black boot until I straightened myself up beside the mini fridge with all the milk cartons. There were chuckles and commentary from behind me, but I was out of range of hearing them and I really didn't care what underclassmen had to say. But I bet before the end of the day, my little slight trip-up would make the rounds and the rumors would have me falling flat on my face.

I *so* loved the gossip machine at Union High.

Fluffing that tiny bit of embarrassment rising up from inside me off, I tossed my carton toward the nearby blue recycling bin so I could grab another.

But instead of landing in the bin—or if I were being honest, landing somewhere probably a foot or so beside it—it went straight into a guy's hand, as if I'd been aiming for that instead.

A tray full of empty dishes in front of his chest in one hand and my empty carton high above his head in another, the guy in the business suit and sunglasses stared straight at me. Or his face turned my way anyway.

Cocking my head, I took a step toward him. "Nice catch."

He smirked. "Nice throw."

"Sure, if I were aiming for your head." I crossed one leg in front of the other and leaned back against the side of the mini fridge.

He lowered the carton. "Were you?" he asked. "Aiming for my head?"

There was something a touch off about his voice. I mean, there was a lot of things "off" about this guy, but I hadn't noticed the voice before. We'd all been so busy when he'd spoken in the kitchen this morning. At least I was pretty sure it was he who'd been in the kitchen this morning.

"It got you talking to me, didn't it?" I said, injecting swagger into my voice to make it seem like that had been the plan all along. From the way his lips turned up just slightly, I could tell he got it and was playing along. *Nice.* My sense of humor or whatever you'd call it usually went over guys' heads. Another reason to skip the Homecoming date.

The guy walked a few steps closer and dropped my carton into the trash, quickly followed by everything on his own tray.

"Wait!" I said, jumping to stand straighter. "You can recycle..."

I stared down at the garbage can. There was spaghetti and chocolate pudding and what I hoped wasn't puke smeared all over it. *Sorry, Mother Earth, I'm not reaching into that.*

He was far from the only student to not bother with sorting the recyclables off their tray before dumping, but the way he stared at me and then looked at the garbage, it was as if he hoped it would speak and clue him in on what was going on. He placed his tray atop the pile of other used ones as he stared at the blue can, the one I'd been aiming for, and reached into the trash.

"Wait!" I said again, putting a hand on his arm. "Now that it's already in there, you don't have to—"

He froze and stared at me with his shades. I hesitated, too, looking down at my pale hand on his dark suit jacket sleeve. A jolt like fire shot through my body at that moment and I might have gotten weak at the knees. Like that actually happened outside of colorful romantic comedies. Laughing nervously, I let go and stepped back. "Next time," I said, nodding toward the trash. "Just be careful next time."

"At the rate pollution is deteriorating the planet, there might not be a next time," he said as we both stepped away from the smelly trash and the occasional student making their way to dump their tray. "I apologize. I'm not always used to..."

He didn't finish his sentence, but I was more focused on how his voice sounded like a professor's. Clipped, maybe New England? But not quite that pronounced. Just a bit off. "So you're a planet saver," I said, for want of something else to talk about. He obviously didn't care enough about the planet to think to recycle without my pointing it out, but I'd never had a simple conversation descend into climate change and the end of the world so easily. "As well as a mover?"

"You remember me?" he asked. As if *he* would be hard to forget.

Pulling out another carton of skim, I let the fridge door shut behind me. "It's hard to remember someone whose name you don't even know, but yeah." I ripped the little straw off and opened the carton to stab it inside. I'd pay. I wasn't a thief—I was just thirsty. "I'm Ivy. Ivy Sheppard."

"The work order said Goodwin."

"That's my new step-mom's last name," I said. "You moved things from the Sheppard home into the Goodwin home. Sorry we weren't at my old place this morning to direct things."

"It was all boxed and ready to go, so we had no complaints." He dug his hands into his pockets and his shoulders slouched just a little. "You know, we do offer packing services as well. We were told it was a rush job—"

I waved the hand not holding the carton. "Up to the fam," I said, and when he didn't say anything, I added, "Family. My parents —not my friends." I supposed it could have been taken either way. Still, he was looking at me how my parents looked at me whenever I slipped into slang from this century. Lost and out of his element. He sure looked that way in more ways than one. Since when did teens wear suits to school? This wasn't a posh boarding school.

"I never caught your name," I said between sips of my milk.

He pulled one of his hands out of his pocket and reached forward, a swagger added to the movement I couldn't quite explain. "Dean Horne."

"Horne, like the—"

"Name of the moving company."

We shook hands then and dang, if I wasn't fighting down another jolt-like feeling. He had sunglasses on. It wasn't the twinkle in his eyes, so what was it? Sure, he looked good. But what guy wouldn't in a suit that fine?

"Your family owns the moving company," I said, and I couldn't help but notice I was the first to let go. "That's why they made you work a couple hours before school." I shook my head. "Parents," I added, the "am I right?" left unsaid.

A couple of girls brushed past us then and once they passed Dean, they both turned back and giggled, but they were still checking him out. It wasn't often one of those cologne model types graced the halls of Union High.

"My aunt is the owner," said Dean, placing his hand back in his pocket. At this range, it was clear he wasn't the Secret Service type at all. He carried himself much more casually, despite the stiff appearance. His suit was baggier than I'd initially thought, too. Not horribly so, but not that skin-tight type of business suit that clung to models like a second skin. Not that it was necessarily off the rack, either. He was a conundrum, that was for sure.

"So if your aunt's the owner, may I make a suggestion?" The milk echoed hollow again. I'd somehow downed the whole thing before paying for it.

"Sure, doll," he said with a grin, making the whole interaction even more bizarre, which apparently had been possible all along.

"Ditch the suits for jeans and T-shirts, maybe? Maybe print the business logo on 'em. Much better for sweat absorption." I cleared my throat and tucked the empty carton against my chest, digging through my purse for a couple of dollars for the cashier.

"It's on me," said Dean, swiping the carton from my grasp. He pulled a ten out of his pocket then, but I had to do a double take because it didn't look right. The last time I'd seen one of those old designs had been in a birthday card from my grandma. It had been very wrinkly and Mom had surmised Grandma had kept it balled up for decades in an empty nut mix tin in the back of her cupboard. Dean "toasted" me with the carton. "For the fashion advice."

"Oh, I wouldn't call it fashion advice," I purred, like a crashy seductress. Something had washed over me, and only half of me liked it. "In most situations, a suit is pretty dang snatched."

He cocked his head.

"Hot?" I ventured. "Gorgeous?" Foot-in-mouth syndrome. In his presence, I was coming down with foot-in-mouth syndrome. Or becoming a total flirt.

He chuckled. "I suppose it doesn't make any less sense than

being 'khaki wacky,'" he said, and I had to agree with him, although I couldn't exactly see his point since I had no clue what he was talking about.

"Ivy," said someone then, and I gazed over Dean's shoulder to see Ember putting her tray atop the pile awaiting the industrial dishwasher. Journey was a few steps behind her, talking to some other seniors.

Milk and money in hand, Dean looked over his shoulder and smiled as if watching the next Top Model approach. *Of course. He's a flirt. No one dresses like that and doesn't walk around with his mind in the gutter and on the next conquest.*

"Do you know the new student?" she asked, approaching.

"New student?" Of course. It would have been hard for this guy not to have been noticed before this, unless he was one of those wallflower types who usually dressed normally enough to blend in. "This is Dean Horne, one of our movers."

"I thought so," said Ember, grinning wildly. *Oh. She has it bad.*

Not about to make waves with my brand-new sister, I thought it best to back off.

"Well, anyway, thanks," I said, plucking the carton back from Dean and pulling the two bucks out of my bag. "But I got this." I nodded toward Ember, suddenly feeling all sorts of awkward and out of place. "See you later."

"Sure," said Ember, her smile falling. "Ivy, um, about tonight..." But despite us all standing there blankly for a bit, she didn't really finish her sentence and I wasn't about to stand there all day, so I forced a chuckle and left.

I didn't really need a boyfriend anyway.

CHAPTER FIVE

EMBER

Ivy ditching me meant I was left alone in front of this hot, odd guy. Journey was somewhere behind me but had gotten caught up in some Model U.N. talk with someone and I'd been counting on Ivy to make things less awkward, but maybe I shouldn't have because really, I didn't know Ivy that well. She seemed nice enough, especially considering without our parents' marriage, I doubt she'd have ever deigned to speak with the likes of me, but I'd already embarrassed myself by asking her to hang out after school and she'd shot it down, more or less. Twice now.

It seemed clearer than ever she was avoiding me. So she may have been nice enough to humor me, but that kindness wasn't going to extend beyond that.

I should have known.

"What happened there?" asked Dean, his face turning slightly, his hand coming out of his pocket and reaching toward my face. It was like he was about to caress my cheek or pat my head, but there must have been surprise painted in my expression because he stopped, balling his hand into a fist and slipping it back into his pocket. He somehow made standing there with his hands in his pockets seem tope, tight and dope—like a boy in a suit at school was an everyday thing.

Then what he was even talking about dawned on me. "Oh, I

bumped into something," I said, cradling my forehead and wincing at the slight bruise that was there. "Something rock hard."

How does he even notice details like that with sunglasses on?

Almost as if reading my mind, he removed a hand from his pocket to slide his sunglasses farther up the tip of his nose. They looked vintage. Classy. But I supposed that made sense. He was obviously a hipster of some sort, though I usually saw them with more mismatched attire and fedoras or page boy caps. Dean's dark hair didn't look mussed enough to have been recently missing a hat, but then again, he had been lifting heavy weights for a couple of hours before coming this way.

"What's with the suit?" I blurted out. "I mean, when moving especially—"

A hint of a smile tugged on his lips. "Horne Movers uniform," he said, as if that explained it all. "And it's pretty versatile."

"I'll say." Before I realized what I was doing, I had pinched a bit of his sleeve between my fingers. "I don't get how you could lift all that and not soak it through."

"What makes you so sure I'm not covered in sweat beneath my jacket?"

"You don't smell, for one," I said, and then I leaned in to make sure, inhaling deeply. "You smell... nice actually." *What on Earth was wrong with me?!*

Dean chuckled, but he strangely didn't back away from the crazy girl tugging on his sleeve and sniffing him. It took me realizing what a dumb move that was to let him go and step back.

"You know, your sister was overly concerned with my attire, too," he said, just as Journey stepped up beside me.

"Hi," she said, extending a hand. She gave me a sly look as he shook it, like she had caught me doing something naughty. Perhaps she had. When was the last time I'd ever spoken to a guy alone outside of working on a class project? "I'm Journey Slowe."

Dean just about made both of our jaws drop by turning the handshake into a kiss on the back of her hand, just like you see in movies set in pre-historic (slight exaggeration) days.

"Enchanted," he said. "Dean Horne."

Journey awkwardly pulled her hand back, absentmindedly running it through her voluminous hair and swallowing visibly. She was shaking a bit, and probably not from rage.

Dean did have that effect on people.

"New here?" she asked, and man, if her voice didn't lower an octave.

Dean nodded, and there was a slight strain of his neck that made me think he was staring over our heads. I turned around and found Ivy and her friends exiting the cafeteria some distance away. "It's a charming school," he said, smiling at both of us. "If you'll excuse me..."

"Wait!" I found myself saying before I even knew why.

Dean was into Ivy. Of course he'd be into Ivy, though I hadn't picked up at that this morning at home. And instead of letting that play out like any girl with half a brain who knew that rejection lay around the corner would, I'd picked up my feet and followed him on his way out of the cafeteria, Journey doing a double take and lagging a few steps behind me.

Dean was fast, though, able to slide around people milling about—even avoiding colliding with one guy who shot up from his chair suddenly to catch a plastic fruit cup that someone else had tossed his way—but I pumped my legs hard until they burned and I found myself beside Dean in the largely empty hallway.

Instead of pursuing Ivy and her friends, who turned around the corner at the far end of the hallway, he stopped.

He was actually waiting for me.

"I just, I... I'm not sure I introduced myself," I said as Journey, panting, walked up behind us. "Ember Goodwin," I said, extending a hand and realizing right then and there that he might have thought I wanted him to kiss mine, too.

Okay, so I did, actually.

"I know you, Miss Goodwin," he said, smirking, and he did kiss it. I was about to melt right then and there. "You're Ivy's new step-sister."

And right back to Ivy. I wished I'd had the good sense to recognize a lost cause, but there was something about this way-too-pale strange kind of hipster that just made me lose my mind.

"Do you—that is, has anyone shown you around school?" I looked to Journey, silently pleading with her to help me out. She seemed to have regained her own sensibilities by then and she nodded, picking right up.

"Ember's a great tour guide," she said. She was far more likely to offer a new student a tour than I was and we both knew it. Hopefully, Dean wouldn't figure that out. Journey pointed a finger at me as she backed away down the hall. "So, uh, I'll see you sixth period, Em."

"Yup," I said, grinning from ear to ear. "And don't forget after school!"

"What's going on after school?" asked Dean, his head tilted. "The jit and jive? Are you cookin' with helium?"

I stared blankly at him for a second. I'd forgive a fair amount of harmless weird behavior from someone cute, apparently. *I'm going to assume that means something like a party, and no, I'd just planned to do homework with Journey, but...* "Maybe," I said as we started traveling down the hall. More and more other people were exiting the cafeteria and crowding the hallways, but a part of me felt like we were the only two people in the world. "Depends if Ivy and her friends are coming, I guess." *Dang. I forgot about not fanning the flames of his interest in my step-sister.*

"What's a guy got to do to get an invite?"

I burst out laughing. I couldn't help it. He spoke weirdly.

"Sorry, um..." I wiped my mouth with my wrist, hoping he hadn't seen any spittle. "You're welcome. You know the address."

"Well, thank you, doll," he said. "What time?"

Uh... What time did normal people do these things? On a school night? And how did they get their parents to agree to it?

Something to worry about later.

"How about seven?"

"Seems on the beam."

I guffawed then. Kind of like a donkey. This guy watched a lot of old movies. Like movies older than my grandpa.

This is one of those excuses to exchange numbers, right? Be cool, Ember. Be casual. "Do you want to exchange...?" I stopped. I'd left my phone in my locker, and I wasn't sure I had the number memorized.

Before I could open my mouth again to figure out how I was going to do this, I heard a voice from behind me. "Ember, I'm sorry again about this mor—" The voice went so high at the end, it sounded like some guy had slipped and screamed as he lost balance.

When I turned around, though, I just found Calder Poole frozen stiff.

My not-so-knight-in-shining-armor.

Calder lifted a finger in the air like he was about to explain himself more and then quickly drew that finger back in. "I'll see you around," he mumbled, and he turned.

What on Earth is with this guy?

"Wait," said Dean, and Calder froze again. "I was just leaving. You're welcome to speak with Miss Goodwin."

That made me frown. *Thanks. So glad he has your permission. And thank you, Calder, for scaring this hot guy away.*

Calder practically warped to my side then. "If you insist," he said. He stepped slightly between Dean and me. Like he was trying to block my view of him.

Dean chuckled—his teeth were so, so white—and did a tip of an imaginary hat. "I'll see you this evening. Thank you for the invite."

"Sure," I said, wiggling my fingers to wave goodbye. "Bye," I whispered. Squeezing my hands together in front of my thigh, I might have squealed just a little and bounced on the balls of my heels. Maybe.

"What's he talking about—what invite?" Calder sounded extremely concerned. Freak-out levels of concern. Like the bleach in his cute little spiky hair had suddenly reached his brain.

I stared at him. He swallowed noticeably, his Adam's apple bobbing up and down. I didn't think I'd ever had that effect on a man.

Was he actually going to ask me to the dance? I thought. Maybe he was panicking because it looked like I had a date with Dean.

"Just hanging out at my place," I said, shuffling toward my locker. "There are these cool woods behind my house and I thought about asking Ivy to invite her friends and—oh, Ivy Sheppard's my new step-sister, by the way. I don't know if you know—"

"Can I come?"

There was definitely something that had gotten his goat.

"Sure," I said, tucking a strand of hair behind my ear. Now to just explain this to Mom somehow. But what were the chances of Ivy actually showing up, let alone with friends in tow? If I kept it just to me, Journey, Dean, and Calder...

"What time?" he asked. He didn't seem grateful at all. He was clearly panicked.

"Seven..." Despite the sudden interest from the cute male variety, this was weirding me out and not in a very good way.

"I'll be there," he said, nodding at me as he started walking away.

"Okay, but don't you want to... know... where I... live?" He didn't hear the last few words and I grew quieter as I spoke them, realizing he'd never hear me as he melted into the buzz of the gathering crowd in the hallway.

So either he was daft enough to forget to ask that question or obsessed enough to already know the answer to that question.

At least with the former, I could try my hand at flirting with Dean with no one else around. Journey would give me some space, I was sure of it.

But if it were the latter...

The first bell rang for fifth period.

Whatever, I told myself, turning the dial on my lock. No one could possibly be that obsessed with me. I'd have had more than a handful of pity dances to show for it if that were the case. My imagination was getting the worst of me.

And besides, if he did show without ever asking where to go, I could confront him there—with plenty of other people around to keep me safe.

As I plopped my tablet against my calculus workbook, my eyes wandered, catching sight of Ivy near the lockers at the other end of the hallway with her friends.

I'd only thought of this idea to get to know her a bit better and now I had not one, but two hot guys potentially showing up at my house. I wasn't sure how I felt about that.

The second bell rang and I cleared my mind. Class first. Then figuring out what the heck was going on with my life. And if I'd ever have time to catch up with *Riverdale*.

CHAPTER SIX

IVY

The clump of grass I'd plucked and laid beside me where I sat atop the picnic table was for the little grass bracelet I was shaping between my fingers. The strands were staining my fingertips green, but I didn't really care. I shivered just a little as Ashton whooped and hollered following a big splash. He, Grey, and the other guys were taking turns skipping stones across the pond in the park and apparently, he was the new victor.

"*Boys*," sneered Lyric dismissively. She tended to get a little grumpier on days when Raelynn had half a dozen after-school activities and she couldn't join us. But Lyric almost always came herself. I wondered how she and Rae ever had time to themselves —the same for Paisley and Grey, for that matter. But the answer to the latter was probably "they just never have alone time" because Grey didn't do *anything* without his baseball bros. Even if it was months and months before baseball season even started.

"Eh," I said, shrugging. "They could be skinny dipping or tossing one another in or any number of stupider things right now."

Paisley giggled and I wondered if they'd all done exactly that at one point when I hadn't been there to witness it. But hopefully in the summer when it was warmer and not the fall. Hopefully not at all, actually. Who knew what kind of grody stuff grew in that pond?

"Is that for Autumn?" asked Lyric.

I stared at the little grass bracelet in my grasp. It was awfully petite. Shrugging, I tossed it beside me atop the worn and weathered table, scraping my feet against the bench Lyric sat on to sit up straighter. "It's for the faeries," I said, smirking. It was really for lack of anything better to do.

Holding back a sigh, I dug my phone out of my purse and checked to see if Autumn had texted me. She hadn't, so I texted her first. *Get home okay?* I asked. *Did Ember get you?*

Dad and Noelle both worked until five, so they'd thought it ideal for Ember (and me) to get there earlier to pick up Autumn from after-school care. Dad used to have Autumn stay there for hours, which always irritated her, but now she could get home relatively early. Ember was the one with the car, though, so there wasn't much my added presence could do.

She's a sucky driver, came the reply back. *We're home now, but she got lost so many times.* There was a pause as she kept typing. *She slammed on the breaks*, she wrote, getting "brake" wrong, *I almost died.*

I winced. *We can talk to Dad.*

Autumn sent a disgusted emoji face.

A pang of guilt shot through me just then. To tell the truth, I'd sort of forgotten Ember and I were supposed to get her after school, so used to Dad doing it was I, and yet Ember had remembered and stepped up, even when I'd kind of brushed her off. More than once.

Of course, if this morning's car ride was any indication, I got why Autumn was terrified. I really did. But it wasn't so much that Ember was a terrible driver. She was just kind of a tense, ditzy driver. Which I supposed could be just as bad.

I knew what Dad's—and even Ember's—solution was likely to be, though. Let me drive.

No more after-school hangouts. Or my friends would have to

come pick me up at home, which I knew they were all too lazy to do.

I'll talk to Ember, I wrote, as if I could lecture her into being a more chill driver. *It'll be okay.*

I slid my phone back into my purse pocket and swapped it for a hairbrush. The breeze wasn't exactly freezing yet, but it was just annoying enough to keep ruffling my hair.

Paisley was in the midst of showing Lyric something on her phone. "I don't know." Her nose wrinkled. "I told Mom the rose accents were a bit much."

"I think it suits you," said Lyric, leaning back and laying her elbows on the table behind her.

"I don't know if that's really a compliment, though," said Paisley, sighing. "Ivy, what do you think?"

I scooched over on my butt to get a look at her phone screen, which had a picture of a cute white dress with fabric roses atop the shoulders on one of those sewing dummies. "It's nice," I said, truthfully. "The roses complete the piece."

Clearly utterly unconvinced, Paisley swiped the image away and began scrolling through her notifications.

"So are you going to enlighten us as to what was going on with you and sunglasses man at lunch?" asked Lyric, not for the first time since the cafeteria.

"Not everything is some grand conspiracy," I said. "He introduced himself. I asked him a bit about his choice of attire. He dodged the question."

"Sounds kind of creepy," said Paisley, which jarred me. Since when was Paisley an expert on these things? She shuddered. "He's too pale. And what's with the suit and the sunglasses? He's not blind, so he's just being a douche."

"Paisley hates hipsters," said Lyric, and Paisley laughed. Probably some inside joke that was lost on me.

I didn't usually have a type—hipsters and jocks repelled and attracted me alike, and repelled more often than not—but I didn't want to have to feel guilty because I had a crush on a guy my friends found gross. "Lyric, you said he was hot." I laid my hair-brush next to my thigh, trying to keep it casual.

"He is, I guess," said Lyric. She tapped a finger to her bottom lip. "Or he makes an impression at first, I suppose. But the longer you see him walking around like some zoot suit gangster, the dumber it looks after all."

"Zoot suit?" asked Paisley, and her fingers flew over her phone, and I guessed she was Googling it.

Nodding, she chuckled. "That's a bit baggier than his, but yeah... He does look like he's from the forties. With added sunglasses."

"I think vintage looks are cool," I said, gesturing to my punk rock attire.

"That's timeless," said Lyric, stretching her arms above her. She could have knocked over a passing-by bird like that. "Punk is always for the fringe, the rebel."

That described me all right. At least I liked to think it did sometimes. Sometimes I knew I was just making a fashion state-ment my actions couldn't always back up.

"All you're missing is the cigarette," said Paisley.

"Ew," I said, thinking of my grandpa's last few months on Earth. He had tanks and a voice box and all those years of smoking to thank. "No thank you. I'm not *that* much of a rebel."

"Pais!" Grey ascended the hill leading down to the pond, cupping his hands around his lips. When she jumped down off the picnic table bench and ran toward him, he rubbed his shoulders and shivered, bouncing in place until he scooped her into his arms and peppered her face with kisses.

"The boys got cold, so that's our cue to go," said Lyric dryly. She looked at the guys—some in letter jackets, some in just T-shirts—and rolled her eyes. Whether at the ones in jackets complaining about the cold or the ones in just T-shirts being stupid enough not to try to combat the cold, I didn't know. I'd assume both.

Lyric patted my boot. "Let's go get something to eat," she said. "Unless you and the new family have something planned."

Shaking my head, I slid off the table, landing directly on the ground. "Dad and Noelle said they'd take Autumn out later but that they knew we 'older girls' probably had things we wanted to do." I grabbed my purse and slid it over my head and across my body.

"So what *is* your dorky new step-sister up to?" asked Lyric as we slowly made our way to the cars in the parking lot.

Crossing my arms, I shrugged, the movement helping to take some of the bite out of the autumn air. "She's at home, I guess. Seems like the type to mostly stay home."

"Is she watching Autumn then?"

"Yeah," I said, the stab of guilt driving into my chest again. "Until Dad and Noelle come pick her up."

"That's nice of her," said Lyric, and I might have actually jumped at hearing her say anything complimentary.

"Well, she wanted to have like a mini party or something," I said, tripping over my words to paint my new step-sister as less holy than she seemed to be. Because really, I knew Autumn was supposed to be *my* responsibility.

Lyric stopped and grabbed me by the arm. "What, tonight?"

"Yeah," I said as Ashton walked up, Grey and Devam punching each other's shoulders over Paisley's head. I tried to keep my voice quiet. "I guess. She said to bring whoever and we'd go exploring in the woods behind the house or something."

"Ooo," said Lyric and her voice suddenly grew several octaves louder. "Guys, Ivy's inviting us to her new house!"

"What? No." I tried to grab Lyric by the arm to pull her back to me and our *private* conversation, but she was already backing up and making sure she got everyone's attention.

"Wood-exploring party at Ivy's new house!" she called out loudly.

"Come on," I said, laughing nervously. "It was Ember's idea. I'm sure it'll be lame."

"Sounds fun to me," said Paisley, grinning from her spot glued to Grey's side.

"I'm up for it," said Ashton, shrugging. He glanced straight at me then, a shine in his eye, and I wondered if our will-they-or-won't-they (they won't) from last school year was back on.

"The woods aren't even my step-mom's," I said. "Ember said they belong to the neighbor."

Lyric's shoulders bobbed as her nose wrinkled. "Trespassing makes it even more exciting."

"*Fine*," I said, resolved. "But we have to make it quick—during that window my dad is gone with my step-mom and sister. I don't think Ember exactly got permission."

"Oo, so you're not the only *rebel* in the family," teased Lyric.

Me and my big mouth.

I fished for my phone so I could give Ember a heads-up—we'd exchanged numbers last week but hadn't sent a single text—and to ask Autumn if she was gone yet. I wouldn't ask her to lie for me, just keep it casual and make it seem like I was merely curious.

But as I was digging, I noticed my brush wasn't there. "I left my brush at the picnic table," I said, pointing over my shoulder. "Just hold up, okay?"

"We can stop at the dollar store and get you a new hairbrush," said Lyric, clearly exasperated. And clearly insulting my choice in hairstyling tools.

That wasn't the point. That fold-up brush was one of the first things my mom and dad had given me together as a kid. It was purple and there was glitter suspended in the clunky plastic and it was missing a couple of teeth. It had clearly seen many, many better days. But so had my parents' marriage, for that matter, and sometimes I liked to close my eyes and pretend we were all happy again. Pretend Autumn wasn't some last-minute attempt to fix what couldn't be fixed, pretend my poor sister had ever known what it was like to have both parents in the same building for more than twenty minutes.

Pumping my arms and legs until they ached, I rushed forward. Lyric would wait for me, but some of the guys might hop in their cars and if Paisley or Lyric gave them my new address, they could be there before me and I had texting and making sure the coast was clear to do beforehand, so that wouldn't do at all. Luckily, the picnic table wasn't too far ahead, just down the slope, overlooking the expanse of the pond.

As my hand clasped the plastic piece of lovable junk, I froze. There was someone swimming. In the pond. Which couldn't have been at pleasurable temperatures.

"Who the—? Hey!" Like he could hear me. I ran down the hill then, my brush still in my grip, not believing I hadn't noticed someone missing from our group. There was a letterman jacket hanging to the side of the sand surrounding the pond, hung up and out of the way on the branch of a pine tree.

"Hey!" I said again, but the yellow head was halfway to the tiny island in the middle of the pond now, and it bobbed beneath the waters.

And as I stood there, dumbfounded, a brush in my hand, my brain racing through the blond boys in the baseball team who sometimes flitted in and out of our group, I realized it had been way too long and he hadn't come up.

Oh, shiste.

I was the only one for yards. There was no way any of the guys in the parking lot would see me. But surely *they* would notice one of their friends missing? *No, no those idiots might not.* I had my phone —I should have called the police first—but the longer I waited to dive in the water, the more his brain would get damaged and the less time he had. But was I ever a champion swimmer? Crap. If I went down without texting anyone, they wouldn't even think to look for me here until it was too late.

I dropped the brush into the sand and whipped my phone out, determined to at least send a *"HELP! POND!"* text to the whole group before I dived, but just as my fingers moved across the keys, swiping away the aggravating notifications that got in my way—he surfaced.

A Guinness-record amount of time for holding breath later.

His hands reached for the edge of the little island, his broad shoulders lifting himself up as he shook the water from his locks like a model in slow motion.

He was all right.

He was all right.

How the freaking heck was he all right?

As he settled himself onto the edge of the island, he seemed... sad. Sullen. Like if someone had asked me to paint a picture of a man contemplating life's greatest tragedies, I'd arrange it just like this. He gazed off at the sky above him, not even seeming to notice me at first.

A sharp instinct to want to go and stroke him—his head, his cheek, his back—took over me. He needed comfort and I—inexplicably—wanted to offer it.

But then he finished lifting himself up entirely out of the water and a long, sky-blue fish tail launched up out of the pond, the fins shaking out like a dog's floppy ears as he turned over and settled himself atop the edge of the island. Everything from the waist down was entirely fish.

CHAPTER SEVEN

EMBER

I had less than an hour before one or more strange young men appeared at my front door and Mom and Easton were still here.

The sensible part of me knew to fess up—Mom might even allow it, considering that Journey was with me—but there was that chance that she'd say 'no' and then I'd have the embarrassing task of telling the boys to take a hike after they'd made the trek over. Because I had neither of their phone numbers.

Then again, by all rights, Calder shouldn't have my address, either. Unless he was one of Ivy's friends. I supposed that was possible, but Ivy had made it more or less clear she and her friends had no interest in hanging out at the house with Journey and me.

Even though it startled the sleepy white kitty on my lap, Journey pinched my forearm as Archie crept down the dark hallway where the serial killer might have been waiting for him. Yeah, it was hard for me to reconcile Grandma's stack of old-school comics full of innocent three-way dates at the malt shoppe and clumsy hijinks with this show, too, but I was pretty darn hooked.

"Em, are you sure you don't want to come?" Mom walked into the living room, fastening an earring. Her idea of "dressing down" for a casual dinner was still pretty over-the-top; she had on a silky blouse and a pencil skirt, but she looked amazing.

I hit *pause* on the remote, which made Journey groan, although she'd already seen it, so I didn't know where that disappointment came from. Arty took advantage of the moment of silence to roll his head upside down and cover his eyes with the back of his adorably bean-toed paw.

"Yeah," I said, lightly scratching him under his chin. "After all that activity this weekend, I just want to unwind."

Mom bit her lip as she stared at the front door. "I was really hoping you and Ivy would change your mind and come with us. It's a celebratory dinner for all that packing and moving." She glanced around the living room, which was far less packed than the bedrooms upstairs, but which still had a number of boxes from Easton's old house surrounding the couch. "Before we tackle all the unpacking."

"Once we finish with this, I can get started with that," I offered. *Stupid, stupid.* I just didn't want her to even *suspect* I was having more company and, like, Dean was a professional mover, right? Maybe he'd know where to put everything.

Sure, sure. Invite a hot guy over to have him help with chores.

"Not unless you're finished with your homework," said Mom. As if unpacking were a reward for that. She walked nearer the couch and ruffled my hair. Cringing, I tried to smooth it out.

"Don't watch TV too late, girls," she said.

"Yes, Ms. Goodwin... Mrs. Sheppard?" said Journey, suddenly confused.

"Ms. Goodwin-Sheppard," Mom answered. "But you can just call me 'Noelle,' dear."

Journey grinned. She loved when adults treated her like one of their own. She certainly acted mature and responsible enough to be one. Mom would have never suspected she was in on my naughty little secret.

"You ready?" asked Easton, walking in. He was dressed a bit more sensibly in a navy polo and khakis.

Mom grabbed him by the collar and kissed him because apparently *that* was the type of environment I'd be rewarded with for my last year at home before college. PDA central.

"Are you sure you don't want to call Ivy and invite her again?" asked Mom.

Easton snorted as he pulled away and fished his keys out of his pockets. "Have her daddy call her when she's with friends? She'd kill me." He glanced at Journey and me then, as if for confirmation.

We met each other's eyes and shrugged. Journey and I got calls from our moms all the time when with each other, and neither of us cared.

"You could text her," said Mom, grabbing her purse off the table near the front door. "Then her friends wouldn't even know."

"It's fine," said Easton before leaning back into the hallway. "Autumn, come on, let's go! If you want to stop for ice cream after, we need to get going!" He turned back to my mom. "Ivy spends most evenings with her friends. But she's good at being back by curfew, so I don't have a problem with it."

Mom frowned. I could tell she wanted to say something but didn't.

"Before you ask, Glory knows and says the same thing," said Easton, referring, I assumed, to Ivy and Autumn's mom. "Ivy's a good kid."

"You said her report card could use some work..." Mom snapped her mouth shut as Autumn descended the stairs, a little bright red plastic purse hanging off her shoulder clashing oddly with her dark brown *Pokémon* shirt. "Come on, sport," said Easton, either totally ignoring what Mom had said or genuinely not hearing it. I didn't think it was great to have these kinds of parenting conversations in front of kids anyway. *Should I warn Ivy or would that just make her hate my mom?*

Autumn padded over to the front door to put on her shoes and I was just about to hit *play* again—Journey was scrolling through her Twitter feed and the DVR had shut off the picture, blasting a cooking show that was on live feed, which had made Arty jump up until Journey started lazily petting him with her free hand—when Autumn's phone buzzed loudly. One foot in a shoe, one foot out, she slowly unzipped her chunky purse and my eyes darted impatiently to the cable box clock, knowing that if either guy turned up early, I'd have a heck of a lot of explaining to do.

Mom and Easton were murmuring to one another and Autumn looked puzzled as she read her screen.

"What is it, champ?" asked Easton. He was turning out to be the perfect replica of those dorky TV dads who gave little kids weird sports-related nicknames.

"Ivy," said Autumn. "She just wants to know if we left yet."

"See?" said Mom. She turned toward Journey and me. "Girls, why don't you both come with us too? Tell Ivy she can bring a friend."

Easton rolled his eyes and snatched the phone from Autumn. She looked perturbed but didn't say anything. Since my mom hadn't allowed me to have one until seventh grade, I wondered how parents handled elementary school kids with phones—assuming they allowed them, period. But she did have two separate parents to keep up with, I supposed.

Easton chunkily typed on the screen and then put the phone down on the table by the entryway. "I told her her curfew is still in effect, even if we're gone when she's supposed to come back." He nodded at me as he put on his jacket. "I'm counting on you to be my enforcer, sport."

"Sure," I said, hoping he didn't notice me swallowing. If Ivy got back a little late and the guys were still here, I wasn't about to tell on her, assuming she'd extend me the same courtesy.

"Call me if you need anything," said Mom, sighing. I guessed she really wanted us to go. "And there's some leftover Chinese from last night in the fridge."

"Thank you, Ms. Goodwin... Noelle," said Journey.

"Right. 'Bye, Mom. Have a nice time." I brought back up my show and clicked *play*.

It took a few more minutes for Mom and Autumn to finish adding layers and then another few minutes before Easton's car pulled out of the driveway and Archie was uncovering some rather shocking news, but I had a hard time paying attention to it. It was 6:40.

Journey squealed as the killer's knife gleamed in the beams of moonlight penetrating the holes in the decrepit house's windows. I kind of spaced on how he'd gotten there again—but then the credits rolled. Arty's claws digging into my thigh as he headed for the hills (or the kitchen) at Journey's outburst snapped me back into the moment.

"Be *so* grateful you don't have to wait as many days before the next episode as I've had to," said Journey, completely countering her argument that I should have watched it ASAP.

I chuckled and deleted the show, switching the TV off. "So," I said.

"So," said Journey, and we both looked out the front window. The sun was setting, but there was still an ember glow over the sky.

"Are you really going to take them to the woods?" Journey asked. She looked down at her clothes—jean shorts and a sweater, not exactly woods-exploring attire—and I stared similarly at mine.

"Let's go change," I said. "You can borrow some of my sweats." We were a similar enough size, even if Journey filled out her clothes more nicely.

"I still can't believe you'd do that," she said as we headed up the stairs, avoiding the boxes that leaked out of my new sisters' bedrooms onto the landing. "We haven't gone in those woods since, god, I don't know? We were young enough to pretend they were the Forbidden Forest behind Hogwarts."

"And Mom got so mad at us," I said. "Er, at me at least." I dug through my closet, looking for the cutest sweats I owned. I pulled out a pair of slightly-too-tight jeans for myself.

"Oh, my mom was angry, too." Journey plopped onto my bed. My room was practically the only place in the house where there weren't any boxes to trip over, but admittedly, it was kind of cramped. I liked to think of it as "eclectically decorated." The timer on the old Christmas lights I'd hung over my bed clicked on and Journey lay back, looking for all the world like a princess in a magical slumber watched overhead by faeries. I started changing, swapping my skirt and leggings for jeans and throwing a sweatshirt on. Maybe Dean wouldn't even care about the woods, anyway. Maybe he really would help us with the boxes. Though I could always say Journey and I had had too much homework to get to it. Truth was, we were both good at getting our homework done during breaks and study hall, and I could count the times we'd brought it home on one hand. Mostly, we just brainstormed for future projects when we weren't watching TV or videos online or just talking.

Besides, Journey wasn't always available to hang out these days, with all her after-school commitments. But she'd made a point of coming today, skipping on Model U.N. or something. Just on the off chance a boy or two actually showed up.

There was still the matter of how I'd kind of promised Dean that Ivy would be here and how I'd handle it if he cared too much that she never showed.

"I'm going to the bathroom," I said. "I left some clothes on the chair. If they don't suffice, you can dig around, but don't pick out anything too nice."

"Aye, aye, captain." Journey saluted me like a soldier, which looked especially weird from her position as Sleeping Beauty on the bed. As I stepped into the hallway, I breathed in the beautiful silence that I'd already come to miss and took my time in the bathroom, fussing with my hair and everything, like there was anything I could do to tame those frizzies at this point.

When I got out, I heard a crash from downstairs. I bolted down, clutching the handrail. "Journey? You all right?"

But instead of Journey, there was Dean, his hands in his pockets and a navy fedora atop his head.

He was in my house. Ten minutes early.

Despite the weirdness of the situation, a smile shoved itself onto my lips. I couldn't help it around him. "Did Journey let you in?" I asked as I finished descending the stairs. I threaded my fingers together, suddenly bashful for no good reason. I still hadn't figured out what had caused the crash.

Dean fished out keys from his pocket. House keys. *My* house keys. "My aunt said the guys locked up after they finished and then forgot to leave the keys at your mom's office. I told her I could drop them off tonight."

I stepped forward and let him drop them atop my palm. "Thanks," I said, and despite the alarm bells going off somewhere in the back of my head, my legs were turning to goo.

Dean took his hat off and held it in both hands in front of his waist. "I hope you don't mind that I let myself in," he said. "I knocked and there was no answer and it's starting to get cold..."

"We were upstairs," I said, pointing behind me. I dropped the keys on the table by the door and then offered to take his hat. "You can hang that here if you want," I said, pointing to the coat rack.

"Thank you," he said and he did just that. "I didn't want to wear it to school because... These hats have a different meaning these days, don't they?"

I chuckled. He sounded like a grandpa. "If you mean that hipsters and sometimes rather douchey guys wear them a lot, I guess," I said. Then I realized what it sounded like and I scrambled to cover my tracks. "But I think that's a shame because it looks good."

Grinning, he gripped the temple of his sunglasses and *oh my god*, I realized he was about to take them off.

"I have light sensitivity," he said then, hesitating. "It runs in the family."

"Are all the movers at your company in the family?"

"More or less." The corner of his lips turned up. "My aunt also thinks they just look good, so..." He nodded toward the light switch. "Do you mind dimming the lights in here? With the sun setting, I can usually handle the indoors fine if it's not too bright."

"Sure," I said, turning the dial to control the brightness.

"Whoa, okay, I'm going to trip here in the dark," said Journey from the top of the stairs. "Oh, hello." She pulled on the hoodie I'd lent her as she came down. "I take it we're not going to the woods?"

"Why not?" asked Dean as he took off those sunglasses. Journey froze and I found myself unable to move, too.

His eyes were gorgeous. The light wasn't that bright, but it wasn't so dim that you couldn't tell once your eyes adjusted. Deep blue—a violet maybe. And they kind of shone, even without much light to reflect.

He seemed to notice our staring and turned, putting the sunglasses down on the table beside my house keys.

I cleared my throat. "I think Journey means... Well, you're still in a suit."

He studied us. "You both changed."

"Yeah," I said, finally moving closer. "I mean, I don't want you to get your suit dirty."

He waved a hand. "I have dozens of these. I don't mind. I want to do what you all want to do."

Journey and I exchanged a look. If it was down to what we *really* wanted to do, exploring the neighbor's woods in the dark wasn't exactly on the top of either of our lists. *Dang, we could have looked a lot cuter, then.*

"Do you have a cat or a dog?" asked Dean, leaning around me and looking into the kitchen. "I think I may have startled it."

The crash. "Arty," I called out, heading back to check on him. "Arty, are you okay?"

There was no sign of him, but his food bowl was totally flipped over, like he'd had one of his post-poo runs through the kitchen and mowed right into his own feeding area.

Bending over to pick it up, I grabbed a dish towel to dab the spilled water from the nearby water bowl.

"Where'd that little stinker go?" asked Journey.

"He's been spooked lately," I said. "With the movers and the new people moving in..." I glanced toward the door that led to the basement and sure enough, I saw those shining eyes staring back up at me from the darkness. "It's okay, sweet pea," I cooed, but as I approached, Dean entered the kitchen behind Journey and Arty hissed, retreating farther back into darkness.

"I'm sorry," said Dean. "Animals don't seem to like me much."

I chuckled at the joke, but he wasn't laughing. Something primal in him seemed to be aching to roar from just beneath the surface and my heart beat faster and faster in response.

The doorbell rang, echoing out throughout the whole house. I wondered for a moment why Dean hadn't tried that before walking in, but I brushed the thought from my mind.

"That must be Calder," I said.

"Calder Poole?" asked Dean, his dark eyebrow arching on his pale, pale face. "You invited that dead hoofer?"

"Yeah," I said, looping a strand of hair around my finger, wondering again what kind of thesaurus this guy used. "Or he kind of invited himself..." I exchanged a look with Journey and then headed toward the door.

I swung it open to find Ivy, a sea of guys and girls behind her.

"I forgot my new key," she said, shivering.

I stood there in shock.

Ivy looked as if I'd lost my mind and she waved a hand in front of my face. "Can we come in?"

I mentally went over the numbers—two other girls, six or seven boys, *oh, crap*—and I found Calder at the back.

So he did know Ivy. That was why he'd known where I lived. It wasn't him being a creepy stalker or anything.

"Ember?" asked Ivy.

"Um, yeah, of course, sorry." I backed up to let them all in. One of Ivy's friends snorted as she passed by, staring me down.

Ivy looked over her shoulder as her friends piled in, her face serious enough to slice through stone, and right before it was Calder's turn, she cut in front of him and grabbed me by the forearm, dragging me through the crowd in the hallway, past the bewildered Journey and curious Dean in the kitchen, and into—of all places—the basement, slamming the door shut behind us.

CHAPTER EIGHT

IVY

No sooner had the door slammed and I'd let go of Ember's arm than I stepped on something soft, like a pillow, and I got treated to a blood-curdling screech.

"Arty!" said Ember, running down the stairs after the streak of movement in the dark that was likely her cat. Blinking, my eyes trying to adjust to the darkness, I fumbled at the wall near the top of the stairs until I found a light switch.

The illuminated basement showed Ember on her knees on the hard basement floor, reaching one arm out toward the feline, which had backed into a small space between two boxes, its fur and tail straight up.

"I'm sorry," I said, rubbing my arm nervously as I finished descending the stairs. "I didn't even know he was there." The closer I got, the more shaken the cat became until it outright started hissing.

"So much for getting him to like me," I said.

Sighing, Ember stood back up on her feet. "Let's just leave him be. He may forgive you. It's just... He's not used to all this activity. He never really saw anyone much besides me, Mom, and Journey before this."

"I have a cat at Mom's," I said. "A calico. Her name's Blossom. I'm usually great with cats."

"I'd hate to have to be parted from Arty for half the week," said Ember. She bit her lip then, like she thought she was insulting me or bringing up a source of great pain or something.

You got used to it. It was annoying at times, but a house was so often just a place to sleep for me anyway. It was a bonus that I got to see Mom and Dad on an alternate basis. And there was always Autumn.

"So," said Ember, turning toward a nearby shelf and moving aside bottles of sunscreen and a rolled-up tent, "you decided to come after all?"

Right. I never warned her. And I'd dragged her down here rather abruptly.

"Yeah, but about that, the reason I brought you down here was because I wanted to talk where no one could see us—"

Ember said "Aha!" and then pulled out two bottles of bug spray. "Deep woods DEET," she said, "which may or may not be poisonous or something, but there are ticks to worry about and that could lead to a bunch more problems than one night's application of bug spray, right?"

The woods. That was the whole purpose of this thing, wasn't it? I looked down at my outfit—it was torn in strategic places, sure, but that didn't mean I wanted to get it dirty.

"Maybe you and your friends should change," said Ember, handing me one of the spray cans. "I lent Journey some of my clothes, but no one—*no one*—else looks ready to hike. Especially not Dean."

"Dean Horne's here?" The question moved past my lips before I even had a chance to remind myself I had more pressing matters to discuss with her. *Much, much* more pressing matters.

Grinning, Ember tossed the remaining can from one hand to the other and back again, which didn't really strike me as safe. "Yeah. In his suit. But he finally took those sunglasses off. He has bad light sensitivity, I guess."

"Is that why it was so dark when we walked in?"

"We have a dimmer switch in the hallway and dining room," explained Ember.

"Yeah, okay," I said, practically smacking my temple to get myself to focus. "Are you aware that Calder Poole is a merman?"

The smile on Ember's face died as she failed to catch the can. It dropped straight to the floor, rolling away from her with such a clatter that Arty screeched again even from the relative safety of his hiding place.

"I'm sorry, baby," said Ember, snapping back to life to peek through the crack through which Arty's eyes were shining.

"I'm not joking," I said, pacing the room, clutching the can she'd handed me, not even caring when my toes sent the other can rolling once more into the wall, resulting in Arty's hiss.

Ember turned to me, clearly annoyed, and *clearly not taking a second to consider the bombshell I was dropping on her.*

I stopped and slammed the can of bug spray atop a pile of boxes, sending dust flying. "Calder. Has. A fish tail."

"It looked like he had legs to me when he came here," she said. She sighed then, stepping away from Arty's hiding place and bending over to pick up the can she'd dropped.

"I know he has legs now, everyone and their mother has assured me that he has legs now, I can *see* he has legs now, but I freaking saw him in the pond at Standing Springs Park—"

"It's a lake," said Ember, like that even mattered right then. "There's a small river joining it at the back that most people miss —the same river that goes through the woods behind the house somewhere, but I've never ventured deep enough to see it."

"I don't *care* if it's a pond or a lake! Oh my god, are you *listening* to what I'm saying?"

Ember placed the can she'd picked up next to the one she'd handed me—gingerly, as if afraid I might blow, or the cat might wail again, I supposed. "So you've been going around telling your friends Calder's a merman—"

"Not *everyone*," I said, pacing again and pulling the very edges of my sweater sleeves down over my palms with my fingers. The tightness of the fabric against my arms and shoulder made me feel a bit more alert. "I'm aware that makes me sound crazy, and *no one* is buying it anyway."

"But you thought I would?"

I stopped, slamming my palm against my forehead. "Did you, or did you not, invite Calder to this party?"

She fidgeted then, bouncing on her heels. "I don't know if I'd call it a *party* exactly—"

"Yes or no."

"Yes, I guess?" Her voice went unsteady at the end of her statement. "But he's your friend, isn't he?"

"Why would you think that?"

She cocked her head. "He came with you guys."

"Yeah, just because we met him at the park right before we left. When he was *swimming in a pond with a tail instead of legs*."

"A lake."

My eyes went wide as I halted my pacing and Ember shirked back.

"*Okay*," she said, her voice jittery. "I just talked to him today for, like, the first time ever, okay? He's a junior. He's a jock, so I thought he must be your friend."

"Because I'm automatically friends with every jock in school." I scoffed.

Sending up another layer of dust, Ember sat back in an old rocking chair covered with a couple of ancient-looking folded blankets. "Let's get back to the topic of the lake. Tell me what you saw."

Biting my lip, I tried to think of how I'd phrased it to Lyric, Paisley, and Grey before they'd laughed their butts off. "I went back to a picnic table near the po-*lake* to grab something and I looked out and saw a guy swimming in the water and freaked out because he dived under for a long, *long* time." I took a deep breath. "And just when I was about to call for help or dive in after him, he broke through the surface and sat on the shores of that little island in the middle. With a merman tail."

"Was his torso naked?"

I stumbled a step backward, literally taken aback. "Does that matter?"

She shrugged. "Well, I mean, was his whole body a fish or... No, I didn't mean it like *that*."

Closing my eyelids, I searched that moment in my brain. "I—yes, I guess? Yes to him being half-naked. His jacket was on a branch near where I was standing and I guess his shirt was there, too. He had a human head, I know that, because it turned right toward me and then he leaped back into the water."

"And then what?" asked Ember, breaking into my focus as I tried so hard to picture that moment, which was clouded by that feeling of panic and anxiety and dumbfoundedness all rolled into one. Calder being cute—noticing his abs or not—had been the *least* important thing on my mind.

"I don't know how long it took him—the whole thing was surreal—but he appeared out of the water in front of me and asked me to close my eyes for a bit because I'd supposedly caught him *skinny-dipping*. On instinct, I did and next thing I knew, he said to open them and he had his clothes back on and he was damp and that was it." The words flew out of my mouth a mile a minute as I paced back and forth.

"So you never saw him exit the water with a tail when he was up close?"

"No, but..." I pounded my fist against my thighs. "Penis or no penis, I should have kept my eyes open and *seen* whether what I found there was merely scandalous or freaking paranormal." I growled in frustration at myself. Ember looked aghast that I'd spoken the name of male genitalia aloud. I ignored that. "And he acted like it was all so *normal*, asked if I was heading home to your party, and I was like—who are you again and why do you know about that? But by then, some of my friends came looking for me and they knew him from swim team or something and I just..." I leaned against a pillar in the middle of the room then. "As soon as he walked off with Ashton, Devam, and the other guys, I told some of my friends and they laughed at me..."

"Well," said Ember, slapping her palms on the rocking chair armrests and standing up. "I'm not laughing at you."

"You're not?" Hope fluttered in my stomach.

"It was just a mistake. Wasn't the sun setting about then? Probably some reflection off the water made you see things weirdly."

"That *wasn't* what happened."

"The island is some distance from the shore, right?" She tapped a finger to her lip, an honest-to-goodness Nancy Drew. "Do you have 20/20 vision?"

"I don't know!" I started pacing again. "I don't need glasses, I guess—"

"But even so, that's a great distance. Too great for the average human eye to see clearly."

This was getting nowhere. I didn't know if this was even an improvement over being laughed at because my new step-sister, unlike my friends, who'd thought I'd been joking, actually thought I *was hallucinating*.

She put the back of her hand to my forehead then and I flinched, jumping back.

"You're not feverish."

"Well, that's good to know—that me seeing a junior turn into a freaking *merman* hasn't caused a fever."

Ember sighed and picked up both bottles of bug spray, shoving them at me until I took them and then digging through the shelves to pull out a battery-operated lantern and two flashlights. "Maybe you should sit this out. Someone should watch for Mom and Easton, anyway. And I don't have enough flashlights..."

"We're still doing this?" I asked. "I told you Calder is a freak who—at *minimum*, assuming he is in fact incapable of gaining fish flesh—goes skinny-dipping in a park in chilly autumn weather and is also a guy I barely know who just tagged along and you're like, 'all righty, let's go into the dark, dangerous woods where the ticks might feast on our blood'?"

"Yes, I guess?" Her nose scrunched. "You said your friends knew him, right?"

"Yeah, but..."

"Then let's do this." She turned to look at an ancient, dusty miniature grandfather clock that was on a table in the corner. "Before Mom, Easton, and Autumn get back. I *kind of* didn't tell

Mom we'd be having company. Let alone boys. Let alone so many of them."

Half-sighing, half-growling, I stomped up the stairs, clutching the bug spray cans as if they were Molotov cocktails I was about to throw.

———

If Ember thought I was going to sit by the fire and play housesitter while she did whatever this was with all *my* friends, she had another think coming.

So I put my name into the random pairing app Journey Slowe had on her phone. And guess who I got paired with?

Calder Poole.

I bounced on the balls of my feet as I waited for our turn to go. Journey was timing everyone, sending us in every five minutes as pairs. The first three pairs had taken the flashlights and lantern, so the rest of us just had the apps on our phones.

The pungent sharp odor of DEET clung to one of my favorite sweaters. I hadn't been sure where my jackets were packed, so I hadn't bothered to grab one. I was shivering and about to walk through some crappy woods not even intended for foot traffic with only a phone light to guide the way.

Fun. My new step-sister certainly knew how to have fun.

I glowered at her. She'd been paired with Dean—Dean, whose eyes were amazingly sharp and bright without the sunglasses, I'd managed to notice, despite all the crap going on right then. Then again, Ember's best friend had been in charge of the pairing, and she hadn't exactly *shown* us the results.

"Are you sure you don't want my coat?" Calder asked for the fifth time as we waited for the five-minute head start for Lyric and Grey—oh, that had been a fun pairing to witness—to run out.

"I'm fine," I snapped, letting my gaze wander toward him for just a fraction of a second. He didn't seem any worse for wear despite having been soaked and slapping all those clothes on without drying off first. His hair still looked damp, but he wasn't even shivering.

"You don't look fine—"

"Well, I *am*."

Calder's eyes widened as if just now discovering he'd been walking toward a snarling, chomping dog. He dug his hands into his letter jacket pocket, taking a few steps away from me and pausing to stare in Dean and Ember's direction.

Ember had a smile on her face that threatened to slice right through her cheeks and off into the horizon. Smirking, Dean was speaking to her in low whispers, a coin in one hand that he kept flicking up and down like Two-Face.

"Ivy and Calder, time to go." Journey stood at the edge of the woods—Noelle's property ended at the mowed grass, but there were autumn leaves encroaching onto her lawn that crunched like brittle bones beneath our feet as we approached.

"Have fun," said Journey, grinning like the proprietress of a haunted house. She'd been paired with Devam, who had his nose in his phone. "Come back after an hour—or sooner, if you want. But whichever pair spends the most time there wins."

Wins what, exactly? Pneumonia and Lyme disease? I broke through the line of trees. No map, no trail... And supposedly these woods didn't end until the *lake* all the way at the park that took twenty minutes to drive to from here. Oh, this was a *very* smart idea.

"Hold up," said Calder, but I didn't. I just walked, my flashlight app lending a too-bright light over the tangle of leaves and branches and moss in front of us.

Calder caught up after about ten minutes anyway, the first time I had to slow down to lift my leg over a huge fallen branch. "I get the feeling you don't like me much."

"I don't even *know* you," I said, as if that explained everything.

"Then you have no reason to hate me."

I shone my phone screen at his face and his grin died instantly as he shielded his eyes with his hand.

"Look, I'm sorry you caught me skinny-dipping. I only jumped in after I was sure you and your friends had left—"

"You often skinny-dip in forty-degree weather?" I said, straddling the branch like it was a horse.

"Sure," he said, and I could see his leg swing out so he straddled it too—facing me. "I'm on the swim team."

"There are indoor pools. Like at school."

"I like being outdoors," he said, and he took a deep breath. "Doesn't that air feel great in your lungs?"

I was hit then with a wave of ice that coursed through my insides and I shivered harder. "Sure. Great. That's what I'd call it."

He rustled and I figured out he was taking off that jacket. "For the last time, will you wear my coat?"

"No," I said, slapping the extended coat away. Dang it, I really needed that coat, but I was so angry with him for... For having a freaking fish tail and making me question my sanity.

We struggled slightly, him pushing the coat toward me and me pushing his arm away, until his arm swung out, his coat went flying —his *letterman* jacket—and I felt a pinch of guilt.

I reached out to grab it for him.

"Wait," he said, "I don't think we're in a safe place—"

But it was too late. I leaned too far and realized after I'd lost my balance that this huge branch was at the edge of a gully.

I went tumbling down, rolling through wet, damp leaves, twigs scratching my face and poking into my sides, my arm slammed protectively against my eyes maybe a bit too late. I wasn't sure how long it took or exactly what Calder called out then, but it hurt and even when I finally stopped, my body ached and I rolled onto my back, groaning.

"Ivy!" The sounds of crunching leaves and snapping branches continued a moment more and I realized that accidentally or on purpose, Calder had rolled down the hill after me.

I rolled up to a sitting position, groaning the whole time, and Calder swooped in to guide me up, gingerly gripping me on my side and shoulder. I stared at whatever it was that I'd clutched so tightly in my hand.

Calder's stupid coat.

I screamed and tossed it aside. Calder wouldn't let the thing rot amongst the foliage and picked it up, sliding it around my shoulders with minimal protest from me for once.

I blinked. "Where are we?"

Calder looked around. "Wherever we are, we're not going back up the way we came."

"Great," I muttered. I stood on shaking feet, allowing Mr. Prince Charming Wannabe to swoop in and lend me support. How come *he* was relatively unscathed? The fall had barely mussed his hair.

I looked around. "Where's my phone?" Panic shot threw me. "Where's my phone?!"

Calder frowned and let go of me as I started to look around. "Up there somewhere maybe?"

"Well, that's just *great*." I started pacing back and forth, as much to warm myself up as to express my anger. "My mom's going to kill me—or my dad's going to when he comes home any minute and realizes we were all throwing a stupid party on a school night and trespassing on a neighbor's property—"

"It's mine," said Calder. "That is... It's my family's."

That made me stop. I pulled his coat tighter around my neck and then just gave up all pretense and slid my arms through it, lifting one leg and then the other in place to keep my blood flowing. "What do you mean, it's yours?"

"These woods are my family's property," he said. "So I give you all permission to be here. Well, I give most of you permission, I guess..." He looked over his shoulder. At what—a deer? No one else was coming this way.

"Well, that solves *one* of many problems if that's true..." I finally took in the area around us more. We were on a path. Still woodsy and quaint and all that but an actual cleared path. "We can follow this out," I said, suddenly excited for the first time in hours—days—years, maybe.

"Yeah..." Calder looked one way and then the other.

"Don't you know the way?"

He kept looking one way and then the other. "We got sort of turned around when we fell," he said. "And just because we own the woods doesn't mean I spend a huge amount of time traveling through them. And you know, by the looks of things, this might be the small section of the woods that the family sold to someone else..."

"You. Are. Kidding. Me." I growled as I stomped down one direction, sure it was the general direction from which we'd started this whole mess.

"Ivy, hold up! Let me think."

"No, thank you. I've had enough of that." I stomped forward, stumbling a little on the damp dirt. I pounded ahead a few minutes, not saying anything, letting my anger build like the sound of trickling water that seemed to grow louder as I moved until at last I found myself retorting. "But if I get shot at for trespassing or for resembling a deer, I'll have you to—"

When I reached the end of the path, it opened to a clearing.

There was a cottage there in the middle of the woods at the edge of a river.

A beautiful, cozy, not-at-all-rundown cottage. With lights on.

"Um, yeah," said Calder as he caught up, his breaths grown slightly shallow. "This is that patch of land..."

The moonlight shone brightly through the clearing surrounding the cottage and I could see Calder's expression plainly.

He looked horrified.

CHAPTER NINE

EMBER

"You're shivering," said Dean as my sneaker kicked up another clump of leaves. "Do you want my jacket?"

I could feel my face flushing—and with the dampness in the air, that was definitely a plus. "Sure, thanks."

Though tree branches threatened to scrape his arms with the simple movement, Dean removed his suit jacket with finesse and wrapped it around my shoulders. I poked my arms through the sleeves and was instantly hit with a sense of warmth and comfort. He might have been wearing some cologne that smelled like fresh-baked cookies—or my sinuses were out of whack after thirty minutes of wandering through the near-darkness, branches slapping against my face, tripping over rocks I didn't realize were right in front of me.

On any other day, I'd have been miserable, but my heart wouldn't stop pounding. I clutched at my chest then, like I'd be able to stop my overactive organ from flying the coop.

Rustling from up ahead caught my attention. Dean's arm shot out in front of me and he took a careful step forward, putting himself between me and whatever was approaching.

Like it might be a bear or wolf instead of just another kid from Union High. The most dangerous beasts in these woods were coyotes.

Sure enough, it didn't take long for the rustling to be joined by laughter, though strangely, the tension in Dean's body didn't seem to loosen.

A scream. One of Ivy's girlfriends stumbled right in front of us. "Oh, it's just you," she said, looking us up and down. From behind her, one of the few flashlights I'd been able to pass out bobbed up and down and a guy in a letterman's jacket tumbled out of the bushes behind her.

It wasn't Calder.

For some reason, I was actually a touch disappointed.

Hotter guy right in front of you, I reminded myself.

The guy roared like a lion, like there was any chance of stumbling upon *that* in these woods.

"Shut up, Ashton," said the girl. "It's Ember Goodwin and..." She stared at Dean then, blinking. He might have robbed her of her powers of speech.

"Dean Horne," he said, nodding his head toward her and shoving his hands in his pockets.

"Paisley Parr," she said dreamily, extending her hand. I waited for him to kiss it, but Dean looked at me, as if asking for permission.

As if asking for *my* permission?

"Ivy's friend," I said, wondering if that was what he wanted me to say.

Paisley seemed to feel awkward then and raised both arms above her head to stretch. "Have you seen anyone else?" she asked, turning to me. Even just in the flashlight glow, her eyes were clearly darting to Dean every few seconds.

"No," I said. "How long ago did you go in?"

"We were the second pair to go," said Ashton, pulling out his phone then and scrolling through it one-handed. The flashlight pointed down at our feet as he slipped it under his arm and started typing. "There's nothing much to see. Just trees, leaves, and more trees."

"I wanted to find the river," said Paisley, rubbing her arms and bouncing on her toes, "but it's too freaking cold."

Ashton looked up. "She's just not used to being out of the arms of her boyfriend."

"Quiet," said Paisley, shoving his shoulder. "Anyway, I'm done." She grabbed the flashlight out from under Ashton's arm. "Want to come? We have a light."

Letting out a deep breath, I looked toward Dean for confirmation. "Okay," I said, once I got none. Truth was, I was cold and had had more alone time with a guy not related to me than I'd ever had since I'd taken my first breaths in this world. I could slow it the heck down, right? I was already overwhelmed after today.

I wondered how Ivy was faring with Calder out here somewhere. After her freakout in the basement, I would have guessed she wouldn't have wanted to be near the skinny-dipper even if she had a ten-foot pole to keep him at bay. But maybe the trip into the woods would afford her more time to talk to him. To snap out of whatever had made her so antsy.

Paisley led the way and Ashton followed suit, not looking up from his phone until he tripped and dropped it—only for Dean to swoop in and catch it before Ashton had to join the ranks of those with shattered screens.

"Thanks," said Ashton, a grin obvious even in the trickle of moonlight through the trees overhead. He took his phone back and slid it into his jeans pocket. "You play?"

That might have made sense to jock boy because the best I could guess was that it referred to something sportsy.

"No," said Dean, straightening.

"Ever think about trying out? For baseball."

"I don't have time," said Dean. "I work. But thank you."

"That blows," said Ashton. "Me and the squad could use a better shortstop."

Dean dug into his pocket and pulled out that coin he'd been fiddling with earlier, tossing it up once and catching it with ease. I realized then that he hadn't brought his own phone into the woods —I supposed neither had I, but I'd left it back in my room. I hadn't seen him or anyone else set them on my kitchen table or anything. Then again, the piles of boxes still there throughout the house made for good camouflage.

Piles of boxes. Okay, so Journey and I not getting around to any unpacking was something Mom could totally forgive, especially since none of it was my stuff anyway. But I *did* want this rather large crowd of teenagers long gone off the property before Easton's car pulled up.

I just didn't know how I'd pull that off without looking like more of a dork than they probably all pegged me for. I'd have to talk to Ivy, I supposed. Surely, she'd share some of the blame if we were caught.

"Did you see Ivy in there?" I asked. "She's with Calder Poole."

A loud snap of a twig behind me made me jump, but when I turned around, all I saw was the shine of Dean's eyes.

"No," said Paisley. "We only ran into Grey and Lyric." Her voice took on a sour note. "And they weren't ready to head back yet."

"We told them there was nothing much left to see," said Ashton, shrugging as he stuffed his hands into his letterman pockets.

"Grey's the type who never takes anyone else's word for anything," spat Paisley.

Ashton made a sound like someone had just been schooled. Not being able to put a face to the name, I couldn't comment on it.

We didn't have much else to talk about as we worked our way back. I could feel my poor sneakers getting more and more caked with mud, but Paisley was even less dressed for woods exploring and she didn't seem to be complaining, so I grimaced and kept moving forward. The only sound was the occasional scrape of Dean's nails against the coin. I had no idea how—or why, for that matter—he was flipping a coin with limited light on uneven terrain without a jacket and not even doing his best to warm up like I was.

When we broke through the line of trees at last, I could see a bunch of kids in my dining room through the sliding glass door.

Dean shirked instantly, catching his coin in midair and stuffing it back in his pocket.

"Your light sensitivity," I said, turning toward him. "I'll tell them to dim it for you."

"Thanks, doll," he said, smiling. His eyes seemed to glow even brighter in the full depths of the moonlight.

Paisley and Ashton were already half-jogging toward the sliding door, probably eager to put this cold long behind them.

Dean stayed at the edge of the woods and I trailed after them. Ashton slammed himself against the glass door—*thanks, don't know how I'll explain the streaks to Mom*—and made the guys inside jump while Journey shrieked before opening the door to let them in.

"Thanks," said Paisley, and she strolled right in with her muddy shoes.

There was mud *everywhere*. I'd never have time to kick everyone out *and* clean away all the evidence.

Journey and I exchanged a look where she seemed to read my mind. I kicked my filthy sneakers off.

"Let's get paper towels," she said and I followed her into the kitchen.

"You weren't there long," I said, rubbing my arms and trying to get some circulation back into them. "You and..." A gurgle of laughter escaped my throat. She *had* to have paired herself with her crush and me with Dean on purpose, right?

"Devam," said Journey, grinning as she bent down beneath the sink to grab a roll.

"You two were the last to go in, right?"

She ripped off a few and handed me the roll. "Yeah. We got like a minute in and I tripped and got mud all over your clothes." She gestured to her whole body then and I just realized there was a light brown faded blotch all over her front. "I tried to spot clean it." She winced as she looked down.

"Don't worry about it," I said. "But are you okay?"

Journey ran her fingers through her hair and pulled out a tiny twig. "I think so." She wrinkled her nose. "It didn't really hurt for more than a minute."

"I'm sorry," I said. "This was all my dumb idea..." I stopped when I saw she had a bandage on her forehead.

Shrugging, she started walking slowly back toward the dining room. "No, it was a good idea. This was fun."

"My mom is going to kill me," I said, staring down the open basement door and finding Arty's shiny eyes reflecting back up at me.

"My mom will if yours does," she said. "No way Noelle's keeping this from her." She bit her lip. "But we'll be fine. We'll just say we went out in the yard for a bit, I fell, we made a bit of a mess inside... We'll get everyone out of here as soon as they get back." She grabbed my arm then. "Um, so before we go back in there..."

I stopped. She took a deep breath. "I still want you to come to Homecoming with me as my BFF and actually, I think you might be hitting some kind of blossoming phase where you're about to beat them all off with a stick anyway, so maybe you'll have a date..."

"What?" I asked when Journey suddenly looked sheepish.

"Devam asked me to Homecoming."

"What?!" I repeated, more shocked than confused this time.

"Shh!" she said, grabbing my wrist and giggling. "It just sort of happened."

"Between falling on your face, patching up said face, and spot cleaning my old sweats, that just sort of *happened?*"

She chuckled and bit her lip. I shook my head but gave her a hug, paper towel roll in one hand and all. "That's great," I said. "But I don't know what you mean about me beating them off with a stick."

Journey pulled back and raised her eyebrows. "Really. What, exactly, are you wearing right now then?"

Dean! I'd totally forgotten. I ran down the hall and hit the dimmer switch, plunging the dining room into semi-darkness.

"Hey," said one of the guys.

"Sorry," I said. "Dean has light sensitivity, so I promised him I'd turn the lights down."

I stared at the floor then. The mud had seemed to have vanished along with the light. So much for cleaning it.

There was a pounding on the glass door—the moonlight

revealed so many handprints, darn it—and I jumped, but it was just two of Ivy's friends.

Paisley slid the door open and wrapped her arms around the guy.

"Hey, babe, you miss me?" he said, kissing the top of her head.

The tall girl with him shoved him aside to stride in. "Oh, please. Miss you? How Paisley doesn't need more 'me time' away from your dumb butt, I'll never know."

"*Hey*," snapped Paisley, but she was smiling from her station against the guy's chest. "You're just jealous, Lyric."

"Yes," said Lyric, leaning against the wall and crossing her arms before whipping out her phone from her jacket pocket. "Jealous. Of you and Grey. That's me."

I looked over the crowd. I actually forgot how many people we'd started with, but I knew two faces that were definitely missing.

"Has anyone seen Ivy and Calder?" I asked.

"Who's Calder?" said one guy.

"Swim team guy," said Devam—I definitely knew *his* name—as he came to stand near Journey. "We picked him up at the park, remember?"

"Oh, yeah," said the guy, who went back to talking in hushed tones with his friends.

"Are they the only ones not here?" I asked Journey. She was good at keeping track of stuff like that and she'd had everyone's names on her phone.

Her head bobbed as she did a mental count of everyone present. "Everyone but them and Dean, yeah."

"Dean's just at the edge of the woods," I said. "He was waiting for me to dim the lights."

"No one was there when we came out," said Grey as he swayed back and forth with his hands on his girlfriend's butt.

My face colored and my gaze darted to the clock on the wall. Mom and Easton had been gone two hours. I wasn't sure how much longer they'd be.

"Can someone text Ivy?" I asked. "And tell her they need to get back here?"

"She's not responding," said Lyric, entirely unconcerned. "I just tried."

"Did she have her phone...?" I turned to Journey again.

She nodded. "She was using it as her flashlight. I think Calder had his phone, too."

"Does anyone know his number?" I asked.

Silence.

There was a buzzing noise from near both Lyric and Paisley then and Paisley pulled back from her boyfriend to pull two phones out of her boyfriend's pocket. She handed him one and glanced at the screen of the other.

"It's from that Calder," said Lyric, already engrossed in the message. "He said he got our numbers from Ivy and that she broke her phone when she dropped it in the woods. But they're fine. They're on their way."

Good. I tapped my toes, the time on that digital clock eating at me. I opened my mouth and shut it.

Journey picked up on what I was about to say immediately. "So," she said, stepping toward the table around which most of the people were gathered, "it's been fun"—she turned toward Devam and grinned—"*amazing* even. But Ember kind of invited you all here without parental permission, so maybe you could head on your way?"

That caused a few chuckles as people got up from wherever they were sitting and headed toward the door.

"Tell Ivy I'll see her tomorrow," said Paisley then, nodding at me. "She can text whenever her phone is working again."

I wondered how she'd tell her dad it had broken.

"What about swim team guy?" asked someone. "We gave him a ride."

Right. Dean and Calder would still be here...

"I'll take him home," said Journey. She turned to me for confirmation. "We'll leave before your mom comes back."

Devam looked a *tad* concerned at the idea, but he cleared his throat and jammed his hands into his letterman jacket pockets. "Text me?"

"For sure," said Journey. She smiled like she was posing for a picture and a photographer had just asked her to say, "Cheese."

Journey herded the crowd toward the door, and I slid open the dining room door and jammed on my sneakers again. *This is actually going to work out*, I thought smugly to myself. I headed back to the woods to see where Dean had gone off to and hopefully to intercept Ivy and Calder as soon as they popped out from the trees.

Only Dean was nowhere to be found. So Grey and Lyric hadn't just overlooked him.

"Dean?" I said, crossing my arms tightly and peering a bit into the woods. "Where are you?"

A hand shot out from between two tree trunks and grabbed me by the arm, yanking me into the foliage.

CHAPTER TEN

IVY

My head throbbed so much, it seemed easier to just lie there, ignoring the shrill beeping, ignoring everything. Just give in to the darkness and the pounding of my brain.

There was a knock on a door nearby.

A spark in my mind pushed through the weariness and the pain.

What door?

The knock resounded again.

There was a slight creak and the sound of something scuffing— boxes being pushed over hardwood.

"Mare muu mup? Ma—"

I slapped a forearm over my eyes, but it did little to stop the pounding.

"Pah!" The voice grew clearer. "Sorry, I had my toothbrush in my mouth. Mom was insistent I see if you were up yet because your dad wants to talk to you, like, *now*."

What...?

I shifted my arm to open first one eye and then the other, pushing through the searing pain.

Ember stood at the foot of my bed, dressed and perky and staring down at me, moving a toothbrush up and down and around.

"Morry, mot to mit meady."

She turned around and left the room.

I lifted myself up on my arms and stared. I was in my new room—I supposed, I hadn't spent much time in this place yet—surrounded by boxes. My bed frame had been put together—the movers, no doubt—and I was on top of my mattress with a blanket wrapped tightly around my legs and torso like a burrito, but I hadn't even dug out my bedsheets. There was also a pillowcase-less pillow behind my head.

And there was no Calder. No cold, creepy woods and no lit-up cottage.

Massaging my temples, I strained to think of what had happened after that.

I didn't know. I, Ivy Sheppard, who was savvy enough never to get so drunk as to black out, had a gaping, *gaping* hole in my memories.

Kicking the blanket off, I swung my legs over the side of the bed and noticed that though I was wearing some clean sweats from who-knew-where, my hands were dirty.

I'd gone to bed filthy from that stupid excursion into the woods.

I jumped up, clunking into one of the bedposts as my head strained to catch up with the rest of me, and pounded over to the vanity, shoving aside boxes.

Grabbing a chunk of my hair, I pulled out a leaf, watching as the hair stood straight up and fell back down.

There was a slight scratch on my chin and the bags under my eyes were vicious.

"Ember!" I shouted, pounding out into the hallway. "Ember!"

Autumn, dressed and ready to go for once, yawned as she exited her room. Peeking in, I saw most of her boxes were at least open, her clothes overflowing off a tower of cardboard. "Why aren't you ready yet?" she asked, rubbing an eye.

Autumn was never ready before me.

I grabbed her by the shoulders, snapping her wide awake. "Where's Ember?"

She shook her head. "I don't know… What's the matter?"

The bathroom door opened and Ember stepped out, a washcloth dabbing at her lips. "Sorry, I heard you screaming, but I had to rinse first. What's up? Are you coming to school today?"

I let go of my poor, confused little sister, who scooted past us, staring at me warily as she clutched her backpack straps and descended the stairs.

"What happened last night?!"

Ember's nose scrunched and she glanced downstairs. "Keep your voice down, will you? We actually got away with it—"

Now it was Ember's turn to have her shoulders clutched between my fingers. "*What happened?*"

"Okay, okay, calm down." Looking again down the stairs, she stepped back and grabbed me by the wrist, dragging me into her bedroom and shutting the door behind us.

"You were super sleepy after you got out of the woods, so I lent you some of my sweats and told you just to go to bed." She frowned. "Did you get sick from being in the cold? I'm sorry, it was my stupid idea…"

Stupid in more ways than one.

"No, I… I got lost in the woods with Calder and I lost my phone…"

Ember winced. "Yeah, I haven't told your dad that, by the way. But I did say you got home early enough to go for a walk in the yard with Journey and me and that you both fell on your faces and got all dirty, so if you want to use that as an excuse for why you can't find your phone… Then again, if we supposedly stayed in the yard, it wouldn't be hard to find, so maybe say you lost it at the park?"

"Ember, *please* be quiet. I can't think." I massaged my forehead again as Ember clamped up.

"Girls!" came Noelle's voice up the stairs. "Ivy, please get down here to say 'goodbye' to your father."

Goodbye? My brain grew groggier and groggier, but something about a business trip popped out of the madness.

"You should talk to him now about your phone before he goes—"

"I don't *care* about my phone," I snapped, which wouldn't normally be true except for the whole *missing memory* problem.

Ember headed toward the door, but I snatched her by the back of her sweater. "You saw me come out of the woods with Calder?"

She looked at me as if I'd asked if we'd also both been carrying bathtubs. "Yeah... You were the last pair to come out. Your friends were already gone, but Journey took Calder home, remember?"

No. No, I don't remember at all, thank you.

"You changed and went to bed and I lent you those clothes and a blanket and pillow and by the time Mom and Easton and Autumn came back, you were already asleep."

"Girls!" said Noelle again.

"Coming, Mom!" shouted Ember. She yanked her sweater out of my grasp and opened the door. "Come on," she said. "Even if you're staying home today, you should at least see your dad off."

Staying home? I did have a mother of a headache, but... I followed Ember down the stairs in silence, my bare feet getting icier with each step on the hardwood floors. I ached suddenly for Mom and her townhouse with carpets.

My eyes darted around the room—there was a hipster hat that had no business being on the coat rack that for some reason sent a shiver through me. Instinctively, I found a pair of sunglasses on the little table in the hallway that also made me start to sweat. Oblivious to these thoughts of mine, Noelle walked across the hallway, adjusting a clasp on her bracelet. "Finally... Ivy?" She stopped. "Aren't you getting ready for school?"

"She's sick," said Ember quickly before I could explain anything. As if I *could* explain anything.

Noelle felt my forehead as I got to the bottom of the steps and frowned. "No temperature, I think." She lowered her voice. "That time of month?"

I felt my face flush. It was hard enough ever talking to my dad about that, let alone this woman I'd just met.

"And her throat's sore," said Ember, looping her arm through mine and dragging me past a stack of boxes into the kitchen. "We shouldn't have walked outside in the cold last night."

"I'll say," said Noelle as she entered the kitchen behind us. Fluffy Artemis jumped at our entrance from where he'd been crouched, snacking, but seemed to calm somewhat when he realized it was just us. Still, he took his next few bites warily, staring up at me in particular.

I remembered stepping on him at least. *Sorry, cat.*

"Ivy, why aren't you ready?" asked Dad.

"She's not feeling well," said Noelle. "Might be the stress of the move and everything."

"Or the tumble you took last night?" Dad frowned. "I really wish you girls would have watched where you were going—and would have thought to dress better. Just because it's only a few weeks past summer doesn't mean it's hot enough out to go without extra layers."

Dad tossed a crust of toast onto a plate and stood from the table, ruffling Autumn's hair. She cringed but ignored him, taking a sip of her orange juice.

"I've got to catch my flight," said Dad. "Noelle has my hotel contact information and I also wrote it out and posted it on the fridge. Enter it into your phone, but you can always call me directly and I'll get back to you within an hour or two at the most —just as soon as I'm out of a meeting. Call Noelle or your mom if it's more urgent and I'm not answering." He took his jacket off the back of his chair and put it on. "Don't forget your mom's coming tonight instead of tomorrow since I'm going out of town, but she'll probably stop by the house after dinner. Text her if you feel better and plan to go out."

"I... I lost my phone." My voice sounded croaky, which I supposed went with this story that I was sick, apparently.

Dad froze and stared at me. "What?"

Clearing my throat, I padded forward and took a seat across from Autumn. "I lost it. At the park yesterday."

Dad sighed but finished putting on his coat and picked up his briefcase. "Retrace your footsteps."

Ember's eyes went wide. "It's probably long gone. I mean, if it was where she could easily find it, someone else would have taken it, right?"

Dad picked his briefcase up off the floor and put it on his chair, cracking it open. "Then head to Verizon after school and ask them if they can trace it."

"It was broken before she dropped it," spat out Ember, way too quickly and way too nervously not to arouse suspicion. "That's why she didn't even notice she'd dropped it. For the second time. The first time, it, like, shattered to pieces." But Dad seemed too flustered as he loaded his case up with papers he'd been inspecting.

He snapped it shut and stared at me, shaking his head. "Honey, those are expensive."

"I *know*," I said, glowering at Ember. I wondered if mine really was broken out there in the woods back there or if I went back in the daytime, I'd find it.

The thought of going back sent shivers down my spine.

"Well, it's not like you can just mishandle it and tell me you need a new one." His lips pinched. "We'll discuss this when I get back or you can ask your mom when she picks you up after school." He leaned toward me and kissed the top of my head. "Don't stay home from school too long, okay? If you feel you have to, let Noelle or your mom know and they can take you to the doctor."

"I don't need to go to a doctor," I said, but actually, with this kind of memory loss, I wasn't entirely sure.

"Autumn, text your mom and tell her Ivy doesn't have her phone," he said to Autumn as he gave her her goodbye kiss.

"No, Mom'll kill me," I said without thinking.

Dad chuckled. "It might be just the excuse she needs to push you to get a job like she's been saying you need at your age." He went up to Noelle, who was at the coffee maker, sipping from a mug, and took her in his arms, kissing her once, twice, three times.

I stared at Ember, silently blaming her for this whole debacle. If I would end up having to *work off* the loss of my phone because of her dumb woods idea...

But the idea of looking for that phone in the woods filled me with dread. Besides, I wasn't sure how I'd gotten out of there or where, exactly, that hill was. Or if I could safely climb up or down to retrieve it.

There was one person who'd know better than I would where, exactly, we'd gone to last night.

I shot up. "Give me ten minutes, Ember," I said. "I'm going to school."

Dad pulled away from Noelle to stare at me. "Honey, if you're not feeling well..."

"I'm *fine*," I lied. "I have a test I can't miss."

"Ivy has her period!" singsonged Autumn, grinning, as if she'd caught me doing something naughty.

Mom had just *had* to explain all that to Autumn way too early.

"Shut up," I said, though not too seriously. "Bye, Dad," I said, pivoting on my heel. Then I found myself turning back to him and giving him a hug. "Have a nice trip."

Dad seemed taken aback, but he hugged me anyway. "Take care of yourself, kiddo," he said. "If you feel sick, go to the nurse's. I don't care if it's just your womanly blood—"

"*Dad*," I said before bolting for the stairs. I was *not* going to school without a shower, even if we were running late. Not when I looked like I'd just crawled out of a grave.

I skidded to a stop in my room and rummaged for whatever stupid mismatched outfit I got my hands on first—khaki capri pants and a black sweater with sparkles, good enough—and ran into the bathroom. Tossing it all into a pile in the corner, I started the water and then peeled off Ember's sweats. I caught sight of everything in the mirror. The dirt marks, the scuffs, the slight bruises... I hadn't imagined that tumble down the hill.

Maybe I got brain damage or something. It might have just hit me later.

Still, Calder had a lot to answer for. If I wasn't going to learn anything that made sense from Ember, Calder would have to fill in the blanks.

Weird, potentially-fish-boy Calder Poole.

Sighing, I tested the water temperature and took a tentative step in.

It was fortunate I was still holding the grab bar when I drew my second leg inside the tub and knocked my legs together because both legs collapsed, a shiny, scaly fish tail flopping up and down against the faucet in their place.

CHAPTER ELEVEN

EMBER

My new step-sister was having a breakdown. And she didn't want me to tell anyone.

"I really think I should tell my mom at least if you won't tell your dad," I said as I put the car in park. "She's cool. If we ask her to keep quiet, I think she will, at least as long as we're sure it's not serious..."

Ivy whipped her head toward me. She looked *angry*. Like between vowing to go to school, stepping into the shower, and shrieking like a banshee, she'd somehow become possessed by a spirit who roamed the Earth looking for revenge.

"*No*," said Ivy. "There's nothing to tell her."

"Just that you started screaming in the shower like two seconds after she and Autumn left? And the whole forgetting half of last night?"

Ivy unbuckled her seat belt and let it retract back with more force than necessary. "I'm on my period."

Puzzled, I turned the ignition off, unbuckled my own seatbelt, and reached behind me to grab my backpack. "Your period makes you scream and forget things?"

"Maybe," spat Ivy. "Have we ever lived together before? Would you even know?"

"I suppose not..."

"Then just drop it, okay?" She opened the door, snatching her large bag off the floor with the other hand. "And don't breathe a word of this to anyone. Not even my own friends."

"Ivy, you're acting really weird. Believe me, I don't want to tell my mom *anything* about last night, but if it made you come down with some weird illness—"

But she'd already shut the door.

My conscience wrestled with me as I slowly got out and locked the door behind me. I'd never done *anything* bad like I had last night and really, on the scale of things, how bad had it been? There'd been no alcohol involved even. I mean, didn't other teens drink when doing stupid stuff like that? I'd lucked out to find a group of people who hadn't even brought any with them or raided Mom's liquor cabinets. The woods alone had been enough to entertain them.

My brain sorted through the memories of last night—so much was masked through the darkness, but Ivy was the one who was losing it, right? I *knew* she and Calder had come out of the woods shortly after everyone else had left.

Everyone else but Journey. She stood in front of Dante's locker, showing her cousin something on her phone and laughing as they talked. She smiled when she saw me and walked over, sliding the phone atop her books and tablet.

"Hey, Em," said Journey. Her voice lowered. "So, did Noelle or your step-dad figure anything out?"

"No. I don't think so."

"Double stellar reputation for the win," said Journey, letting go of her stuff with one hand to point at me and herself. "Noelle wouldn't even *picture* us messing around like that."

"She seemed to truly believe we'd all just gone for a walk in the yard. And that the two of you fell flat on your faces." That actually *was* hard to believe the more I thought about it. Mom must have really trusted me.

And I'd betrayed that trust in the name of making new friends. And, to be honest, in the name of spending time with two potential hot new boyfriends. As if I'd go from zero choices to two in three seconds flat.

"Is Ivy doing better today?" asked Journey.

I froze, grabbing hold of Journey by the elbow and pulling her into an alcove between the edge of a row of lockers and a water fountain. There was gum stuck along the rim of the fountain and I shuddered. "You took Calder home, right?"

Journey cocked her head slightly as I finally dropped her elbow. The scratch above her brows didn't need a bandage today, but there was still a thin red line dotting her smooth and perfect skin. "Yeah...?"

Relief washed over me. "Ivy's making me question things."

Journey laughed. "What? What do you mean?"

"She doesn't remember last night." I frowned. "No, I guess she remembers some of it. She said she lost her phone in the woods and got lost with Calder and then... She woke up."

Journey ignored buzzing from the phone in the pile in her arms, which meant she was completely devoting herself to the problem at hand. "Is she feverish?"

"No, I guess not." I waited for a girl to take a sip from the water fountain, wipe her mouth while staring at us, exchange a *hello* with Journey, and then back away before I said more. "But what do *you* remember happening?"

Journey shifted the pile of things tighter against her chest. "Well, I saw everyone off—Devam was the last to leave." She grinned but shook her head as if to clear it. "Then I came back outside to see if you'd found the others yet—oh, you never told me how things went with Dean?"

"What?" The sudden detour in conversation threw me for a loop. "What do you mean?"

Journey's eyebrows scrunched together. "Like... After you went outside to tell him he could come in now that you'd dimmed the lights, did he just say he was going or...?" She stared above me. "He didn't have a car, right? I mean, I didn't think much about it when I left with Calder because I thought he'd left already, but there wasn't an extra car out front when everyone else left. Unless he just got tired of waiting and left before you dimmed the lights?"

"I..." I stared at the floor. What was she talking about? I'd been in the woods with Dean, true, but then... When had he left? And why hadn't I thought about this before now?

"Oh, but you weren't wearing his suit jacket anymore when Ivy and Calder came out of the woods. So you must have seen him. Right?"

It dawned on me just then that I *had* been wearing his suit coat, that he'd lent it to me for warmth during our trek through the woods. But then...

I felt as stupefied as Ivy apparently did. I just remembered going into the backyard, sitting on the wrought-iron bench Mom kept at the edge of her little garden, and watching as Ivy and Calder came out of the woods. Journey had joined us from the house a minute or two later.

Where had Dean been? I rubbed my fingers over the sleeve of my own four-button wool coat now, as if that would explain what had happened to Dean's coat—and what had happened to Dean.

"Well... And then, Ivy and Calder were on their way out of the woods, looking exhausted and, like, maybe their pet dogs had died, and then Ivy said she wanted to go to bed, you said you'd help her, and I took Calder home, and Mr. Talkative he was not..." Journey stared at me and went silent as a guy leaned forward to take a sip from the fountain.

"Ladies," he said, saluting us both with one finger.

Journey smiled, but I couldn't. I didn't recognize him and I didn't care. No-date me didn't care. Something really must have been wrong with me.

I couldn't explain what had happened for a tiny bit last night and I felt as lost and hopeless as Ivy did.

"Oh!" said Journey, bouncing in place. "But you won't believe where Calder lives—practically just around the corner from you. He said those were *his* woods we'd been exploring."

That was like a flick to the forehead. "What...?"

Journey shrugged. "Well, his family's. I don't know if you know that kind of big house half surrounded by trees down the street and to the east of your place?"

"Yeah," I said, my stomach lurching. "Mom said those are the owners of the woods that stretch all the way behind our house and the other neighbors' and right up to the park."

"Well, that's the Pooles' place." She chuckled. "So we weren't trespassing after all! We probably could have just formally organized the whole thing and not have felt an ounce of guilt about it."

"Weird..." I said, thinking.

"I wonder if Dean lives nearby, too?" asked Journey. "Maybe that's why he walked."

"Yeah..." I said, but I didn't know the answer.

First bell rang overhead and I hadn't even stopped at my locker to drop off my coat, but I didn't really care anymore. My legs automatically shuffled toward first period and Journey accompanied me halfway. "Do you have English first today?" asked Journey. English was one of the few classes we didn't share together this year.

"Yeah," I said, but my mind was so far from school, images of that house Calder lived at, those woods, the suit jacket, Dean—all of it flashed through my mind in one wild mix.

"That's your class with Dean, right?"

I nodded—though he hadn't spoken to me much the day before in class. Everyone had stared at him and his weird outfit as the teacher had made introductions since he was a few weeks late to start school, but he'd only opened his mouth once—when the bell rang to say he'd see me at seven.

"Ask him," she said.

Ask him why I can't remember a small chunk of last night?

"If he lives nearby."

Oh. I nodded. Journey frowned while looking at me but dashed away before the final bell could ring out.

I shuffled into class and put my backpack down at my desk. Dean was nowhere to be found.

Just as I was about to peel off my coat, a voice crackled out over the intercom. "Miss Goodwin. Miss Ember Goodwin. Please report to the principal's office immediately."

"Oooo," said Joe, my desk neighbor and sometimes class partner who never did a lick of work himself. "Someone's in trouble."

I turned to look at Miss Meyer, as if she could explain. She looked up from her laptop for a second and said, "Go on, then. You're excused." She scribbled something down on her hall pass pad and ripped it off, holding it out in the air.

I slowly dragged my feet over to grab it from her, shuffling back to get my backpack and loop my arms back through it.

"So what'd you do, Goodwin?" asked Joe. "Drugs? Sex? Rock and roll?"

"That's enough," said Miss Meyer, but she couldn't be bothered to look up. The final bell rang and everyone's conversations began to die down.

Miss Meyer stood up, then looked straight at me, as if I were an interloper who'd come only to disturb her class. "Miss Goodwin, please." She pointed to the door.

With shaking hands, I dragged my feet toward the hallway.

"*Nice,*" whispered Joe, a sleazy smile on his face. He gave me a little thumbs-up, as if there was no question that I was about to face some serious consequences and that was, in his estimation, totally savage.

Only I had no idea what it could be...

And if it was anything like Joe seemed to think it would be, my whole life just might be over.

———

The halls were eerily quiet as I made my way to the principal's office, thinking of how I'd headed to the nurse's office just yesterday morning. That felt like ages ago. But maybe that explained a few things. Maybe that little bump—though I'd forgotten it by the time the whole woods adventure had started— had been responsible for a few diminished brain cells.

Yeah, that was probably it.

I shuffled up to the administration office and stepped inside.

The door to the nurse's office was open and a girl was on the edge of one of the beds getting her temperature taken. A guy with a bright-green streak through his hair was speaking to the secretary, a piece of paper in his hands.

I numbly stood behind him, waiting my turn.

Was this about the party last night? It hadn't really been a party, but what if the neighbors—what if Calder's parents had complained or something?

The door behind the secretary leading to the waiting area in front of the principal's office opened. "Ember," purred a deep and soothing voice. "In here."

It was Dean.

He had on a new pair of sunglasses and he was wearing another just slightly oversized suit, though this one was pinstriped and a different design than his "work uniform."

I slowly shuffled toward him, more in awe than anything. "What are you doing here?"

He held the door for me, then closed it behind us.

"What's going on?" I asked. "Why are we both here, do you know?"

He opened his mouth and I felt my heart thud loudly, threatening to escape up into my throat, something making me dizzy and hot and strange all at once. I wanted to move forward, to put my skin at his lips—*any* part of my skin. Anywhere on my body.

"Dean, Miss Goodwin."

The pale, beautiful woman I'd seen the day before while on my way to the nurse's—the one with the cat's eye sunglasses—stepped out of the principal's office. Had Principal Lawrence gotten a new personal assistant?

"Aunt," said Dean, straightening up and tugging at the knot on his tie, tightening it.

There was no one in the room behind her and the nameplate no longer read, "Principal E. Lawrence." Instead, it read, "Principal W. Horne."

Dean's aunt was the principal?!

CHAPTER TWELVE

IVY

I'd managed to duck into an old computer lab that no one had probably cared about since the 90s before any of my friends could notice me and derail my mission. Not having a phone at the moment had actually worked in my favor because I couldn't be accused of ignoring texts asking where I was. According to Ember, Calder had texted some of them to tell them my phone was broken. Because I'd given him their numbers. As if I had those memorized after entering them as contacts ages ago.

Yet another mystery that junior was going to have to explain.

But far from the most pressing one.

The lights were off in the lab and I settled down in front of a dusty old computer with a square monitor large and chunky enough to house half a dozen other modern monitors stacked back to back. Hugging my bag to my chest, I waited for the traffic outside to subside.

The plan was to wander the halls, dodging monitors and janitors, and glance into the classrooms packed with juniors first period. Once I found Calder, I'd stalk the room, waiting for him to exit and pulling him away before he could blink, hopefully far away from anyone who might be more focused on unimportant things like dances and dresses and schoolwork.

Instead of, you know, fins that took the place of feet in the shower.

I tapped an impatient beat beside the keyboard of the computer. The ancient mouse was so grimy and caked with dried-up sweat, I noticed the light spots amongst the dark plastic even in the dark. I sat there stewing through first bell, not caring about the absence that was going to be noted on my record. Maybe I *should* have had Noelle call in for me after all. Then I could have told Ember I'd changed my mind and ghosted through the halls without being expected to be anywhere.

A voice came over the intercom right before the final bell. "Miss Goodwin. Miss Ember Goodwin. Please report to the principal's office immediately."

I tensed. What on Earth was she being summoned to the principal's office for first thing in the morning?

She's probably just getting some academic goody-goody award, I thought.

But what if it had something to do with last night?

It was about time to search for Calder regardless.

Cautiously, quietly, I made my way for the door and peeked out into the hallway. No one in sight. I wound my way toward the administration office, running into a bathroom when I heard some adult voices up ahead.

Standing behind the door, I waited until the voices and footsteps died out, then opened it again. All clear.

Embarking on my mission once more, I felt for all the world like I was playing one of those mini games in a video game where you had to sneak past guards by ducking just out of sight.

The administration office was just around the corner now. I settled into an alcove between a water fountain and a row of lockers, ready to observe Ember when she went in and then... What, exactly?

Couldn't I just ask Ember what this was all about when I saw her later?

This was a greater risk than I'd calculated, milling about mere feet from the secretary's office.

Turning around, about to head to the wing where I was sure the juniors mostly were this time of day, I opened my mouth to scream.

Calder put his palm against my lips, though, stifling the noise. He lifted a finger to his own lips and then slowly removed his hand from my face.

My heart was beating like mad—whether from the fright or the violation of my personal space or what, I didn't know.

"When did you get there?" I hissed. I hadn't heard him sneak up on me in this alcove. "How did you know where to find me?"

"I wasn't looking for you specifically," he whispered. His eyes darted over my shoulder and he grabbed me by the hand. "But I'm glad to find you. Come on. Quick."

I let him drag me down the hall—this had been my goal all along anyway, although I was none too happy to be the findee and not the finder, thereby losing all control of this situation—and just as we rounded the corner, I glanced over my shoulder and caught sight of Ember heading into the administration office. She must have come from the other end of the hallway.

"Where are we going?" I hissed. Sure, it'd been my idea to find a quiet place where a hall monitor might not come across us, but this was ridiculous. We were passing several empty classrooms and a number of dark alcoves.

"The gym," said Calder curtly. "You probably have questions and it's the best place for answers."

Sure. The gym. Always the best place for answers from sweaty blockheads.

"What about first period?" I asked. There was a little thing called a gym teacher in addition to thirty-plus students who might just get in our way.

"They're not at the pool this period," he said, as if that explained everything.

But... The pool. My shower. The pond.

Grunting, I ripped my hand from Calder's and readjusted my grip on my bag. He stared at me and I nodded, walking beside him the rest of the way.

When we approached the doors leading to the gym, he held up a finger to get me to wait. Cracking the door open, he peered inside and then nodded, and we both ducked into the empty hallway.

The sounds of shouting and cheers punctuated by a shrill whistle every half minute echoed dully from the gym proper at the end of the hallway. We stopped at the door leading to the pool, across from the locker rooms. "Don't they lock the pool when there isn't a class or practice?" I asked, realization dawning on me. "To prevent accidental drowning and all that—okay. Sure."

Calder had whipped out a key from his pocket and inserted it into the deadbolt. It unlocked with a click and he opened the door. I ducked inside after him just as the sounds from the gym grew louder and light shone down the hallway from the open door leading to the gymnasium.

A lot of close calls today. Then again, I'd never skipped before. Well, I had, like, twice, but I had been smart enough not to skip and *stay* on campus. Until now.

The pitch-black room lit up with blue, glowing light from below. Calder was a few feet away at the light switch. "It's better if we just light up the pool," he said. "The overhead light will leak out into the hallway."

"Good to know you're so experienced at sneaking into the pool with a stolen key." Raising an eyebrow, I slowly sashayed over to the lowest bleacher bench.

Grinning, Calder walked toward the edge of the pool at the spot closest to where I'd parked myself. "What makes you so sure it was stolen?" He took his jacket off and tossed it at the bench beside me.

I flinched. "Well, excuse me. I didn't realize you had a special arrangement to skip class and go swimming without adult supervision or a lifeguard—whoa, okay, is that what you're doing right now?"

Calder had flung off his shirt while I'd been talking and was tackling his belt buckle.

I let go of my bag to hold my hands in front of my face as I turned away, but my stupid, treacherous eyes kept squinting toward him, focusing on the slots between my fingers. He was buff, I'd give him that. And he looked really darn fine. His obnoxious gold hair wasn't so spiky right now and he suddenly reminded me of Chris Evans during that part in the first *Captain America* when Hayley Atwell was, like, poking his pecs.

My fingers ached to do some pec-poking.

"Sorry," he said, and I could hear the clanking of a belt buckle as he raised his jeans into the air. He tossed those farther away from me onto the bench, and they landed with a thud. "I don't mind if you look."

"Yes, I've noticed," I said. "And I bet eighty percent of teen boys would feel the same, but, uh, did you ever stop to consider that maybe *I* mind?" My hands were still up, and my eyes kept squinting through those spaces.

I'm looking for a fish tail, I told myself.

Yeah, that was it. I trained those hands lower to get a look at his feet. There were feet all right, and he was removing his socks now.

"Suit yourself," he said. I stared at those feet as they padded to the edge of the water.

Then he jumped in. The splash rocked the pool water, which bobbed up and down in a facsimile of waves.

"Someone's going to hear us," I hissed. My arms had dropped and I was staring straight ahead now, my attempts at maintaining a sense of modesty between us lost as my shoulders tensed at the idea of a gym coach walking by.

"They're more likely to hear you shouting than they were to hear that." Calder stretched his arms behind him and moved them back to his sides in a perfect reverse butterfly stroke. "Come closer. We'll talk."

"You're naked, so, no."

"Half-naked," he said, smirking. "Well, really all naked, but if you don't ask a goldfish to put on pants, I don't think you'll mind."

Fish. The tension reached my neck muscles now and I found myself plodding over to the edge of the pool.

Calder donned such an angelic smile then, the tightness in my muscles washed out and I wanted so badly to jump in with him, clothes and all.

The smile vanished. "Whoa, whoa, wait," he said. His hands popped out of the water, splashing liquid on my feet. "You don't want to get your clothes wet," he said. "Sorry, I'll turn it down."

Cold air slapped hard against my face and all sense of warmth vanished. "Turn what down?"

"Siren call," he said. "It was an instinct. I didn't even realize I was doing it. Not that that's an excuse..."

"Sirens are women," I said, like arguing semantics was the thing to do right now.

"Are they?" he asked. "I didn't know you'd ever met one before." He looked at me then like I... Like I was the most amazing person in the world and like he would be there worshipping me, if only I asked.

Realizing my limbs were shaking, I decided to sit at the edge of the pool, stretching out my legs to the side of me, careful not to get my pants wet from the splash of water at the edge. My hands shook as they ran over my legs then, but I felt them without thinking, as if to make sure they were really there.

Calder beamed sweetly as he swam closer, hooking his forearms on the side of the pool in front of me. "You've seen your tail, haven't you?"

My blood ran cold and I stared at him.

He flexed his legs up and out of the water, except that instead of toes, it was a pair of fins that broke through the surface.

I knew I ought to have screamed, but my mouth hung open and all sound choked.

He let go of the edge to turn his whole body sideways, giving me a full view of him. Sure enough, below that way-too-defined-for-a-teen-boy six-pack was a long, deep blue fish tail that ended in a pair of light blue fins that stretched on twice the length of his feet.

"How are you on the swim team if that happens when you touch the water?" I asked. Because that was the first thought that I managed to find my voice for. Not the whole, you know, *how are you a freaking merman* thing.

Chuckling, he rolled in the water. He took a deep breath and then dove down, and what popped through this time were feet, his toes wriggling in the air as he did some synchronized swimming move and then they were gone, back under water, and his head popped up.

I pointed at where his feet had been as he swam closer, my mouth opening and closing. "Okay, I don't even know where to start with that."

"Try me. Ask anything. Any question that pops into your head." He leaned his forearms against the edge of the pool again.

"Can you breathe underwater?" I asked. "Because I saw you take a breath."

His fingers did a little promenade atop the concrete. "I can, but only when I have my tail instead of legs. Thus, the need to fill up on oxygen before I showed off my lower limbs."

"How do you switch from one to the other?"

"When you saw your own tail, what happened?" he asked, totally cheating because he'd promised to answer *my* questions.

"I was in the shower," I said, feeling my face darkening and suddenly growing shy. "And I fell right to the bottom of the tub."

Calder winced. "Are you okay?"

I rubbed the top of my arm, which had taken on all the strain gripping the grab bar when my legs had suddenly lost their ability to support me. Because they'd been soft and squishy and floppy and fused together. "Yeah," I said, rotating my shoulder. "Mostly."

Calder nodded. "And then?"

"And then I screamed like a mother—" I cut myself short. He widened his eyes, but he seemed more mischievous than disapproving. "And then I *screamed*," I said again. "And screamed and screamed and by the time my step-sister knocked on the door, I looked down and I was sitting in the tub with two perfectly human legs."

Calder bristled at the mention of "step-sister," averting his gaze, but he didn't say anything about her. "Give me your hand," he said.

"What?" Instinctively, I cradled both hands against my sternum, as if afraid to give him what he wanted.

He looked a tad affronted, then nodded. "Put your hand in the water."

"Tail or elephant trunk down there?" I asked.

"What?"

My face flushed harder. "Are your family jewels on display?"

He laughed. "Tail. For me, that's easier."

I rotated and crawled on hands and knees toward him, not entirely unaware of what it might look like were there anyone to observe us just then, and let the knees of my pants get damp in the remnants of water on the hard surface of the pool edge. Lowering a palm toward the water, I hesitated and looked to Calder for confirmation.

"Go ahead," he said. "And think... Think of water."

"Put my hand in water and think of water?" I scratched my jaw.

"I just... That's the best way I can explain it."

I lowered my hand until it was practically grazing the surface. "I'm not about to form a tail here that'll bust through my capris, am I?"

He shook his head. "Not unless your legs are wet. And not unless you really focus. For me, I have to focus to have legs in the water. You... You have to focus to have a tail."

"I wasn't *focusing* on mermaids when I became one in my morning shower," I said. "It just happened."

"It's a little unstable at first," he said, swimming closer, "until you get used to it." He grinned up at me then. "Besides, maybe you were thinking about me in that moment..."

I dunked my hand then, staring at one of the lights beneath the surface of the water to avoid focusing on his dazzling white teeth.

This was ridiculous in so many ways, I didn't even *know* where to start. I didn't believe in ghosts and spirits and all that stuff. No one had ever bothered to ask me if I believed in *mermen*.

"Focus on the water," said Calder quietly.

I stared at my appendage and pushed aside all my racing thoughts. *Water*, I told myself. *Water. Flow. Water on my hand.* I gently moved my fingers up and down.

And then they glowed blue.

"What's going on?" I asked.

"Pull it out of the water," he instructed.

I did. It was still glowing blue. A brighter blue than the light coming up from the bottom of the pool, a brighter blue than the sky on a sunny day. A brighter blue than I'd ever seen—but not so blinding as to need to turn away from it. My hand glowed blue—*water*, I thought again, as I thought I saw it fade—and it was beautiful. I watched it as I turned my appendage back and forth in the air, drawn to it like a moth to flame. Only "flame" wasn't the right word. I felt chilled then, though the cold didn't bother me.

"That's your power," he said, like that made any sense at all.

"Calder, what happened last night?"

The door to the hallway burst open. "What are you two doing in here?"

The light on my hand vanished as I spun around. One of the gym coaches pounded through the room to the light switches.

His eyes went wide as he flicked on the overhead lights. "Are you *skinny-dipping?*"

Then, for some reason, as if he were calling a foul, he put his whistle to his lips and blew.

CHAPTER THIRTEEN

EMBER

"I won't take much of your time," said the new principal as she walked around her desk to take a seat. I exchanged a glance with Dean and he offered a hesitant smile before pulling out one of the seats in front of the principal's desk and staring at me expectantly.

"Oh," I said. "Thank you." No one had ever pulled out a chair for me before.

I slid my backpack off my back and cradled it in front of my chest as I took a seat. Dean pushed the chair in and I startled, not expecting the movement.

Turning to glance up at him over my shoulder, I locked eyes with him—or, stared at his sunglasses anyway—and the corner of his lips curled up into a knowing grin.

Heat rushed down from my head to my toes.

"Dean's told me so much about you," said the principal as Dean took the seat beside me. He crossed one leg over the other, resting his ankle on the opposite knee.

He's been telling her about me?

I laughed nervously. "We just met yesterday..." It *did* feel like a lifetime ago in some ways.

"When it's meant to be, it doesn't take long," said the principal, her plump, bright red lips curling into a smile. "At least it didn't for me and my partner."

Okay... Tittering awkwardly seemed to be the only thing I was capable of at the moment.

"But you must be confused," she said, finally making some sense. "And I haven't introduced myself properly." Her long, long fingers that ended in French manicured tips caught my eye as she extended her hand over the desk. I took it in mine, self-conscious of my stubby nails and dry knuckles. "Wilhelmina Horne. Minnie," she said. "Dean's aunt."

"The aunt who owns the moving company we used...?" I asked.

"One and the same." She dropped the handshake and readjusted her sunglasses. "I have a variety of business interests, but education has long been a passion of mine." She must have caught me staring at her glasses then because she added, "Light sensitivity runs in the family."

"Oh," I said. "I... I didn't mean to stare. Sorry."

"Please, dear," she said. "No need to apologize. I'm just used to anticipating the question."

She shifted slightly to the side to face her computer screen then, clicking her mouse a few times and typing at lightning speed. "All right. Down to business. We received a complaint about your little excursion last night."

My stomach fell through the floor. *What? Who? When?* My mom was going to kill me.

She stopped typing and smiled at me. "Don't worry about it. As far as the school is concerned, it occurred off-property and after school hours. There were no reports of underage drinking, so I see no reason to discuss this with your guardians."

I looked from Dean to Minnie and back again. "So... What was the issue?" I asked. As far as teen "parties" went, I thought this had been kind of tame.

"Well, there was a complaint that you were trespassing. That a group of our students were trespassing," Minnie clarified. "I mentioned it to Dean, and he told me what happened—"

Something Journey had said flashed into my mind. "But the

land belonged to one of the students with us," I protested. "Calder... Calder Poole?"

Minnie's lips went tight and she folded her hands, resting them on the desk in front of her. "Apparently, he didn't have his guardians' permission. Not for every student there." Her head tilted ever-so-slightly toward her nephew.

Dean bounced his leg beside me, running his fingers over his chin.

"But in any case, what's done is done," said Minnie. Her nose went up in the air then, as if she smelled something foul. "But enough of that unpleasant business. I hoped while I had you here that I could extend an invitation to have you over for dinner." Her lips curled upward sweetly. "I don't know if Dean has made you aware, but I'm his guardian. It would be an honor to have you join my family for a meal."

I blinked. "I, uh... Huh?"

The laughter Minnie emitted echoed pleasantly in my ears. Dean turned to look out the open window, pushing his fist against a cheek. He seemed to be stifling a smile. I shivered. It was a warm day for autumn—but still too cold to enjoy the breeze, which sent the deep red curtains swaying back and forth just slightly. I was glad for my coat.

"Dinner, my dear," said Minnie. "I'd love to have Dean's new girlfriend over for dinner."

If I weren't already squeezing my backpack tightly, I would have clung to the armrests on the chair in shock. "Sorry?"

"You can't come?" asked Minnie, her lips growing thin. "I haven't even suggested a date—"

"No, I mean..." I whipped around to face Dean, but he was still staring out the window. "Aren't you going to tell her she's mistaken?"

Dean snapped to attention then, uncrossing his legs and putting his foot down flat on the floor. "Have you changed your mind?" It was hard to tell with the sunglasses on, but his lips went tight, and he seemed to be holding back something like hurt in his voice.

"What do you mean?" I asked.

Dean and Minnie shared a pointed look, a slight shift of their heads to indicate a silent exchange.

"Are you feeling okay, doll?" asked Dean, turning back to me.

"I..." I shook my head. "I just don't... I don't know what you're talking about. We never talked about *dating* last night." *Believe me, I would have remembered that.*

"We did," said Dean. "When you came back out after dimming the lights in the house. And you returned my suit jacket."

The missing few minutes in my memory. I felt nauseous then. There was no way—*no way*—I wouldn't remember that happening.

But the thing was, I didn't remember what had happened at all.

"I thought you... You seemed interested in Ivy." Like that was the important thing right now.

Dean cocked his head. "Your sister?"

"Step-sister," I whispered, clinging to my backpack even more tightly.

"Ember, I told you last night I understood if you thought I was being too forward," said Dean. "If you've been having second thoughts, just tell me."

"No, I..." What was wrong? There was something so wrong hanging in the air. If I'd remembered him asking me out—if he'd asked me out today, I... I knew I'd have said 'yes,' as crazy as it might have been to accept someone I barely knew like that. Because to be honest, a small part of me had hoped for a date to Homecoming.

I just hadn't dared expected something more so quickly.

And I... I didn't like that I was missing this part of my memory. What had happened—to both Ivy and me? Was there some kind of mushroom in those woods that gave off hallucinogenic spores?

"Dean, why don't you take her to the nurse's office?" said Minnie. "She doesn't look well."

"I'm fine," I said, but my heart was beating hard.

"Then just go there and rest, dear." Minnie stood. "We can discuss dinner another time—if you're interested in coming, that is."

I tried to smile then. She seemed so kind. And I felt more at ease as she approached, as Dean stood and stepped behind me. "Thank you," I whispered. I did feel faint.

Dean pulled my chair back and leaned down, his forearm extended. I took hold of it and stood on shaky legs. Dean reached around my other side to grab my backpack. "Let me," he said, and I let go of the thing, left with only his arm to grip on to with my shaky fingers.

Minnie's wedge heels echoed on the floor as she moved around us to get the door.

"Thank you, Aunt," said Dean, nodding to her as we passed. He pronounced it like "ahnt" instead of the garden variety.

"Thank... you..." I said again, but my throat was growing tighter. I stared at the blood-red button on the shoulder of her cute vintage navy dress.

We wove past the secretary's desk and the woman barely spared a glance as we rounded the corner and headed straight for the nurse's.

A beautiful, pale Latina woman in an old-fashioned candy striper outfit looked up from the nurse's desk. "Hello. Is there something you need?"

She had dark, dark eyes—unnaturally so. Like she was wearing black Halloween contacts. The color seemed to spill even into the whites of her eyeballs.

She stood and went to close the door behind us. I followed her movement and caught sight of Ivy—*Ivy of all people right now*—approaching the secretary, a guy with a towel wrapped over his shoulders a short distance behind her. An angry gym teacher leaned over the secretary's desk and started shouting something about the pool and he pointed to Ivy and—*Calder*, it was Calder Poole—and Ivy caught my eye just as the nurse closed the door and blocked my view of her.

"It's noisy out there," said the woman. Clasping her hands together in front of her waist, she looked from me to Dean and back again. "How can I help you?"

"Where's the... nurse?" I asked, finding, for some reason, my strength slightly returning.

"She's ill," said the woman. "I'm her temporary replacement, Ruby."

But I'd just been there the day before and she'd seemed fine. I massaged my forehead, trying hard to remember. I'd peered in here just before going to speak with Minnie and I'd *thought* I'd seen the white lab coat the nurse usually wore, not this, this... *Halloween costume*.

"Let her sit," said Ruby, and she took me by the arm Dean had left vacant and the two of them guided me to the chair beside the nurse's desk like I was a toddler about to topple over on my little awkward feet at any minute.

When I finally landed on my butt and they both stepped back, I simultaneously felt relief and disappointment.

Strength was returning to me, so long as I stopped thinking hard about all the things that didn't make sense.

"What's ailing you?" asked Ruby.

Where do I start? I looked up at Dean, who stood staring down at me, his arms crossed, concern twisting his lips.

Something strange hit me then, something like gravity, a force pulling my head to look down beneath the nurse's desk. A wastebasket was there, nearly overflowing with garbage. Tissues, bandage packaging... A few gauze pads splotched with blood. Red against white.

"Let me take your temperature," said Ruby, pulling an ear thermometer off the wall above her desk and rummaging through a drawer for a little disposable cap. I brushed the hair on my right side behind my ear and she inserted the thermometer.

After a beep, she took a look at the screen. "That looks normal." She reached beneath the desk to pull out the wastebasket and popped off the plastic cap into the garbage. "A little hot, but still within the range of—"

Before I could even begin to stop myself, I grabbed for the bloody gauze pads, and the instant the pads came into contact with my palm, my fingers glowed brightly with a fiery red light.

CHAPTER FOURTEEN

IVY

I had the ability to swap my legs for a mermaid tail and I was about to probably be *expelled* for something that wasn't *quite* like this coach insisted he'd walked in on, and all I could do was stare at the door leading to the nurse's office through which Ember had just disappeared. With Dean Horne.

Had whatever the principal had summoned her for made her sick or was *she* the one who'd caught something in the woods the night before? Maybe we both had. I stared down at my hand—the one that had glowed blue when I'd submerged it in water—and tried to will it back to light again, tuning out the coach who was droning on and on in front of me.

"Are you even listening, young lady?"

Admittedly, no. "What?"

The coach's face flushed red and he snapped back to face the principal's secretary. "Do you see what I mean? Utter disrespect. Skipping first period to *skinny-dip*, putting themselves in danger without supervision—"

The phone rang and the secretary held up a finger, getting up from her desk to prop open the door leading to the principal's office waiting room and using her foot to lower the stopper before heading back to the desk and grabbing the phone receiver. "Okay," she said to the coach. "Have them sit there and I'll explain to the principal."

I exchanged a glance with Calder and we shuffled over to the seats. The coach had shoved towels he'd grabbed from the sidelines at both of us after he'd turned his back—still lecturing us the whole time—but I hadn't really needed one, so I bunched it on my lap and gripped the rough-spun fibers. Calder's towel was wrapped around his shoulders, his hair still wet. I lifted my towel toward him, offering it to him.

He shook his head and frowned, his thoughts clearly elsewhere as a glaze rolled over his eyes.

He seemed different—sad, somehow. The image of him as I'd first noticed him on that little island jumped into my mind. He'd seemed melancholy then, too.

I remembered that urge inside me to want to protect him, to comfort him—it drowned me right then.

The coach had been saying something, I supposed, because he sighed loudly and I caught him sending us a pointed look before he turned on his heels and left.

Good thing I didn't have gym this semester. Not that I'd ever had that guy before anyway. But I did *not* need a gym teacher who'd look at me and think "skinny-dipper" all the time, thank you.

Calder wasn't saying anything—didn't he care that he'd essentially gotten us into this mess?—and I turned over my shoulder to see if Ember had left the nurse's office yet, but the door was still closed.

The secretary finished her call and then dialed a shorter number before diving into a hackneyed explanation of what we'd been up to.

Calder folded his hands together and bounced his knees. He seemed pale.

"Are you all right?" I asked the freaking merman.

"You can go in," said the secretary before he could answer, putting the phone down.

I stood, a barrage of emotions flooding through me. It was only in that moment that I realized that more likely than not, a parent —or both—was going to get a call about all this.

And I wasn't dumb enough to tell them the truth and have them start whispering about putting me in therapy again. Maybe they'd even put me away for this and throw away the key. I might have, had someone come to me with this story sixteen hours earlier.

So kinky falsehood it was.

Dad was on his business trip, so that left Mom to come pick me up if I was suspended and whoo boy, was that sure to be a nightmare.

Was there any chance they might call Noelle instead?

I headed toward the principal's door, one shaking leg at a time. As I touched the doorknob, I turned to see Calder still sitting there, looking for all the world like he was about to be sick.

"Principal Lawrence isn't *that* scary," I said, trying to seem braver than I felt. He wasn't that frightening, but my mom could be.

Calder stood, drawing the towel around his shoulders tighter around his neck, like he needed the warmth.

Who, exactly, was the one who'd just had her mind blown here? Wasn't the fish stuff all old hat to him?

Blinking rapidly, I opened the door, pushing it wide.

It wasn't Principal Lawrence.

A pale redhead in a cute navy dress sat behind the desk donning vintage-style sunglasses. A name plate read, "Principal W. Horne," which made me do a double take, considering the name and the sunglasses. It couldn't be a coincidence.

A breeze fluttered through the billowing burgundy curtains to the side of her, and my gaze snapped to watch the movement.

Just in time to watch as Calder brushed past me, tossed off his towel as he ran past her desk, and jumped right out the open window.

We were on the first floor, but still.

Still.

"What the—?" I said, all thoughts about the strange woman in the principal's seat forgotten. Calder was still moving, nothing more than a dot on the horizon.

I didn't notice the woman get up or approach the doorway.

She pivoted toward the window to watch him vanish from sight before turning back to me. Her head moved up and down and her eyebrows arched before she slammed the door in my face, not speaking a word.

Dumbfounded, I kept staring at the pale oak of the door, as if something—*anything*, for Pete's sake—might just start to make sense.

"Did you see that?" I said, turning to the secretary.

She shrugged and picked up the phone. All in a day's work. Sure. This was all normal.

My feet shook as I made my way back to the hallway. I just felt the need to get *away*—I could make sense of it elsewhere.

Just as I reached it, the door to the nurse's office flew open and Ember, much more full of energy and pep than she had been before, bolted out of there.

"Em—" I started, but I caught sight of Dean Horne standing in the nurse's doorway and I swallowed.

His sunglasses turned in my direction and I felt a chill wrap around my spine.

Someone grabbed my wrist—my hand still clutching the scratchy school towel—and I jumped.

Ember stared then into my eyes. "Let's get out of here," she said. "Now."

She didn't have to tell me twice. I tossed the towel behind me, throwing it at Dean for good measure.

———

"I'm sorry I didn't believe you," said Ember almost the second she closed the driver's side door of her car. She'd been silent as she'd strode determinedly right out the school, her hands shakily digging through the backpack she clutched in front of her until they'd found her car keys.

"About what?" I said. I'd only told her a fraction of it, really. I hadn't had a chance to tell her the rest of the bizarre events that seemed attracted to me like iron shavings to a magnet.

"The mermaid thing, the memory loss, everything."

She looked tense as she squealed her car out of the spot. I clutched on to the dashboard for dear life, quickly slapping on my seatbelt during the brief pause she needed to switch gears.

"So you believe me now?" I said, my shoulders tense as she hit the accelerator. Thank god the parking lot was empty. Because we were ditching class. The good student was driving like a maniac to get far, far away from school while it was still in session.

"Yes." Something had shaken her. Clearly.

She pulled out into traffic, ignoring a car that honked and screeched to a halt to let us cut in and drove faster.

"Ember," I said, tossing a glance over my shoulder to see the driver mouthing something while flipping us off, "as glad as I am to have someone not think I'm off my rocker, can we slow down? I don't want to die in a car accident."

Ember's foot relaxed somewhat and we slowed down just enough to stop breaking the speed limit. But she hunched over the steering wheel like an old lady, her nose pointed forward, her eyes focused like Cruella de Vil after those blasted Dalmatians.

"What happened?" I asked, in no mood to tiptoe around the obvious.

"We need to go back to those woods."

As if that answered anything. And after last night and the fact that a gaping hole existed in my memories? No thanks. "I'll pass, thank you."

She didn't say anything for another minute, hitting the accelerator and barreling through a stale yellow light just as it turned red. Cars honked at us.

"Okay, maybe you should pull over," I said. My palms sweated as I gripped the armrest on the car door. "I can drive."

She didn't reply. I extended a hand toward her shoulder hesitantly and gently placed it atop her sweater. "I'll go to the woods with you. But you have to tell me why."

She took one hand off the steering wheel then and looked at it
—taking her eyes off the road, which sent my heart thumping,
until I took a look at it too.

There were streaks of cracked red on that hand, a mishmash
pattern of dried blood.

CHAPTER FIFTEEN

EMBER

We'd made it home in one piece, though I'd be the first to admit, that hadn't been for lack of (unintentional) trying.

I really shouldn't have driven when upset, but all I'd felt was the need to get out of there.

Now all I felt was the need to wash away the stains on my skin. The dried blood was long gone, but I could *feel* it on my skin, even if I couldn't see it. I could feel the rush of fire that had coursed through my hand, the *need* to pick up disgusting medical waste.

Closing my eyes, I took my hand out from under the water and leaned it against the bathroom wall beside the mirror, not bothering to dry it off or turn off the faucet.

A knock came at the door behind me. "Ember?"

I opened my mouth to speak, and a tightness squeezed at my throat. "I'm okay." That was a lie. But what else could I say?

"You ready to talk about... the blood?"

Sighing, I turned off the faucet and grabbed a towel, scrubbing my hands dry until the skin cracked.

More blood pooled—just slivers, small fragments—but it was enough to drive me wild with fire.

I threw the towel to the ground and ripped open the door. "Bundle up this time," I said, looking over Ivy. She had a sweater and capri pants on but no jacket. "Hats and gloves and everything."

"Hats and gloves aren't exactly going to save us from memory loss," muttered Ivy as she followed me to my room. "So you're saying you forgot some of last night, too?"

"I hadn't thought I had," I said as I opened my closet and started rummaging for some old winter wear. I found a pink hat and a matching set of gloves I'd gotten for free during a cancer walk I'd done in honor of my aunt a few years back. They were too thin, really, but they'd have to do. "Here." I tossed them at her and she caught the hat, but the gloves fell to her feet.

"Look," she said, "I said I'd go with you—I should probably look for my phone anyway—but there's one condition: You have to calm down and *talk* to me first."

Closing my eyes and swallowing, I took some deep breaths—meditative breathing for the win—and sat on the edge of my bed. Ivy shuffled over to sit beside me just as I heard a quiet growl and I opened my eyelids in time to see a white streak dart out from underneath us.

"Arty?" I cooed. "It's okay..." He stopped at the doorway and stared at us, his arched back lowering somewhat at the sound of my voice. "Come here, baby," I said, patting my lap. He reluctantly slinked over and sat down, eyeing Ivy cautiously as he kneaded my lap.

"I don't think he likes me," said Ivy.

"If he didn't like you, he wouldn't even sit near you." I started stroking his forehead as he settled down, drifting off to sleep.

Ivy looked at him but didn't try to pet him, perhaps afraid of scaring him away. "What don't you remember about last night?" she asked.

"Dean... Dean Horne..." As if there were any other "Dean" in our mutual acquaintance. "He said he's my boyfriend now."

Ivy did a "white guy blinking" slight shake of her head in perfect echo of the GIF. "Wait, what? When did that—?"

"Last night. During those missing few... minutes, I guess?" I started massaging my temples. "It couldn't have been long. I remember being in the house and Journey escorting everyone outside to their cars and then I was in the backyard and you and Calder came out of the woods—"

"Allegedly," added Ivy. Like she doubted the fact that she had ever exited the woods? "Sorry," she said when she caught me staring. "Go on."

"Well, I mean, he apparently asked me out, I apparently said 'yes' and gave him back his jacket, then he apparently left on foot in no direction anyone else could witness him—all in a matter of minutes. Because Journey joined me right after, right as you two were—*allegedly*—leaving the woods."

Ivy's lips pinched as she played with the hot pink hat in her grip. "That's a heck of a lot to happen in a handful of minutes. And to not remember."

"Tell me about it." I tucked my right hand under my thigh, leaving only my left one to pet Arty. "After eighteen years of no dates, like, *at all*—unless you count single pity dances—I would make a point of remembering getting my first boyfriend for the rest of my life. Him being gorgeous makes that extra hard to forget."

Ivy didn't say anything for a few moments. "He said *girlfriend?* Like, not that he asked you on a date—that you're his girlfriend?"

All of a sudden, I couldn't remember the exact wording. My heart had been hammering in my chest so much since, it practically drowned out my thoughts. Maybe it wasn't so hard to believe I could forget the whole thing after all. "Yes," I said. "Pretty sure."

"Who does that?" Ivy scrunched her features up like she'd just sniffed a trash can full of rotting garbage.

My heart went cold. "Does what?" *Date me?*

"Meet someone and ask them to be their significant other by the end of the night? I can see *maybe* asking for a date, but..." She chewed on her bottom lip for a moment. "Do you think he was gaslighting you?"

"What?" I laughed. "Why would he do that?"

"I don't know." She pulled the hat over her head. "But there's a lot of stuff that doesn't make sense."

"It still doesn't explain where his coat went—and where he

went. Though I suppose he could have left earlier, right after I left him, and then I could have—chucked the coat in the woods and fallen asleep for a second? I don't know."

"But *would* you have said 'yes' if he asked you? After just meeting him?"

Swinging my legs in front of me, I stared at a hole in the toe of one my socks. Arty shifted cautiously at the movement but didn't budge. "I don't... I don't know. I had it in my head he might ask me to Homecoming. I don't know why. No one ever does." It was hard to admit that to someone who probably had to field off offers with a stick.

Ivy let out a deep breath and jumped up from the bed, swiping the thin pink gloves off the floor. Arty dug into my thigh at the movement but must have decided to stay put when Ivy didn't seem concerned with him. "Okay," she said, putting one on with the panache of a biker pulling on her leather glove. "That at least partially explains the freakout. But why did you say you believe me? And what was with the... was that ink or...?"

"Blood," I answered. "Some dried grody blood from a used gauze in a garbage can."

Ivy really did seem to have smelled rotten garbage at that. "How did that get on your hand?"

"And why did I wait until I got home to wash it off?" I ventured, not fully understanding myself. "Because... I was the one who reached into that garbage can to grab those gauzes. And I can't tell you why. I just *wanted* to. I really, really wanted to."

"Okay..." said Ivy, more slowly pulling on the other glove.

"But that's not all. It... It glowed."

Something like realization morphed the expression on Ivy's face, her features softening. "Your hand?"

"How did you know?" I didn't remember explaining *what* had glowed. I pulled my hand out from under my thigh and stared at it, turning it back and forth. The blood wasn't there anymore—not really—other than those small dry skin cracks, which had hardened into bright red dots. But the longer I focused on it, the more I thought I saw the fiery red glow in my mind. Before I even noticed she'd moved, Ivy sat down beside me, wrapping her pink gloves around my extended palm, closing it. "Because, in the right circumstances, my hand glows too."

Something happened then. My hand didn't glow, but I could feel it almost trying... Staring at the dried drops of blood on my knuckles, I could almost sense the warmth being summoned there.

Arty jumped up, bolting for the door, as if a dog had popped up from behind the bed and started chase. I let him go and stared at Ivy. Mermen and glowing hands and a crazy *need* to touch blood.

What on Earth had happened in the past few days?

The new boyfriend would have been hard enough for me to believe all of two days ago. But this?

My phone buzzed from where I'd left it in my backpack, which I'd tossed on my desk chair.

Ivy stood. "Do you want to get that? We should probably bring your phone with us. In case we get lost." She headed for the door. "I'll dig around the boxes for my winter coat."

Clenching my hand into a fist, refusing to look at it and get all hypnotized by it once more, I nodded, shuffling to my backpack after she left.

It was a text from Journey, asking why I wasn't in second period and what the principal had wanted to see me for.

Please, please tell me we didn't get in trouble for last night.

That was Journey for you. Despite not being summoned to the principal's office and therefore seemingly not a target of any punishment for the whole wild excursion, she simply didn't seem to think of getting away with anything I didn't get away with.

Even though it hadn't been her idea at all. Even though I didn't deserve her support.

The phone buzzed again and the name "Dean" with a heart flashed across the screen.

I hadn't gotten his number. I definitely hadn't inputted his name as a contact and added a heart after it.

Please call me, doll, it said. *I need to know you're all right. You ran out of the office so quickly, I didn't get a chance to speak with you—*

The text just kept going and going, like an old-fashioned letter, only he was careful to use all the right punctuation throughout. I had to turn the phone over. I laid it on my desk, not even wanting to look at it, but I did. I stared at it. Stared at it, willing it to make sense.

"Who was it?" called Ivy from the hallway.

"Journey," I said. "Just asking why I'm not at school." I didn't say anything more.

"You ready?" she asked.

"Yes," I said, walking toward the door. With one last glance over my shoulder at the phone—a wild, thunderous beating of my heart echoed in my mind then, a soft whisper deep down telling me to go back and pick it up and talk to him—I flicked off the lights and left it behind.

"We're lost," said Ivy, not for the first time. She whapped a branch away from her face and scowled at it like that would stop it from smacking her. "I have no idea where that cliff is, where the path is—"

She'd filled me in on what she did remember from the night before. A cliff she tumbled down, a nice clear pathway that ended at a cottage in front of a river that probably led to the "pond" in Standing Springs Park.

Most likely the river that joined up with the *lake* in the park, I'd told her.

She'd scowled at me over my use of "lake" and "pond," and I'd lifted my hands up in surrender.

"I saw where you two went in," I reminded her. "Same place as the rest of us."

"We must have gotten turned around at some point," she insisted, carefully lifting a leg and wrapping it around a big fallen branch. "But I wish we would freaking find it already. I'm in no mood to tumble down the cliff again, but that pathway through the woods would be a lifesaver about now—ow!" A twig snapped and she rubbed her cheek where it had hit.

She sighed, stomping her foot into the mud. "Can you bring up GPS? Like at least if we see how far we are from the river, maybe we can follow it."

"I didn't bring my phone." Guilt ate at the back of my throat as I spoke the words. It had made sense, though, at the time. I'd felt like I would drown under my thunderous heart in that moment if I'd gone back and read the full text from Dean.

From my boyfriend.

The warmness that spread throughout my body at the thought warred with the logic that kept spouting out from my mind. But if I stood still too long, the warmness was winning. I picked up the pace, maneuvering my legs around another big branch with ease. "I forgot, okay?" I said, not wanting to explain. "But I think I hear moving water up ahead."

Ivy muttered something I couldn't hear behind me and I heard the snaps of twigs and the rustles of leaves as she followed.

It was only a few more minutes until we did hit the river. "See?" I said, triumphantly standing in front of it with my hands on my hips.

"Yay, the river," said Ivy, crossing her arms tightly across her chest as she approached the small clearing. "Now we just need to follow it who knows which way for who knows how long and maybe, just *maybe* we'll—"

But I didn't hear the rest of what she had to say. With a loud splash, something shot out from the river behind me—my chin slamming forward into a pile of leaves with a sharp jolt of pain— and dragged me by the legs into the icy current.

CHAPTER SIXTEEN

IVY

I lost sight of her almost instantly. I'd let myself get frozen in shock and those few seconds had turned out to be necessary to have any hope of saving her before she'd fallen in.

Before she had been *pulled* in. I didn't see what had grabbed her, but I knew she hadn't just fallen forward onto her face and then slid backward into the river. Something had taken her. And if I didn't at least *try* to save her, even if I couldn't see her, that something might keep her below water so she couldn't breathe.

"Ember!" I shrieked, though I didn't know why—it wasn't like she could shout back if she were below the depths of the river.

I stared at the water in both directions, looking for any sign of movement. She shouldn't have been hard to find. It wasn't like large creatures typically inhabited small rivers like this one.

Calder said he could breathe when he had his tail.

Where was that obnoxious merman when you actually needed him?

I pulled my gloves off. *Dunk my hand in the water and see if I can get it to glow again?*

Although Calder hadn't exactly told me the point of the glowing hand thing.

The glowing hand thing that my step-sister exhibited as well.

I took a deep breath, steeling myself. I couldn't remember if my hand had glowed in the brief shower this morning—I'd been more freaked out about the *fish tail*—so I'd skip the hand and just... go for it. I took a step back, ready to sprint and just *dive* in—

"Don't you want to remove your pants first?" Someone cleared his throat behind me. "Sorry. That sounds impertinent, but it was truly meant as a practical question. I don't venture it's like the Hulk, whose pants magically grow to proper size. More like the Hulk's upper body, where clothes get shredded. One has to wonder why he doesn't just wear magical T-shirts on top of magical pants, come to think of it."

I whipped around. Some *guy*—pale brown skin; deep, fetching green eyes; and curly, brown hair threaded with highlights of gold and green—stood at the edge of the tree line, his hands behind his back, a casual expression on his face as if just strolling by and wishing me a "good afternoon."

And he was British or something. His accent sounded a bit off, but there were definite British overtones.

Like any of that matters when Ember is drowning right now?

I didn't have time to make a snappy comeback, ask why he knew enough about mermaid tails to make a rambling observation, or even feel embarrassed. I took his point to heart and kicked off my boots, ripping off my socks, and then unfastened my pants.

"Whoa, whoa," said the guy, taking a step forward, his face suddenly aghast, "you don't have to actually undress right in front of me."

"Then turn around," I snapped.

"No, I—" He clamped his mouth shut, lifted a finger hesitatingly in the air as if he had a point to make, opened his mouth as his head slightly twisted, and then closed his mouth again, curling his finger back into his fist.

I let go of my pants and shook my hands in the air. "For cripes-sake, will you just say what you have to say already?" I didn't care what he had to say. I was already back to the pants, peeling first one leg of them and then the other, shaking them off the second foot. The cold air slapped against my bare skin like a whip made of ice.

The pretty boy didn't turn away, despite his *apparent* misgivings. He just stared at my bare legs.

Whatever. I can kick him in the balls for this later. I left my panties on as I approached the water, wishing I hadn't dragged on the pair that read "*SASS*" across my behind. I hadn't been in the mood to fish for my boy shorts in the piles of boxes still overflowing in my room, and this old joke gift from Lyric had been on the top of the pile.

If they broke apart when I swapped my human torso for a fishy one, so be it. I wasn't giving this guy a glimpse of the full monty before then.

Okay. Jump in. Think of water. Yeah, just think of water—it'll be all around you, so you can do that—and think of... Calder? Sure. Okay. I can do this. Clenching my fists, I got ready to jump.

He lunged forward and touched my shoulder, which I swatted away almost instantly.

"Sorry," he said. "It's just... If I can promise you she's unharmed, will you refrain from jumping into the ice-cold waters without a proper guide?"

I stared at him. "What?"

He ran his hands up and down his upper arms then, staring at the river. "It's just... The river is *really* cold this time of year, and frankly, not that deep, so you have to be an experienced swimmer not to get your tail caught on the bottom. There's a lot of debris down there, yeah? Too many litterers at the park, and some of it gets carried into the woods."

I slapped both palms to my face, closing my eyes and massaging my temples. "Will you shut up? Please?"

"Right," he said.

He did. But that wasn't helping and every second that was passing was one more second Ember was probably *dying*—

I let my hands drop. "If it's so dangerous for me, why are you so sure Ember is safe?"

Pretty Boy jutted his chin out toward the moving waters. "Because they'd be breaking the treaty to attack her on *my* strong-hold, all right?" He spoke loudly then, and a gust of wind rushed in behind him, bringing with it fallen detritus that swirled into the air. "I don't care if it's autumn," he added, "I am, and always will be, judge, jury, and *executioner*."

At the last word, the flying leaves and twigs and other bits of dirt from the ground shot into the water with the force of a torpedo.

Flying leaf weapons. Sure. Why not?

The iciness hit my legs again and I shivered, jumping up and down, my toes starting to grow numb even as the pebbles and sand at the bank of the river struck like little daggers into the soles of my feet.

"My place," said Pretty Boy, loudly—and to the water. "Bring her there and we shall discuss punishment."

A shadow moved through the river then—*finally*, something I could see, something I could jump after; I wanted to jump in, I *needed* to jump in—but with a sharp look from Pretty Boy, the urge to jump passed.

He held out his arm to me, as if offering to be my escort. "Shall we?" His gentlemanly smile turned mischievous as his eyes darted down to my legs. "I suppose I should be letting you put on your pants first, Miss *Sass*."

At the next opportunity, these joke panties were going straight into the garbage.

———

Pretty Boy lived in the cottage I'd remembered walking up to the night before—before it had all gone blank.

That was the most welcome news I'd had all day. Something that might finally make sense. Assuming I could get over all the paranormal details, which, okay, I really had no choice about now.

But I wasn't dumb enough to confide in anyone else yet. Not after the reaction and stares I'd gotten yesterday for just the first portion of it.

You don't believe I saw a merman? How would you feel about the fact that I grew a pair of mermaid fins?

Pretty Boy guided me to a bench at the side of the cottage that faced the river. I hadn't wanted to let him physically escort me, but he'd insisted I'd never make my way here without his guidance and permission. Why either of those necessitated us walking arm-in-arm, I didn't know. I'd found the place with Calder and we hadn't been touching. As far as I remembered anyway.

Slinking onto the bench, I let go of him at last. I hadn't been in the mood to argue about it. I'd been hesitant to give him more fodder for his lovely new nickname for me, but that hadn't stopped him from using it twenty times on the way over.

"Until your sister arrives, Miss Sass—"

"Step-sister," I corrected. I tucked both pink-gloved hands into my coat pockets—what was the point of paper-thin gloves like that if they did exactly nothing to keep hands warm?—and huddled my upper body closer to my thighs for warmth. "And it's 'Ivy,' okay? I didn't want to tell you to stop reading my underwear in your mind because you seemed like the type who might find it amusing that I didn't find it amusing, but you don't seem to be stopping naturally on your own." I glared at him and he smiled before sitting alongside me. The bench—one of those "natural"-looking ones that seemed like someone had just split a log in half and forged it into a seat—seemed almost to glow with warmth at the touch of his butt.

Tension released out of my body, my shoulders relaxing, my muscles loosening.

"Ivy," he said, extending his hand toward me. "Orin. I told you this last night, but I bet you don't remember."

"So you did know my name." I scoffed and hesitatingly pulled a hand out of my pocket to shake his. Another burst of warmth spread throughout my body. "You just chose to be a cheeky jerk for the fun of it."

"Touché," said Orin and when he dropped his hand, I was hit with another blast of cold. I'd have asked to go inside, but my need for warmth took second place to knowing Ember was safe.

If she somehow was.

"Oh," said Orin, lifting a finger into the air. "I found this for you."

He shifted in his seat to reach into the back pocket of his brown corduroy pants—a look completed by his fuzzy green sweater—and pulled out a phone.

My phone.

Thank god.

I snatched it from him and hit the "power" button. Of course, it was out of battery.

"Told you I'd find it," he said, but I didn't remember that at all. His nose wrinkled. "It stunk out there. All that foreign, plastic, *metal* material in my woods..."

"Calder said these were *his* woods. His family's."

Orin laid an arm behind me on the bench and crossed one leg over the other, resting his ankle on his knee. "Yes, well, but these parts are *my* woods. My family's."

I glanced behind me at the small window inside, looking for movement. Orin snorted. "You won't find them in there. Believe it or not, I'm the only one who can halfway stand these human innovations."

I jangled my phone in my hand. "Innovations? Like phones that let you talk to someone halfway across the world or watch a video of a celebrity tripping over her own feet in the middle of the woods?"

Chuckling, he bounced his foot in the air. "Yes, like *those* innovations. But hey, I'm not knocking them entirely, all right? I'd be bored out of my mind without movies and books. None of my family care much about those."

I studied the cottage behind us again. "Books, I can see, but—do you get electricity out here?"

Orin grinned and reached into his other back pocket, not even dropping his arm from the bench. He took out a phone and jangled it at me as I'd jangled mine at him. "Innovations like these. Long battery life. I only need to charge it when in town."

I raised an eyebrow. *Okay, then...* Nice to know my phone caused him to give me the stink eye, but his own was just hunkydory. He seemed to read my mind then as he shifted and put the phone back into place, his eyes roving to the side, at the tree line of the woods across the river. "I'm a complicated fellow," he said, the corner of his lips twitching.

I'll say.

"So," I said, too casually for the situation, "I know you said we met yesterday and I believe you—because why the heck not? That's the most believable thing that's happened to me today. But, uh, care to fill me in on everything I need to know again?"

"That's not my place," he said, slowly dropping his arm and leg and shifting to stand. "I can do it for the blood because they don't predate me, but the water invokes ancient rites, and despite my impartiality, I have no choice but to bow to them on this."

Sure, sure... That made perfect sense. I sighed as Orin walked over toward the water, deciding it best I follow him.

As I approached, he held a hand out toward me without turning to look at me, and I froze.

The trickle of the water was growing louder then, like a rushing current.

Something shot through me—a feeling of desire. A desire to rush out and dive into those waters.

I must have moved because I found myself at Orin's side, his extended arm now cupping around my side to keep me affixed in place.

"Return the champion of the blood first," he said. "*Nerida.*"

The water rose up from the surface then and a figure went flying toward the bank. Ember. She landed in a pile of wet and soppy orange, brittle leaves.

"Ember!"

Orin let go of me and I ran past him to take hold of Ember's arms and flip her over onto her back. She was pale—*so* pale—and soaked through to the bone. I didn't know if she was even still living.

"Ember!" I said again, leaning my head toward her chest to listen for a heartbeat.

"Stay away from her!" shrieked a woman from behind me. Her voice vibrated through the air, shaking me where I knelt on the ground.

Orin slid in beside me as I turned. "It's all right," he said. "She's in stasis. I promise I can make her right."

My gaze darted from his beautiful bright eyes to the river, where the surge of water still extended up out of the surface. A woman with long, auburn hair that covered her breasts sat atop the surge. A pair of fins moved in and out of the surge below her, about where her feet would be.

If she'd had them. But of course she didn't because she was a freaking mermaid.

Orin moved his hands over Ember's body beside me and her eyes shot open. She screamed and I jumped back, tumbling onto my butt.

She breathed hard, her eyes darting between me, Orin, and the mermaid floating above the river. "Ivy? Where—what happened?"

"Come," spoke the woman in a stern, commanding voice. "Come, champion of the water. Orin, I have done as promised—"

Orin shot to his feet. "Yes, but there's still the matter of punishment for this transgression to discuss."

"There was no transgression," the mermaid spat. "She ventured into *our* lands, not yours. She forfeited her safety—"

"Don't be blooming ridiculous," said Orin. "She's freshly turned and didn't know any better. You *know* this. Your champion fares little better. Would you not lodge a complaint if the blood stole her because she accidentally strolled into their strongholds?"

The mermaid's lips pinched tightly together and the surge of water started slowly lowering back into the river. "This is a mistake she will not make twice."

Orin nodded. "Very well. But *you* will think on what you've done. A fortnight. A fortnight of no movement in these woods, no stepping foot nor fin in my territories."

The mermaid tossed her long, thick hair over her shoulder, nonplussed. "I have little need to spend time here. Very well, Son of Bloom. A fortnight."

"Ivy, what's going on?" asked Ember in a hushed voice beside me.

I stared at her. Something tugged at my insides then, something that made me ill to think about. I was piecing together just slightly more than she was, and if I was right—

"Come, child," said the mermaid, now back atop the water level proper, her torso the only thing in sight. She held a hand out toward me. "Don't be afraid." Her voice was like honey, the thought of joining her a comfort.

Orin exchanged a look with me and nodded, but his hand shot out and caught me by the wrist as I started to move toward the woman. He held out his other hand as I tore my eyes from the mermaid to spare him a look. "Hand over your phone again. I'll give it to your sister. I don't think it'll make it where you're going."

The mermaid whipped her tail against the surface of the river behind me, sending a splash of cold, icy water across my face.

CHAPTER SEVENTEEN

EMBER

Cold and wet, I shuddered as I watched my new step-sister spare a forlorn glance my way before removing her shoes, socks, and pants and then diving into the water. The scary mermaid woman caught her in her arms and then that rush of water surged around them again. With a scathing look my way, she whispered in Ivy's ear and then they both submerged themselves into the depths.

After a rush of water like a torrent headed down the river in the opposite direction, everything quieted and the river resumed its slow, melodic trickle.

And there was another hot guy in front of me. Which made three in two days, but I oughtn't to have been counting. Considering the mermaid and the blood and the memory loss and all.

"Orin," he said, kneeling in front of me and extending his hand. "Let's get you inside and warmed up."

Taking his hand, I already felt warmer—calmer. Things somehow seemed to make more sense.

They didn't really. Not if I thought too hard about any of it.

"What about Ivy?" I asked, letting go of Orin once I stood and hitching a thumb over my shoulder in the direction she'd disappeared. "I don't remember what just happened, really, but it was cold and dark and—"

"She'll be fine," said Orin. A playful smile tugged at the corner of his lips. "Better than fine, actually. They'll treat her much differently than they'd treat you."

I had to take his word on that. I bent down to pick up the pile of clothing and shoes Ivy had left behind. Orin watched me skeptically as I brushed past him and shuffled the pile in my arms to open the cottage door.

"We were looking for you," I explained. "Or this cottage—and I suppose you come with it." I nodded inside. "I take it you can give me some answers? Let's get to it."

"Very take-charge, the women in your family." He tucked both hands into his front pockets—he'd put Ivy's phone in his back— and headed in.

Cute British guy living in the woods behind my house. Why not? It made about as much sense as anything else.

It was so much warmer inside the cottage, especially after he shut the door behind us. It was so cozy—so *earthy*—inside. A fire was crackling in a little stone fireplace with two rocking chairs placed in front of it. Both chairs looked like they'd be at home in the middle of a forest floor. They were made of wood that barely looked processed and even had small vines and flowers twisting and growing up around the legs and slats that made up the backs of the chairs. The floor—*ground*, really—was just dirt. Dirt swept clean of debris, but dirt nonetheless. A small wooden bed against the wall beneath one of the cottage's two small windows was covered with a no-frills, fluffy green mattress and pillow. At the foot of the bed was a massive bookshelf that practically took up half the cottage's wall space on its own, its unfinished wood resembling something more like the wood you'd find in a decrepit old barn, the books on its shelves numerous and stuffed both vertically and horizontally to use as much space as possible, almost every one a paperback that was cracked on its spine. The only other piece of furniture was a small wooden table with a single wooden chair. Orin gestured to it and took Ivy's phone out of his pocket. "You can put her things here."

I did, fitting them beside the phone and a small pile of wooden bowls, cups, and utensils at the back of the table. I hesitated to put her shoes on his dining table, but it didn't seem like any dirt on her boots could make the place any filthier.

I supposed that wasn't fair. It didn't feel *dirty*, per se, but...

"I wash dishes in the river," he said. "And I just haven't gotten around to it in a few days, all right?" It wasn't combative, just matter of fact, his accent making the statement slightly upbeat even. He put his hands back into his pockets and nodded at the fireplace. "And that's my stove."

He had one of those iron bars and a pot over the fire. "Kind of limiting," I said, making my way over there. "A microwave could get the job done in about a hundredth the time." I let my palms hover over the fire, feeling the warmth surge through me down into my toes.

"That'd require electricity, though," said Orin, taking a seat in one of the rocking chairs and smacking both armrests. "Grab that for me and have a seat, all right?" I followed his pointed finger to the mantel of the fireplace, where a round lump of glass lay. *Why hadn't I noticed that before?*

I reached for it. It was a tad heavy in my hands, like a rock, only it seemed to be made from three shades of glass fused together at the center—red, blue, and green.

I went to hand it to Orin, but then I hesitated, bringing the lump of colored glass back to me.

Orin grinned. "Tempting, yeah? But it's just a symbol. It'll do you no good to hold on to."

I hadn't meant to hold on to his piece of junk anyway. But as I began to give it to him, the red glass caught my eye, a trick of the light causing the glass to almost glow.

Orin leaned up, one arm still on the armrest, and took it from me, gently prying it from my clutched fingers.

"Little champion of blood, relinquish your hold on that."

I did, sitting down on the rocking chair across from him, folding my arms and turning back toward the fire. "You've mentioned 'champions,'" I said, all business. "Explain."

Orin lightly tossed the ball of glass from one hand to the other, which seemed a disaster waiting to happen, but it was his glass rock. His shiny, shiny glass rock. "Do you remember coming here last night?"

That snapped me back to reality. "What? No. I mean... Ivy was the one who told me about this place. Not that she remembered it, either."

Orin caught the glass and ceased his tossing. "She was here, too. Before you."

"Before...?" I chuckled. "She came out of the woods after me."

"And when is the gap in your memories exactly?"

"Right before she came out." My heart thundered in my chest as I willed myself to stare at the fire instead of the red line emanating from the ball in his hand. "After I... left the woods."

He twirled the glass ball across his fingertips like a basketball, though it was a third one's size. Balancing the ball atop one finger, he held it up. "And that's when I saw you. Your vampire prince at your side."

"My... what?" I swallowed, drawn to that red light. A burning in my toes spread all the way up to my throat.

Orin placed the ball back between both hands, running his palms over it like magic—or like a contact juggler. "The vampire prince you pledged to champion."

Squeezing my eyelids tight, I tried to breathe deep and put the sight of that blood red light flickering off the glass orb behind me. Mermaids undoubtedly existed. So why not vampires? "I wish I remembered that."

"It's not your fault," answered Orin. When I opened my eyes, he had placed the glass orb securely on his lap, leaning forward to shield most of it from view. But there was still the faintest tint of a red glow from his abdomen. "Your sister forgot her pledge, too."

"Let me guess," I said, wracking my brain for the most ridiculous thing I could add to this story. "She's the champion of a merman prince?"

"Right," said Orin, leaning back into his chair and tapping his temple with his forefinger. "See? You're quicker than you let on."

"Thanks," I said, only realizing after I said it that he was saying I *didn't* seem that smart. "But I was joking."

"Even so, it's the truth." He held his glass ball up again. "See, this orb, it can identify potential champions."

"Okay..." I shivered and remembered to scooch closer to the fire. I was getting drier, but flashes of images of the cold, dark, and wet kept shooting through me and chilling me to the bone.

"Your sister showed signs of reacting with both blood and water." Orin pointed to the red and blue parts of the glass in turn. His mouth dipped into a frown as his finger traced the edge of the green glass, but he shook it off. "But it was the merman prince who brought her here, so it was to him she made her pledge."

Swallowing, I tried to stare at the rest of the orb, to ignore that pulsating red. "And I was only the red?"

"The blood," corrected Orin. "But I can't say with any certainty either way. Since the water had been claimed before you entered, the orb would not show whether or not you'd been suited for it." A friendly faint smile danced on his lips as he stood and put the orb where I'd taken it from atop the mantel. "Personally, I don't see why you wouldn't have been suited for either."

My thoughts raced wildly over yesterday—a lifetime ago. The attention both Calder and Dean had paid to me—the attention Dean had paid to Ivy, too.

"I don't understand," I said. "Why yesterday? And why... *How* is it possible I came here and got back to my backyard in a matter of minutes?"

Chuckling to himself, Orin walked away from the fireplace and went over to his bookcase, running his finger over the spines on one shelf. "This is why I wish becoming champion wasn't such an ordeal for humans," he said. "All these questions and I have to explain everything twice—three or four times, really."

Gritting my teeth, I clutched the armrests of the chair harder. Taking a deep breath, I let the fire pass through. This wasn't like me. I didn't get annoyed with hot guys. He might have been a year or two older, but hot was hot. "I'm sorry for the inconvenience," I said, once I was sure the irritation had faded from my voice. "But this is something I really need to know—and remember."

Orin selected a book and spun around to face me as he opened the tome. "These woods and the surrounding area are consummate lands to faefolk, merfolk, and the blood children." He spoke as if reading from the book, but I squinted and saw the word *Dracula* on the cover.

"Consummate lands?"

"Great magic can be performed here."

"In... flyover suburban Midwest country?" I wasn't the type who thought moving to NYC or LA was the end all of existence, but even I had to admit the comparison between that type of place and here left "here" a bit lacking in more ways than one.

He smiled and slammed the book shut. "Your infant country means little to the ancients. Or the more recent children of our magic."

"You keep going on about 'children,'" I said, tugging on an earlobe as I tried to make sense of it.

"Not children as you would think of them." He walked closer and handed me the book. "But children compared to my own folk."

I took the battered copy of *Dracula* from him. "Vampires," I said, realizing all at once that this book was a hint. "Vampire princes."

"Well, only one prince, to be sure." He scratched his chin. There was a hint of a shadow of dark stubble there. "Dean Horne has been looking for his champion since almost as soon as he turned."

"Turned?" I asked, running a finger over a crack on the corner of the cover of the book.

"When he became a vampire."

"And that would be..."

Orin wore a pensive expression. "1942 in your calendar, I suppose."

My finger froze. I didn't know whether to laugh or to throw up.

"So Dean is a vampire. From the 1940s. Not like the nineteenth century or the ancient days or...?"

"Nope," said Orin, a twinkle of amusement in his beautiful, magnetic eyes. "Children, they are."

"'They'?"

"Well, he's not the only vampire you've met recently, surely." He tapped his temple then. "They're easy to spot."

The sunglasses. "But he took them off at night..."

"It's only daylight that makes them go blind unless they protect their eyes with the darkest of shades." Orin sat back down in the rocking chair across from me. "They don't particularly like electrical light, either, though the effect isn't as devastating." He pointed to the book on my lap. "These vampires aren't like the ones you've read about. The sun won't kill them, only temporarily blind them if they're not careful."

A surge of irritation coursed through me again and I felt like biting out a response like, "Thanks for the tip," but I held my tongue and let the fire die down.

I was struck immediately again by how gorgeous Orin was. I had no business dating anyone when I'd been drooling over three new guys in all of two days. I cleared my throat. "You never explained—why now? Why us?"

"They've been waiting," said Orin, a stern look taking over his face, "for two women of the right age to claim roots within a certain distance of our consummate land."

I snorted. "Can you explain that in... Non-magic human speak?"

Orin started rocking in his chair, threading his fingers together in front of him. "They waited for two young women to live in your house."

My jaw dropped. "What?"

He raised his eyebrows. "I told them to wait, that the second girl had *just* moved in, that her roots wouldn't be as strong—"

I pointed to my chest then, confused. "They were waiting for my mom to get remarried?"

Orin pinched his lips and kept rocking. "They considered using both you and your mother, but the difference in age was too great. It affects the magic and it wouldn't have been fair to one side, you see."

Scoffing, I crossed my arms again and stared at the fire. "And if she'd never gotten remarried? Or if her husband hadn't had a daughter my age?"

"Then they'd continue to wait." Orin stopped rocking. "You can see they were getting impatient. It explains their haste to claim one of you."

Yesterday made a whole lot more sense now. No guy *ever* seemed interested in me, so why on Earth would two hot guys have been all up in my face? *Question these things, Ember, you idiot.* Not that *vampires and mermen* would have been the explanation I'd have come up with, but I could have at least been aware of the fact that there were ulterior motives behind it all.

"Champion of blood," said Orin, all of a sudden at my side. He picked a strand of damp hair that stuck to the side of my cheek and pulled it back behind my ear. I shivered, melting at his touch. "Do not be forlorn. By all rights, your roots are stronger—will continue to be stronger. You were a prize to be had for sure."

I felt like crying, despite the warmth his presence spread throughout my body. "What woman doesn't want to be a 'prize'?" I said, my voice shaking. I kind of did, to be honest. Not like *this*, per se, but... I'd longed for a man to think of me as his prize. His treasure. I sighed and he stepped back. "You said Ivy could have been either's... champion."

"Perhaps you could have been too." Orin shrugged and approached his orb again. "But she got here first."

"Dean was clearly more interested in Ivy for a bit." I chewed on my bottom lip. "He must have known she was the better choice..."

"Is that what concerns you?" asked Orin, his eyebrow lifted.

"No, I... You just... Ivy's not like me," I said. "I'm a nobody. I mean, I do well in school and I have Journey and well, I... It's just when it comes to *dating*, no one's ever looked at me."

"Becoming a champion of blood or water is more than mere *courting*."

"Right," I said. "Because it being about something more is the only way me having a boyfriend makes sense."

Orin seemed amused, but then his smile fell and he changed topics. "Your other question—the matter of time?"

Right. If I came here in those few minutes missing from my memory...

"One of the powers of blood is to manipulate time—or, I suppose, *pause* it is more accurate." He grabbed the orb with both hands, almost petting it. "You wouldn't be an expert on the skill by any means, though your new *boyfriend* certainly is." He picked up the orb and started tossing it up and down again like it was made of rubber instead of glass. "Though I imagine there's a part of you that understands how it works in a pinch."

He chucked the glass orb straight at my head.

And though my hands went up to shield my face, nothing happened.

Peeking through my fingers, I found the orb suspended in air, the sound of the fire in the fireplace gone mute, the flames frozen mid-movement.

And my right hand glowing red.

CHAPTER EIGHTEEN

IVY

Almost as soon as the strange mermaid had taken me into her arms, my legs had fused together, transforming into a tail—ripping to shreds the "*SASS*" underpants much like Orin had predicted.

Good riddance.

My sweater weighed heavily on my upper chest. The woman—Nerida, I supposed—dove with me underwater and motioned for me to remove my top. Catching sight of her bare breast, I shook my head, instinctively covering my already-covered chest with my arms. She shrugged one shoulder as if to say it was my funeral and looped an arm around my back, gripping me by the stomach.

Before I could ask her for some personal space—assuming I *could* ask her for some personal space underwater—we were off, swimming at record speed in the direction opposite the cottage.

Without even thinking, my tail—my *tail*—thrashed in time with hers, propelling us forward. My hair had fallen out of its ponytail holder, the dark, wavy tendrils floating behind me.

It was only then that I realized the water felt good on my face. That the burst of cold I'd felt when I'd leaped in had vanished, that the muscles in my shoulders had relaxed as if I were taking a warm soak.

And I hadn't had to come up for air once. Just as Calder had told me—mermaid tail, breathing underwater.

Despite our speed, I was able to bring up one hand and feel for gills around my neck, but there were none. I had no idea *how* I was breathing, then, other than it didn't even feel like water was entering my nose and mouth. It just felt like being outside on a warm, cozy day—if I'd submerged myself in a warm pool and somehow managed to swap my lungs from filtering oxygen to water molecules.

Our pace slowed just as the river seemed to open up. It grew brighter, and I saw the river floor grow deeper as the river met the pond—*lake*—near the park, I presumed. The shadow of the small island hung over the open space in the middle. But there were other merpeople all around us, some swimming, some sitting on outcroppings of rocks and talking. One mermaid held a little merbaby to her breast, letting it suckle as she lazily swam round in place. There were about two dozen merpeople all around, though the picture seemed off in my mind's eye. There was no brightly colored coral reef here, no clamshells with pearls. The fish that swam amongst the people were drab and lanky and boring, nothing at all like the tropical schools of fish that seemed more at home with a race of merbeings.

A merchild, probably about nine or ten, swam past, his arms held in front of his head like a point. A merman chased him and I heard laughter—actually *heard* a sound clearly beneath the water— as the merman caught up, his fingers reaching for the boy's tail and snatching it.

Then his head snapped toward us and his face fell, his fingers letting go of the scaly fins.

The merboy kept laughing and swam back, circling the merman—circling Calder. "That doesn't count," said the boy. "You have to hold on for ten seconds flat." Seeing Calder's somber expression, the boy's own smile died. "Queen Nerida," he said, turning toward us.

The mermaid beside me beamed—warmly—but there was

something more behind the smile that sent a chill through my body, soggy sweater or not.

"Everyone," called Nerida, and her voice seemed to echo across the waters. "Please, gather round."

They did, merpeople from all corners of the lake turning toward us. I didn't recognize any of them, so I affixed my stare on Calder, hoping for some sort of recognition from him, some kind of acknowledgement that he'd literally ditched me to face punishment alone, but he simply held on to one elbow with the opposite hand, his gaze focused on the lake floor.

"We have a big announcement," said Nerida, once everyone seemed to have settled nearby at last, "though I have no doubt many of you expected this." She clapped—the sound more a dull echo than I'd have expected—and sent small pockets of air flying out from between her palms. "We have found our champion." She gestured toward me.

All these faces focused on me then—though half of them had been curiously checking me out since they'd swum closer. Seeing all these naked torsos, I suddenly felt like the person who'd overdressed at a party. Subconsciously, I twiddled with the sleeve of my sopping sweater. My eyes caught Calder's briefly and I felt better having kept it on.

"Introduce yourself, dear," said Nerida, leaning forward.

"What? Me?" My voice sounded strange underwater—a shade of normal, but a sense of something warm and almost bubbly beneath the sound as it left my throat.

"Yes, of course," said Nerida. She swam to the other side of me and rested a gentle hand on my upper arm. The crowd burst into life then, clapping in that hollow, heavy way that sent more air pockets floating upward. Some cheered and some sang and my ears echoed with the warmth of their cacophony.

Nerida nodded and smiled until her gaze came to a rest on Calder. "Er, what's her name, dear?"

I raised an eyebrow, both at the fact that she was treating me like her long-lost daughter without even knowing my name and at the fact that she seemed to think I wasn't capable of uttering it myself. Okay, so maybe I wasn't. I was a little distracted by the fact that I was a mermaid at the moment.

Calder cleared his throat. Bubbles escaped from his mouth along with the sound. "Ivy."

Nerida's lips pinched. "She's the newer one, then?"

Calder nodded, his face fallen, as if struck.

Nerida threaded her arm through mine. "Well, no matter. What's done is done. The other one felt a bit *faint* for my tastes regardless."

At a sauntering pace not unlike walking, she guided me through the crowd of gathered merpeople, brushing past Calder, heading toward the shadow beneath the small cover of the island overhead. The rest of the crowd dispersed, though I tossed a glance over my shoulder to see Calder following us, his eyes still low, his face grim, as if heading for his own execution.

The island above reached all the way to the lake floor, a dense wall of rock coming into view as we approached. She took us through a door-sized hole in the wall inside to a hollow chamber, a long, empty grand ballroom-like space, if the interior decorator had insisted on eschewing all color and using only earthy materials. Light streamed in from several openings in the wall of the rock and from glowing, floating orbs that moved back and forth from the floor to the ceiling in a soothing, repetitive pattern. At the back of the grand room was a small alcove carved into the wall in which there were several seats made of stone.

Nerida placed me beside one and then let go, perching herself on the seat nearby. Calder leaned his back against the wall right beside her, his eyes looking out over the grand space, at the ceiling, at the ground—anywhere but right at me.

Nerida seemed to notice I was staring at him and she looked at him, a fluttering smile tracing her lips, before she turned back to me. She leaned closer, her fins lazily kicking lightly to the side. "You must have many questions, Ivy," she said, seemingly proud of herself for using my name.

I chuckled, ignoring how the sound boiled and languished in my throat in the water. "Oh, you have *no* idea," I said.

Nerida clapped her hands together. "Well, where should we begin?"

I looked to Calder for help, but *big surprise*, he provided exactly zero assistance.

"What's going on, for starters?" I asked. I gestured to my tail and really *looked* at it for the first time ever. It was a deep blue, the fins a lighter, more translucent color. I consciously tried to wiggle my toes and got a curl of the fins instead.

"How much has my son told you?"

That got my attention. So Calder was her son. That was why he'd tagged along like a sullen teenager. But Calder didn't blink, just turned his head, not facing my way.

"Next to nothing," I said through gritted teeth. The grinding took a little more effort than it would have normally, but the situation more than called for it. "I'm still kind of reeling from the shock that merfolk exist." I stared back at my tail and gave my fins a whack against the stone. It stung and I winced. "And that I can be one of them."

Nerida reached forward to pat the bend in my tail where there might have been knees, if that made sense. I wondered what the bones looked like underneath it. It wasn't like fish had a bend right in the midst of its tail quite like this one. "It's a lot to adjust to," she said, "but it's just the beginning."

She sighed, the sound echoing out on an air bubble like a haunting song. "What do you remember about your ascension to champion last night?"

"Nothing," I said, my eyes narrowing at Calder. "We got lost in the woods, we came upon what I suppose now is Orin's cottage, and then boom, I woke up the next day."

Calder snapped to attention at the name *Orin*. I smiled smugly when his eyes finally met mine.

Nerida didn't seem to notice. "Well, you consummated with my son, Calder, to become champion of water."

I choked on the water for the first time since I'd been submerged, the cool liquid hitting my throat. Nerida took my hand in hers in a flash, somehow sending a soothing sensation through my body, relaxing my muscles.

Calder made an aggravated growl and finally fully faced us both. "She meant *consummate* in a spiritual sense," he said. His fists clenched tightly at his sides.

"For now," said Nerida sweetly as she sat back, the curl of her lips as innocent as if she'd just pet a puppy instead of holding the hand of the girl she'd just hinted ought to make love to her son.

I worked out a kink in my neck, rubbing my hand there absentmindedly. "For forever," I muttered, snatching a glance at Calder and hoping he heard me.

His face fell, so he probably had.

"In any case," said Nerida, "you became the one who'll stand by the prince's side to drive the forces of evil from these, our consummate lands, at last."

"What?" I asked, genuinely lost.

Nerida cleared her throat. "The vampires, dear."

"*What?*" I repeated.

"Many, many years ago," continued Nerida, "long before any of us swam these waters—or walked this Earth"—she nodded at me—"there were two powers beyond that of human reach on this planet: the merfolk and the faefolk."

Calder jutted his chin out then. "Orin is the prince of the faefolk. Though you'll not find the rest of his kind so eager to take human form."

Nerida's gaze darted to Calder then and he shrunk back, assuming his place leaning against the wall and brooding.

"Yes, well, the bloom—the faefolk—being so disinterested in things that interest the rest of us, they have stayed out of all conflict, officiating as judges of sorts to this battle."

"The battle with... the vampires?"

"Yes!" said Nerida, her sea-green irises sparkling as if she were a teacher making a breakthrough at last with a rather dim student. "Long, long ago, these foul creatures came to life from the humans themselves. Not *born* as themselves as we are, but created when one human life dies and keeps on walking through the foulest venom pumping through their veins."

I was lost. But I felt that if I kept interrupting, I'd be here all day.

"No one knows from whence they came, but we know they grow their numbers through—"

"Sucking blood?" I ventured. "Piercing flesh with their fangs?"

Calder, at least, seemed amused, though he crossed his arms and cleared his throat to try to hide it.

Nerida seemed aghast at being interrupted. "Indeed," she said sourly, "though there's a bit more to it than that." She lifted her chin, her lecture resumed. "Our people defeated them once, long, long ago—drove them to extinction, so we thought." She gestured around her. "We broke free from our pocket of consummate lands and ventured the waters of the world freely."

"The world was your oyster," I said.

Calder snickered audibly then, bringing a hand to his mouth.

Nerida sent him a scathing look and he nonchalantly took that hand and scratched the top of his scalp, his grin at war with the sharp expression in his eyes for dominance.

"Yes, well... We lived freely for millennia. Saw humanity evolve from dull, infant-like, grunting things to the rather proud-of-themselves children you are today, polluting our planet with no thought to anything but instant gratification." She sneered.

But I wasn't focused on the effects of climate change on merfolk, no matter how important a subject it might be. "You've lived for millennia?"

"Not us personally, dear," said Nerida, her face softening once more into her teacher's smile. "Our kind. Sadly, our life spans don't seem much longer than your own." The knuckles on one of her hands grew white as she clutched the other hand tightly. "A disadvantage in the war against the blood, to be certain."

"So if the vampires were vanquished...?" The alliteration of my sentence seemed to give Calder's smile another advantage because it broke out freely on his face now.

"Millennia ago," snapped Nerida. "They came back less than a century ago. In the 1940s."

I opened my mouth to ask, but I wasn't sure *what* to ask. "World War II?" I ventured.

Nerida shrugged. "Perhaps. Perhaps they just bided their time; perhaps they fed on the chaos of an evil of humanity spreading and thriving across the world. We are not privy to the origins of these dark creatures. All we know is that when the humans' war at last ended, those foul creatures were back." She looked ready to throttle an imaginary enemy. "My grandfather was the first royal to die at their hands."

Calder grew serious at that, even going so far as to swim closer to his mother and lay a hand on her shoulder. She took it in her own and patted it. "The bloom awoke, then, returned to the human realm, and interfered—reminding the blood that this was never a war to be decided directly with fang against fin." She stared at me directly. "Once they'd submitted to... proper punishment for the transgression, they agreed to follow our ancestors' example. In the first war, a prince of water and a princess of blood took from among the tribes a champion each."

I looked from Calder to Nerida, not following. "Why?"

"Power flowing to a champion is different than power in a merperson or vampire proper." Nerida cleared her throat in her sing-song way. "It evens the playing field somewhat, lessens the... impact on the rest of our people."

"But you said the vampires were eradicated," I said, in no mood for jokes this time.

"Yes, well, having the prince and princess and their champions do the battling while the others merely supported them ensured that there were no casualties among our people before war's end. But when the champion of blood fell..." Nerida's eyes narrowed. "So fell the entire vampire race with it."

"I... I don't understand." My throat was growing dry. Surrounded by water and my throat was cracking.

Calder swum closer to me. "You and me—and that pompous vampire prince and... And Ember."

"What?" I asked, twisting to face him. I didn't know what "vampire prince" he meant, though my mind was racing and coming up with the most likely candidate:

Dean Horne.

Though I couldn't say why, other than he was odd and new and... Ember claimed he'd said she was dating him, despite her having no recollection of that fact.

My stomach sank as I examined Calder. Did he think the same of us? Were we... A couple? Consummated, even if not really physically?

Why on Earth would I have ever agreed to that?

Calder took his time answering, eventually deciding just to stare at my light-blue fins instead.

"You will fight to the death, my dear," said Nerida sweetly. "Our entire race depends on it."

CHAPTER NINETEEN

EMBER

Ivy had been distant with me when she'd finally come home the night before. Straining to smile when Mom spoke to her, more at ease around Autumn.

She'd slid into the house without me even noticing, taking a shower and dressing before I could see if she'd been waltzing in without pants on, considering I'd dropped off the last pair she'd had in the laundry room upon my own return.

"I *found* your phone," I said, clearing my throat and handing it to her in the hallway outside our rooms after supper. Mom was downstairs on her laptop, music from the '90s softly playing from her stereo, but Autumn was in her room nearby, the door open.

Ivy froze. "Thanks." She grabbed it from me.

"It wasn't broken after all," I said loudly as we passed by Autumn's room. She was on her stomach on her bed, one hand acting as a chin rest, the other swiping on a tablet almost flat up against her nose.

Ivy reached her room and turned around, her fingers wrapped around the edge of the door. There were still mounds of opened and closed boxes behind her.

"Do you want any help unpacking?" I asked, for an excuse to step inside and speak more with her.

She opened her mouth, then let her gaze fall. "I just... I need some time. To myself."

Arty startled me as he slinked by, brushing my calves. I went to pet him with my right hand, then hesitated as I glanced at it, remembering the red glow the moment the orb had stopped moving.

"We really need to—" I started, but she closed the door.

"Mom's almost here!" Autumn padded into the hallway, still staring at her tablet, but she seemed to almost instinctively pet Arty as she neared Ivy's door, not once tearing her eyes from her screen.

Right. Easton apparently had them on Tuesdays and rotated which Wednesdays he had them, but because he was on his business trip, that meant their mom was getting them early this week. It just messed with her usual schedule with her bosses, so she couldn't pick them up right after school.

Good thing, since Ivy and I weren't exactly in school.

"I'll... I'll be there in a second," said Ivy, her voice muffled by the door.

Autumn finally tore herself from her tablet, resting it on an end table near the banister and crouching to rub Arty's cheeks. He lapped it up, purring loudly from the attention.

"He's cute," said Autumn, smiling up at me.

I grinned and crouched beside her, letting Arty head-bump my arm and forgetting, for all of one second, everything unnatural about the last couple of days.

The doorbell rang and Arty froze, but Autumn scooped him up before he could bolt. "Can I show him to my mom?" she asked.

"Sure," I said, standing. "But he's skittish around strangers, just so you know." I rested a hand on my hip. "But he adores you, I can tell."

The door to Ivy's room burst open and she came out, a duffle bag stuffed to capacity over her shoulder. "Come on, Aut," she said, using a rather unattractive nickname for a pretty name. She spared me a single glance and her back practically stiffened. Footsteps echoed in the hallway downstairs and the door opened.

Though her voice was distant and unclear, I could make out the tones of Mom at her friendliest.

"...don't stand outside. It's getting chillier these days. Come in, come in." Mom appeared in the hallway and I watched through the slats in the banister as another woman—shorter, with dark brown, almost black, hair—entered behind her. She had a brown store apron on, like one of the greeters or cashiers did at a number of places. She looked tired, but she smiled nervously as she stood beside Mom, clutching the strap of a purse that hung in front of her knees.

"C'mon, Autumn," said Ivy. "Put the cat down and get your things."

"I'm going to show Mom," said Autumn, but Arty was getting one of his panicked looks about him, his gaze darting between Ivy and me and the stairs.

"Let him go and let's *go*," said Ivy, more sternly this time, before she headed down the stairs herself.

"Ivy, I still think we need to talk," I said, almost tripping over Arty as he darted out in front of my legs into the master bedroom to hide under Mom and Easton's bed.

"Ivy," said Mom, clasping her hands together, "are you feeling better?" She turned to Ivy's mom. "She almost didn't go to school today," she said.

Ivy's mom narrowed her eyes on her daughter. Ivy certainly looked the part—already in pajamas, her dark hair a mess, puffy redness around her sockets. Her mom seemed to soften after closer inspection. "What's wrong?"

"Nothing," Ivy snapped. She crossed her arms and stared out the front door. "I'll go wait in the car."

"Say 'goodbye' to your step-mom and sister," said Ivy's mom as I put my foot on the bottom step. I gave Ivy's mom a genuinely warm smile, though it faltered a bit when I glanced at the coat rack and something hit me—like something was missing. But what? Easton's coat? Like I'd care about that.

The hat. When had Dean gotten his hat back? Or his other pair of sunglasses, for that matter. They were conspicuously absent from the table in the hallway. Perhaps Mom had moved them.

The slam of the front door snapped me out of my reverie. Ivy traipsed across the front lawn to the driveway.

"I'm so sorry," said Ivy's mom. She extended a hand toward me. "Glory."

"Gloria?" I said, taking her hand. She was wearing fingerless gloves.

"Oh," she said, chuckling, "not Gloria. Morning Glory." Her nervous titter as she looked between my mom and me also made me laugh. "Hippie parents."

"Oh, but I think it's so pretty," said Mom. "And pretty, nature names for your girls, too."

"Yeah," said Glory. She stared pointedly at me. "Easton hasn't told me your name."

"Ember."

"Another pretty name," she said, and then the air between us got uncomfortably quiet.

"Say, is Ivy going to Homecoming?" Mom asked Glory. "I've been trying to get Ember to go. I mean, I don't want her to regret it—"

"I'm going," I said, swallowing as I ran a finger over my shirt sleeve.

"Oh, good," said Mom. She looked about to burst. "Maybe we can arrange something for the girls to do together beforehand."

Before she could take that thought any further, Autumn puttered down the stairs. She brightened as she spotted her mom, rushing past me to embrace her.

"Hi, sweetheart," said Glory, but Autumn had already launched into speaking a mile a minute.

"Mom, they have a cat and it's a boy and he's mostly white and I was going to show him to you, but Ivy scared him away—"

Glory patted her hair as another chuckle escaped her lips. "Slow down, pumpkin. You have plenty of time to tell me."

"Did Blossom miss me?" asked Autumn, undeterred.

"That's our cat," said Glory to my mom and me. She turned back to Autumn. "Yes, dear, of course she—"

"Oh, but I forgot to text you about the ice cream place we went to last night! They let you get your own and add sprinkles and toppings and everything, but Dad said not to put too much because they charged you by the pound—"

"The ounce," said Mom, grinning.

"Maybe 'the pound' with her love for ice cream?" suggested Glory as she put an arm behind Autumn's back and directed her toward the door. "Thank you," she said to Mom and me, though I wasn't sure for what. "Nice... Nice meeting you. Very nice house." Her eyes darted above her at the elaborate light fixture near the front doorway.

"Thank you," said Mom, sliding in behind Glory and Autumn. "We'll see you soon, dear," she said to her new step-daughter.

And then, the door was shut, Glory's rust-stained tan sedan had pulled out of the driveway, and they were gone.

"Almost like it was all a dream, huh?" said Mom as she went to the dimmer switch to turn off the hallway light. "Back to being just you and me for a bit?"

"Yeah..." I stared out the glass of the front door even as the light went out. "A dream."

Mom couldn't possibly begin to imagine the half of it.

———

I feigned sickness the next morning, opting to stay home. I'd almost forgotten Ivy's excuse had wound up being that time of the month and said I must have caught something from her. But Mom felt my forehead and frowned, saying it felt a bit warm, and that my cheek felt a bit too cold.

She let me stay behind regardless, and I actually intended to. There was a hot guy living in the woods behind our house, but I had, like, zero interest in paying him a visit.

And even less in seeing my supposed boyfriend.

The image of his charming face, those beautiful irises... That did something to me, so I tried hard not to think about him.

Too bad Journey wasn't making it easy for me.

Okay, the WHOLE SCHOOL is talking about you and the new boy hooking up.

Journey's text buzzed, interrupting my mindless browsing of a reddit forum with theories on *Riverdale*. Sighing, I pulled the comforter tighter up over my head, my face and hand, which held the phone, the only things sticking out.

Yeah, I wrote. *I guess. He asked me out anyway.*

Why didn't you tell me?

I grunted. There was so much I wasn't telling her. But if I told her about the memory loss, the time pausing, the *vampires*... Ivy was the only one who could possibly understand, and she pointedly refused to speak to me. I never did get her number, even after I'd charged her phone for her.

Well, he's been asked out by half a dozen girls and a guy in the past few hours alone, and he keeps telling everyone he's your "beau."

Who gets asked out by half the school in a single morning? I thought to myself, though that clearly wasn't the issue here.

That swagger. That face... I could see why people couldn't help but be tempted by him.

I tried to think of what to write back that didn't incorporate fishpeople and champions and all that, but my phone rang, blaring out Mom's favorite song, that schmaltzy sad song from *Titanic*.

"Hi, Mom," I said, putting her on speaker.

"Just checking on you, Em," she said. I glanced at the clock. It was 12:15 already. Mom was probably having lunch.

"I'm fine," I said. "Feeling a bit better. Been sleeping." I hadn't slept a wink all night, actually.

"There are some leftovers in the fridge," she said. "If not that, make sure to at least have some oatmeal or chicken noodle soup."

"Okay," I said, knowing I had no appetite.

"Do you think you'll feel well enough to go to your new job tonight? I told Yvonne I wasn't sure if you could make it if you couldn't make it to school."

My blood ran cold. *What and what?* "What are you talking about?" Mom had never pestered me to get a job.

"Did you forget or...?" Mom hesitated. "I did think it was weird you'd offer to help out, but when Yvonne explained you were dating her nephew..." She laughed. "Now I know why you changed your mind about Homecoming."

I shot up in bed, kicking the comforter off and swiping away a notification about a text from Journey. "Yvonne? Or do you mean Minnie?"

"Huh? No. Definitely Yvonne. I know my secretary's name." Then she must have gotten a new one since I'd been there last a few months back. There were sounds of a drawer opening and shutting. "She told me she recommended her sister's moving company and then you met her nephew when he moved things to the house and he just transferred to your school and you offered to show him around." She paused. "I'm very proud of you for being so... sociable, Ember. So proactive. More like Journey."

Gee, thanks, I thought. I sighed. I didn't feel at all like myself—I felt lost, adrift, *emotional*—but whatever it was, it was apparently an improvement over the quiet, unassuming me I'd been last week.

"Do be careful, though. Promise me you'll use protection."

"*Mom*." I squeezed my temples between my thumb and forefinger. Would it be too weird if I asked Mom if her new secretary wore sunglasses to work? "What job are they talking about?" I asked instead.

Enough hiding. Ivy was no help. Orin had said everything he was willing to. Time for some answers.

"At their moving service office," she said. "Apparently, her nephew mentioned they'd been bogged down in spreadsheets and you'd offered to help a few hours a week?" She sounded unsure.

"Right," I said, just diving into the lie. "I'd just... forgotten. I'll be there. I'm feeling better already."

"Okay," said Mom, but she still seemed unsure. "Will you be home for supper?"

"I don't think so," I said. "I've been invited to their place for dinner." Truth was, I didn't know where to go to have dinner with them, but it was going to happen at some point. Staring at my right hand, I could almost feel the redness emanating from it, though my hand remained entirely glow-free. I flexed it, stretching my fingers. "And I intend to take them up on that."

CHAPTER TWENTY

IVY

"How did your step-sister score the new hottie?" asked Lyric as she dropped her plastic fork into her salad. "Just from partnering up with him the other night for that lame woods adventure?"

Wasn't she one of the ones who pushed to go on said adventure? I kept swirling the same fry in ketchup. When the table went silent, I just shrugged.

"She's like... I mean, it's not that she's ugly or anything, but..." Paisley stared at Grey, apparently hoping for a male's point of view, but he was busy laughing at something Devam had said. Paisley twirled the straw in her milkshake. "She's just kind of a nerd. And she barely tries to look halfway decent. I'm just surprised she caught his eye."

"Wow, is Paisley acknowledging the existence of good-looking people besides her dull-and-dumb-as-a-rock boyfriend? No offense." Lyric added the last bit for Grey's benefit, but to the surprise of no one, he still wasn't even paying attention.

Paisley looked angry for a second, but when Grey dropped his hand from her shoulder to catch a baseball Ashton had tossed his way in the middle of the mall food court, she snorted, letting her guard down. She and Lyric both laughed.

I stood up, pushing my chair in and grabbing my tote bag. "I gotta go."

Lyric raised an eyebrow at me. "Where do you need to go so badly? And what are you going to do—walk there?"

I *had* thought about walking... Anywhere. Just walking with no particular purpose. Find somewhere where I could think and be alone and...

The idea of being alone with my thoughts just now was unbearable. But trying to paste over those thoughts with the laughter of my friends was possibly worse.

"We haven't even found you a dress yet," said Paisley. I could tell she was genuinely sad at that.

"I'm just going to wear one of my old dresses," I said, shrugging. "It's not like they go bad after one event."

Paisley looked as puzzled as if I'd meant that dresses were made of food that did indeed have an expiration date.

"Okay," said Lyric, slapping her palms against the table, "when are you going to tell us what you've got stuck up your butt?"

Ashton had looked over just in time to hear that, and he snorted, whispering something to Devam.

Thanks for that, Lyric.

"Are you still feeling sick?" asked Paisley, at least caring enough to be a little concerned. I'd told *no one* I'd even been at school yesterday, let alone everything that had happened.

I *was* feeling sick, but not in any of the ways they could even imagine.

Lyric chortled and stole a fry from my plate. "Ooo, I wonder if she's under that merman's spell—the one who eschews the ocean and hangs out at the park pond."

That got just about everyone laughing, other than Paisley.

"It's a *lake*," I said, suddenly caring about that unimportant distinction. "It... runs out to the ocean. Eventually. After traversing many more lakes and rivers." I swallowed and stood. Lyric looked half-impressed, half-amused by my sudden interest in marine biology.

"Hey, why don't we split off from the guys?" asked Paisley,

standing up beside me. She bent down to lock lips with Grey before jutting her chin toward Lyric. "Want to come? Or don't you have a thing with Raelynn later today?"

Lyric poached another fry before standing up and grabbing her coat off the back of her chair. "We're going book shopping."

Paisley laughed and even I forgot my anxiety for a second. "You?" said Paisley. "In a bookstore?"

"Shut it," said Lyric, pulling on her second sleeve. She tugged the front of the coat down so the slim-fitting faux leather coated her svelte, muscular form as if it'd been poured on. "I'll go to any number of dull places if I can spend time with my bae. She's taking her own car, so I can give you guys a lift there if you're interested..."

I couldn't tell if she wanted us to give her some space and was just offering to be nice, or if she was genuine. In either case, I didn't care. I wanted out of here. "Sounds great," I said, grabbing hold of both Paisley's and Lyric's arms. True, I wouldn't exactly be alone with the two of them, but at least I was paring the group down and could stop flinching every time I looked across the table and caught sight of a letterman's jacket.

———

I certainly didn't dislike books or anything, but I typically went to the library or ordered the rare volume of something I just *had* to own online. The little mom-and-pop shop Lyric pulled her car up to was nothing I'd really paid attention to before.

It was quaint, though. Cute. The exterior almost seemed like a log cabin, but it seemed so out of place plopped here a short drive around the corner from the park entrance, half a mile from the nearest strip mall. There was nothing else on this stretch of road but that old-fashioned diner I hadn't been to in ages—though something about it niggled at me when I thought on it now. I usually associated bookstores with downtown and uptown areas, but I know the few that had tried there in town hadn't lasted long.

Actually, I hadn't even known we still had a bookstore. Unless it was new.

Paisley made a cooing sound as Lyric turned off the ignition, like we were staring at a kitten instead of a store. "Oo, The Hollow Tree. I haven't been here in forever. My mom used to take my brother and me here all the time when we were kids."

Okay, so not new.

"I've never been," said Lyric, puckering into her visor mirror and grabbing some lip gloss from the console to apply it.

A car pulled up next to us and Lyric flailed her hands at us. "Now, shoo, shoo. This place doesn't look that huge, so I'll need some alone time with Rae before we go in. Go on."

"All right, all right," said Paisley, giggling. I wasn't in the mood for laughing.

We both nodded at Raelynn as she stepped out of her car, her cheerleader outfit still on. *Does Lyric's girlfriend participate in everything?*

Paisley knocked her arm against mine as we ascended the couple of wooden stairs leading up to a porch with a cozy hanging bench suspended from the overhang. "Dance team," she said, as if somehow taking note of my interest in Raelynn's uniform. "Slightly different colors from the cheerleading squad. They practice once a week instead of every day like the cheer clique." She rolled her eyes at the last two words as she opened the door and the bell hanging overhead chimed. Over my shoulder, I caught a glimpse of Lyric and Raelynn embracing one another and exchanging kisses before the door shut closed behind me.

Everyone else lived such peaceful, simple lives.

"Wow," said Paisley under her breath. She looked around. "This place hasn't changed." She walked up to a display table with an array of books that could hardly be confused for the latest releases. Picking one up and blowing off a coat of dust, she turned the wrinkled, yellow paper. "It *really* hasn't changed."

Her voice practically echoed in the space. There had been no other cars upfront—one might wonder how they stayed in business—but still, the quiet felt unsettling. It sent a chill down my spine.

I walked off on my own, weaving through aisles and aisles of books. Was it a used bookstore? Nothing seemed up to date, and the spines were cracked more often than not. Definitely a used one, then.

The door chime rang again and I heard Lyric giggling under her breath and whispering something. Raelynn shushed her like this was a library instead of a place of commerce.

When I rounded the corner to make another loop through an aisle, I smacked right into a guy with a book in front of his face, Belle-style.

The book jostled his thick, rectangular hipster glasses as he uttered a small cry. "All right? Sorry. Just faffing," he said, his British-esque accent on display. "I didn't hear anyone come in."

It was Orin. Wearing glasses and somehow looking even hotter —not that geek had ever been my thing. Nor had jock, though. I didn't really have "a thing."

I wanted to ask how he hadn't heard four teenagers walk into this utterly quiet store despite the jangle of the bell over the door and the still-audible whispering of the most recent pair to enter, but I had more important questions on my mind. "What are you doing here?"

Orin slammed his book shut, oblivious to the little gust of dust that popped out of it, and tore his glasses off his face. "I could ask you the same thing." He rubbed his scarf against the lenses because of course he was wearing a scarf indoors. It completed the whole hipster ensemble.

I readjusted my tote bag on my shoulder and slipped my arms over my chest. "I'm at a bookstore with friends. Not unusual for a normal teenager. You should be in the woods, like, telling girls to take their pants off before jumping into the river or something."

Orin seemed amused as he dropped the glasses into a front pocket of his flannel shirt. "Well, I'm surprised to find you here instead of at the bottom of the lake. No mafia implication intended."

Paisley's squeal carried throughout the bookstore and I bit my tongue, trying hard to remind myself that there were people nearby who already seemed to think it possible I was losing my mind.

"You still have a bookstore cat!" cried Paisley. She sneezed—she was allergic to cats. "Is this the same bookstore cat?"

Orin put his book down on a nearby windowsill and went to see what Paisley was up to. I followed, but not before taking a peek at the book he'd put down. *The Count of Monte Cristo.* "Feilia. She's an old lady," he said. "Been here at least a dozen years. Though the truth is, she comes and goes. Can't keep that one caged up."

Paisley, who'd been grinning from ear to ear as she pet the fluffy brown Maine Coon curled up in a sunbeam that shone atop a plush chair, looked up and her jaw dropped. "Hi..." she said, suddenly struck numb. "I, uh... Are you...? Do you have a brother who used to work here?"

Petting the cat's cheek, Orin chuckled. "Yeah. Older brother. Went off to college and lives in a commune in California somewhere."

"I thought so," said Paisley, smiling. Her cheeks were flushing. Since when did Paisley have eyes for anyone besides Grey? "You look so much like him. Either that, or my memory is fuzzy."

I didn't have to know much about Orin to figure out that maybe, just maybe, he *was* the "older brother" Paisley was referring to.

Because non-aging faefolk wasn't that surprising in a world with merfolk and vampires. Orin looked to be in his late teens or early twenties, but he carried himself with a sense of bemusement that made him seem much older.

"I remember Mom saying he looked *just* like your dad—I guess you do too." Paisley giggled, annoying the shop cat, who opened one sleepy eye and pivoted an ear as she glared at her.

That settled it. Orin was one of those never-aging hot immortals. Because why not? "Cheers. Looking good just runs in the family, I suppose." Then he turned to me and winked. "It's a family business. Been here ages."

I glanced around. It was quaint, but with any other owner, I'd see it closing within a year. Raelynn and Lyric climbed up a rickety set of stairs to visit a loft full of books I hadn't even noticed yet. "It's a wonder this place stays *in* business," I spat.

"*Ivy*," said Paisley, as sharply as if I'd insulted her beloved Grey in front of her.

Orin laughed and the cat got annoyed, flicking its tail and covering its eyes with its arm. The laugh was rather... entrancing to a human listener, though. "It's not our only source of income. We keep odd hours, after all, so we can't expect any more." He turned to Paisley. "Though I'd be happy to order anything you need and let you know when it's arrived."

Paisley took a visible deep breath, as if reminding herself she was taken. "No, not for me. Just browsing. My friend is the one looking for something." She nodded up toward the loft, from which a soft set of giggles emanated.

"I'll see if I can help," he said, lifting a hand to his temple and flourishing it at Paisley as he bowed. "Let me know if you have any questions."

He walked off toward the stairs and I watched him, pinching my lips tightly so my jaw didn't drop.

What were the odds of running into him in town right after all this started?

"So he's cute," said Paisley, as if her reaction to his every movement hadn't made her opinion obvious. "Why don't you ask him to the dance?"

Snorting, I glanced at a shelf of battered romance paperbacks, the painted models on the few turned out to face passersby evidence these books were at least several decades old.

"What?" asked Paisley. "Do you think your mom and dad would have a fit if he's over eighteen?" She frowned. "I can't really place his age—"

"I don't need a date to the dance." The way I said it, I knew almost immediately how she'd misinterpret it.

"You found one already?" Paisley grabbed my wrist, excited. "Who?"

Images of Calder flashed through my mind, and I didn't realize until that moment I'd been staring at a romance set on a cove, the violent waves battering a cliffside and my whole body thinking *water*.

My hand grew cold and I thought I saw the faintest hint of a blue glow. Before Paisley could notice, I ripped it out of her grasp and walked away, tucking the treacherous hand in the opposite armpit. "No one," I snapped, harsher than I'd meant to.

"*Fine*," muttered Paisley from behind me, a little of Lyric's trademark touchiness evident in her voice, "keep your secret."

I didn't want to explain I couldn't care less about the dance right now—that I'd only cared a little to begin with and now it all seemed so... pointless, stupid. Everything seemed pointless. Staring out the window affording the cat the sunbeam, I heard Paisley walk away, but I didn't move. I didn't try to smooth things over with her.

My phone buzzed in my tote bag and that only made me think about more inanity. Though my phone had been recovered, Dad had checked in with Mom about my losing it, and I'd still gotten a lecture about responsibility and earning my own way when I'd gotten to Mom's snug three-bedroom townhouse. Even when I'd dangled the phone in front of her, she'd still gone on and on about how I shouldn't have lost it in the first place, how I needed structure, how *she*'d had a part-time job at my age *and* little siblings to help take care of. Toward the middle of her lecture, I'd tuned her out.

I *had* heard her command that I find a job or an activity after school as she'd finally walked away, though. *"No more just putzing around with your friends."*

Because I'd given exactly zero trucks at that point, I'd done exactly that—"putzing around"—after school again today, texting my mom I was "off to look for jobs at the mall." It wasn't like she could even get off work to pick me up until five. Poor Autumn had to stay in an after-school program until then. If Dad were home, I wondered if they'd have had Ember pick her up and take her to his shiny new place for a few hours instead, even if Wednesday was "Mom's day" this week.

The thought of Ember and Dad's house made me feel sick to my stomach. My abdomen cramped and I realized my hand had warmed again and I pulled it out from under my arm to find no traces of blue light. I focused on the small diner some distance down the road—how it looked like another pitiful truck stop-esque standalone building—and let my mind go blank for some time.

Until I watched a blue pickup truck pull up to the little diner and a teen in a letterman's jacket from my school get out. He had blond hair, and though I couldn't make out every detail of him from this distance, the way my heart hurt as if in a vise told me everything I needed to know.

Sure enough, he shut the car door behind him and paused, simply facing this direction.

Calder.

He hadn't been to school since his window-jumping and I'd been ignoring his texts—how he'd gotten my number, I didn't know, and how he'd gotten my friends' numbers the other night, I didn't know that, either—and I'd been ignoring him. I wondered how he'd even known I'd gotten my phone back. After learning what he and his falsely sweet mother expected me to do...

I hadn't wanted to hear anything more. I'd simply swum off until I'd reached the edges of the shore and climbed out into the park—fortunately with no one around to see me.

Nerida had wanted to stop me, but Calder had finally stood up and asked her to stop, to give me some space. He'd followed me up, and though he'd asked me to go back to his home for some clothes, I'd refused. I'd intended to walk home, shivering and half-naked—the half that really counted at that—but I'd at least let him convince me to drive me home, to offer up a towel and a pair of spare sweatpants from the back of his truck. He'd been half-naked himself at that moment and I hadn't even cared to look—he'd kept his own pair of pants behind a rock nearby.

I'd let him offer me pants and a ride on one condition: He didn't say a word more to me the rest of the day.

He'd made the promise, laying a gentle hand on mine, his eyes pointedly avoiding looking down, and he'd kept it—but I hadn't promised I'd speak to him after that.

"I might be able to help you," spoke Orin in his unmistakable voice from behind me. I jumped, ripping my eyes from the spectacle of Calder just staring this way. I didn't know how long I'd been standing there as he approached.

My gaze flitted around. Paisley and the cat were in another corner of the store now, sitting on a rocking chair near picture books together, Paisley smiling as she pet the cat in her lap even as she kept rubbing her nose with a tissue. Raelynn and Lyric were milling about near the cash register, a bag in Raelynn's grip, Lyric's arm around Rae's back.

I hadn't noticed any of the movement.

Orin jutted his chin toward the window, his eyes focused on the diner behind me. "If you want to avoid him for more than a day, you only really have one option forward."

"Run off to Paris?" I suggested, feeling utterly defeated. "Hide out off the grid in the mountains in Tibet?"

Orin took me seriously. "No, he could easily find you in either place. As the impartial judge, I can offer you sanctuary for a while." He gestured toward the cashier's counter. "If you'll take a job here. His mother made a sacred vow to not have her people set foot in my territories for almost two weeks."

He turned back and extended his hand, watching me curiously. I didn't know if that was a joke, but if it could solve two of my current problems...

"Deal," I said, shaking his hand. Like a balm to frostbitten skin, I felt a warmth surge through my hand and up to my heart.

CHAPTER TWENTY-ONE

EMBER

Horne Moving Co. looked plain enough from the outside of the building—an unremarkable single-story building with stained bricks and a flat roof and a small, almost nondescript sign indicating the business name. Attached was a large warehouse, and one of the garage doors leading inside was open, a "Horne Moving Co." truck parked inside beside a stack of flattened cardboard boxes.

Turning off the ignition, I tossed my keys in the little back-pack-style purse I used when not at school and checked my appearance in the visor mirror.

I might have resembled a zombie in early stages of decomposition.

For a second, my heart went cold at the idea of Dean possibly seeing me like this.

Common sense shrieked somewhere deep in the back of my mind, but I stuffed it down there, lost in a sudden memory of Dean's sparkling blue irises.

Sighing, I raised the visor back up and got out of the car. I'd put on a cute red sweater, a jean skirt, and opaque black tights. For some reason, I couldn't stop thinking about how I wanted to look good for my new "boyfriend"—Ivy's lectures notwithstanding.

This didn't feel real. On so many levels, it didn't feel real.

My fingers rested on the plain, metal door handle for a moment as I took a deep breath and then I pulled.

A woman with dark, dark eyes looked up as I entered. Her long, wavy dark blonde hair hung over half of her face, her porcelain skin marked by the bright red, plump lips that formed her mouth. On closer inspection, she didn't look much older than me—she might have been younger, even, but she carried herself much more maturely. "May I help you?" she asked, looking me up and down.

I swung the mini-backpack over my shoulders and looped my arms through the straps. "Apparently, I work here now? Part-time?"

The woman's eyes widened at that and she pressed a button on the desk phone in front of her. "She came." She said it as if that were a surprise. Maybe it was to me, too, the more I thought about it.

The door to the side of her desk swung open and Principal Horne stepped out. My eyes flitted to the clock on the wall. It was 4:30, after school had let out, but most administration staff stayed until five, I thought. But what was time to someone who apparently had the gift of pausing it on occasion?

"Ember, dear," said Minnie as she approached. She looked stunning again, her sunglasses distracting from an hourglass-shaped body in a tight-fitting dress. She looped her arms through mine. "I'd have preferred to have this talk at our home—the office is rather sterile and uncomfortable, in my opinion—but I applaud Yvonne for her ingenuity in getting you to come see us." We bypassed her office and headed toward a door at the end of a long hallway that I'd have guessed led to the warehouse with the trucks and boxes.

"My mom thinks I'm going to be working here part-time."

Minnie patted my arm. She had on silky gloves the same emerald color as her dress. "And so you shall. Or it shall be your excuse whenever you might need time for other, more important things." She nodded over her shoulder and I realized the secretary had been following us, a clipboard in hand. "Zelda, get her a biweekly paycheck," she said. "Minimum wage—make it all look official." Leaning toward my ear, she whispered, "Of course, if you need more money for anything, you just need ask."

I chuckled. But she didn't admit she was joking. Because apparently, being the blood champion of whatever I was exactly meant that my new "boyfriend's" family could act as a personal ATM.

The secretary scribbled something on a notepad she carried as she brushed past us to the door. Only instead of opening it, she knocked and a muscular man in a white tank top, navy pants, and suspenders stepped out, training those otherworldly dark eyes I'd seen now on three people on me as he held the door for Minnie and me and then Zelda.

"Thank you, Leopold," said Minnie as she guided me between stacks of packaging supplies to the center of the room. Men lounged around the room in all manner of activity, some loading the back of an open truck, others gathered around a small table playing cards, still more leaning on shelves or walls and just talking. Music from a bygone era rung out in the warehouse, and I followed the source to find a rather old-fashioned—like pre-TV days—radio on an upper shelf. Though on closer inspection, I recognized it to be more of a replica, as it was flashing some track information on a digital screen. They didn't have those in my great-grandparents' days.

They were all dressed like from a black and white movie, the men's hair slicked back with grease. They had those slightly baggy suits Dean tended to favor, some with hats, others without, but a number of hats hung nearby on the backs of chairs. And like in a black and white movie, their skin was unnaturally pale, though it varied in shade of pale, almost as if they'd started with different skin tones before they'd suddenly become washed out. They were a black and white movie brought to life—except almost all of them wore sunglasses and those who didn't had eyes unnaturally black.

At our approach, one of the men looked over his shoulder and walked down a hallway that led to a break room of sorts, appearing back a few seconds later with a few women in tow. Women dressed like bombshells, but that was no surprise.

"Thank you, everyone," said Minnie as the group went quiet

and everyone gathered around us in a circle. Zelda pulled out a remote from in front of her clipboard and closed the open garage door. Everyone waited silently while it was in operation. Some had their hands tucked into their pockets like Dean was wont to do, others leaned nonchalantly on a shelf. Still others crossed their arms as if ready to encounter some bull. Minnie gestured broadly to me before bringing her hands back together in front of her chest, clearly excited about something. "This is she. Our champion."

Excited about me. But she didn't really know much about me yet.

"Hey," I said, wiggling a few fingers casually before slipping both hands around my mini-backpack straps. Everyone stared at me, and no one spoke a word. The only sound was the crooning of a Rat Pack-esque song from the radio. The only reason I could vaguely recognize that was because Grandma had said her mom had taught her a love for Sinatra. My gaze rested on Minnie. "Yeah, about that, though..." Before I could finish, the sound of a door opening from behind us echoed throughout the warehouse, followed shortly by the heavy, methodical footsteps I associated with the gait of a man in formal wear.

I looked over my shoulder as Dean approached and my heart—already thundering—melted while one corner of his lips upturned into a charmer's smile.

"Hey, doll," he said, his hands stuffed into his pockets. "So glad you could make it."

My immediate instinct was to stare at the floor, clearing my throat, determined to bring some sense back to my mind. "About *everything*," I said, emphasizing the latter word as much to remind myself there was no way I had a handsome, vampire boyfriend, whether he insisted that was the case or not, "I... Look, I don't know what you expect from me..."

Minnie stepped back to my side again, touching my shoulder. "We expect great things, of course, as we—"

"Then you have the wrong person," I spat, taking a careful step away from her. I purposefully kept my gaze affixed to the floor all the while.

Dean's footsteps echoed again and I *felt* him before I saw the tips of his shiny dress shoes enter my field of vision. "Orin told me you and he had a chat yesterday."

I scoffed. "At least I *remember* that one." There was a heat burning inside me, running up through my body and out through my right hand, an anger I wasn't accustomed to feeling but had become more and more familiar with over the past few days. Dropping my backpack strap, I clenched my fist at my side, willing the fire to settle before my hand started glowing.

Dean's palm rested on my shoulder then, a chill spreading through me, almost working to cool the anger. "The shock of the consummation can be traumatic," he said. "Minnie told me to expect... Well..." He paused and I lifted my head just slightly to see him exchange a nod with his supposed vampire aunt. "I was too hopeful that you would remember it all." My eyes met his sunglasses and his smile faltered, though he struggled to keep it on his face. "It was... Magical. I'm sorry you don't remember it. I'll never forget the moment you told me you would be mine."

My mouth opened to scoff again, but no sound came out. "I don't even know you," I said when I'd at last regained function. I stepped away so his grip on me would break. The song ended and another one began, this one a degree sadder, the jazz music breathing melancholy life to the woman singer's soulful sound. I was hit with an overwhelming urge to cry, but I held it together, biting my lip hard.

As if offering to lead me in a dance, Dean slipped in closer, taking my hand in his. "I know enough about you to know you're the one. I've waited... Ember, I've waited longer than you can imagine for you. It was an empty, vacant life all those years before you came."

My knees buckled and Dean swooped in to steady me at the small of my back, keeping the other hand clasped tightly around mine. There was fire and ice in that grip, a meeting of polarities that made me stumble as a wave of searing force jolted through me.

"She's faint," said a woman, and I recognized her. Ruby. The substitute nurse. Of course. She directed one of the men to grab his chair and bring it behind me. Dean gently lowered me into it and I leaned over, my mind racing through everything—these weird *vampires*, partially frozen in time; the way Dean looked at me though I hadn't even known he existed a few days before; the feeling inside me, a flurry of passion I'd never thought myself capable of before. I knew in some sense I was a "late bloomer." I hadn't given much thought to it—assumed I'd known what having a crush was because I'd had no shortage of those. I'd never imagined this whirlwind of emotions, this *intensity*. I wanted Dean—I wanted all of him as soon as possible. I wanted a *vampire*. I didn't have to be a paranormal expert to know that was a bad, bad idea.

The sound of another chair's legs scraping the warehouse floor made me lift my head to see Minnie seated in front of me, her legs crossed at the ankles so demurely, it almost looked like she was riding it side-saddle. "I know you have questions," she said and she looked up above me—to where Dean was still standing, his gentle grip on my shoulder. "And I know the fae gave you some answers, but... I want you hear it from us. What do you want to know?"

I cracked my knuckles, willing the bit of discomfort to snap me out of my raging, dominating thoughts. "What's with the glowing hand?" I asked, remembering the feel that had coursed through those fingers.

"It's a sign of your power," answered Minnie. "In time, you'll learn to control it, to channel it into a weapon you can use to defend our people."

I laughed, but it rung out hollowly. One of the men went up to that vintage radio and turned it down. Tension permeated the air so thickly, you could cut it with a knife. All that nonsense Orin had told me about a war, and the way she looked at me, it was like... The war wasn't a metaphor or some battle of the minds.

"A *weapon*?" I said once it was clear no one else intended to elaborate. "Like the... time pause thing."

Minnie rested a palm on her knee, her eyebrow raised in what was clearly amusement. "The fae explained quite a bit, it seems." She looked over her shoulder and nodded at Zelda. Zelda picked up her pen from the clipboard and held it like a dart, tossing it straight at Minnie's head.

Despite what I knew about vampires and magic being real and all that, I gasped.

But a slight shock ran through the room like a sound wave and the pen went stock still, suspended in the air, as the room drowned in pure silence. Smiling, Minnie grabbed the writing utensil and held it like a pointer, gesturing behind her.

Everyone else was stock still. I hadn't noticed at first because they'd been so guarded with their movements ever since she'd gathered them around, but they were like statues now. Dean squeezed my shoulder, though, and I turned around to find him smiling down at me.

"Select members of our family can pause time," said Minnie. "The more skilled you are at it, the longer you can hold the moment." She put the eraser on the cap to her lips, almost contemplating. "The wider your reach, too. I included you and Dean in the action because you were near me, but if I'd wanted, I could have included the entire room." She waved the pen in a slight circle above her and the soft music returned, the other people resuming their slight movements.

"She's the only one who could pull in others that far, though," said Dean from behind me. "Not even I can match that kind of distance."

"You flatter me, child," said Minnie. She casually swapped her legs' position, crossing the back ankle in front of the other. "Our prince just doesn't realize his potential yet."

The way his fingers dug into my shoulder then—it didn't seem like a gesture of support, like the other squeezes had been.

Shoes echoed throughout the room as Zelda went down a hallway. Moments later, the lights in the warehouse—already not overly bright—dimmed.

Minnie slowly and methodically removed her sunglasses, and

everyone else wearing them followed suit. When Zelda returned, she popped contacts out of one eye and then the other, right there in the middle of the group.

So some choose to wear dark contacts? Seems less noticeable than sunglasses. Then again, their eyes *had* seemed unnaturally black.

"Forgive our little interruption, but it's nearing twilight and we do love to give our eyes a breather after the sun sets." Minnie's sparkling blue irises peered at me, shining even in the dim light. "You will learn to pause time, too," she said.

"I already have," I said, surprising myself with my bravado. Ever since that night in the woods, there were moments where intense feelings rode like a wave out from the back of my mind to the front of it. I faltered, remembering myself. "At least, I... I did it once. Briefly. With Orin in the woods."

"Impressive." Minnie's focus flicked above my shoulder again. "And was the fae included in your reach?"

"He could move while everything else froze, if that's what you mean."

She nodded. She held up the pen and Zelda stepped forward to take it from her, scribbling on her clipboard.

The room fell into a near silence again, but the soft sound of music and the glow of bright blue irises from all corners of the warehouse almost distracted me from my purpose here.

My gaze fell on Nurse Ruby. "Why did... Why did I reach for that blood in the garbage?"

Minnie tittered, and the sound was sweet, like a bird. "Blood makes you stronger, my dear. It calls to you. Thinking about it will help you bring your powers to the forefront—and *feeling* it will make summoning your powers all the easier."

Gross. If it meant I never touched another dirtied bandage, I could live without going the easy route.

"What's the purpose of this?" I asked, trying hard not to turn around and gaze at those beautiful eyes I knew Dean had trained on me. "Why do I need... a weapon? Why pause time? Why...?" The question died on my throat. "Do you... Do you drink blood?"

"So inquisitive," said Minnie. "I like that." As if anyone else in my shoes wouldn't ask all these questions and then some. She straightened in her chair. "You are the chosen one. The one who will enact revenge upon the foul creatures of the sea who denied our existence."

"The... mermaids?"

"Merfolk," said Dean from behind me and Minnie's gaze darted pointedly to him. He went quiet.

"Yes," said Minnie, returning her focus to me. "The merfolk."

"Why are you fighting?" I asked, still completely lost.

"I doubt any of *them* remember," said Minnie, and her lips went tight, as if that was all she had to say on the matter. "As for drinking blood, we do, but not so greedily as you see depicted in the fictitious portrayals that might form your opinion of us." She tapped her long fingers atop her knee. "For us, blood is not a matter of survival, but... More of a fine wine. I'm sure you'll grow to understand once you develop a taste for it."

Develop a taste for it?

Minnie looked behind her and nodded. "Why don't we offer you a sample?"

"I'm too young to drink. Legally anyway." Mom *had* shared a sip of her rosé on occasion, but... I chuckled nervously, but no one else laughed.

Two of the men disappeared down the long hallway and we all waited quietly for their return. My stomach turned at the idea of a blood bag or a blood sample poured into a wine glass, like an air of sophistication might erase the fact that it was freaking *blood* about to pass someone's lips.

My hand grew hot and I covered it instantly, almost on instinct to shelter myself from the glowing red there, the desire spreading from my fingers to my toes.

Footfalls echoed from the hallway. "Bon appétit," said Minnie as the two men returned with a woman between them, her wrists tied with rope in front of her, a stick between her teeth that she was clamping down on.

The entire group sprang into action, like animals—like

monsters—and I... I screamed, freezing the moment in time, as much to stop myself as to stop any of them.

CHAPTER TWENTY-TWO

IVY

Two days into my new "job," and on any other week, I'd be thanking the skies for the lack of anything to do and the boss who didn't seem to care less if I just browsed the Internet on my phone with the cracked screen. But this week, I was just glad that being here afforded me an escape from two environments I'd rather not be in right now: my mom's place when she gets her mind set on something, like me working, and the little drab sea kingdom under the park lake.

The fingers on my free hand traced soothing, repetitive patterns at the back of Feilia's neck. She curled up beside the register, having popped in through the cat door at the back of the store when I'd arrived and hung up my coat. Since this place was so peaceful, I got why this cat liked to hang out. The Hollow Tree had, like, *no* customers. Unless they all came in during the school day. Though, apparently, Orin came in on a whim whenever it suited him. And his whim extended to offering me rides to and from work because it was a bit of a drive from Mom's and she was too busy anyway.

After a long bout of petting, I gave the cat a break. "How do you keep the lights on in this place again?" I asked, my voice somewhat muffled by the fact that I rested my cheek on one palm, my elbow on the counter beside Feilia, as the thumb on my other hand brushed aside a text message from Lyric and went back to scrolling through obscure facts about films from before I'd even been born.

Orin, seated in a plush chair at the end of the counter and engrossed in one of his beat-up paperbacks, didn't respond.

I did my best imitation of a bird whistle and his curly head jerked.

"Is someone here?" he asked, getting up and removing his reading glasses. Because apparently never-aging fae needed those.

"No, you would have heard the jingle." I pointed to the bell dangling over the front door.

Shrugging, Orin sat back down. Before he could get his glasses back on, though, I set my phone down.

"Hey," I said. "Answer the question."

"What question?"

Argh. I never considered myself someone who *had* to be part of a conversation constantly, but after years with Lyric and Paisley and the rest, I had to admit I found absolute silence rather disconcerting. "How do you keep this place open with no customers?"

Orin lifted his book above his head as he put those glasses on anyway. "I look at it as more of a hobby. It's my personal library away from home."

"But how do you have the money for that?"

"Investments."

The idea of this fae who looked like a twenty-year-old guy at most walking into a financial advisor's office with a losing business plan and a goal to make it happen made less sense to me than the fact that merfolk existed. Then there was the idea of him with an accountant to pay his taxes, him at the town hall to get his business license—

"I wouldn't worry about it," he said, almost as if guessing the trajectory of my thoughts. He turned the page, the wrinkle of the paper the only sound echoing in this silent chamber.

"I wasn't exactly *worried* about it." I walked around the counter, ambling through the aisles and pushing any book that seemed slightly out of line back into the shelf. He'd gotten one shipment while I'd been here—they often came on Fridays, he'd said—but it had all of two books in it, one he put beneath the counter and the other he was reading right then.

"You know, an e-reader would save you a lot of space."

Though I couldn't see him entirely over the shelf in front of me, I did see the phone he stuck up into the air. "When I'm away from books, I have this."

"For movies," I said. He'd already explained it.

"And TV shows," he added. "I *love* streaming, all right? Never could bring myself to get cable and a TV and a hookup and all that. Ah, the wonders of satellite. Still, books were the first thing to keep me sane all alone in that cabin and I'm not the type to abandon a first love." The phone disappeared, presumably back into his pocket, and I kept meandering down the aisle.

Before I even acknowledged I wasn't just wandering aimlessly, I found myself at the window through which I could see that old-fashioned trucker's diner. "He's there again," I said, noticing the blue pickup truck. He wasn't leaning against the truck today. Perhaps it had finally gotten too cold. But something in my heart seemed to whisper that he was certainly nearby.

"Of course," said Orin. "He knows he can't come in here without my permission, but he won't want to be apart from you for long." He yawned, the sound echoing even across the room. "Boy, I'm shattered, mate."

Nice to know this hardly fazes you. I stormed back to face Orin, taking a seat in front of him on the edge of a display table full of mystery books. "What's to stop him from entering my mom's place at night?"

Orin actually looked up from his book for that, his eyebrow raised. "What indeed."

Shuddering, I ran a hand up and down my arm.

"Rest easy," said Orin, turning back to his book and flipping a page. "The prince of water is rather... *milquetoast* in my opinion. He has no desire to ravage you in the night, not if he hopes to earn your trust, all right?"

Milquetoast. That's a word you don't hear often. I sighed, shifting slightly back toward the window, my chin resting on my shoulder, though I couldn't see through it from here.

"Is the prince of... blood... more of a ravager?"

Orin snorted. "Do I detect a hint of envy?"

I snapped back to face him. "I don't—That's not..." My fist clenched, and I had to take a deep breath to will the iciness away. "I just... I don't like that I'm just supposed to take this all in and fight on their side and... I won't... I don't care what they say. I'm not hurting Ember."

Dog-earing a page, Orin shut the book. "What if she hurts you first?"

My hair whipped across my face as I abruptly turned. For some reason, I hadn't even thought about that. I didn't have a response.

"How are things at school?" asked Orin, steepling his hands and leaning back in the chair.

"Fine, I guess?" I nodded backward toward the window. "You know Calder has skipped ever since Tuesday?"

"I'm not surprised," said Orin. His eyes widened exaggeratedly, as if about to tell a spooky Halloween story. "Vampires wander your halls."

I shivered again. "The new principal," I said.

Orin ticked off a list on his fingers. "And the nurse. And a custodian. I wouldn't be surprised if they added a lunch lady by next week."

"Why?"

"To stay close to Ember—to keep an eye on you."

"She's been skipping school, too." Shaking my head, I picked up one of the mystery novels just to have something for my fingers to pick at. It was one of those "cozy" mysteries with a brightly colored, painted cover of a cheery-looking garden—except for the bloody knife growing out of the ground next to the tomatoes. "Well, I guess she came back today, but... I don't know. I didn't see her. I just heard about her being draped all over Dean Horne and..." *Did I really care about stuff like that, considering everything else at stake at the moment?* "She looked ill. No one seemed to question why she'd have been gone for half the week before this."

"Interesting," said Orin. He pulled his glasses off and tucked them inside his front pocket.

"Is that fair?" I asked. "Can one side like... take over our school like that?"

"If it weren't allowed, I'd have stepped in by now."

Right. All-mighty overseer here. I felt more comfortable around him than I did anyone else involved, though. Which brought me to another point. "And it's not unfair that you've been spending so much time with me and none with Ember?"

Orin gestured around him. "I offer neutral sanctuary to both champions when necessary. If Ember were so inclined, she'd be welcome here, too."

Huh. For some reason, it hadn't occurred to me until that moment to plead with Ember, to make her run here, too, to escape all this madness.

"I won't see her until Sunday," I said, already formulating a plan. "But can I tell her about your job offer to work here?"

Orin stretched, raising his arms high above him. "You want me to be open on Sunday? You girls will be the death of me."

I'd yet to ask if death was on the table for a fae who at times hinted he was older than dirt.

After he finished his stretch, Orin nodded at me. "She's already had my offer." *Oh, yeah. He spoke to her in his cabin that day.* "But you're welcome to nudge her to reconsider it. She didn't turn me down outright. She just had a lot to think about." He pulled his glasses back out of his pocket and produced a wipe from his jean pocket and began moving the cloth in circular motions over the lenses.

The bell over the door jangled and I jumped, actually dropping the mystery book I'd been cradling. Feilia let out a little mew and jumped off the counter, retreating to the back room.

"Hello...?" spoke someone, unsurety clear as day in her voice.

"Yes, hello," I said, swooping down to pick up the book and toss it back on its display. "Can I help you?" I rounded the corner and came face-to-face with Journey Slowe.

Her face brightened. "Oh, *hi*! I didn't know you worked here."

Caught unawares, I shuffled my weight from one leg to the other. "Just since yesterday."

"Cool," said Journey. She cocked her head. "Then you... Are you the 'girl at the bookstore' this is for?" She reached into her purse and pulled out a folded piece of paper.

"I guess...?" The paper hung in the air between us as I hesitated to take it. "Where did you get that?"

Journey nodded over her shoulder at the door. "I stopped by my dad and Nana's diner for takeout for my mom and me. Calder Poole was there—on his third slice of apple pie, Nana told me— and he asked me if I'd give you this."

Ember had mentioned something about Journey and that diner, I remembered now. I smiled warily and snatched the paper from Journey's waiting hand. "Sorry you had to go out of your way—"

"No, I was headed here already. Nana told me The Hollow Tree had been open a lot this week, so I had to stop in."

"Miss Slowe. It's been ages. Welcome." Orin appeared out of nowhere behind me, as quiet as a mouse. I startled, but he ignored the way I'd almost jumped out of my boots. "I have just the thing for you." He raised a finger in the air and then rushed behind the counter.

"Okay..." said Journey, chuckling nervously. She leaned closer to me and whispered conspiratorially. "He's *so* cute, isn't he?"

"I hear his older brother was, too," I said, smiling awkwardly.

"What older brother?" asked Journey. She did a double take as she watched Orin pull a book out from under the counter. The book we'd just gotten in today.

"His older brother used to work here," I said, going ahead and perpetuating the lie Orin had let Paisley think. "It's a family-run business."

Journey chuckled. "I don't know about all that, but Orin has been hot stuff here since I was a kid anyway." She pursed her lips as he approached. "He's got to be at least thirty by now."

Orin put the book in her hands. It was a hardcover fantasy, a beautiful young woman in a pale pink ball gown carrying a magic wand that lit her way through a dense forest.

Journey gasped. "Pretty!"

Orin jutted his chin toward her and looked at me, his irises sparkling. "She always judges a book by its cover."

"You remembered!" Journey smiled. Her teeth were sparkling white and dimples appeared on her cheeks. Clutching the book to her chest, she practically swooned. "If only you were ten years younger..."

I snorted and Orin raised an eyebrow at me. Taking that as my cue to leave, I made my excuses. "I'll just... take my break now," I said. "See you at school."

"Sure," said Journey, her eyes lost on Orin. "Oh, hey, Ivy!" she called and I turned around to see her snapped back to reality. "Have you spoken to Ember lately?"

Wouldn't *she* have spoken to her more recently than I would have? "Not really. I'm at my mom's until Sunday."

"Oh," said Journey, and she seemed sad. "It's just... She's been acting a little strange."

No, really? I sighed. Like this poor girl could even begin to imagine what was going on with Ember.

"Yeah..." I said at last. "But I don't... I didn't really know her well before our parents got hitched and all that."

"True." Journey frowned, but then her face brightened. "Hey, are you going to get ready with us for Homecoming?" The dance was a week away—a week after tomorrow. And it was the *last* thing on my mind, considering everything else.

"I don't know," I said. "Saturday's my day at Mom's and I'll probably be with Lyric and Paisley beforehand..." I hadn't exactly finetuned the details because I hadn't cared. But I was certain one or both of them had mentioned some kind of preparation plans.

"Why don't they come, too?" Journey was practically bouncing on her feet. "My mom and Mrs.—er, Noelle are the best at prep. Mom does hair, Noelle does makeup—they both cook up a wicked pre-dance meal."

I laughed. I'd have found hanging with moms right before a dance a ridiculous thing to do before last week.

"Devam's already coming to join us for the dinner part," she said, and that snapped me back to the moment. Right. He'd told everyone he was taking her, and the guys had all given him high-fives. Journey *was* really cute, do-gooder though she might have been.

"Maybe," I said, more to get her out of my hair than anything. "But I'd have to ask Lyric and Paisley."

Journey whipped out her phone. "Will do," she said. I didn't even know she had their numbers.

Shrugging, I headed to the back room, which was hardly the stark, white-walled dull place one would expect in the back of a business. It was decked out as lusciously as the rest of the store behind the door, but it was overloaded with boxes spilling over with unshelved used books—one of which had a fluffy Maine Coon tail popping out of it. It was like Orin was hoarding them. Maybe he *had* dug them all out of trash bins. It would help keep his overhead manageable at the very least.

Ignoring the electric tea kettle atop the large table in the midst of the room that Orin had said I was free to use at any time, I sunk into the comfortable high-backed chair beside the table. It wasn't until I sat there for a full minute that I remembered I'd left my phone out there on the counter—and that I was clutching a folded piece of paper.

You hungry? it read. *Please join me for dinner at the diner.* The "please" was underlined. *I promise... I promise I'm not like my mom. Please.*

My stomach rumbled then, almost as if in answer to the request, the traitorous thing, and I heard the door bell jingle and Orin exchange goodbyes with Journey, whose diner takeout was probably getting cold.

My stomach lurched again. I *was* hungry...

"So," said Orin, joining me in the back room, "I'm closing up shop."

Leaning forward, my nose wrinkled. "It's like... 6:30."

"And this is a small business," he said, smiling. "And it's open and closed on a whim."

"But what about—?"

"I'll pay you for the full three hours," he said, taking my jacket off the nearby coat rack and tossing it to me. That wasn't exactly what I'd been concerned about, and he knew it.

"Sorry," he said, wincing. "Just... if you need me, I'll be at home."

Sure, I'll go for a stroll in the labyrinthine-like woods behind my stepmom's house the next time I'm in danger. "What about my ride first?"

"What about it?" he said, his eye twinkling. He nodded at the paper still in my fingers.

"Okay..." I stared at him, daring him to get a hint. "Fine. I have a... dinner invitation."

Orin darted his eyes away at that, and I thought I saw a slight bob to his throat before he clicked off the lights in the back room. A rustle of movement from Feilia beside me made me jump. "Don't forget your phone," he said. In the outline of the open doorway, he fished into his pockets and drew out some keys. "And lock up, will you? I've got some business to attend to for a bit. I'll see you Monday. If you feel like coming."

"Wait, Monday? But what about before then? And how will you know I want to come Monday without—"

But he was gone, the jangle of the front door bell my only reply.

CHAPTER TWENTY-THREE

EMBER

When I'd daydreamed about having my first boyfriend, I'd pictured Elizabeth and Darcy, Jane and Rochester—maybe Edward and Bella. But I hadn't meant the latter one *literally*.

Besides, I'd always been more of a Jacob girl. But Journey could never know that; I'd never live it down.

My vampire boyfriend strolled through my bedroom, his hands behind his back, his sunglasses in his pocket—it was early evening now and with just my old white Christmas lights on in my room, he seemed unbothered enough by the light. He ran a finger over a picture I had fastened to my corkboard—Journey and me on our first day of kindergarten, already best friends, our arms wrapped around each other's shoulders, toothy smiles on our faces.

"You and Miss Slowe have known each other a long time," said Dean.

"Yeah." I bit my lip, tearing my eyes away from him. Part of me wanted to stare at him and never look away—but there was a quieter part, louder when he wasn't near me, that wasn't ready to give up everything that had mattered to me less than a week before just because I couldn't stop picturing my hands running over the front of his suit. My phone—on the nightstand beside me —buzzed then and I forced myself to look at it instead of Dean. Another message from Journey. We'd talked at school today, but...

I knew she knew I was hiding something. I just didn't know what I could possibly tell her. I didn't want her involved in all of this.

Just finished takeout I got from Pop and Nana's, Journey wrote. *We have extras. You want some?*

Mom was going to be late—she was picking up Easton from the airport and they were stopping for a bite to eat on the way home. I hadn't eaten much in the past few days, but the thought of food had my stomach grumbling.

"Hey," said Dean, suddenly standing next to the bed where I'd parked myself awkwardly, not daring to get comfortable in case he got the wrong idea about *why* I'd let him come up to my bedroom, an idea I wasn't so sure *was* the wrong idea, if I was being honest with myself, but my brain was kicking in with warning bells. One of my legs hung at an angle off the bed and my back strained from the lack of support I'd forced on myself. "Why don't you and Miss Slowe enjoy a Friday night together? You look... pale... and you didn't eat much at lunch." He reached a wary hand toward my shoulder but pulled back at my flinch, his brightly colored eyes flashing with hurt. Sliding his fingers as casually as he could into his pocket, he produced the coin he liked to fidget with when his hands seemed to lack something better to do. "I can eat, but I don't always bother," he said. "I prefer a liquid diet." His smile languished awkwardly on his face and I realized with a pang I'd been searching for hints of the fangs I'd seen protrude from the open mouths of the people in his aunt's warehouse. "That... sounds terrible. But I actually did mean liquids. Human liquids."

"Blood's a human liquid," I said, standing.

"Liquids humans enjoy. Tea. Coffee. Soda on occasion."

He hadn't eaten anything at lunch, but neither had I, really. There'd been so many people staring at us and whispering that I'd asked to go somewhere more private. We'd ended up behind a dark tree topped with bright orange leaves off to the side of the baseball diamond, me laying my back against his chest, him wrapping his arms around me, neither of us speaking.

"Ember, if you want to talk about what happened the other day—"

A wave of dizziness descended on my brain as I pictured the other day, the woman, the fangs bared, the way I'd held them all—except Dean and Minnie—frozen in time, but how it'd been useless, how it'd only delayed the inevitable. The debacle had made me never want to eat again, despite the weakness that permeated my body.

"She *wanted* us to drink her," he began.

I shot up, my knees going weak, and Dean swooping in to steady me. I pushed him away, despite the intoxicating desire I had to pull him close. "Minnie said you only drink blood for pleasure, not for survival."

"True, but it's so much more than that..." He sighed, flipping his coin in the air as he paced back and forth in front of me. "It makes us stronger, more alert—more..."

"Alive?"

He froze, a timid smile on his face. "If only."

I turned, clutching the back of my desk chair for support. "You didn't... You didn't drink any."

"Because I could tell it upset you. I mean, even without the attempt to pause time." The gentle smack and whoosh of his coin flipping in the air made it clear he'd picked his habit back up. "It was more important I escort you home so you didn't have to witness more of it."

He'd insisted on driving my car for me—had insisted on even opening the passenger door for me, and I'd numbly climbed in and let him do as he pleased. I'd felt powerless then—powerless to resist, powerless to do anything. I'd asked for him to leave me alone the next day and had spent it binge watching shows I'd already seen all of on Netflix. He'd respected my wishes for one day and then had shown up at the door early this morning, chatting with my mom before I'd even come downstairs, Mom beaming when she informed me that he'd *walked* over to see if I'd like to ride to school together. He'd driven my car today for me, too. "I *did* pause time," I pointed out. I *had*. Briefly.

"Yes, you did." His voice grew louder and I could feel his presence behind me, my body practically crying for his. "And in future, with more practice, you'll pause it for longer and learn... To change things to suit your objective."

I scoffed. "Like get the woman out of there before any of your *family* could drink from her?"

"Well, maybe not like that." He grabbed me by the arms and spun me around, his nose close to my brow, my heart hammering as I gazed up into his bright blue irises. "She's okay," he said. "The woman."

I laughed, tearing my gaze from his

"I'm serious, doll," he said. "She's at my house with the rest of them."

"The rest of what?" Rage coursed through me and my right hand burned hot. I shoved his chest and moved away, putting a few paces between us. "The rest of your... blood hostages?"

"That's not how we see them, but..." He stopped, closing his lips tightly as he stared at me.

"But what?" I asked, my arm growing hotter and hotter as the Christmas lights glowed brighter—no, that was my hand. I held it out in front of me. It was glowing red again, just slightly.

"You're amazing, Ember," he said, stepping toward me, but I ripped my arm out from his reach and put it behind my back.

"Answer the question," I spat.

He stared at me, then sighed and stepped away, walking back toward my cork board on the other side of the desk.

"Some people agree to offer up their blood to us on occasion in exchange for the chance to... become one of us someday. A number of those you met at the warehouse were turned in such a way."

"And you?" I asked, my heart thundering wildly.

"I'm different," he said, shoving both hands into his pocket, his oversized suit jacket being pushed back to reveal a dress shirt that clung to muscles like paint. I had to look away, the fire coursing from my abdomen.

"But," I said, leaving my vampire boyfriend's origins aside for the moment, "if she was *volunteering* to be there, why was she tied up?"

"Quenching can be frightening—perhaps a touch painful." He

moved then toward the door and I was compelled to watch him again. "It's safer for them if they can't move much while it happens."

"Oh, sign me up for *that*," I said, crossing my arms and almost forgetting the redness in my hand. I yelped as my right hand came into contact with my left arm. Even through the sweater, it was like a hot burner scorching my skin.

"Are you all right?" asked Dean, suddenly at my side. He took my right hand in both of his and the fire seemed to meet ice, a soothing balm soaring through my fingers to the tips of my toes, the heat cooling. Once the red glow had gone entirely, he massaged my palm. "As champion of blood, you will wield fire," he said. "With enough practice, you'll win this and bring survival to our family—"

"Survival to undead *vampires*," I said, and I could feel the jolt in his body through his touch. Sighing, I let my hand slip from his, my brain fighting off the desire to keep his skin on mine.

"We deserve to live, too," he said quietly. "That's all we ever wanted. But the merfolk... They'd deny us our entire existence."

I was certain they saw it differently. When did anyone in war ever think they were on the wrong side? "And for that, you'd have me... fight my new step-sister. Literally battle her. I don't even do that well in gym, Dean."

"You're a champion," said Dean, swooping in closer, "and you will wield power you never thought yourself capable of."

I snorted. He was right about that already. Silence descended over the room as my phone buzzed again over by the nightstand. "Would I... How do I win?" I asked, my throat suddenly dry. "I just need to ask her to surrender?"

"She may not," he said. "In fact, I... I doubt she would."

"So then...?" I left the rest unsaid.

"You have to do what you can to *make* her surrender."

I shook my head and brushed past him, picking up my phone. "I'm not fighting her, Dean. I don't... I don't care what reasons you and your family have. I'm not like that—and I'm not involved."

"You're our champion," he repeated. "Our... princess. You and I —we're key to the vampires' survival."

Journey had sent another message. *I saw Ivy at The Hollow Tree —you know, that never-open bookstore by Pop and Nana's diner? Did you know she works there?*

And the other message... was from Ivy. It came up "Unknown," but it was clear immediately whose number it was. Had she asked Journey for my number? *There's a way to stay neutral*, she wrote, not bothering with preamble. *Orin said he spoke to you about his bookstore —his home and his bookstore are neutral ground. Neither vampire nor merperson can set foot in them without his permission, and the merfolk don't have that for over a week. Truce? Can we talk?*

Dean appeared over my shoulder and I realized that even this close, I wasn't sure if he was breathing.

"It could be a trick," he said, and I felt weird, violated.

I put the phone to my chest so he couldn't read it anymore. "But Orin is the overseer," I said. "You'll admit that much?"

He bit his lip and I thought I saw just the tip of an overly long incisor. "Yes."

"And his house and... bookstore... are places you can't go?"

"Not without his permission."

"Then I'll take my chances." I reached for the little backpack purse I'd tossed beside my nightstand. Dean moved to stand between me and the door.

"I just want to talk to her," I said, gripping my backpack handles tightly. He didn't move. "She's going to be here half the week anyway. It's not like I'm going to avoid her entirely."

Sighing, Dean stepped back to let me pass, opening the door and holding it for me, though it wasn't like doors in houses were ever in danger of swinging shut. "Just promise me you'll be careful."

I watched him warily and nodded, sending a quick text back. *Where do you want to talk?*

CHAPTER TWENTY-FOUR

IVY

Once I saw Ember's response to my text, relief washed through me. It wasn't too late. Despite all these crazy, unbelievable things going on all around us, we could rise above and fight for the normal lives we ought to have had. These monsters would just have to get used to the idea. They couldn't very well follow us to college, could they?

"I take it you got a good reply?" Calder wrapped his mouth around the straw in his third chocolate shake since I'd sat down across him and I shook my head at the bottomless pit that was his stomach. I wondered briefly what happened to his innards when he transformed—or mine, for that matter. I didn't want to think about it, but maybe the stomach morphed and all the food vanished in the process. It would explain why he was strappingly fit despite putting all these sweets away.

I grunted my reply. A young-looking waitress brought my BLT and potato wedges and I thanked her, but she was too busy trying to catch Calder's eye. A part of me bristled at that, but then I remembered—she was welcome to him. Someone else could have this whole mess to deal with. I didn't need a boyfriend, anyway, let alone a merman prince one.

A message from Paisley popped up on my screen and I almost swiped it away, but it gave me an idea. Orin had gone who-knew-where, and though he'd left me with the keys to his shop, I hadn't had the chance to ask if his neutrality only applied to places where he was currently parked behind his obnoxious hipster glasses reading a book. So the bookstore might not have worked regardless. Besides, this—this would seem more *normal*, more *real*, which was the point of all of this.

Want to go shopping for Homecoming dresses? I wrote to Ember. *Paisley and Lyric keep wanting to turn me into their dress-up doll.* I didn't add that I didn't really care at this point whether or not I went to the dance, even if I bought a dress. I didn't actually have to buy anything, so why not? I texted Paisley back to get the okay from her, and she texted back right away, seemingly flabbergasted that I'd agreed at all.

The hollow echo of Calder's straw sucking at an empty shake glass grated in my ear. "So you're going to broker peace, huh?"

"My step-sister and I don't have stakes in this nonsense."

"You sure about that?" Calder leaned over and snatched a potato wedge from my plate. I sent him a death glare and he actually shirked back. But he still ate the wedge. "Maybe not you—not yet—but how deep do you think the Hornes might have their fangs sunk into Ember by now?"

I shuddered. I didn't know if he meant that metaphorically or literally, and I wasn't sure I wanted to think about it. "That's what I need to find out," I said. "And what I need to stop from progressing further."

I texted Ember back and took a few mouthfuls of my sandwich before she replied. *I'm bringing Journey*, she wrote. *I'm just stopping at her place first for a bite and we'll meet you there. Dress Castle. An hour.*

A bite? I cringed at myself, thinking that might be literal, her knowing *vampires* and all. But it was done. I put the phone next to me on the booth seat, my finger running over the crack on the screen and cringing. If Orin kept his word and gave me an actual paycheck, maybe some good would come out of this mess after all.

"'The best laid schemes o' mice an' men,'" said Calder, drumming his fingers on the table.

"What?" I asked as I finished the first half of my sandwich. I stared at him cautiously as I pulled the toothpick out of the second half, my grip on the pick getting tense, like I'd use the sharp end of the stick as a dagger if he tried anything.

He shrugged. "Nothing. I just... I want you to be careful is all."

"You're not following me to meet her," I said. "It's bad enough you stake this place out for hours on end just because I'm down the road." I stared at the waitress, who was taking the order of a trucker who'd sat down at the counter shortly after she'd served me my BLT. "I think you're giving the poor waitress the wrong signals. She clearly likes you." I took a giant bite.

"There's only one woman for me," said Calder, and he somehow managed to turn on some kind of roguish charm with a smile that made my toes curl in their shoes. I put the last quarter of my sandwich down, my face suddenly hot under the power of his pale green irises.

My right hand, though, went cold, and I had to clench it into a fist and ignore it, afraid to look down and find it glowing blue. Taking a deep breath, I started working on my potato wedges with my left hand.

"Ivy, I know my mom can be... overwhelming." He chuckled and ran fingers through his hair. It looked even messier, but it suited him. "So I told her to step back. I want to be the one to watch over you. I want you to feel like you're safe with me."

I scoffed. "Safe from my nerdy new step-sister. Sure."

"Not just her." Calder clamped his mouth shut as the waitress came back and asked if we needed refills or anything.

"Another shake, sweet stuff?" she asked.

I stifled a laugh and Calder flushed somewhat. "I've had enough, thank you," he said. "But another pop for the lady."

She bristled and walked away, clutching my half-empty glass like she wanted to shatter it.

"Soda," I said, chomping on another wedge.

"What?" he asked.

"I hate 'pop.' It makes me feel like I'm a bobbysoxer about to drink something from the 1950s."

Calder gestured around us to the kitschy vintage-style diner.

"Touché," I admitted, just as the waitress returned and rather unceremoniously slammed my glass on the counter before stepping away.

"You know," said Calder, resting his forearms on the table and leaning forward, "I'm sixteen. Like actually sixteen."

Snorting, I grabbed for my glass, and, hoping the waitress didn't take her jealousies out in the form of a root beer and spit float, took a sip from the straw. "That's great," I said, once I'd finished. "What a big boy you are."

He didn't laugh at my joke. Biting his lip, his eyes darted to the table surface. "Merfolk... We don't really live much longer than the average human. That's part of the... Well, that is... Our population is dwindling and the vampires... They just never die."

"What?" I said, putting my glass back on the table and laughing. "Like... You're serious?"

Calder stole another of my potato wedges and this time I didn't have the heart to glare at him. "You've breathed underwater and grown a fish tail and immortal vampires surprise you?"

"Well, no, but..." I ignored the buzzing of my phone to rub a hand up my arm. I'd suddenly experienced a chill, and my palm grew icier still with the movement. My voice grew quiet. "They're really, like, blood-sucking vampires?"

"Yup," said Calder, grabbing a napkin and wiping his fingers. I lost my appetite and shoved my plate closer to him.

"But they can walk around in sunlight."

Calder pointed toward his temple with a potato wedge. "That's what the glasses are for. Though some prefer scarily dark contact lenses."

I shook my head, confused. "How do glasses save them from turning to ash in a sunbeam?"

He shrugged. "If only it were that easy. But they don't die in the sunlight. They just... can't see well unless their eyes are shaded like a hundred times over. They don't particularly like artificial light, either, but they can deal with it."

"Okay..." I chewed on the bottom of my lip and flexed the

fingers on my right hand, something coming over me like I was itching for a fight. "So you tell me *you're* really sixteen—"

"Right."

"Like... someone isn't?"

"Well," said Calder, finishing off the last of the potatoes with a four-wedge grab all at once, "I imagine Dean's trying to pass himself off as a senior, so he'd say he's seventeen or eighteen, but he's really an old man."

I chuckled, but Calder didn't laugh with me. "You're serious? But he looks like a hot older teen—"

Calder's eyes narrowed at that and I bit my tongue, suddenly distracted from what I was saying.

"And the people he hangs with look young, too, for the most part. They look the ages they were when they died."

"When they... died?" I could barely hear myself speak the last word.

"You know, *undead* and all that. Stories got that part right." He pulled another napkin out of the dispenser on our table and wiped his mouth.

I shook my head in amazement. "So Ember's new 'boyfriend'—"

"Is like seventy years her senior."

I blinked. True, that always was a bit of a problem in those vampire romance stories. Or in a fairy love story. A mythical creature boyfriend could be thousands of years older than you.

But me? I got stuck robbing the cradle. "You know I'm seventeen. I'll be eighteen in a few months."

Calder grinned. "I like older women. So long as they're not seventy *years* older."

That was like a slap to the face, a reminder of what exactly was going on here. "Your mom mentioned us... mating?"

He shook his head heartily. "Don't worry about that. It's just... a dumb wish on her part. Like part of a prophesy. I'm more concerned about the immediate threat: those undead, blood-sucking interlopers. They threaten not just my people, but all of humanity." He sighed. "We just want to live in peace. We don't pose a threat to people. We don't walk the Earth and swim its oceans an absurdly long time like they do." He turned his eyes on me and they were sad, almost puppy-like. "I promise, no matter what stupid and embarrassing things my mom says, that if you help me win this conflict, I'll do everything in my power to help you walk away. No questions asked. No pressure. Just help liberate my people and I promise you I'll never speak to you again if that's what you want."

The waitress came back with a check and started collecting Calder's glasses and my plate. Numb, I didn't react as Calder pulled out his wallet and got the bill in full. "Keep the change," he said to the waitress, grabbing her hand to place three ten-dollar bills in her palm. When she beamed down at him, his smile and grip dropped and he just nodded at her awkwardly.

"I don't want to kill Ember," I whispered once the waitress had finally walked away.

"If she doesn't fight for them, you won't have to," said Calder.

"Then how would we win?" I asked, the words catching in my throat. A dull, blue glow came from beneath the table where my fist clenched in my lap.

"If only one side has a champion, it wins by default," said Calder. "The deadline of sorts for the champions to declare themselves for real and seal the deal is a fortnight from the initial consummation."

"Declare themselves for real?" I asked, the ice in my hand warming somewhat. "Are you ever going to explain what happened that night in the woods?"

Calder swallowed. "There's a reason why the champions, like, forget the initial pact?"

I stared at him, waiting for him to continue.

If he'd had a collared shirt, he would have been grasping at it as he squirmed under my glare. "The champions don't exactly volunteer the first time? You just have to get one to the orb."

Of course. I folded my arms. Things were making more sense. Like I'd ever *agree* to this nonsense for the weird fish boy I barely knew? "And would any girl have done?" I didn't know why the idea of him answering positively bothered me. It was the least of my concerns at the moment.

"No, not exactly..." Calder sighed and ran a hand through his hair again. Pretty soon, he'd muss his follicles into complete disarray. "She has to put down roots within a certain distance of the consummate lands."

"Okay..." I almost didn't get what he meant, but then it dawned on me. "She has to live at my step-mom's house?"

"Yes?" said Calder, like it was a question. He scratched the back of his head.

"So Ember would have done just as fine for you."

Calder cleared his throat, his gaze darting to the napkin dispenser. That was answer enough.

I blew air out of my mouth. "And why not Noelle then, huh? Why wait until I moved in?"

"We thought about Ember's mother, but Orin was insistent the champion had to be far younger. A better willingness to believe in the magic that might sprout in the heart or something."

A thought struck me and made my blood ran cold. "What about Autumn?"

Calder's nose scrunched up. "You mean your littler sister? If we waited a few years, maybe, but I had no desire to get a little kid involved in this. Fortunately, the bloodsuckers seemed to think the same."

A wave of relief washed over me and I checked my phone to see if Autumn herself had sent any updates. There was a text from Mom asking if I'd need a ride from work timestamped a few minutes back, so I quickly told her I'd made plans with friends and I'd be back before curfew. If anything had happened to Autumn, Mom would have definitely known. She'd be with her by now.

Calder chuckled, but there was a shaky nervousness to his laugh. "So what do you think of my trick? Did you know you can use it yourself?"

It might prove more useful than growing a fish tail, that was true. I stared at the phone. Calder had explained how he'd gotten all my friends' phone numbers that night in the woods to send the text by producing Ember's phone number for me to text out of thin air, a pretext of peace to allow me to meet with my step-sister and hash things out. Somehow, we still hadn't actually exchanged numbers. I was surprised she didn't even find it weird I'd texted her.

"It works for anyone you come into contact with. Anyone you've touched even once." He stared over at the waitress, who was taking the truck driver's order down from the service window leading back to the kitchen. He fished his own phone out of his pocket, and as he had done with mine, he touched the screen with four fingers, making it light up. His digits flew across the screen and after a minute, he turned it around to face me. A name, an age, an address, a phone number... I'd have no way of confirming they applied to the waitress, but I believed him. Apparently, merfolk were like semi-psychic stalkers.

"Any information in the subconscious mind," he said and I noticed he made a point of dismissing the memo without saving the information. "Anything they're not thinking of that moment, but they know deep down. Search for it as your skin comes into contact with theirs, and you'll know—and they won't even know you were nosing around in their brain."

"I don't know how useful that *skill* will be in a war against vampires, but okay..." I shook my head as Lyric's familiar burgundy car pulled into the parking lot and honked at me. "That's my ride," I told my sort-of-uselessly-psychic-sort-of-would-be-merman-boyfriend.

"Stay alert," he said, his smile faltering.

I stood, gathering my coat and tote bag. "You mean watch for supernatural creatures that would draft me into a war against my will? Thanks. Already on alert for that." I cleared my throat. "Thanks for dinner."

Calder's puppy dog eyes suddenly went sorrowful and I had to turn on my heel and leave before my toes had another chance to curl like some cartoon wolf in front of an overly sexy animated babe.

CHAPTER TWENTY-FIVE

EMBER

"I think it's cool that you and Ivy are getting along so well," said Journey as she fiddled with the Sirius radio on her dashboard. "I always thought she was pretty cool—and Lyric and Paisley. Raelynn Kelly is dating Lyric, you know, and though Lyric herself may not be that, like, active around school, Raelynn says she's a sweetheart under all that bravado."

I stared out the passenger window of Journey's car, the leftover chicken fried steak her mom had offered me from her dad and grandma's diner settling uncomfortably in my heavy stomach. I'd only eaten because I'd known I'd been long overdue, and Mrs. Slowe had commented on my appearance, saying I "still" looked sick and I needed some protein before she'd let me set foot out of her house.

I'd nibbled on my steak, trying hard not to imagine the pale anachronistic people digging into that gagged woman's flesh.

"Okay," said Journey—maybe after she'd spoken some more. I couldn't be sure. "You have to tell me what's been bothering you."

I shrugged. If I spoke to her about all of this, she'd laugh at me. Or worse—get hurt.

"Uh-uh," she said, pulling into The Dress Castle's parking lot. "As my mom would tell me, you're not going to get away with clamming up and giving me attitude."

I bristled. She was worried about my *attitude* when I'd been concerned for her safety? I clenched my right fist again and again, willing the heat and the anger coursing through me to escape. "I've been sick."

"You've also been dating the hot new guy at our school behind my back and you haven't said a *word* about it to me." She put the car in park and turned off the ignition.

I went to unlock my door and she clicked it locked again. I stared at her and the irritation on her face melted.

"Em, talk to me. You weren't just sick the past few days, were you?"

Letting out a deep breath, I plunked my elbow on the armrest and stuck my chin on my palm, my gaze focused on the door of the store. "What else do you imagine there could be?"

"The boyfriend, for starters." Journey's nails made a distinct clacking sound against her steering wheel. "The Ember I know would have never in a million years gotten a date, let alone a Romeo-and-Juliet-style-can't-keep-their-hands-off-one-another boyfriend, without volunteering every last detail."

Was I really so different from the Ember of last week? Tomorrow was only one week since Mom had gotten married. It felt like eons ago. "Who says we can't keep our hands off each other?" My mind raced over the day. Dean had been by my side as often as possible, but...

Lunch break at the tree. I'd thought we'd found a place where no one would bother us, but I supposed it was visible enough from half the windows in school. I felt myself growing irritable. Love had hardly been the most prominent feeling on my mind then. "It just... It's not like that."

"It sure seemed *like that*. You barely even talked to me today. You didn't answer my texts while you were out sick. It's just... I'm worried about you."

I finally turned around to look at Journey and she worried her lip. When I didn't have much else to say, she sighed, her gaze flickering out the windshield. "They're here," she said. She turned on her Model-U.N. smile. "Shopping for dresses is fun. Let's have fun."

"Don't you already have a dress for Homecoming?"

"I *do*, but I don't mind looking with you. Weren't you going to wear your spring formal dress?"

"If I went at all," I said under my breath. I'd planned to go before all this. I was just in a testy mood as of late. I clenched my too-warm hand again as I looked out the window to watch Ivy, Lyric, and Paisley enter the store. Paisley and Lyric talked and laughed without a care in the world. Ivy walked behind sullenly, her arms folded, a smile appearing on her lips when Paisley turned around to say something to her—and a frown replacing it the instant her friend looked away.

She seemed half as miserable as I felt at least. But *she*'d been the one to cut off contact with me, to ignore my attempts to extend an olive branch, so to speak.

It could be a trap, Dean had told me. But what choice did I have? I had to live with her half the week from now on.

Journey unlocked the doors and I exited, falling in step behind her and walking toward the store at a sluggish pace.

The girls were still near the entrance when we stepped in, Paisley already holding a hanger with a deep-blue dress and dangling it in front of Ivy as Lyric clung to the tip of the skirt. Ivy looked as happy to be there as a teen on a family vacation with a set of overly enthusiastic parents.

Her eyes locked with mine and she swallowed visibly.

"Hey," said Journey, shuffling up beside Lyric. "How's it going?"

"Ivy didn't tell us you were coming." Lyric let go of the pretty dress and slapped Ivy's shoulder. "But I'm so glad you're here. You'll be more fun to hang out with than this wet blanket."

For a second, I thought she meant me, but she nudged Ivy's shoulder again. Ivy kept looking at me, unmoved.

"Want to try it on?" asked Paisley, unbothered by Ivy's lack of expression.

"Sure," said Ivy, extending her elbow away from her torso and allowing Paisley to drape it over her arm.

I wasn't sure she'd even looked at the thing.

She turned around, grabbed a fiery red dress off the rack without even glancing at it, and shoved it at me as I approached. "Ember, why don't you try this on with me?"

Before I could do more than take the silky material in my fingers—the hanger settling against my clavicle with a clunk—Ivy had grabbed me by the wrist and started dragging me toward the dressing room. She checked us both in with the attendant, the fingers on her free hand tapping the counter in a rapid succession, and instead of going into one booth on her own, she dragged me into the farthest booth with her and shut the door behind us.

We stared at one another a moment and then she finally let my wrist go.

It stung a little, as if she'd wrapped an ice pack around my skin. Blinking, I found the heat burning from my core and outward, radiating to that hand to warm up the cold skin.

The hand glowed red at the edges.

"So you can really do it, too..." It wasn't a question. Ivy tossed the blue dress onto the chair in the room, closed her eyelids and held her hand out. Seconds later, it glowed faintly blue.

So it wasn't quite the same thing.

Something hot pulsated from deep inside me, and I had to look away from Ivy before the fire went out, my hand fading to normal temperature. I stared into the mirror, the red dress held awkwardly in front of me, and I held it upright to get a better look. Not a bad pick for a clear excuse to talk to me alone.

"Really?" said Ivy, and in the mirror I saw her hand's blue glow spark out. "You're hanging out with a pack of vampires and you're still actually worried about what you're going to wear to Homecoming?"

Raising an eyebrow, I tossed the red dress atop hers. Chewing my bottom lip, I gave Ivy a onceover, Dean's words about this being a trap echoing in my mind. "Why wouldn't you talk to me Tuesday evening, but you will today?"

Ivy looked affronted. "I... I didn't know what to do about all this... All this..." Her hands flailed and then she clenched them into fists at her side. "But I do now. Orin has a bookstore and apparently, if you or I are in it or in his cottage, we're safe from... From them."

"Safe from who exactly?"

Ivy growled. "Merpeople! Vampires! What do you think?"

I thought back to Dean's admission. "I don't remember it, but Dean said he'd been in Orin's cottage before."

She cringed. "Calder, too, apparently. They can enter when Orin gives them permission."

"And what's to stop Orin from giving them permission while you think you're safe in there?"

"He wouldn't—he..." She swallowed visibly. "I thought he told you all about being the impartial judge or whatever and offering us sanctuary—"

"He did, it's just... Why should he be the one you trust when you don't trust your own prince?"

She seemed taken aback by that and began to pace the tiny space, though it didn't offer much more room than a closet. "I never said I didn't trust Calder... I just don't accept this." She stopped, her voice growing quieter as a group of girls giggling echoed from the fitting room at large. "Do you? Do you want to fight me... to the death?"

I waited for the laughter to subside, though the girls kept talking, their chatter a muffled mumble as doors slammed closed. "It's not to the death," I said quietly, running a hand up and down my arms and staring pointedly at Ivy's feet. "It doesn't need to be. Just... One needs to make the other surrender?"

Ivy scoffed. "And how do you suppose you or I will do that? Seemed pretty clear to me that fighting was involved."

The idea of trading blows with the girl standing before me was laughable. "You could just surrender," I pointed out. "It's obvious you don't want to be involved."

Ivy's mouth went slack. "And you do? You're capable of being the one to surrender too." When at first I didn't respond, she sighed and placed a hand atop the chair.

I opened my mouth. "Look, I know you agreed to this. I did, too, apparently, but it's not too late—"

"You didn't agree. Probably. Not yet."

"What do you mean?"

"The first 'consummation' that neither of us remembers is just preliminary," she said. "We get time to think about whether or not we want to fight. We have a fortnight. Apparently." She hardly seemed an "expert" with the way her voice shook.

"I..." I blinked rapidly. "No one told me that."

Ivy's face lit up. "Well, then... That takes care of that."

"What do you mean?" I swallowed, not sure I'd like the answer.

"We just don't agree to this nonsense. Put it all behind us."

Silence lingered in the air between us as a new crop of giggling echoed into the dressing room. "Ivy?" called one girl—Paisley, I thought. "How'd it look?"

Ivy sighed and ripped her sweater off her head. I jumped and turned my back to her to give her some privacy.

"Fine," she said, tossing the sweater on the chair beside me and grabbing the light blue dress. "I'll get this one," she added, and I peeked back at her. She wore it over her pants and her black bra straps were clear as day, but even like that, the dress looked good on her. The pants and straps might have even given it more character.

"Em, you in here still too?" Journey.

Ivy tossed the red dress at me and I flinched, but I caught it anyway. "Yeah," I said. "I had to get Ivy to help me with my zipper." I turned around, removed my own sweater and my skirt, too, so I could slip the red dress over my head. I looked over my shoulder to confirm Ivy would actually give me a hand. She shook her head and grabbed hold of the zipper.

"She looks great," said Ivy, raising her voice for the others to hear.

I took a look at the mirror, my deep-blue step-sister standing slightly behind me. We both looked great. Somehow in the mess of more important things, we'd gotten our hands on the best possible dresses.

I jumped. I thought the other girls had entered just then—it *felt* like a group was standing right behind me, someone more than just Ivy—but there was no one there.

"Let me see," said one of Ivy's friends—probably Lyric. She jostled at the door and Ivy went to unlock it, but she must have forgotten to lock it to begin with because it was already opened slightly. All three girls spilled inside, their arms covered in various sweaters, jeans, and dresses.

"Nice," said Journey. She reached for the price tag dangling under my armpit. "Not too bad."

She showed it to me. $80. Not exactly cheap, but Mom had spent over a hundred on a dress for one of my dances before and it had been wasted spending so much time on the sidelines.

"Ouch," said Ivy, taking a look at her own price tag. I peered over to get a look. $50. How much cheaper could she possibly wish her dress to be? She started sliding it over her head, brazenly not caring about the crowd around her and the open fitting room door.

"Oh, but come on," said Paisley, taking it from her and checking the price herself. "What about your new job?"

Ivy flinched and slid her sweater back on. "Payday's not until after Homecoming."

I cleared my throat. "I can put it on Mom's card," I said. "I'm sure she won't mind."

Ivy frowned. "It'd get back to my mom," she said, as if that said everything.

What, that Ivy had allowed her step-mom to buy her something? Was she supposed to buy things like that herself? But what about her dad?

"Oh, just let her," said Lyric, shaking her head and tossing her pile of clothes at the chair. I had to push them aside to get the clothes I'd worn in as Lyric started removing her top. Journey and I exchanged a look. We'd never actually changed in the same room together. I shuffled toward the door, intent on claiming another room for myself, and Journey followed behind.

Before I could leave, Lyric-in-her-bra tossed the blue dress on top of the clothes in my arms. "Super sweet of you, Ember. Ivy needs to learn to accept generosity sometimes. And you look cute," she said.

The way she looked at me, her dark eyes heavily lidded, I couldn't help but blush.

I scrambled to an open room and Journey followed. "Need help with the zipper?" she asked loudly. I nodded.

She shut the door behind us and unzipped me as I put the pile on the empty chair. "What's up with Ivy?" she asked, more quietly.

I tensed. I knew if I deflected, it might just be one deflection too many. "She's irritated about Dean and me."

"So 'Dean and you' is indeed a thing."

I pursed my lips and caught her eye in the fitting room mirror. "On a trial basis," I admitted at last.

"Okay…" said Journey. "Is that so I can't say you're moving too fast?"

"You're going to Homecoming with Devam," I said. "You hardly ever spoke to him before that night." Was it really just earlier this week?

"Yeah, but I knew him. I *had* spoken to him. I've known him for years and I crushed on him for months. And, I might add, I'm also not draping myself all over him. I haven't even had time to see him since then outside of a head nod at school." She looked crestfallen.

Holding tightly to the front of my dress so it wouldn't fall, I felt all thoughts about crazy, unbelievable things fly straight out of my brain for once. "I'm sorry," I said. "I wanted to hear more about how he asked you."

She shrugged. "I guess there isn't much more to tell? We've been texting. Nothing too suggestive…"

"Maybe he crushed on you just as long as you crushed on him." I smiled, enjoying teasing her, and her eyes fell to the floor, as they often did when she was embarrassed. "I guess at least one good thing came out of our reckless woods adventure."

Journey looked back up at me and cocked her head. "You and Dean isn't a 'good thing'?"

I stiffened. "It's… It's something different anyway."

Journey tossed her own pile of clothes to try on onto the chair and grabbed me by both shoulders. "My little Ember is growing up."

"Oh, come on," I said, but I wasn't angry. This was more like I'd pictured life with my first boyfriend going—gossiping with my best friend about our boys, shopping for dresses together, not keeping any secrets...

But a shot of heat soared through me as I thought of that woman and the fangs in her flesh and the danger Journey would be in if I let even the smallest hint slip.

Moving out of Journey's grasp, I turned around and slid out of the dress. "So my mom wants Ivy and her friends to hang with us before Homecoming."

"I know," said Journey. "Your mom told my mom—I was trying to talk to you about it." It grew quiet and I heard Lyric snort with laughter from several booths over. "That could be fun, right? They're all pretty awesome girls. And Raelynn is a friend. I'd have invited her myself if I didn't think she was already doing something. And if it weren't, like, a Goodwin-Slowe duo tradition."

Tossing the dress atop the back of the chair, I grabbed my clothes out from under the pile and slipped my skirt on first. Homecoming was still a week away. A lot could happen before then. But either way, it'd probably be best to keep Ivy close, keep an eye on her activities. "You cool with it then?"

"If they are," said Journey. She retrieved her pile of clothes as I slipped my sweater on overhead. "I'm surprised you're cool with it."

"Why?" I asked, dragging my hair out of the collar and checking out its arrangement in the mirror.

"Ember and big gatherings never mixed. Before this week anyway."

"Well, as you said, little Ember has grown up." I smoothed out the bumps in the fabric of my sweater as I readjusted it.

The lights overhead flickered.

"Uh-oh," said Journey, instinctively looking overhead. "Power outage? With clear skies?"

Several other women in the fitting room shrieked and started laughing as the lights flickered again, this time plunging the store into darkness.

The fitting room door flung open and a hand enveloped in a slight blue light reached out to grab my wrist.

"Come on," whispered Ivy. "Something's wrong."

Now she was reading bigger problems into the most minor of inconveniences. Not that I could entirely blame her.

Journey looked down, and I grabbed Ivy's arm, dragging her hand behind me so Journey wouldn't notice the faded light. Ivy stumbled and seemed upset but then noticed what I was doing.

"Do you think you can still buy things with the power out?" Journey asked, with all the concern of a young woman who wouldn't even begin to imagine the kinds of things Ivy and I had seen this past week.

Ivy let go and I saw her light had faded, so I scooped the dresses into my arms. "Only one way to find out," I said, brushing past Ivy and heading out the dressing room to the front counter.

"Wait," said Ivy, but she was waylaid by Lyric, who shouted "Boo!" and glomped on to her arm as we reached the end of the fitting room. Ivy screamed and Paisley giggled.

Though the evening light had faded, the dark in the store didn't scare me. A woman's voice called out from near the front door. "Please don't panic," she said. "There's a power outage on our block. If you would make your way to an employee with a flashlight or to the front counter, we can still accept cash payment or take down your card information for a later charge or accept items on layaway. We apologize for the inconvenience."

A flashlight beam flickered in front of me and I jolted, the light harsh to my eyes. At the feeling, my brain kicked in with some important information. If Ivy was right and this wasn't just an accident, darkness could mean only one thing.

Dean.

So I'd be fine, but Ivy...

I turned around. But she wasn't the champion yet, not more

than the preliminary one. I'd told him to leave us be, that there was no way this was a trap...

A palm clamped down over my mouth from behind me, another hand grabbing me around the waist. "Don't scream," said the voice, husky and hot beside my ear.

I didn't move, considering the possibilities and my chances for escape. Pausing time was an option, if I could get my thoughts to focus. Not that I'd been practicing. Besides, my heart was hammering, my palms sweaty.

"I just want to talk," he said. The hand on my mouth shifted slightly, almost weakening, but it didn't move.

I could feel the warmth in that hand, fighting to break through a chill of ice. A pulse throbbing.

That was when my incisors grew and I pierced that flesh in front of me, sucking in the delectably tangy taste of his blood.

CHAPTER TWENTY-SIX

IVY

Was she seriously concerned about buying these dresses right now?

Maybe it was the chill that coursed up my arm from the tips of my fingers or the fact that I seemed more aware of just how crazy this was, but the moment the lights went out in the store, my thoughts went immediately to vampires. Mr. Shades and his ilk didn't like light.

But... What did Ember have to fear from vampires?

Then again, what did *I* have to fear rightly? I'd never agreed to any of this.

"Do you think they'll notice if I just walk out with this blouse under my shirt?" Lyric said from somewhere behind me.

Paisley snorted. "The power goes out and the first thing you think is, 'Hmm. What a great chance to shoplift'?"

"Shut it. I wasn't serious," she said. Something moved in the darkness to our right. "I took it off. Just going to chuck it here," Lyric added.

We were somewhere near the front of the fitting room, where there'd once been an attendant, and I jolted when a group of people slipped past us, whispering and chortling all the while.

Somebody's phone rang. Only once my heart stopped hammering did I recognize the song Lyric used for Raelynn's calls.

"Why is she calling you instead of texting?" wondered Paisley, taking her own phone out of her pocket and using it as a flashlight. I squinted at the intensity of the glare. "Bae asked if the lights are out by me, too." Her fingers flew over the screen. Her face looked haunted in the darkness, illuminated only by the glow.

"Yes, it's out by us, too." Lyric looked somewhat irritated at the edges of the halo of light coming from Paisley's phone. "We're at Dress Castle. Shopping with Ivy and her new sister for dresses. Yes, I told you that—you know I already have one, and I thought you already did—okay, maybe next time—"

So it was a large-scale outage? That made the tension in my neck and shoulders ease slightly. Maybe I'd been so wrapped up in all this paranormal nonsense that I'd been missing the forest for the trees. Life had been normal before I'd known about all of this and there would still be normal, perfectly rational things going on.

"Have you guys seen Ember?"

Journey appearing from behind me, a pile of clothes tucked against her chest, made me let out a yelp.

"Sorry," she said, putting a gentle hand on my shoulder. "Didn't mean to scare you."

Paisley looked up at me in her ghostly glow like I had just broken into a tap dance. So sue me. I was jumpy.

"That was Ivy," said Lyric into her phone. "She just got spooked." She ran a palm over her forehead and up through her hair. "Babe, I *know* you're kind of afraid of the dark, but you're not five—no, no one else is in earshot, so they couldn't have heard—ugh." She held up one finger to us and shook her head, peeling off from the group and making her way to the front door of the store. Now that my eyes had adjusted somewhat, I could tell there were shadowy forms gathered near there and light from the moon made it so it wasn't pitch black in the few feet around the door.

"I'll make sure she doesn't get so caught up in her argument that she leaves without us," said Paisley, her fingers still flying over her screen.

"Oh, you can ride with Ember and me if need be—" started

Journey, but Paisley was already gone, her focus on her glowing screen as she expertly weaved her way around obstacles. I followed her glowing form to the door until she exited and turned the corner.

I scanned the room as someone appeared behind the counter, another glowing phone screen in hand. A number of customers had decided to rely on their phones' lights to get around the place.

Journey pulled her own out and frowned, her expression clear in the brightness of her screen. "My mom says I should stay put, that traffic lights are out all over town and there could be more accidents. Something about an explosion at a power substation..." Her fingers flew over the screen.

That put the tension right back where it had eased from. How often did a substation *explode*? This was no act of nature or a car spinning out.

"An accident, not terrorism, authorities think," said Journey, and again I was reminded of the real dangers in real life—away from the fantastical creatures that lurked in the shadows. "And no injuries, but authorities are putting out the fire before they switch to auxiliary power and can begin the repairs."

"Let's tell the others," I said, knowing full well both Lyric and Paisley would be more concerned with their significant others than the world at large. And then there was Ember...

My hand grew cold again and I shoved it into my pocket before Journey could see it glow blue. There'd be no hiding that in the darkness. My phone buzzed in my bag and I figured it was Mom or Dad or both of them, checking up on me in the wake of the outage, but my raging pulse made me less concerned with assuaging their fears than I ought to have been.

"Everyone, if you could please make your way to the front," said the clerk beside me. "We just heard word from the manager and we're closing until this power situation is sorted. If you'd like to make a purchase, we're taking cash and card numbers at the front—"

I didn't hear the rest as I made my way forward in mostly darkness, pushing aside fuzzy sweater sleeves and jangling racks of jeans whenever I strayed too far from the narrow paths on the sales floor. Where was Calder when I needed him? True, I'd told him to stay away, but... All I could think about was a town full of darkness and vampires growing bolder in the night—

"Miss Shepherd, hello."

I ground to a halt, jumping when Journey bumped into my back.

At the edge of the glow of her phone screen, Dean Horne shirked, taking a careful step back.

A fedora hat not unlike the one that had been hanging on my step-mom's coat rack adorned his head, but he wasn't wearing his sunglasses for once. His eyes practically glowed in the darkness, a bright blue that reminded me of the glow of my hand.

"Dean," said Journey, stepping around me and completely oblivious, "did Ember call you?"

"Yes," said Dean, and his tight smile broke through the darkness as my vision adjusted to the edge beyond Journey's phone light. She pointed the phone down and he relaxed visibly, taking a step closer. "I'm worried about her—" he started.

But I pulled my hand out of my pocket, about to go for my own phone to shine the screen right in his face, but I didn't have to—my hand was already faintly glowing.

Dean took a step back, both palms extended. "Miss Shepherd, you don't understand."

Journey shook her head, as if unsure she was actually seeing what she was seeing. "Ivy, what's wrong with your—"

Then the fire alarm rung out. At first I actually thought it was a school bell.

"Please exit the building!" said a woman loudly. "Forget the purchases and make an orderly line to the front."

Dean whipped his head around and I was about to karate chop him with my blue hand, as if I'd had any experience in doing such a thing, but my eyes darted toward the glowing red light to the side of the front door that had drawn his attention—a fire. And in its glow, Ember.

And Calder.

He was gripping her left arm tightly, and she was clearly trying to get away from him.

My heart sank.

I thought he... I thought he understood. I didn't want this. But what I wanted didn't matter. He didn't care what I wanted. He didn't respect me. He was *not* going to be my mate or whatever he and his family thought.

I shook my head. This wasn't about me. Calder had his reasons —the survival of his family—to consider.

And one of the people standing in the way of that was right in front of me.

"Oh my god, Em is right by the fire." Journey clutched my arm then. I'd almost forgotten she was still there.

Before I could speak, something strange happened.

I blinked and Dean was gone—no, he was over by Ember and Calder, standing between them, his hands out to either side of him.

How had he moved so quickly?

"When did he get there...?" Journey sounded as confused as I felt. "I am *not* seeing well in the dark." Good. She was going to dismiss all this weirdness as a trick of the light maybe.

But I had more context. Whatever the reason, it couldn't have been more unbelievable than my legs turning into a tail.

Ember's hand was on fire and my own hand grew icy as if calling to it.

Her *hand* was on fire, the two stupid dresses still draped over her other arm.

"Please exit—" began the employee nearest the door, but before she could finish, a loud tittering sound rang out, followed by clicks just as the sprinkler system started raining down overhead.

Journey shrieked and squeezed her eyes together tightly, jumping in place and tossing the pile of clothes she'd been carrying as if it'd been what was on fire, clutching her phone to her chest to shelter it from the water.

Other patrons screeched and screamed and even the employee who'd been shouting headed for the door, a small stampede knocking racks of clothes and tables filled with odds and ends asunder.

But what no one else seemed to notice was that the source of the fire—Ember's freaking *hand*—was never doused by the drops showering down from overhead. She may have escaped becoming wet entirely.

Because one second she and Dean were there and the next, they were gone, taking the fire with them.

I couldn't find them anywhere.

"We have to go," said Journey, already pushing her way forward. Her arm was strewn futilely over her head, like that would protect her hair from the shower.

My gaze darted back to where Ember and Dean had been—and Calder. But Calder was still there until he wasn't. Only he hadn't vanished. I saw *him* slip to the floor.

My own knees went wobbly. *Oh, no. Not now.*

I jogged behind Journey.

"Where's Ember?" she asked as she strained to open one eye.

"She got out," I said, sure that was true. "With Dean."

"Good," said Journey. "Let's go."

But I veered slightly to the side, away from the door, to where Calder had sunk somewhere between racks of bras and negligee.

The sprinkler water poured over me, like a rain shower that spurt out in bizarre, uniform patterns. It was cold and it soaked through to my bones, but I didn't shiver. My hand grew brighter and brighter and I used it to light the way.

"I'm fine," grunted a voice from below me.

I held my hand aloft over the source of the sound. Calder was there, his jeans torn and stuck partway over his deep blue merman tail, his letterman jacket soaked and his blond hair limp with wetness. He held splayed fingers up to block his eyes, as if he found my glowing hand too bright to look at. "Turn that down, would you?"

I shook my head. I didn't know how and I didn't exactly care just then.

He rolled over onto his elbows, and it looked like the effort strained him. I glanced again at that tail and my mind exploded with images—*Calder, merman, water*—and I felt a tingling run down from my waist to my toes.

"No, be careful!" said Calder, rolling back over. He squinted and with a shimmer, his tail turned into a pair of well-toned legs, his thigh twisted just so to hide his nether regions from view.

It was like a splash of cold water to the face—though that was exactly what had been happening for minutes and it didn't seem to have had much of an effect on me. The tingling stopped and I looked down at my legs, realizing I may have been moments away from busting out of my jeans and growing a tail as well.

"I thought you could control it," I said, diverting my eyes as he rolled once more and brought himself to a standing position.

"I wasn't expecting to get soaked in the middle of the ladies' undergarments department, okay?" He ran fingers through his hair to get those too-long soaked bangs out of his eyes, stumbling as he did.

A fire roared through me then, at odds with the coldness that had coursed through my body. I stared pointedly at his pants, then gestured over my shoulder. "Grab some baggy sweats or something —quick."

"There are no men's clothes here."

"Would you rather the firemen find you standing here half-naked? Let's *go*."

Grunting, he slapped his bare feet on the soaked carpet and went off behind me. That reminded me to bend down to grab his sneakers, which seemed to be intact.

When he returned half a moment later, he was wearing slightly-too-small pajama pants that rose up above his ankles, hugged his package rather tightly, and, I noticed as he grabbed a shoe from my grip and shifted to slap it on his feet, read *"Frisky"* across his butt.

"Frisky?" I asked, a vision of a similar conversation with Orin in the woods playing out with embarrassing compunction in my head. "Was 'juicy' not in your color or something?"

Calder practically sneered as he snatched the other sneaker, though he seemed more frustrated at the situation than he was at me. "I'm sure you have better questions for me than that."

Oh, he was right. He was *so* right.

CHAPTER TWENTY-SEVEN

EMBER

I spun out of Dean's grip as we darted down the alley beside The Dress Castle. The faint conversation and pounding footfalls of other patrons as they rushed to exit the nearby strip mall threatened to drown out anything I might have had to say.

The fire alarm rang out, the flashing lights relying on some kind of generator. In the distance, sirens sounded, but there was no need. The fire was gone.

The fire had been me.

I stared down at my hand, only faintly red now. It had been on fire when I'd confronted Calder about... whatever it was he'd been about to do to me.

The dresses over my arm slipped to the ground and Dean darted forward to grab them before they could get dirty.

"I didn't pay for those yet," I said, like that was what mattered just then.

Dean pulled out his wallet, fished out two hundred-dollar bills, then, with a strange pressurizing feeling, he did it again—pausing time, leaving only us cognizant enough to know what he'd done. The world went eerily silent at that moment, as if to confirm what I could only suspect with no others in sight. He dashed around the corner, and I followed suit, but I froze when I saw Lyric and Paisley leaning against a car, one with her phone to her ear, the

218

other with her phone in both hands, her focus on the screen. In the time I stared at their statue-like forms, Dean appeared at my side, a Dress Castle bag in hand. He wrapped an arm around my waist and guided me back to the alley.

The pressurizing feeling lifted and I took a deep breath. All the sounds and activities burst to life once more. He lifted the bag. "I left the money on the counter."

I massaged my temples, turning my back to him, jumping slightly at the pure heat that still radiated from my fingertips. "I don't *care* about the dresses," I said. I didn't think tossing money—albeit more than the dresses cost—at a counter and calling it a day counted as properly purchasing them, either. But that was the least of my problems.

"Well, I think you and Ivy looked ravishing in them," he said. "So I wanted to make sure you took them home."

A chill ran down my spine—so at odds with the heat trying to radiate out from my hand. I spun on my heel. "How would you know what we looked like?"

Dean visibly bristled. It was then that I realized his blue irises were shining at me, his glasses nowhere in sight. My own eyes had become adjusted to the darkness.

"I was merely keeping an eye on you," he said. "Remember, I warned you it could be a trap."

And it was. Or Calder was working on his own. I really felt like that had to be the more reasonable explanation. Ivy had seemed so... sincere. And really. Why would she be any more invested in this insanity than I was? It'd been less than a week since it had all started.

A week ago tomorrow, Mom and Easton had tied the knot at the courthouse. A week ago, I'd thought my biggest concern was adjusting to my new sisters for half the week.

Something else struck me then. "But we only tried them on in the *fitting room*."

Dean jammed his free hand into his pocket. "I checked in on you from time to time."

"You paused time... To check on me in the *fitting room*?"

"I made sure you were decent before I did more than peek, I promise." He shifted and started fiddling with that infernal coin again and I put my hand over his to stop him.

His skin was like ice, though it warmed at my touch. He grinned.

I dropped my grip, angry at myself for feeling light as a feather at the physical contact between us, at his smile. "How am I going to know you're not always creepily watching me?" My stomach roiled at how I'd once found it so romantic when fictional vampires snuck into bedrooms to watch their human beloveds in their sleep. I *wanted* to love Dean like that, I *might* have been starting to love Dean like that, but this was all so fast.

"I promise I don't. This was just for your safety."

A loud exhale escaped my lips. "And what about this nonsense about a trial period?" I retorted. "Did you not tell me about *that* for 'my safety'?"

"You know?" he asked. He bounced in place, letting a soft curse escape his lips. "Ember, I'd have told you as soon as I thought you'd be... Ready. To accept it. To choose to be my champion for however long this takes."

"You mean because I didn't *choose* to be before, like you said I did." My voice went quiet. "Did I even say I'd be your girlfriend? Are you lying to me?"

"No, doll, *no*... You and me, we're meant to be." I could feel him step closer to me as the sirens grew louder and fire trucks and police cars rolled up to the strip mall before cutting their sirens out, their flashing lights still blinding in the darkness of the city.

Dean staggered behind me, covering his eyes with his arm. His coin went rolling down the alleyway with a clang. Despite being angry with him, I stepped forward to steer him farther down the alley, out of the emergency lights' reach. The shouted voices were distant now. In the dark shadow, Dean lowered his arm, his blue irises focused in on me, his fingertips at my cheek like ice that melted into a warm bath. "I'd never forgive myself if anything happened to you," he said, his voice quiet.

I closed my eyes and just let my mind get carried away by his soft touch. I felt the distance close between us, moved my chin upward instinctively, ready to receive his lips on mine—

"Ember!"

Journey's familiar voice snapped me back to reality. When my eyes shot open, I found Dean's face so close, his lips slightly parted, the tips of sharp incisors protruding.

I pushed on his chest, my stomach sickened. "Were you going to bite me?" I hissed.

Dean stepped back, as if struck. "Never. Not you. Not even if you asked me to." His foot shuffling backward, his heel clicked up against his coin, and he bent down to retrieve it, pocketing it.

I chewed my lip, wondering if I'd mistaken his intentions.

Something else bounced off my brain, though. *Why would I ever ask him to bite me?*

"Oh, thank goodness," said Journey, running up beside me. She stared at Dean, who shrunk back slightly, the glow of Journey's phone screen clearly an irritant to him. "I see you found her," she said. "I... lost track of you in there."

He tipped his hat to her. "Glad you made it out safely as well."

"Just in time," said Journey, looking over her shoulder. "The sprinklers went off."

I winced, then hoped Journey didn't see it. I dug into my purse for my own phone. I had a few missed messages. "How did Mom find out...?" I wondered.

"Power's out all over town," said Journey, turning her attention back to her own phone. Her fingers moved brusquely over the screen. "I texted my mom to text your mom we're both fine," she said, then tucked the phone in her pocket and grabbed me by the hand. "But we should get out of here in case the fire spreads."

Dean and I exchanged a glance. The fire would go with me. I hadn't had a chance to burn anything—or anyone—with it. It had just... happened.

"Do you need a ride, Dean?" asked Journey.

"You're a doll, thank you," he answered.

Journey lifted her eyebrows but nodded and we made our way back to the parking lot. Dean reached into his inner coat pocket and pulled out his sunglasses. Neither Journey nor I made a comment about it, despite the near darkness as far as one could see. There were still the flashing siren lights and I supposed we'd both gotten used to Dean's eccentricities by now.

Naturally, Journey's car was halfway across the lot, meaning there was no avoiding Lyric and Paisley where they stood against another car. Not unless I was ready to practice time pausing again—not that I'd do that with Journey here. Thinking back to the dresses and the two hundred bucks, I wondered how often Dean used it for trivial matters.

Paisley waved us down and came jogging over. Lyric nodded but turned, her attention focused on her phone conversation. "Is Ivy with you?"

Journey stooped as she paced a little, her shoulders bending forward. "She *was*, but we got—oh my god." I followed her line of sight. Ivy limped out of the door to The Dress Castle, Calder beside her. Both were soaked through.

"Oh, crap," said Paisley. "What happened?"

"There was a fire," Journey answered. "Apparently."

So she hadn't seen the fire emanating from my hand. That made sense, I supposed. She certainly would have made a comment about it earlier.

"And they got caught up in the sprinklers?" Paisley stared as a firefighter went up to Ivy and Calder, blankets in hand. "Holy cow, this day..." She looked from the shivering couple to Dean and back. "And what are you two doing here anyway? This is a *girls'* night."

Dean shrugged, stuffing his free hand into his pocket. "In the neighborhood," he answered.

"Are Ivy and Calder dating?" asked Journey. Oh, to be as naïve once more.

"I... don't know," said Paisley, the tone of her voice rising a pitch, as if she were considering the possibility. Calder stepped closer to Ivy and grabbed her by both of her upper arms, though Ivy pointedly looked away.

She'd been the bait. She had to have been. I didn't know her that well, but I refused to believe she'd been lying. Calder had just taken advantage of her calling me and—

What was it he'd wanted to do exactly? He'd claimed he wanted to talk, but the way he'd grabbed me had startled me and I'd gone on the defensive before he could talk much.

"Whoa, Ember..." Calder dropped me and stepped back, holding his hands out. He shook his right hand then, and even in the darkness, I knew it was dripping blood. "I meant it. I just wanted to talk."

"Then why did you just grab me as if you were about to kidnap me?" My hand burned and my throat ached then. The darkness couldn't conceal the warmth of his blood. I licked my lips, surprised to find my tongue caught on the tip of one of my teeth.

Calder lowered his arms, his gaze darting to the glow of my appendage. "Are you a... Have you turned into one of them?"

I launched forward, ready to pounce, ready to grab his throat between my teeth and dig into the sweet, juicy flow of the iron between his veins.

Calder shoved me off. "Have you lost your mind?! Are you one of them already? You still have time to drop out of this, you know, it hasn't been a fortnight—"

I froze, leaning backward, away from his supple throat, away from his skin. People kept murmuring around us, but my heart thundered so loudly, I couldn't make out what they said.

"You know about the fortnight?" I asked. "The trial period?"

"Of course I do," he said, shaking his hand again. "Though we'd hardly call it a 'trial period.'"

"I didn't know," I said. "Ivy had to tell me." My voice cracked.

"I don't believe in lying to my champion," said Calder, suddenly sheepish. "Not... Not for long anyway." He froze, his gaze drifting somewhere over my shoulder. "He's here," he said quietly.

I didn't know who he meant, but I recognized the primal anger that rushed through my body as he went to grab me again.

My hand burst to life, bright and powerful—on fire. Calder took a step back.

And before I could even so much as think of what to do next, I'd been out in the alleyway, Dean having used his magic trick to whisk me out of danger.

Calder wanted me not to commit to the vampires. But that was exactly what the merman prince set on eradicating a whole group of people *would* want. He didn't care about me. He only cared about himself—and Ivy.

"Lyric's not going to like Ivy getting her seat all wet," mumbled Paisley, strangely concerned with the least important of things.

Dean hovered over my shoulder, whispering in my ear. "Water gives them power."

I put a hand on Journey's wrist. "We should go."

Journey's neck bent forward slightly. "Don't you want to make sure Ivy's okay first? You can't exactly show up home without her and mention you left her soaked at the strip mall, can you?"

"She's at her mom's tonight," I said. Considering everything else going on between us at the moment, I doubted Ivy would be in the mood to tattle.

Lyric shouted from over by her car. "Pais, come on! Get Ivy and let's go. Rae's in a mood..." She hadn't noticed her water-soaked friend, then. She merely opened the driver's side door and got in.

"See you at school," said Paisley, nodding toward us.

I nodded back. A week ago she never would have spoken to me. Journey, maybe, but not me. A week ago I might have cared.

"All right..." said Journey, though she didn't sound sure at all as Paisley trotted over toward Ivy and Calder. "Mom actually wanted us to stay put." She shivered. "But I just want to go home..."

Ivy turned and across the distance, caught my eye. I whipped my head around and strode over toward Journey's car. "Let's get home," I said. "Our moms are probably still freaking out."

True enough. Dean got to the car first and held the door open for me, rushing around to the other side of the car to get the driver's side for Journey.

Journey gave him a onceover. "Manners even in the craziest of times," she said. She winked at me across the top of the car. "He's a keeper."

If she only knew.

CHAPTER TWENTY-EIGHT

IVY

It'd been almost a week since Ember had even looked at me, let alone discussed the impending deadline on the war between fangs and fins that we really were no part of but that had threatened to put our lives at stake regardless.

Even when at Dad's, Ember had always been too busy to talk—off to Journey's, she said. Or to some job she'd apparently gotten last week.

Probably off to her blood-sucking boyfriend's.

At school, she walked the hallways with her nose in the air, Dean's arm often around her waist, his head the only one that dipped slightly in my direction. His sunglasses obnoxiously obscured his eyes.

Calder theorized the vampires had had something to do with the city-wide outage last weekend, but I didn't know what. It wasn't like they'd used the opportunity to attack anyone. Every fishy scale was accounted for and Dean had barely made a move at The Dress Castle.

Calder had been the one to confront the other champion, his actions more threatening than Dean's had been.

Besides, the power had been patched by morning. It had taken another few days to fully replace the damaged transformer, but everything was right as rain in our sleepy suburb once more.

Everything but the impending decision and the battle that awaited me against a stubborn step-sister.

"Why do *you* think Calder 'failed' to mention originally I had a fortnight to fully commit to this thing?" I asked Orin from the counter of The Hollow Tree. A mom and her kid had left an hour earlier, the kid cradling a vintage Dr. Seuss under his arm, but the place had been dead ever since.

"Political strategy, I imagine." Orin didn't look up from his book. Feilia was snuggled on his lap.

"What does that even mean?" I sighed and hunkered my elbows down on the counter, leaning my chin on my palms. "And why didn't *you* tell me?"

Orin turned a page, licking his pointer finger beforehand. "I told you, the merfolk have the right to explain to their champion as they please."

"Yet you could tell the vampire champion anything?"

"Not *anything*, but... They're mere children, these vampires. They sometimes lack... social graces." He shut his tome and put it on a table cluttered with books beside him, picking up one volume and then the next as he examined their spines. "Besides, I wasn't the one to tell Ember that little wrinkle, either. Personally, I find it better for the champions to wrap their heads around what's to come before they make a decision as to whether or not they want to commit to it."

I snorted and stood up, crossing my arms. "Let them think they have no choice in the matter and just as they're about to get used to it, just as they're ready to *accept* it, you ask if they're willing to fight? Cheap move."

"Politics in action," said Orin, finally settling on another book and flipping it open to a page two-thirds through. He seemed to enjoy that. Reading a book in chunks and then picking up another volume, never fully finishing what he'd started. Feilia opened one eye warily at the sound of pages rapidly turning.

"Why did you kick me out of the store last week?" I asked. I'd had a week to get some answers, but personally, I'd hoped he'd have volunteered them by now.

"Business to attend to," he said, adjusting his glasses.

"Business like sabotaging a substation?" I ventured. Calder may have had a more vampiric theory as to who had been responsible, but I thought I'd say what I could to get the man's attention.

"Oy." Orin snapped shut his latest book and placed it on the table beside him. The Maine Coon jumped off his lap and stretched, first her front legs and then her back. "You think I'm that dodgy?"

I casually ventured around the corner of the counter and leaned against the side of it, closer to Orin's little reading station. Feilia meandered off to a sun beam farther down the aisle. "I don't know you that well." I gestured around me. "You say I'm safe among your little kingdom of books and then you up and kick me out of it one day last week. Then some serious stuff went down. Coincidence?"

Orin ripped his glasses off his face. "I told you I was neutral."

Shrugging, I ran a finger over a stack of pamphlets touting the work of a local wild animal rescue. It was faded from the sunlight, its images grainy and more at home in an earlier decade. "So you say, but I just learned about this ridiculous war a week and a half ago. I'm just taking a lot of this bullcrap on faith. If it wasn't you, it was the bloodsuckers. Had to be."

"Bullcrap," said Orin, tucking his glasses into his shirt pocket. He stared pointedly at me. "A thousands-year war is bullcrap to you." He shook his head. "Kids."

"You sound like an old man."

It was his turn to shrug. Then he sighed. "Okay, the issue of my involvement aside, why so certain the vampires had anything to do with the outage? Why can't it just have been an unrelated accident?"

"While you were unaccounted for?" I pointed out, letting a bit of playfulness sneak into my tone. "I don't know. Because they can see better without overhead lights?" My chest grew tight at my next thought. "That's what Calder thought anyway."

Orin shifted in his seat to dig his phone out of his back pocket.

"First of all, I was at my cottage, not noticing the town was without lights because my cabin doesn't use any."

"Sure. Away from all the action. As any responsible *observer* of a millennia-old conflict should be."

Orin ignored that, though he paused long enough to stare pointedly at me. He glanced at his phone screen, then put it beside him atop the books on the table. Crossing one leg over the other, he rested his ankle on his thigh and clasped his hands together. "What, pray tell, did the vampires accomplish?" He gestured toward me. "From what you tell me, it was Calder who tried to attack the champion of blood first."

"He says he didn't *attack* her," I mumbled, though my irritation with the boy still made me wonder. It was easy enough to avoid him at school—since vampires had woven their way into the administration, Calder had transferred to Central, the school in my mom's house's district—but I knew that as long as I kept coming here, he'd be there staking me out at the diner down the road. With his eating habits, I was surprised his tail hadn't grown three sizes at this rate.

"Regardless, he got chastened quickly, the vampire prince swooped in to take his champion away and—what? Then what happened?"

"I got soaked," I said, as if that would help my case.

"Any big events happen around town? Any other fires? People going missing?"

"Not that I know of," I admitted. I shook my head. "But you have to admit it was too much of a coincidence. The biggest power outage in city history? Not even during a storm or a hot day?"

"A mechanical malfunction," said Orin, his voice clipped.

"Which was initially reported as an accident at a substation," I pointed out.

"Mere chaos and rumors during a stressful time," he said.

True. The media had explained it had all just been a mechanical mishap after all, old equipment in need of replacement.

Calder hadn't bought it. Not that night, nor in the dozen or so texts he'd sent me since. Sighing, I started strolling down the aisles again, pushing in an errant book spine here and there to even out the shelves.

"Have you been to the Pooles' home yet?" Orin asked from across the room.

"Nope," I said. "Not unless you count the underwater cove." I shuddered at the memory of the experience, which had practically faded to a dream at this point. My brain was good at trying to compartmentalize all this bullcrap in a vain effort to make sense.

"No, the human one," he said. "At the edge of the woods."

"Nope," I reiterated. I found myself at the window overlooking the diner and I pouted in its general direction, sending angry vibes Calder's way.

He'd tried to gain my trust by telling me he understood my desire not to be involved, he understood my desire to be left alone, to try to talk Ember out of this, and what had I discovered? He'd tried to handle Ember on his own. And he and his mom had "omitted" the detail about me still having a chance to get out of this arrangement.

I hoped he was good and bored in that diner every day. And maybe a touch desperate—desperate enough to suffer for it all, but not enough to do something stupid. Again.

"The Pooles are... overly paranoid, to say the least."

That caught my attention. I turned around and made my way around a shelf to peer more closely at Orin. He leaned an elbow on the chair's armrest, a few fingers cradling his chin as his foot bounced across his thigh.

"First you tell me vampires are out to eradicate the merfolk and then you tell me they're paranoid?" I shook my head. "Even I would grant you that if I were in this for the long haul—which I'm not"—the slight smile Orin sent me at that almost made my blood boil—"I'd be a touch *paranoid* too."

Orin's foot stopped bouncing and he shrugged. "Their home is a fortress," he said. "And they rely on solar panels for power—not just because they care more about the Earth than you monkey creatures seem to"—I bristled at the condescending way he said that—"but because they've lived in fear of just such an event. A power outage where vampires roam the town, ruling supreme. If the panels get broken, they have backup gas-powered generators. If those go, they have UV lamps. Of course, they can always dive into the water, too." He stretched both arms over his head, leaning first one way and then the other. "So it's no surprise to me that the first thing they think of when there's a power outage is vampires at work."

It seemed to me if they were *that* paranoid, they'd carry those UV lamps with them wherever they went. That actually seemed like an easy enough way to win this mess, though I supposed if it really came down to Ember and me, that wasn't going to be much help.

Not unless Calder was right and she could turn into one of them.

I shook my head. She didn't wear sunglasses. She was no more pale and pasty than usual, and I would have noticed if she'd asked her mom for blood protein shakes, but she'd eaten like normally too. She just walked out of a room as soon as I walked into it.

Clapping his hands together, Orin put his foot back on the ground and leaned forward. "So you going to the dance tomorrow?"

I laughed. After all that, I'd almost forgotten about Homecoming. Paisley and Lyric never shut up about it, but I'd managed to tune it all out. Besides, the main focus of their conversation had been the fact that Raelynn had practically been traumatized by the outage—so much so, she and Lyric had fought over her freak out and had been *this* close to calling it quits before the big day.

Then there was the discussion between Mom and Dad about me coming over to Dad's on Saturday. They hadn't even asked if I'd wanted to, but all of a sudden, Mom was telling me she was taking Autumn to Chuck E. Cheese's for the day and dropping me off at Paisley's beforehand—but she'd drop by Dad's later to get pics of me in my dress. The dress I'd lied to her and told her I'd gotten for it. I'd figured I'd dig an old one out of the half a dozen boxes that I hadn't finished unpacking in my room at Dad's. Would anyone really notice or care if I showed up in the same old thing?

"Everyone seems to think I am," I said, answering Orin's question at last. "I'd just as soon come here."

"Closed tomorrow," he said curtly. "You've had me here quite often, I'll have you know. It was more on a whim before."

"So then I'll come to your cottage and stay in neutral territory there," I said, jutting my chin out toward him. "I'll be at my dad's anyway. I'll do this beforehand prep with everyone and then tell Paisley and Lyric to cover for me and just escape to the woods."

The corners of Orin's lips curled upward. "As much as I'd appreciate your company, I won't be home, either, and until you're the proper champion, you're not going to be able to find it on your own."

"Well, I'm not *going* to be a proper champion ever anyway." I sighed, pointedly ignoring the twinkle in Orin's eye.

"Why not just go, yeah?"

"Because it was a dull enough event before I got stuck in this crazy nightmare," I said.

"Calder would escort you, you know."

"Oh, *that's* such a relief. The only reason I've been hesitating was because *I didn't have a date*. Not because of blood suckers and fin flappers roaming the halls or anything."

Orin snorted.

But then what he'd said puzzled me. "*Would* Calder go? He seems terrified of the school ever since he discovered vampires transferred in."

"He would," said Orin. "And I'm going as well."

"You," I said. "An ancient old faery. Are going to a high school dance."

He pretended to fix the knot on an imaginary tie. "I happen to cut a fine figure in a suit."

I'd imagine so. I shook my head. Thoughts of a guy's hotness had no place in my mind just then. "*Why*, pray tell, are you going?"

"To observe," he answered succinctly. "If I'm to do my job, that's where I'll need to be."

I frowned. If I didn't go... Would the vampires win without

opposition? Would that take care of all of this? As much as he annoyed me, could I let Calder and all those merfolk just... die?

Merfolk might not have been entirely human, but they lived human life spans.

Vampires had had their chance at life once. They were complete aberrations, zombies brought back to life.

It didn't seem fair. Or natural. Or right.

"I still need a date," said Orin and I froze.

Was he seriously asking what I thought he was?

Calder would be hurt—and for some reason, despite it all, that bothered me a little. Even if he knew I wasn't some soulless "mate." He seemed... invested in this, in making something between us work, even if it was just a friendship. But I supposed that made sense, considering his family's lives were at stake.

Orin stood and raised a finger. "And I have just the thing for the girl on my arm to wear."

He disappeared into the back room and came back with a bag from The Dress Castle, holding it out toward me as I raised an eyebrow. "You have interesting taste in clothes," I said, snickering when I remembered Calder's "*Frisky*" rear end.

Orin just jostled the bag toward me again and I took it from him. I looked inside and pulled out a deep-blue dress—a dress that hit me at once as familiar, a material that made my fingertips grow cold, a faint blue light at the edges of my skin. "Where did you get this?" I demanded to know.

"Your sister," he said, smiling. "She dropped it off earlier this week, said she'd gotten it for you."

"My... sister." Autumn made no sense. "Ember."

His head bobbed up and down. "Said you might actually accept it coming from me. So," he said, scratching the back of his scalp. His thick hair bounced cutely and I had to rip my gaze from him before he noticed me blush. "Ivy Marie Shepherd, will you go with me to the Homecoming dance?"

"My middle name isn't 'Marie,'" I said, my brow scrunching.

He shrugged. "I figured. But I thought I'd be cheeky and take a shot. It makes the promposal sound better, doesn't it?"

"It's Homecoming."

"Whatever," he said, the 't' sound almost entirely silent in that cockney-esque lilt of his.

Letting out a deep breath, I pulled the dress out of the bag completely, my mind racing with thoughts about what Ember could have meant by this "gift," and why, if she'd been so determined to give it to me, she hadn't just done it at home like a normal person.

Because she wasn't a normal person. Not anymore. And neither was I.

This weekend was the last time I had any hope of convincing her we could be normal again, that we needed to just put this all behind us.

"Fine," I said. "But I'm not buying you a boutonniere." I thumbed my nose at him. "My boss hasn't paid me yet."

His smile reminded me spookily of a textbook villain about to see his plans come to fruition. All he was missing were the fingertips tapping together.

What had I just gotten myself into?

CHAPTER TWENTY-NINE

EMBER

"Ember, your guests are all here!" Mom called up the stairs. I could hear her through my closed door, over the sound of the straightener steaming as Mrs. Slowe ran it through Journey's hair.

"Em, what do you think about this look?" said Journey, twisting her head back and forth where she sat before my vanity mirror. Her hair was half-straight—and much longer than it usually appeared, as it didn't often touch her shoulders—and half-voluminous. To tell the truth, she looked gorgeous both ways. Her mom dipped her hands in some styling goop and kept rubbing it through the flat side of Journey's hair.

"I like it," I said from where I sat on my bed, sweats on to go with the bouncy curls in my yellow hair that Mrs. Slowe had given me before setting her sights on Journey. "Very punk."

Journey chuckled and my mom called my name again.

"Go and greet them," said Mrs. Slowe—the two women always had each other's backs. "Let them know the hairstyle station is up here."

Mom would still help me with makeup, though Journey was a wiz now at her own. I had the basics down, but when I applied it, it looked like nothing had changed except the scratchy, heavy sensation that plagued my cheeks, so I must have been doing something wrong. I stood, wondering if the buffer of all these other girls would work so I wouldn't have to talk to Ivy.

After what Calder had done—surprised me like that, during what was supposed to be a truce—I wasn't sure I wanted her to get in my head.

I knew this was crazy. I knew it was too much for the two of us and I had no wish to see her hurt or... But Dean had offered me something no one else ever had. To be adored, to be protected... And besides, his whole family's existence was at stake. Could I blame him for being a little pushy?

"What time is your dinner?" asked Mrs. Slowe as my hand reached the knob.

Dean had invited Journey and me for a pre-dance dinner at his place. It'd be the first time I went to his home. He'd even told Journey to invite Devam, and though he'd had some taco dinner planned with his friends—which included Ivy, I supposed—he'd been easily swayed with the promise of a gourmet steak dinner cooked by Dean's apparent full-time chef.

A chef who cooked for vampires. I wasn't sure I liked to think too hard about what they might be serving up any other day.

"Five," I answered, turning the door.

"Do you need a lift?" she asked.

"*Mom*," said Journey as her mom ran the straightener back through her hair, "it's bad enough we have moms helping us in the afternoon. Please don't embarrass us in front of our dates."

Mrs. Slowe mumbled something about copping an attitude and I went downstairs. Lyric, Paisley, and Ivy were gathered in the kitchen, munching on the chips and salsa Mom had set out for the group. Easton was in the TV room, ignoring some sports game in favor of playing some colorful game on his Kindle.

Ivy was the only one not smiling, the only one not munching on chips. Even Mom kept jutting her hand into the bowl.

"Ember!" said Paisley, rushing forward like we were old friends. She had curlers in her hair and I noticed two garment bags haphazardly draped over the kitchen table. She and Lyric were wearing pajamas. Ivy had changed... into the deep-blue dress I'd left at Orin's bookstore for her.

"I thought you both looked lovely," Dean had said, encouraging me to make the drop. "I hold no ill will against her. In fact, I feel bad for her, being forced on the wrong side of this... Be cautious but extend the olive branch. Offer the dress as a gesture of good will. There's still time."

She had on makeup that made her lips even redder against her pale face, but her hair was just twisted into a messy bun and she had on mid-thigh-high black boots over black fishnet stockings instead of anything resembling dress shoes. A pang of jealousy shot through me at how great her messy look came together.

"Did *you* know Ivy got herself a date?" asked Paisley.

"No..." I said, letting my eyes flit toward Ivy's. She turned away at first, but then she crossed her arms and stared at me blankly. We were hardly on "gossiping about boys" terms. Besides, considering everything that was happening between us, it didn't take much to figure out her date was Calder.

Paisley lowered her voice. "He's her *bo*—" she started.

Lyric elbowed her and let out a squeal. "You *must* give me your salsa recipe, Mrs. Ivy's-step-mom!"

Paisley giggled and turned, whispering, "Sorry" to Ivy as they both gazed in the direction of Ivy's dad.

What was the big deal about keeping Calder a secret from him? Did he not approve of her dating yet?

He might not approve of her dating a merman, but I highly doubted Ivy had been any more eager to share that kind of detail with her friends than I had been.

Mom laughed, not noticing anything being covered up. "Oh, it's just store-bought, dear. Let me find you the bottle." She opened the fridge and began rummaging through it. Lyric raised her eyebrows at Ivy and obediently shuffled over toward the open fridge door to learn about Mom's grocery shopping habits.

I cleared my throat. "Journey's mom is doing hair upstairs." I looked between Paisley's curlers and Ivy's sloppy bun. "If you need it."

Paisley laughed and patted her hair. "Maybe she can help me get the frizz down when I unveil it."

"I'm good," said Ivy. She tapped the back of one of the kitchen chairs with blue-tipped fingernails.

"How's Autumn?" I asked, trying to be sisterly. I had nothing against Autumn, to be sure. I just wasn't sure how much of a relationship we'd have if her sister and I wound up going at it.

Which wouldn't have to happen if she just didn't get involved.

"Fine," muttered Ivy. "She and Mom are going to Chuck E. Cheese."

Mom turned around, Lyric now holding a half-empty bottle of salsa. She put both hands on Ivy's shoulders. "Tell your mother 'thank you' again, dear. It was so nice of her to understand about wanting to get our girls together before Homecoming."

Ivy glared at me, not even flinching from Mom's touch. "Yes. So nice."

"Easton!" said Mom, releasing Ivy's shoulders and heading into the living room to stand between Easton and the TV. It didn't matter much, though, since his attention was still focused on the tablet in his grip. Arty was on the couch beside him, a paw on his leg, a cautious eye opening and closing anytime anyone walked past. "Get the nice camera."

"No cameras yet, Mrs. S.," said Paisley, though Mom had hyphenated my dad's name and her new husband's. True, she hadn't been married to Dad in forever, but she'd built a reputation with that name and she felt it was as much hers as it was his at this point. She'd probably emailed Dad to tell him it was my "big dance," like he would care. I was lucky if I saw him once over the summer and once over the holidays—and I saw Daryl even less, but Big Half-Bro had college to worry about and to tell the truth, I could count the number of times we'd both been at Dad's growing up on half a hand.

His mom didn't like my mom—perhaps for good reason, though I thought she was the greatest in so many ways—so there was that hovering between us, too.

"Oh, come on," said Lyric, placing the salsa jar down next to the chips and shaking Paisley by the shoulders. "We need to preserve this curler-and-jammies look for all ages. Maybe we can add a mineral mask."

"No!" shrieked Paisley, running down the hallway.

"Mom," I said. "Just let it go until we're all ready." I glanced at Ivy again. "Some of us need some more time."

Ivy shrugged. "Thanks for the dress," she said, her voice clipped.

Something stuck in my throat. "Thank Dean. He bought it. But you're welcome."

Ivy choked on nothing, some of that sheer attitude dropping from her features, but she finished coughing and covered up her apparent surprise as Mom came back in, grabbing another chip.

"Maybe I can thank him later," said Ivy, and Mom must not have heard about the weirdness of my boyfriend buying my new step-sister a dress. "Are you guys coming to Jorge's?"

At first I thought she was referring to one of her friends. Then I remembered the Mexican restaurant Journey had mentioned she'd peeled Devam away from.

"No, oh my god," said Paisley as she and Lyric entered the kitchen once more, the chase at an end. "Didn't you hear from Devam? He and Journey and Ember and Dean are eating at his ritzy mansion."

I cocked my head. I actually hadn't been to Dean's yet, so hearing it was a mansion was news to me. Though not to my best friend's date apparently.

"I see," said Ivy, her lips drawn tight.

Mom rummaged through a big Ulta bag on the counter and drew out several cases full of makeup. "Who's ready for me?" she asked.

"Oo, what do you have?" asked Lyric. I couldn't tell if she was wearing makeup or not. She was just one of those natural beauties.

"Me, me!" said Paisley, practically champing at the bit.

Ivy, her dark red lipstick clear as day, simply walked out of the room and crashed on the couch next to her dad, grabbing the remote from him with barely a nod of acknowledgement.

———

"1, 2, 3!" Mom clicked her digital camera for what had to be the fortieth time. Mrs. Slowe—now joined by Mr. Slowe—was taking pics with her camera and Easton was taking some pics with the Kindle that had barely left his hip all day. Ivy's mom had stopped by along with Autumn. Autumn was running around like a nut and Glory kept stepping in between clicks to fuss with a stray chunk of hair that hung over Ivy's face.

"Mom, that's enough pictures," I said.

Another car pulled up and I realized Mom had given permission for the girls' dates to meet them here—and from the looks of the couple who got out of the second car, another set of parents too.

"Oo, my bae is here!" screamed Paisley, heading outside.

"Don't forget your coat, young lady," said Mom, but she was gone, her bare shoulders in her beautiful princess ball gown surely ill-suited to the cooling temps outside, sunshine or no.

"We need more pics with everyone," said Mom, stepping up to me and picking a piece of lint off my bodice. "Em, Journey, where are your boys?" I could tell by the way her mouth curled up that she was excited I finally had a date, though she was keen not to let it show.

"That's my *girl*," said Lyric then as another car pulled up, this one with Raelynn, her dad, I presumed, and yet another set of girls inside.

We weren't going to have room for all of these people.

"Dean said he'd pick us up," I said. "I don't know if he'll do pictures."

"Nonsense," said Mom, just as a new car pulled up and Devam and another boy got out along with a girl. At least they hadn't brought any parents.

Journey squeezed her mom's hand and grabbed her shoulder wrap before heading outside to greet him.

Ivy stared at me, clearly ignoring whatever her mom was telling her.

"Mom," I whispered. "Don't forget Dean's... light sensitivity."

"Ah," said Mom. "Yvonne has the same thing. Must run in the family." She shook her head. "But she can take *pictures*, for Pete's sake. Tell him he can keep his shades on."

I sighed. I wondered when Calder was showing and if Mom—oblivious and pushy and used to getting her own way—would snap a picture of the four of us, just days before the fortnight was up that would decide the fate of us all.

Someone knocked on the front door and I startled. I hadn't heard another car pull up.

When I saw who it was, it made perfect sense why. No car necessary.

"Orin...?" I asked aloud.

Ivy snapped her head around. "My date." She went to open the door.

"He's cute," said Mom, bumping arms with Ivy's mom. Glory smiled awkwardly up at her. "He looks familiar, too..." said Mom, cocking her head.

Ivy was going to the dance with Orin? Not Calder. Oh, so her friends thought the big deal was he was her "boss." And much, *much* older, though he barely looked older than twenty. Ivy was still a minor, though. I wondered if Journey would notice and spill the beans that the man was "at least thirty" in her opinion, as she'd told me multiple times about the guy at The Hollow Tree. If only.

"You look pretty."

I almost jumped at the tug at the back of my dress.

"Thanks," I said, smiling awkwardly down at Autumn. She had Artemis in her arms and the cat was squirming, trying to run away.

Mom brushed past Glory and reached over Ivy's head to open the door wider. "Well, come in. Introduce us, Ivy, dear."

Grimacing, I shifted backward as Ivy and Orin shuffled into the entryway. He looked cute—as always—though he'd just thrown a dark green blazer over a beige dress shirt and khakis. No wonder Ivy hadn't gone out of her way to doll herself up.

Arty howled and managed to jump down from Autumn's grip, scurrying for the kitchen and the basement door.

Orin chuckled. "Ember, all right?" he said in his oddly lilting accent. He dug both hands into his pockets.

Mom looked to me and back again. "Noelle," she said, reaching a hand out to shake Orin's. She turned over her shoulder to call Easton in from where he'd wandered back to the living room, then turned back to Orin. "Do you all know each other from school?"

Orin shrugged. "The book—"

"Club," I finished for him. "He's in Book Club. At the bookstore Ivy works at."

Mom beamed and Easton made his introductions, his attention still darting to the TV on in the living room. "Are you also in Book Club?" Mom asked me, but I shook my head and brushed past her to grab my dress jacket.

"Well, I'm happy to hear you're all making new friends," said Mom after Glory finished making her introductions to Orin.

A long, black limo pulled up along the street. Some of the others out on the lawn started bouncing in place and pointing to it.

It parked and a driver came out. Naturally, he had sunglasses and a suit on—and he was pallid to boot. But that looked less out of place on a limo driver than it did on a mover, for example.

It wasn't until he opened the back door and Dean slid out—sunglasses, top hat, and tuxedo, complete with a long tail—that my heart skipped a beat.

"Wow," said Glory. Her eyes had grown as wide as saucers and it took her a moment to acknowledge Autumn, who was jumping in place and tugging on her sleeve. "We'll go as soon as they all leave, honey," she said.

"No! I want to see the limo!" Autumn replied, as if that were obvious.

Glory laughed and let Autumn lead her out the front door as Easton rejoined Mr. Slowe in the living room. "Have fun, girls," he called over his shoulder. "You both look great. Like a million bucks."

Ivy rolled her eyes and Mom frowned but turned her attention back to us, laying a hand on my back and ushering me toward the door. "Pictures," she said.

Well, if Dean honestly wanted me to save his family, I supposed the least he could do was placate mine.

Dean was busy nodding at the group of teens who'd gathered round him, a bemused grin on his face. Journey ran up to me and slid her arm through mine. "Someone splurged," she whispered.

Devam trailed a few steps behind her, talking with another guy and his date. Journey looked over her shoulder at him. "He cleans up nice, doesn't he?" She jutted her chin toward Dean. "Though not as nice as yours."

Tell me about it. As we drew nearer to Dean, my heart threatened to burst through my rib cage. The smoldering look I imagined him giving me even with those sunglasses on his face made my toes curl and I had to take a deep breath to cool the fiery feeling tingling in my fingertips.

Then his smile faded and he stepped forward, sliding a hand to the small of my back. "Orin." His lips were in a thin line.

"All right?" asked Orin by way of greeting. He nonchalantly walked toward the limo, admiring it. "Nice car. Splash out a bit on it, mate?"

"I didn't know you were..." Dean's head twisted toward Ivy and he stopped himself.

Ivy raised an eyebrow and nodded toward him, only showing life when her sister ran up to her and hugged her legs.

"Nice to see you, Dean," said Mom, oblivious to anything more meaningful than a pre-dance get-together going on around her. She turned toward the group. "Pictures, everyone!" Someone groaned, but Mom was insistent, herding even kids I didn't know that well like a flock of sheep. "Just one more set of pictures and we'll let you be on your way."

She turned toward Dean again and said more quietly, "I expect her home before dawn," she said.

"*Mom*." I slapped my forehead. Only my mom could simultaneously act like an imposing parent without actually requesting something that unreasonable. Wasn't I usually home by one after dances? Or midnight. It got kind of tiring sitting on the sidelines, sipping too-sweet punch.

Mom pinched my upper arm and winked, then stepped back. A gaggle of other parents joined her.

Dean's hand never left my back and he drew me closer to him once Mom's attention seemed diverted. "Do you know why he's here instead of...?" He left the rest unsaid.

"No," I admitted, watching as Ivy disentangled from Autumn to nudge Orin away from the limo.

"Okay, kids," said Mom, still giggling after tearing herself away from Journey's mom. They seemed to be loving this—so many teenagers, even though it always used to be just Journey and me. And her dates. Sometimes her cousin.

Everyone lined up like suspects, the line so long, Mom and the other parents had to back up to fit everyone in frame.

Dean squeezed my waist and something strange shot through me, a vision of how different my life had been just two weeks before. It was like an out-of-body experience, and for a brief moment, I felt sure I was living a life meant for someone else.

"Say, 'cheese'!" said Mom.

Smiling, my gaze darted to Autumn, who had taken up running along the side of the limo. Only when she bent down to inspect the shiny rim of a front tire did I notice down the sidewalk at the end of the block...

A guy in a navy suit, his suit jacket a little too tight. His sea-green necktie against a dark blue shirt should have clashed horribly, but with his messy, blond hair and swimmer's tan even in the fall, he looked like he could have rocked plaid or polka dot pants if he'd wanted.

Calder. Watching us from down the street, just staring at us.

"I know," said Dean then, squeezing me tighter against him. Mom's first flash went off, followed by half a dozen others. "He's hanging back... for now."

The second part of that sentence was what worried me, but Ivy and Orin didn't so much as glance in Calder's direction.

Though Ivy's friends regretted the fact that they all had to cram into multiple cars to get to their Mexican restaurant while the four of us—Dean, me, Journey, and Devam—spread out with enough space to seat a basketball team in the back of Dean's limo, it was a short ride to Dean's place, so it wasn't like I had much time to get used to it. Dean and Devam tried to make small talk, but it was like a great-uncle trying to find a way to relate to a modern teen.

"So, you fancy any footballers?" Dean asked at one point.

"Sorry?" Devam asked.

"A team? You rooting for the home team?"

"Oh, uh, more college football than NFL," said Devam. "But more baseball than anything."

An awkward pause hung in the air.

It *was* like a great-uncle trying to relate to a young kid. As Dean strummed the back of the seat from behind my shoulders, I tried to push that thought away. Teen girls were always with super ancient guys in all the vampire stories, right? Besides, at least he was less than a hundred. Barely, but...

"What's wrong?" asked Journey as Dean mentioned something about liking any new "flicks" to Devam.

I shook my head. "Nothing. Everything..."

Journey leaned closer and whispered. "Are things not going well with Dean? Let me know if there's someone I need to punch."

Though Dean's head was turned to Devam, he squeezed my shoulder then and I shook my head at Journey. "It's really nothing. Everything's just so... different. It's overwhelming."

Her head bobbed as she hummed a tune. "Different but good," she said. "Hey, what was up with Ivy and her *boss*? Do her parents know how old he is?"

My jaw hung open a second, but I snapped it shut.

She tugged on her earlobe, nearly jostling her earring. "I guess he looks young enough they might not have known. *Dang*, girl, though, you know?"

"Here we are!" said Dean and we pulled into a long driveway.

"Mansion" wasn't far off. It wasn't like one of those grand estates with no other house for miles, but we were clearly in the doctor/lawyer part of town, the houses two- to three-stories and spilling out twice as far back as one would reasonably expect them to. Dean's looked a little older than the other houses, a Victorian-ish beauty that might have been more at home on a New England street, but it was well-maintained and looked like it might not have aged a day since it had been built. Much like the vampires themselves, I supposed. There were two stories, but a third-story window—the attic perhaps—was squeezed between the second floor and the roof over the middle of the house. A crowd had gathered on the front porch, all wearing sunglasses or those dark contacts, even though the sun was on its way out.

"Well, that's..." Devam started, but he didn't finish, his jaw growing tight.

I wondered if he had been about to say something like, "that's creepy." The line of well-dressed vampires certainly did look like an unearthly band of paranormal entities.

"My aunts and uncles and their friends," said Dean. "Sorry, I should have asked if it was okay, but Aunt Minnie figured if we were having a big meal, she may as well make the most of it. We have a rather large dining room table." His head swiveled toward me, and I tried not to detect anything in that comment about the size of his dining room table, but I couldn't help but picture someone strewn across the surface, their blood being sucked from their veins, that whole crowd gathered around them.

Journey fidgeted, tugging down on her dress. "Oh, okay..." She seemed to be getting some creepy vibes from the place, too.

But Dean wouldn't do anything to them. He *couldn't* do anything. He knew how upset I'd been at witnessing the "feast" at the moving company. With only two days left before I had to make my decision, he wouldn't dare risk it.

Besides, he'd assured me they only munched on volunteers.

As we parked and the driver walked around to hold the door, my stomach churned.

For a brief moment, I'd considered how *good* it might feel to munch on people myself.

I threw a palm over my mouth.

"Are you okay?" asked Journey just as she was about to disembark.

"She's fine," said Dean, taking my hand from my mouth and squeezing it. The mesh of his cold skin on my hot flesh sent a wave of calmness through me.

"Right," I said, smiling. He rewarded me with a row of pearly whites—no fangs in sight.

Dean escorted me like an old-fashioned movie starlet toward the house, his arm through mine. Journey clutched Devam's elbow in a pale imitation. As we approached the row of pallid undead welcoming us, Minnie ran up to me on delicate feet, taking my hands in hers and air kissing either side of my face. "Ember, darling, I'm so glad you came." She winked at Dean. "It looks like my nephew finally learned to put that charm of his to good use."

Dean's brows arched over the top of his sunglasses. Minnie ignored the movement. "And who are these fine young students? I know I've seen their bright and cheery faces in the Union halls."

"Why didn't you tell me Dean's aunt was the new principal?" hissed Journey in my ear before she turned on her dazzle-face. "Journey Slowe," she said. "Model U.N., student council—"

"Ah, yes, of course, Miss Slowe." Minnie gripped Journey's hands. "It's a pleasure to meet such a distinguished student as yourself." She looked at Devam, waiting for an answer.

"Devam Kapoor," he said, scratching his cheek in what seemed to be a nervous habit. "Varsity baseball."

"How do you think the boys will do this year?" asked Minnie as she slipped her arm through Devam's. He seemed taken aback for a second, then almost seemed... like he was counting himself lucky. Minnie *was* gorgeous in a slinky, black-and-white movie star kind of way. But Devam seemed a little *too* into counting his lucky stars, only taking Journey on his other arm when she slid herself there inside the foyer, her lips in a tight line.

With everything going on, I hadn't given Journey enough time to gush about Devam, and after this, it looked like there might not be another chance.

But Journey's jaw dropped when she looked around at the elegant décor.

"Please," said Minnie, brushing past us as the line of pallid vintage vampires filed in behind her. "It's this way."

Journey stepped to my side and giggled as we let ourselves be led down the hall and into an elaborate dining room, complete with a dimmed candelabra and dark, velvet curtains that made the whole room seem a set from the likes of *Dracula*. Which I supposed was true enough. Minnie gestured to two chairs on either side toward the end of the table, gripping the back of the chair at the end. "Please. As our guests of honor, you'll dine near me up here."

Dean moved smoothly to pull my chair out, and I sat, giving him a smile and a "thank you." When Devam wandered to the other side of the table, his gaze on everywhere but his date—the candelabra, the fancy dinnerware on the table, the heavy curtains, the beautiful vampire women—and he moved to sit down, Dean *tsked* and jogged to the other side to pull out a chair for Journey. Journey raised her eyebrows at me but took a seat, thanking my gentlemanly vampire.

Dean made his way back to me and Devam crouched halfway to his seat, observing the room as all the men held out chairs for all the women and then stood behind them like their bodyguards. Minnie looked over the room and nodded as a sallow dark-skinned man pulled out the chair for her and she made herself comfortable. Once she sat, the men pulled out their own chairs in unison—the one who'd guided Minnie to her seat walking around the table to take the other end—and were seated, leaving Devam still hovering and scrunching his brows together before he finally let his rear fall on the chair beside his date.

"You must forgive us, dear," said Minnie, extending a delicate hand with blood-red fingernails toward Devam's plate, "we're a bit old-fashioned here."

Devam nodded wordlessly, still confused.

"Men don't seat themselves until the women are all seated," I said, remembering a comedic sketch in one of those old movies Grandma liked. The women kept excusing themselves and leaving the table and the men had to stand each time. The joke had been lost on me until Grandma had explained how things had been in the time of her parents. Journey frowned and I realized I'd embarrassed Devam, who hung his head, entirely lost and out of place. I laughed nervously. "I just mean in old-fashioned days."

Minnie's head bobbed. "As the years pass, some things may improve, but there are still traditions that had it right the first time."

Journey clearly bristled, laying a gentle hand on Devam's arm. "I think men holding doors and pulling out chairs—I mean, everyone should hold doors, not just men anyway—can be demeaning." She gave her date a half-shrug. "As long as a guy is polite and considerate, I can do without all those trappings that put women in a cage on a pedestal."

It was my turn to raise my brows. Journey *was* on Model U.N. But hadn't she complained to me about how rude Avon had been toward the end of their relationship? Holding doors to a car might have been a bit much, but weren't her exact words that she wished he were more of a gentleman?

My fingers wore at the cloth napkin I'd slipped off my plate and laid on my lap. My body was a flutter of emotions, from being proud of my gentlemanly supernatural boyfriend to being reminded full-stop that this wasn't a world I belonged in.

Dean seemed to sense my discomfort and brushed my wrist gently, stopping my fingers from moving.

Minnie gestured over her shoulder and two figures I hadn't noticed lingering in the darkness made their way out a back door, the dim glow of muted light pouring into the dining room. They returned with trays and two others to help them serve. As the doors closed, those wearing sunglasses at the table removed them, slipping them onto their laps or into their breast pockets. Dean tucked his into his lapel.

"Thank you," said Minnie as she was served a small, fancy-restaurant-sized portion consisting of a chunk of red meat and a drizzle of sauce. Dark, dark red sauce.

The thundering call of my heart made me flinch and Dean kept running his fingers over my skin.

My gaze flit to the servers—anything to clear my head—and I noticed the somber expressions on them. None were pallid and none had the bright blue eyes that shined all around the table.

Like the woman at the moving company.

Dean leaned into my ear. "It's red wine sauce," he said, as if reading my mind. "We wouldn't... Not in front of your friends."

I felt hot then, my brain buzzing as I felt a chill run through me and a flash of cold sweat.

"You okay, Em?" asked Journey, squinting in the dim light over the table. "You look a little ill."

"Fine," I said through clenched teeth. I forced a smile on my face as a pair of servants reached my plate. One—a man—stuck a tong into a large serving dish to remove a piece of meat and put it on my plate. Then he put the tong down and grabbed for the ladle to drizzle the sauce over it.

"You'll have to forgive us skipping the salad course," said Minnie, smiling deviously at Devam in particular. "We're not much for vegetarian diets."

Journey wrinkled her nose at her own portion of meat but didn't say anything more.

"It's just the appetizer," said a woman two seats down from Journey. Zelda, I remembered. The secretary. Her gaze roved over to the man standing behind me. "We'll have something more satisfying before the end of the night."

I felt myself blush, but staring at the dark red wine sauce as it pooled around my meat, I couldn't think. Now I felt hot and dizzy and as my gaze wandered around the table at the glowing, blue irises interspersed with those with dark contacts, I felt like I was about to vomit all over my pretty Homecoming dress.

You don't belong here.

"Darling, you do look unwell," said Minnie, her attention on me. "Do you need the restroom?"

"Yes!" I said, jumping to my feet. The men at the table—minus Devam—scrambled to stand then just as they had in the old movie.

Journey looked from one to another, a look of bewilderment on her face, and then pushed her own chair back, tossing her napkin onto her seat. "I'll go with you."

"No, I—well, maybe." I turned and bumped into the serving man, slamming my face into his shoulder. His blood thrummed loudly through his veins at such a short distance and my gaze slid slowly up to find multiple sets of scabbed puncture wounds all over his neck. Sets of two, spaced perfectly apart like incisors.

"Em, what's wrong?" started Journey, who'd somehow arrived around the table while I'd been staring at the man's puncture wounds, my blood roaring in my ears, my hand hot and fiery.

I opened my mouth to speak and instead I felt my top incisors grow longer.

"You look—what the?" said Journey, stepping back.

I grabbed hold of the serving man, causing him to drop his tongs, and I dug my teeth into his neck. He shouted out and thrashed his arms before growing still.

Everything went still, even the movement of the blood that had so enticed me.

"Ember, you're caught in blood lust," said Dean, the only moving thing beside me. He laid a gentle hand on my shoulder, causing me to pull back, to take my teeth out of the man's flesh. "Rick will let you feed on him, but this is neither the time nor the place—"

A haughty echo of laughter sounded from behind him. Minnie was also moving in this moment, unaffected by Dean's time pause. "This is progressing so well," she said, a smile as wide as her face taking over her lips. "Oh, do let her go, Dean. Let her *feel* it."

"But her friends are here."

Minnie ran a finger over her lips as she stared at Devam. "I know," she said. "And I was thinking of asking this morsel what he thought of immortality regardless."

"No!" I said, a cold splash of reality hitting my face. It was hard to speak with these awkward teeth extending out of my mouth. "Leave them out of this."

Minnie chuckled. "Darling, you brought them into this. I'd promised Dean a night of good behavior." She tilted her head toward him. "Though I disagreed with the approach, considering how close it is to the day of reckoning."

Dean looked sad, but he nodded and then with a whoosh, time unpaused.

Journey screamed as she looked at the serving man's neck, from which there now coursed two small streams of blood. He put his hand to it but seemed unbothered when he pulled away blood-dipped fingers.

"Ember, what did you *do*?" asked Journey, rushing to grab a napkin from the table and put it to the man's neck. She turned to face me, the muscles in her arms and neck turned rigid. "Have you gone mad?"

Her own neck throbbed then, there between me and the meal I'd started.

I opened my mouth to warn her to get out of there, to leave the guy behind.

But instead I launched myself at her, sinking my incisors into the curve of her neck just where it reached the shoulder.

Devam shouted in alarm as Minnie's cool laughter echoed, echoed in my head.

CHAPTER THIRTY

IVY

Even the best green enchiladas in town hadn't done much to get me in the mood for this dance.

"He's been staring at you like a puppy dog all night," said Lyric as she brushed past me to get at the punch bowl. I'd taken up root against a wall near the refreshments, content to let my hot date accumulate a crowd of interested onlookers a few paces away. He was doing something with cherry stems with his tongue that was driving girls wild.

"I doubt that. He's occupied," I said. "But it's cool. We're not like that. Just... friends. Of sorts."

Lyric downed her punch, then dabbed her lips with a napkin, leaving dark pink splotches all over the stiff white paper. "Not your date. Though, yeah, I kind of have to wonder why you're so cool with that." She chucked her cup into the overflowing bin beside the table and nodded over her shoulder. She was wearing a strapless black and white number and part of me regretted not asking Paisley's mom for an outfit after all. But I hadn't even been sure I'd be coming. And worrying about what I looked like at a dance was so pre-merfolk and bloodsuckers.

It took me a second to look past all the faces—familiar and unfamiliar, Raelynn giggling in the corner with some of her friends, Paisley and Grey half-attached at the hip, Ashton with his arm around some girl probably a year or two younger, which sent a jolt I wasn't expecting down my spine—to see the guy Lyric was talking about.

I supposed I should have figured that out sooner.

Calder was at the dance, slouched against a wall of his own over by the doors to the gym that led down the hallway to the pool and locker rooms. Every so often he nodded at someone who called his name and I even saw him talking to a girl—a freshman, maybe— who seemed to be asking him to dance, but he'd shaken his head, a kind smile on his face the whole time, and eventually, the offers had dried up and people had let him be.

Much like an echo of what had happened over on this side of the gym with me and the friends and guys I didn't know who'd asked me for a spin around the floor.

I wasn't much in the mood to dance, considering the music had been blasting for well over an hour and Ember, Journey, Devam, and all the pale, creepy vampires were still nowhere to be seen.

They could be preparing to drive their vehicles into power substations at this very moment. Though I still didn't know why they'd need to, considering the sun had gone down and the gym was barely lit.

"Didn't he transfer to another school?" Lyric asked, raising her voice to be heard over the bouncing beats of a Lorde track. "That's what Rae told me, anyway."

"Yeah, I think," I said, shrugging and looking away. I didn't know how he'd pulled that off if he supposedly lived right by my dad's, but maybe Central had taken a special application for him.

"Then doesn't he have to come with a date who attends the school? It looks like he came stag to me." Lyric slid next to me on the wall.

"He might have asked to come with me," I said casually, remembering how the texts had gone silent when I'd told him I was going with Orin. He already knew he was in trouble with me for his stunt with Ember. I just had to ride the next few days out and it would all be over. If I didn't agree to participate in this nonsense, I wouldn't need Orin's presence for protection, I wouldn't have this puppy-eyed fish man dogging my every move, and I wouldn't have to consider fighting my own step-sister. Or worrying about watching my back around her.

"And yet, you seem content to hang back here." Lyric tapped a fingertip against her lips, then nodded my way. She left, heading toward Raelynn and slipping an arm around her before whispering in her ear. Raelynn turned to the friends standing behind her, who nodded and dispersed, joining the small crowd gathered around Orin as he did some dance move that lit up the faces of those gathered around him and made them break out into applause. Meanwhile, Lyric and Raelynn both crossed the dance floor, seemingly concerned with swaying to the music. Just when all the tension about what Lyric might have been up to started slipping from my shoulders, she and Raelynn arrived at Calder's claimed spot of the wall. Lyric talked to him while Raelynn kept glancing my way and then Calder's face grew tight. He squared his shoulders and wove through the various bouncing couples to make his way toward me.

I felt a cold sweat break out on my back and regretted not wearing a wrap over my shoulders.

He made a beeline for me, ignoring the refreshments, and my gaze went to Orin. But he wasn't a few paces away with a crowd gathered around him. He was clear across the room, Raelynn's friends completely surrounding him, bouncing as a conga line pushed him to the back corner.

Lyric had planned that somehow. She couldn't have known of any supernatural reason Calder may have been keeping his distance, but she probably had her petty normal teen reason in her head. She saw me, being grumpy, not even spending much time with my supposed date, and him staring at me all night, looking much the same.

Only it wasn't because he loved me. It was because by ignoring him, I was dooming him and all his salt water friends.

"Why are you here?" I asked, staring around his side at the mass of people surrounding my date.

Calder followed my gaze. "I tried to get your attention earlier," he said. "Back when you were posing for pictures at the house."

My attention snapped back to Calder. "Were you spying on us earlier?"

He shrugged. "I thought you saw me."

I shook my head. So maybe I had. That didn't make it right. I counted my lucky stars that he hadn't followed us to the restaurant after. At least I was pretty sure he hadn't.

I would have felt his eyes on me, even if I couldn't see him. It was a hard feeling to shake.

I changed the subject. "Orin said if he came with me, he could keep me out of this nonsense."

"I'm glad you think it's nonsense." Calder took the place beside me on the wall that Lyric had previously occupied. I sent a silent sneer her way when she looked over from where she was dancing with Raelynn. She just smiled broadly. "To me, it's the survival of my species," added Calder quietly.

Sighing, I wrung my fingers in front of me. "That's a lot of pressure to put on a girl you hardly know."

"I realize that," said Calder. His own gaze spread out over the crowd, surveying the scene of gyrating teens—and one totally unhelpful ancient forest dweller—with a sense of detachment. "I'm sorry. I wouldn't be doing this if there were any other way."

"I thought we went over this. The other way is convincing Ember not to participate, too. No champions, no winners—but no losers, either."

Calder nodded toward the dance floor. "And do you see your step-sister dropping out of the battle?"

A sharp feeling raced across my chest at that. "She's not here yet..."

"And when she comes, she'll be happily on the arm of a vampire. She may be missing a friend or two."

That was like a slap to the face. "What?"

Calder turned to face me, resting a shoulder on the wall and crossing his arms. "She's changing, Ivy." He held up one palm before tucking it back against his side. "She bit me. Using vampire fangs. Before she relied on fire to fight me—"

I laughed, cutting him off. "If she bit you as a vampire, you'd *be* one."

Calder clearly shuddered. "A vampire merperson. That would be a new one." He shook his head. "It doesn't work that quickly. A vampire needs to feed for days—weeks, even. Months if they choose to belabor it. Then the venom takes effect."

"Okay..." Shaking my head, I tapped the sole of one of my shoes harder against the wall. "So how come I haven't noticed the fangs?"

"They turn them on and off, much like we can with our fins. Their trigger is blood, like ours is water."

We. I stared at the remaining foot holding me up and remembered how it had become a fin, the tip of a tail that was utterly useless everywhere but in a body of water. A couple more days and I'd be done with that, too. "So Ember's like... training? Getting ready for this... battle?"

"Seems so." A visible twinge affected the lump at Calder's throat.

"And your mom hasn't decided to kidnap me again and *force* me to start training of my own?"

"I told her I'd handle it." He shifted against the wall and threaded fingers through his messy golden hair. "I begged her to let me try the soft approach."

Scoffing, I put my foot down and straightened up, giving my head a rest from being pushed against the concrete wall for over an hour. "And you're not desperate enough to tell her it's not working?"

"Not yet. I'm still holding out hope." The hollow shade of happiness on his faltering smile did something crazy to my heart, spurring it to beat rapidly.

I moved to step away. "Well, I'm sorry—really, I am. It's not that I don't feel an ounce of guilt walking away, it's just—you can't... I mean..." I swallowed, my tirade lost on my tongue as I stared up at him. He'd taken a step away from the wall, too, and he had this smoldering look in his eyes, on the tightness of his lips, as he stared down at me, clearly eager to hear more.

Eager and amused.

"Vampires have another power," said Calder, as if I hadn't even spoken my objections to the whole thing. "They used it on me to get out of the store last week—before I could talk to Ember."

Gulping, I took a step back, this feeling that if I didn't put some space between us, my next instinct would be to erase that space and step into him. "What power?"

"Time pausing," said Calder. He scanned the room, then looked back. "They appear to move quickly from time to time, but that's because they can pause time and move before releasing it."

I chortled. Another step back. "You're joking."

Calder took a step forward. "I'm not."

I had to pointedly stare at his knees. He had a nice suit and tie on—nothing super special, but on him, it was poured like hot, melted butter. I cleared my throat. "Then you guys are fu—"

"Freaking in a pinch?" finished Calder. I waggled an eyebrow at him. I didn't know mermen cared so much about language. He grinned. "Yeah. We know, thanks."

Somehow he'd taken another step forward without me noticing and we were right on top of one another, just a hair's breadth away from lifting our arms and wrapping them around each other and taking a twirl around the room.

He seemed to notice, too. "Shall we?" he asked, just as a slow song came on. One of those boy band tunes Mom still played from the '90s. He held his arms out to either side of me.

I opened my mouth to reject him. "Okay," I said instead.

Stupid.

He slipped his palms on either side of my waist. I put my hands tentatively on both his shoulders and he guided me toward the edge of the dance floor. We just swayed for a few moments in silence, my gaze roving around, eager not to spend too long drowning in his big puppy-dog eyes.

"So," I said, my palms suddenly clammy and going cold, "how does this psychic thing work to help at all? Is that all you guys got?"

"That and an advantage in water," said Calder. "There's the

siren call, too, but that only works in water, and vampires basically have their own version of that anytime. Helps them lure in prey."

That got an eye roll. "Great. So water-based powers, which will definitely come in handy, considering all the vampires have to do to win is avoid a shower."

Calder cocked his head. "I wonder if any of them *do* shower," he said. "Maybe they're afraid we'll pop out of the faucet from the sewers or something."

"Or maybe you stop stinking once undead," I offered. We caught each other's eyes and laughed then. Since when were corpses known for smelling fresh?

Calder's smile dropped. "Our telepathy is limited and, well, it doesn't offer as much of an advantage. We don't actively read current thoughts. We have to be near the person—touching them even." He shook his head. "We may as well not have the power at all."

"But you said I have it—for now at least."

"You can draw on it if need be, yes. At least until Monday evening, when time's up."

"And my free trial is over." I smirked, then I thought over what he'd said. "You can't actively read thoughts?" He'd explained this at the diner, but I felt it best to be sure.

"We can search minds, looking for specific things. Things that dwell in the subconscious that even the conscious mind might not know."

"Things like my friends' phone numbers that I glance at from time to time but never bother to commit to memory."

"Right," he said.

I frowned. This really was a useless power.

But I might as well explore it. Might as well get the most out of my free limited time trial. "How do I...?"

Calder's grin threatened to reach his ear. "Touch my skin."

"What?"

"Your hands are on my suit jacket now. For this to work, you need to touch my skin directly."

"Then you—?"

"Hands," he said, answering before I could accuse him of anything. "Hands to hands works just fine."

The song ended and it would have been an ideal time to take his hand in mine and slip back to my safe spot along the wall, but another slow song—a more recent one this time—started up and I shifted my hands up the back of his bare neck, drawing him closer. "Will this work?"

Clearly flustered, his gaze darted downward as his own hands moved from my waist to the small of my back. "Sure."

"Now what?" I asked after a moment of nothing but dancing.

"What do you want to know?"

"Huh?"

"What do you want to find out from me?"

Scoffing, I shook my head. "I don't know. A whole lot."

"Pick something."

This power got more and more useless. Sighing, I settled on learning more about his dad since I hadn't met a Mr. Kidnapping Mermatron in my time under the lake. My mouth opened—

"Don't tell me," he said. "It works better when your target doesn't know. That way you can swim through the subconscious."

"Okay..." I closed my eyes and flattened my palms even harder against his neck, the tips of my fingers curling up into his hair. I felt him twitch beneath my grasp, but I ignored the feeling, thinking hard about his dad, his dad, his dad...

My right hand went cold, sizzling like ice on a hot radiator, and then I saw it.

Images of a man with a tail, swimming hand in hand with me, my hand much, much smaller than it ought to be. The merman with long, blond hair grinned as he looked back, then flapped his tail and pushed forward, causing a boyish giggle to erupt from my throat.

My eyes snapped open.

"It worked," said Calder, a statement instead of a fact.

"Yes..." I said.

"What did you want to know?" he asked quietly.

"You don't know what I saw?"

He shook his head. "I suppose that might give us an advantage. If we need to read someone's mind to uncover a plan or something, they won't necessarily be able to guess what it is we took from them."

"But if they know about these powers and how they work, they'll know you took *something*," I said. I let out a long exhale. "Does this even work on vampires?"

Calder nodded. "If you can get close enough to one."

"You *know* it works?"

He nodded again. I didn't bother asking how; I'd just assume he or one of his people had done it before.

"It's... useless," I said. Before he could open his mouth, I shook my head. "But it's magical." I smiled. I'd felt like I had been him in that moment, like I was happy and free and comforted and safe holding the hand of "my" father.

Calder leaned closer to me. "What did you see...?"

But before I could answer, Orin popped up behind Calder and made me jump and let out a *gack*. His entourage was nowhere to be found.

"What...?" asked Calder, turning around. His smile dropped when he saw Orin. "Look, she let me approach her. I'm not doing anything against the rules—"

"May I cut in?" asked Orin, putting one palm to his chest and bowing slightly in perfect imitation of some historical romance hero. As weird and out of place as that was in a dimly lit modern gym decorated with drooping balloons and marker-colored banners.

"It's okay," I told Orin, "Calder and I—" But the next few words caught in my throat. My hands went limp and slid off Calder's neck as his own grip on my waist went loose and Orin slid in to take his place in front of me. Orin seemed unperturbed, but both Calder and I stared slack-jawed at the doors that led to the parking lot. Ember had arrived wearing a different dress, a more vintage red number—her hair voluminous, her skin a shade or two paler, her eyes a shade or two brighter, even from here. Dean was on her arm, his blue irises practically glowing in the dim overhead light. Journey and Devam were nowhere to be found. Instead, they were accompanied by a gaggle of men and women—young and beautiful but not so young as to appear at home at a high school dance—a veritable four-member battalion.

Ember had brought more than just one vampire to this dance.

Orin guided me by the hips around the edge of the dance floor. He called over his shoulder to the frozen Calder. "I'd move if I were you," he said. "Isn't there a place nearby that might offer you an advantage?"

Calder stared straight at me.

"I have her," Orin promised, and I wasn't even sure what that meant. He would protect me against blood-sucking vampires?

Who were going to attack here—and now? At a school dance?

I laughed at the wild train of my thoughts. But the way Calder's eyes met mine, then...

He bolted across the room, heading for the hallway, pushing aside one couple after another until he managed to exit the room down the hallway leading to the lockers.

CHAPTER THIRTY-ONE

EMBER

Walking into the high school gym, I felt out of place. Not like I used to feel out of place, like I would have felt had I come to the dance never having met Dean. I'd have stuck to the bleachers, checking in with Journey every so often, maybe getting a pity dance or two from Dante if Journey nudged him hard enough. I'd have jumped in for some of the fast dances where dancing in a group was an option, but I would have probably headed home early, my absence unremarked upon by anyone else.

Now I was standing in the middle of the group that was turning all the heads.

"Let me take your coat," said Dean, slipping his arms around me as I shrugged out of the dainty wrap.

Minnie had lent me the dress after... After... My heart beat wildly in my chest, a sense of warmth spreading through my veins.

"Easy," said Dean to me as he handed off my coat to Zelda. Her date guided her to the table where the Homecoming committee had a coat check set up. I watched them go—watched the way the heads turned to look at them as they moved—and felt lost. They might have looked young, but there was no question they were out of place here.

And if I was one of them... Out of place again, just in a different way.

Another of the vampire men who'd joined us—Herbert, Dean had called him—leaned over to whisper in Dean's ear. But I caught what he said, despite the thunderous beating of my heart, the way the world around me threatened to skid off-balance.

"He's here."

Calder. He broke away from where Ivy and Orin stood, dashed across the dance floor, startling couples along the way, and headed straight for the hallway that led down to the locker rooms.

A teacher—one of the gym coaches, I thought—put down his glass of punch to follow, shouting after him, probably warning Calder that the dark hallways were off-limits during the dance.

Dean straightened his shoulders and then fiddled with the cuffs of his sleeves, even as he slid his arm through mine. "He's alone?" he asked casually.

Herbert nodded toward the dance floor. "She's here."

"But she's with the bloom," said Dean, unconcerned. "That likely means she won't be champion. Leave her be. The merfolk's days are numbered." He smiled down at me, and a shade of something like fire jolted through me, waging war against the dizziness, the disorientation, that wracked my bones.

Giving a curt bob of his head, Herbert joined his date—Mary Ellen—and knelt toward her ear. Zelda and her date—Leopold, I thought—joined them, and they all conferred.

About what, I didn't know.

What were we here for again?

"Do you need to sit?" asked Dean, guiding me toward the bleachers. "You look pale."

I giggled at that—this from the palest man I'd ever encountered—and let myself be guided on somewhat wobbly feet. I stared down at my feet and found them slipped into a bright red pair of high heels. I never wore high heels. I couldn't walk down the block in them, let alone dance in them.

I leaned against Dean once we sat, his fingers twirling a lock of my hair as he looked out over the dance floor. The stares were dying off now, the curiosity satisfied, the crowd of teens more concerned with things other than the super handsome pale guy and his bizarre choice of girlfriend.

"Music certainly has evolved since my time," said Dean, his voice low, his body stiff as he turned his head this way and that.

Squeezing his arm, I chuckled, still feeling the warmth of that tingling sensation in my throat.

"You sound like an old man," I said.

He shrugged. "Maybe it's just my old man ears, but I haven't been able to listen to any of the hottest tunes since the fifties."

I couldn't have heard that right. "Are you kidding me? What about The Beatles? The Rolling Stones? David Bowie?"

"Now *you* sound like an old person."

Sniggering, I ran a finger over his cuff. "I'm not saying they're my favorite musicians or anything, but I just can't believe you dismissed even the likes of them."

Dean gestured to the dance floor. "So you like this modern stuff? This... electric beat?"

"I don't know. This sounds like something from the '80s. That's a lifetime ago."

Dean shook his head. "How fast time flies." He tensed beneath my touch.

In the heat of the quiet moment between Dean and me, I hadn't noticed who was approaching.

Ivy stood in front of us, her arm through Orin's. Orin gave me a shrug and a nod, like he wasn't at all bothered.

"Ember!" Ivy bent over to snap fingers in front of my face. I shook my head, trying to get away from the annoying click of her fingers, but finding my reactions slow.

"What have you done to her?" barked Ivy. Her attention was turned to Dean.

Dean looked straight at Orin, not Ivy. "I didn't do anything," he said.

"That's clearly a lie," said Ivy, removing her arm from Orin's and clenching her hands into fists.

"I'm fine," I said, though the words were slow to come out. My throat became scratchy at that moment, and the boiling anger at this girl in front of me roared up to call to me, to remind me of the red deliciousness that coursed through her veins.

She grabbed me by the shoulders, shaking me, and Dean moved to jump up, but Orin slapped a hand out to stop him. "Where are Devam and Journey?" asked Ivy.

Those names... Those names meant something to me.

People standing nearby were staring at us again, their movements slowing down, along with the inner echo in my ears.

"I..." My right hand began to burn, my left chilled like ice.

The taste of blood in my throat. On my tongue, on my... I ran my tongue over my incisors and found them to be normal, but as Ivy kept shaking me, they grew in an instant, piercing my tongue.

I cried out and bent forward, bringing a palm to my mouth.

"I have to insist you stop that," said Dean, and Orin let him slide in between Ivy and me, pushing Ivy backward.

Only everything grew clearer then with the throbbing of my tongue, the tang of my own blood on my taste buds. I remembered then—my teeth sinking into Journey's shoulder, the taste of blood in my throat. Minnie laughing and having Devam escorted away.

I felt sick.

Dean moved to wrap an arm around my shoulder and I shoved back at him, removing the appendage from my mouth to find the palm dripping with blood.

That hand began to glow. "Where is she?" I hissed. "Where's Journey? What have you done with her and Devam?"

Dean stood straighter and looked over his shoulder at Orin. Orin shrugged as the other vampires approached, putting themselves between us and the crowd forming. Ivy looked left and right, her nostrils flaring as her jaw muscles clenched.

Leaning in, Dean grabbed me by both shoulders. "Ember, calm yourself," he said. "We've as good as won."

I slapped the hand across my mouth again, the fire practically searing my lips. "Where are they?" I mumbled, but I kept picturing my teeth pierced into Journey's flesh.

Into my best friend's shoulder.

Orin was saying something, waving his arms and getting the

crowd to push back, to stop hovering, though heads kept turning in our direction.

Dean went on his knees before me, gently taking my hand from my lips and putting it between his. "Ember, my champion, my princess. They are fine. We didn't do anything to them that..." He went silent, his lips thin as he lowered my hand.

My hand cooled. "But I—"

He looked over his shoulder and nodded toward Herbert. I noticed Leopold and Mary Ellen were missing. "She will recover," Dean said.

"Then why aren't they here?" My head throbbed and my throat ached.

"My aunt thought it best they remain at my home for the evening," he said.

A loud scoff drew my attention back to Ivy. Dean turned to face her, looking straight at her for the first time all evening. His fingers went lightly to his throat then, massaging his skin for a moment. "Don't flip your wig. They are fine. I assure you. My aunt is attending to Miss Slowe and if she and Mr. Kapoor decline our offer, then they'll be sent on their way so long as they keep their word to keep their traps shut."

"What offer?" both Ivy and I said at once.

Dean looked back at me. "The offer we extend to all our servants," he said.

"To become...?" My mouth was so dry. "No," I said. "No! Dean, I didn't want this! I—I want to help your people, but that doesn't mean—"

Dean rested his cheek against my palm. "If we are meant to thrive, sweet Ember, then that means we shall *thrive*. We need to reproduce. We don't have our foes' ability to breed in quite the same way."

"*No!*" I said, trying to stand. I was weak on my legs and Dean swooped in to steady me. "Not Journey!"

"If not her, then *someone*," said Ivy. Zelda and Herbert tensed, but Dean held up a finger and sent them a stern look, ready to stop them. Ivy seemed wary but stood her ground. "You're siding with these *monsters*," she hissed, "and that will lead to more people becoming like them."

"Shut your trap, water whore," said Herbert then. "You don't know nothing about it."

Ever so slightly, Dean shook his head at him and Ivy sent a cold stare in his direction.

"We're not monsters," said Dean quietly. "The merfolk are. If you only knew—"

"Knew what?" demanded Ivy. "I know they're at least living creatures, not some freaks of nature who rose from the dead."

Dean's lips went tight again and he looked to Herbert and Zelda, speaking at them, even as he continued his conversation with Ivy. "So have you made your choice? You'll fight for them?"

"No!" snapped Ivy, launching forward to grab my arm. She started tugging and I tumbled against her, though Dean moved to wrap his arms around me. "But if she refuses to fight for *you*, it's just back to a stalemate, isn't it? Neither of you has to perish." She pulled harder. "So leave us out of it."

"Miss Shepherd," said Dean, "you need to get your mitts off her and *listen* to me, listen to what we have to say—"

A loud clicking sound erupted overhead. The vampires' heads snapped up and Orin looked around cautiously, straining to hear.

Ivy used the distraction to tug harder on me, and I tumbled forward, free of Dean's grip.

A fire alarm went off and the crowd of teens looked shell-shocked, some still dancing, though slowly, others looking around.

"All right!" shouted one of the teachers from the corner of the room. "Please exit in an orderly fashion to the parking lot—"

Before she could finish, the sprinklers turned on, sending showers everywhere down on the proceedings.

People shouted and laughed and started stampeding for the door.

The DJ's equipment sparked and sputtered, flames shooting up from the stage, causing people to scream and rush forward faster toward the exit, even if the flames were quickly vanquished.

Then, everything stopped, a spark halfway to the ceiling, a crowd of people frozen on their way to the door.

Dean swooped in beside me, his hair soaked, his tuxedo wet, his flesh almost smoking at spots. What on Earth...? "It's an attack by the merprince," he said. "We need to get you out of here."

My head swished back and forth. "No." My gaze flicked to Ivy, who stood frozen beside me, squinting, an arm over her head in a vain attempt to stave off the water.

What she didn't realize was that if neither of us chose a side, the stalemate might continue, but...

The war would never end. And vampires and merfolk alike would choose new champions by any means they knew how.

If there was a shot at ending this without much conflict...

"I go with you," I said, straightening my back. "I'm your champion."

Dean peeled Ivy's fingers off of my bare arm, a grin forming on his lips. "Is that a promise?" he asked.

I wrapped my arms around him. "It is. On one condition."

"Anything." If looks could melt...

"We leave my loved ones out of this."

Dean nodded. "Done. We'll get your friends out of the manor, even if Minnie's worked her whiles."

Just as well. I was positive neither Journey nor Devam would have told Minnie to sign them up for the vampire lifestyle after one mess of a dinner.

"How do we do this?" I asked.

Dean let go of my back with one hand to rest his fingers above my breast. "You feel it in your heart," he said. "Your determination, your fealty."

I nodded, summoning both, dropping my right hand from his back then as it burned with fire—literally erupting into a red glow.

Chuckling, Dean moved his face closer to mine. "And then we seal it with a kiss."

I kissed him then, and though I had to keep my fiery hand away from his body, he more than made up for it, pulling me tight against him, the tip of his tongue moving between my lips, running over the incisors that hadn't yet vanished. He didn't spill blood into my mouth, but something sweeter, something intoxicating. I pushed my own tongue between his lips and his fangs punctured it lightly, gently, taking my blood down his throat.

I pushed into the kiss, well aware that though the world was frozen around us, we would never have enough time for this, to feel his essence and mine as one, even if the world never reset for all of eternity.

CHAPTER THIRTY-TWO

IVY

One second there were images flowing through my mind—Ember filled with hunger for some server in a crisp suit, Journey stepping between them, Ember's teeth sinking into her flesh—and then my fingers curled in on themselves, my hand no longer gripping Ember's bare arm.

Vampires no longer anywhere in sight.

I blinked through the drops of water clinging to my eyelashes from the sprinklers overhead.

That made twice in a little over a week I'd been drenched by overhead sprinklers, something I never would have imagined would have happened once, let alone twice, in my life. That was certainly one thing. My life before all this had been so much drier.

"You're not so out of the game after all, are ya, mate?" Orin shuffled next to me, the last other soul still at my side, the shrieking of the other students dying out as they poured through the doors to the parking lot and away from all this.

About to ask what he meant, I stared at my cold right hand instead. It sent a chill down to my bones. And it was deep, dazzling blue.

"You used the telepathy, too," he said, digging his hands into his pockets and jutting his chin toward me. He looked none the worse for wear for being absolutely soaked.

"Kids! Let's go!"

I whipped my head around to see one of the teachers near the exit to the parking lot, gesturing wildly for us to follow her. Mrs. Marton. She was shielding her eyes with her arm and I wondered if she could make us out clearly, if she noticed the unnatural hue of my hand.

Just then, the door leading back to the locker rooms slowly slammed shut.

I turned to Orin.

"It's your choice," he said. "I'm just here to give you another option."

"*Kids*! Hey! Come on!"

I clenched my fist and bolted for the locker room hallway.

Orin fell in step behind me, pulling the hefty door shut after we passed through. In the darkened hallway, the fire alarm echoed even louder, the red and white flashes from the end of the hall dizzying, lending a sense of urgency to my task, though I had no doubt this wasn't a normal fire I had to flee.

A loud clang echoed behind me and I turned to find Orin dragging a metal chair leg through the double handles of the door to the gym. He grinned, the water dripping off the ends of a curl that hung over his face. "Figured you don't want the chaperone's company."

I shook my head. I prayed Mrs. Marton hadn't recognized me. I'd barely recognized her through all that water and I wasn't exactly a standout student.

I took a step down the hall, the ice in my fist surprisingly refreshing, my hand neither numb nor bothered by the dampness even as a chill set in to the rest of my bones.

Orin slid in beside me. "So what did you see?"

"Huh?" My focus was on the doors on either side of the hall up ahead, straining for sounds.

"When you used telepathy on your sister."

Step-sister. "She hurt her friend," I said. It was what I'd been searching for—confirmation of what had happened to Journey. I hadn't had time to see the fate of Devam, but I supposed it had to have been something similar. It had only been for a moment, and I was half-concerned with just dragging her out of there and then she'd been gone.

"She used the vamp time cheat?" I asked.

Orin chuckled. "Dean did, but yeah. I don't know if I'd call it a *cheat*, but—"

"It offers way more advantage than skin-to-skin fish snooping," I said. Before Orin could retort, I flung my left arm out to stop him.

Sounds echoed beyond the alarms, beyond the cascade of water. Beyond the rattling of the door and the pounding from behind us.

Shouts and a splash.

The pool. Of course.

I bolted down the hall until I reached the pool door, but it wouldn't budge. Locked.

I started pounding on the door. "Calder! Ember!"

I didn't know if Ember was past saving or not, but there was no way I wouldn't try.

Slamming my hand harder against the wooden surface, I let out a grunt and kicked at the door, sending water droplets flying everywhere. "Let me in!"

"Might he be of assistance?" Orin pointed to the wall across the way, where the gym teacher I'd seen chase after Calder—the same one who'd sent us to the office for playing around in the pool the other week—lay slumped on the ground.

My palm went to my mouth and I jumped, my lips not expecting the icy cold. "Is he alive?" I scrambled to his side. His head lolled backward at my touch and I yelped.

Orin slid in beside me, a sour look on his face. He ran his fingers over the man's neck and his fingers flinched to find two nail-head-sized wounds. "He has a pulse," he said, shaking his head. "Good thing, too, because direct civilian casualties in the midst of the conflict is breaking at least a half dozen treaty terms."

"Only that many?" I barked. The "direct casualty" line niggled at the back of my mind, but I shoved it down. "We need to get him out of here."

Orin cocked his head. "Your friend needs you first."

My lips pinched. *Friend?* I assumed he meant Calder, but... "The conflict is as good as over," I said. "He's outnumbered, and I..."

"*You* have the power to even the score," said Orin. "It's supposed to be you against the champion of blood, not all the vampires ganging up on one merprince."

"Then why aren't you doing something?" I asked. "You're the referee, aren't you? Get in there and lay out some ground rules or something."

I reached for the key ring at the gym teacher's hip pocket, flipping through the keys, hoping to find one that rang a bell, that reminded me of the one Calder had had made for himself. "How did the vampires get in there?" I asked.

"Maybe Calder left it unlocked for them to find him." He nodded toward the door. "It *is* a pool, right?"

"And then the vampires thought to lock it behind them?"

"Probably." He shrugged. "They didn't want *you* to join them, official champion or no."

I had no idea which key I needed, so I stopped my nervous hands from fumbling and went straight to the lock, trying to jam the first one I found in. It wouldn't go in more than partway.

Orin flinched.

"What?" I asked, exasperated. I tried another key and felt my hopes soar when it seemed to go in, but it jammed before I could even try turning it.

"They keep pausing time." He shivered. "It tickles."

Shaking my head, I went for the next key. I hadn't felt a thing, but I'd take his word for it.

Calder was a dead man walking—or swimming—at this point.

My blood ran cold. "Will they kill him?" I asked, fumbling for yet another key.

Orin shrugged, a drop from the sprinkler overhead flinging off his shoulder. "If they want to deal with my punishment, I suppose it's not entirely out of the realm of possibility."

I wasn't in the mood to figure out all the details just then—if they expected the champions to die instead or if either side would find the "punishment" worthwhile to just put an end to the heir of their enemies. A key I'd tried slid in at last and I turned the bolt, ripping the door open.

The overhead lights were off, though there was a glowing light coming from the bottom of the pool. The vampires spread out around all four sides of the water, glaring down at a sole figure within. *Calder*.

"Hey!" I shouted, my nostrils filling with a burnt, sour scent—and I noticed in the corner a stack of soggy gym jerseys, the tiniest bit of smoke sizzling from the clothes as water streamed down from above. There were holes in them edged in brown. Someone—Calder, no doubt—had set them aflame.

Why?

"Fire set the sprinklers off, I'd wager," said Orin, sliding in beside me.

But I had more pressing things to worry about. Nearest to me, Ember stood hand-in-hand with Dean. She looked proud, pale, confident—not unsteady on her feet and wary like she'd been in the gym.

Their eyes were drawn to me.

Ember spoke first. "Stay out of this," she hissed, and when her lips pulled back, there were sharp edges protruding from two of her upper teeth. "You said it yourself—if you don't decide to become the champion, you don't have to get hurt."

Scoffing, I crossed one foot in front of the other, edging carefully toward the water's edge. "The same goes for you."

"She's already a part of this." Dean pulled Ember to his chest roughly, every inch the black-and-white-movie romantic lead, and Ember fell into it, her head lolling, delight on her face, where I'd be about ready to slap a mofo in her position.

But something felt off. There wasn't even a hint of hesitance in her expression, not an ounce of hope.

Orin whistled audibly beside me. "She's become the champion."

"*What*—?" But before I could ask more, a loud crash spurred me to spin around. "The door!" I shouted to Orin, tossing the key ring at him.

Firefighters and/or teachers had fought their way into the hall by now.

Raising his eyebrows, Orin made his way to bolt the door behind us, the keys actually proving superfluous to the task at hand. I couldn't think straight. My blood ran cold from top to bottom, accumulating in the pulsating blue glow of my right hand. The bolt on the door wouldn't hold them for long—but I was less afraid of what that might mean for a bunch of teens and supposed-teens and more afraid of what that might have meant for the unsuspecting humans making their way in.

The shadowy figures seemed to be *steaming* a little, mist rising up around their forms as water kept falling from the sprinklers overhead. Half a dozen bright blue eyes sparkled out from around the pool—and I realized that included Ember's eyes among them.

"How...?" I shook my head. Right now, that didn't matter.

"Ivy!" called Calder. A splash drew my attention. The light-blue fins reached up out of the water and then descended down again.

So that was his solution? Just dive in and hide, surrounded by enemies? And what... wait them out? I bet the vampires could be patient. And call in reinforcements. And dine on every passerby that made their way in here.

And maybe grow a spine and just jump into the water. They were already plenty wet.

"Leave," said Dean to me, and it was clear from his tone that he wouldn't say it again.

I looked at Orin, but he simply leaned against the wall. He dug his glasses out of his front pocket and wiped them with the bottom of his sopping-wet dress shirt, blowing on them.

The sprinklers overhead stopped, and the resounding echo of the fire alarm died out. The pounding on the door continued, though, muffled cries to open up or at least get out of the way.

Dean and Ember shook their heads like dogs and their glam, undead entourage shook out limbs to get the sopping wetness off. The steam seemed to dissipate.

There was a fire exit across the way. I could make for it, probably get away unspotted. This could be the end of my involvement entirely.

I'd just have to get used to having a vampire for a step-sister and having some blood on my hands.

And knowing that I'd failed Calder. Calder, who'd been a part of this from the start, but who'd tried to give me space. Even though the survival of his people depended on him persuading me this was all worthwhile.

"Crap," I said, clenching my fists and sprinting toward the fire exit door. I could feel Dean and the others watch me go, heard the slight snort of laughter, the splash of water from the pool as Calder resurfaced...

And then, just as I skirted the edge of the pool, I jumped in sideways, diving in without so much as pivoting so as not to set the vampires on their haunches.

"No!" shouted Dean. Whatever else he or the others said died out into mumbles as I felt strong, muscled arms wrap around me and I sunk into the water.

My eyelids snapped open and I felt my body flood with panic at the thought of being dragged down here, not even having taken a deep breath to prepare myself.

Calder let go of my side and cradled my cheek, gently drawing my face to his. His mouth opened and I heard a sound, but I couldn't make it out.

He spoke again and it snapped in my brain at that moment— *water*. Think of water. Embrace the water. Think of... Calder.

That should have proven easy, considering the position I was in.

With a rush of icy cold, my legs squeezed together and my tights and panties ripped, my boots sinking to the bottom of the pool, as my legs merged into my own, sparkling mermaid tail. My dress remained on top in tact—though soaked into a heavy, sopping mess—and I spun back from Calder, admiring my look as a mermaid dolled up for the Homecoming dance.

Calder smiled, though the grin died quickly on his lips. He swam next to me as echoing booms resounded overhead. I looked up to see the sky above the water aglow with red.

"Ivy," said Calder—clearly to my ears this time. He grabbed my hand.

I locked eyes with him.

"Thank you," he said.

I nodded. It hadn't been for just him, but...

My heart raced. I didn't know what was happening above us, above the safety of the waters, but just for this moment, I could revel in the safety of these shallow depths.

Maneuvering out of his grip and taking both sides of his face in my palms, I leaned forward, guiding his lips toward mine.

He pulled back, bringing a finger up between his lips and mine. "You have to be sure."

Taken aback, I cocked my head, not letting him go. "It's just a kiss," I said. The words felt foreign on my tongue, the water massaging every syllable into a singsong pattern.

He shook his head. "Not with me. Not right now." He stared intently at me. "Kiss me now and we'll seal the pact. You'll become the champion of water."

The sounds continued to echo dully overhead. As comfortable as this was, I couldn't stay hidden here forever. We were trapped, like rats in a cage. It was only a matter of time.

The water came to life, moving on its own, bubbles shooting to the surface.

Clearly panicked, Calder pulled my hands down and looked around—and then up at the red surface glow. "They're trying to heat the water," he said. "Use Ember's fire to scald us, get us out of here."

I'd deal with that in a moment. I'd deal with how that made me feel—going up against my step-sister, risking my life for people I barely knew—in the moment after.

Right then, I needed his lips on mine.

Clutching his face again, I pulled him to me—quickly this time, harshly, whatever I needed to do to get it done. My lips moved forward to meet his and it was like a refreshing rain in the tropics, a blast of air conditioning after a jog on a sweltering hot day. Iciness curled my fins and imbued my fingertips. The warmth of the water no longer bothered me.

And I could have kissed him forever—literally, I must have been breathing through magical gills because I didn't need to come up for air—but there was work to be done.

I pulled back and took note of the awe on Calder's face as he stared at me, followed by the twitch of his Adam's apple and the look of guilt that washed over him as he looked away. "Ivy, I—"

But we didn't have time to talk about it. I propelled myself backward, lifting my hand radiating dark blue light above my head. Then I shot upward, breaking the surface. My icy power radiated outward, meeting hot water with cold, sending steam into the air all around me. I stared out at the bright blue eyes boring down on me, finding the only pair that mattered right then.

Ember stood from where she'd crouched at the edge of the pool, removing her fire-red hand from beneath the water.

I hurled my blue hand back and sent a blast of icy energy her way.

CHAPTER THIRTY-THREE

EMBER

I'd just wanted to get them out of the water—before the people pounding on the door made their way in here. Herbert and Mary Ellen were covering the door, stacking chairs from a pile beside the bleachers in front of it like magic, seemingly zipping across the room and back again as Orin just watched with amusement.

"Ember, keep it up!" said Dean, ripping my focus back to the task at hand.

Heat them up. Boil them out. And then... And then...

Ivy could still be saved, right? But what about Calder?

"If he admits defeat, it's over," Dean had whispered into my ear after Ivy had dove—or fallen?—into the pool. "If he doesn't make her his champion, we'll win by default."

So there was a way to end this without bloodshed. They just needed to get out of the water. Vampires, apparently, couldn't swim. No time pause would help with that.

Still, the more I forced the heat to flourish in my hand, the more it seemed to burn—searingly. Painfully. Steam floated out from the pool's surface. The heat had never done that before.

"It's the water," said Dean, leaning down beside me. He wrapped an arm around my back. "When you're in vampire form, you won't like it." He shook out his other arm, sending droplets out over the water. "But you'll be stronger this way," he added. "Stay in this form. You can do it."

"Dean!" someone shouted. Zelda, I thought. "They're breaking though. Should we—?"

Dean's facial muscles tensed and he jumped to his feet. "No," he started, zipping across the room toward her with a time pause he didn't pull me into.

I forced heat into my hand harder and then, just as I felt the heat soar, as the bubbles boiled over, breaking the surface of the water, something shot up and outward. Cold as ice, like a brain freeze that started at my fingertips and worked its way up to my gray matter.

Ivy. Soaring up above the middle of the pool on a platform of ice.

"Ivy...?" I asked, falling backward onto my butt as I shook my numb hand.

"She's sealed her fate!" said someone—Leopold, I supposed.

Ivy drew her raised hand backward and flung it forward, a blast of blue headed my way.

Even from here, I could see the anger on her face. She was livid. Changed.

"Watch out!"

Before I could even think to react, the ball of light went still, the sounds of pounding, of voices, of water splashing—all silent. Dean swooped in front of me and I realized he'd done what I hadn't thought to do in the heat of the moment: a time pause. He scooped me into his arms, launching to his feet and carrying me off to the side of the bleachers like a princess in distress.

His clothes a soggy mess, his hair damp and clinging to his forehead, he looked ragged—the remaining drops from the sprinkler shower looking for all the world like sweat. I doubted he sweated anymore. My fingers were drawn to his brow, where I pushed aside a lock of dark hair.

Panic clouded his bright blue eyes. I'd never seen that emotion on his face before.

He gently put my feet back on the ground and took my hand

from his brow, bringing it to his lips, laying a gentle kiss on my knuckles. "She's gone," he said quietly as he pulled his lips away. "Ember, if she's chosen to be the champion of water—"

I shook my head. "I know."

It was over. The war was on.

Somehow, I... would have to make my step-sister surrender.

He stumbled a little, catching himself on the wall. "I can't hold it," he said. "Too much water." He shook his head. "I'm too wet... Tired..."

I moved in under his arm, keeping him from slumping down the wall. The silence popped, and the chaos resumed. The blue blast went right through where I'd been standing and into the pile of chairs in front of the door. Herbert and Mary Ellen jumped back, but they both slumped somewhat, the sprinkler water obviously catching up with them as well. Shouts resounded from behind the door as the pounding stopped and the door was iced shut, a coating of frozen water splashed like a snowball across the door frame. I thought I heard the word "explosives." The blast hitting the door had sounded like one. They'd call in the bomb squad at this rate.

My gaze flew across the room to Orin, who'd seated himself atop one of the bleachers for some reason, his hands clasped between his legs as he leaned forward watching us, for all the world an eager spectator about to see some goal scored.

Straightening my back, I stepped away from the wall to let Ivy find me. *She could have killed me if I hadn't moved.* "I'm here!"

Ivy spun, the water around her spilling over with steam as ice began to form along the hot water. That chicken Calder popped up a little behind her, making his "champion" position herself between him and the threat.

I could have gone over there and slapped him. Something like rage bubbled up from inside me, radiating outward. Without even thinking, I flung my own right hand over my head, the heat gathering at my fingertips, and shot the fireball out at them.

As they flinched—Ivy moving to drag Calder out of the way—I ran forward, toward the pool, the "no running" warning painted on the wall at my side an irony I quickly dismissed—and just as I reached the edge and Ivy turned around, one arm around Calder, the other poised to strike at me with the icy blue glow, I went to pause time.

"Ember!" called out Dean weakly behind me. "Ember, you're not ready—"

But if he was referring to me not being ready for an assault via time pause, it was too late. The sight of Ivy's hand glowing brighter, the fizzle of my fireball as it hit the thin sheet of ice with which she'd coated the pool surface, kicked my instinct into action.

Time froze, the sudden stillness of the steam from the ice evaporating the first sensation to hit me.

I looked around. Orin leaned forward slightly more, clearly intrigued, one elbow on his knee, his fist holding his chin up. Mary Ellen and Herbert slunk over near the iced door, half-standing, trying to make their way to me. Zelda and Leopold were near the fire exit door, Zelda reaching for the handle and the door slightly open a crack. Had the firefighters and officials decided to bust through that door? Dean was halfway to me, his head slightly turned toward the commotion going on at the fire exit, his trajectory clearly aimed toward me, the look of exhaustion on his face overwritten by determination.

And then there was Ivy, a snarl on her lips as she moved to ready her ice ball.

And Calder, somehow closer to me than I remembered, his hand reaching up from out of the water—just inches from grabbing hold of my bare ankle.

I screamed into the silence, startled at the sight of him there— how? When?

But then I lost control of the time pause, and just as Dean's voice burst back into the air—"Stand back!"—I felt the cool grip around my ankles and the tug into the water.

The loss of balance struck me first, then the feel of chilled water on my feet. The tug of his grip on my ankle as he threatened to take me lower.

And then I realized my upper body—my head—was about to slam into the concrete edge of the pool.

I closed my eyes, everything I would regret flashing through my mind, and I felt the hold on my leg slip somewhat. The ice ball Ivy had summoned flung out above me just as a pair of strong arms wrapped under my arms, tight across my back.

My eyes opened. Dean's gaze bore through me. He didn't seem composed, mature. He looked lost, scared.

And it was then that the ice ball struck him on the temple.

"Dean!" I screamed, but he lost his balance and tumbled forward, both of us hitting the water, my body just barely clear of the concrete's edge.

The grip on my ankle vanished, but it didn't matter. With Dean's arms around me, we were sinking, falling to the bottom of the pool's deep end like iron weights.

Dean was unconscious, and when I tried to speak his name, my voice choked on the icy, stinging waters around me. My eyeballs burned with the chlorine, but I fought to keep them open.

A halo of blood spread out above Dean's head, floating upward. It wasn't just from the ice ball, though—his pale skin seemed to go even paler, even bluer at the pressure of the water, and a fine red mist spread out from his entire body, like a robe.

No, I thought, certain it was all at an end.

His grip went loose, but instead of taking advantage of that and swimming back up to the surface, I surged forward, wrapping my own arms tightly around him, squeezing my eyelids shut.

I didn't know how much time passed before I felt two sets of hands on me, tugging me upward. I squeezed Dean harder, but the hands ripped my arms away with force.

The word "no" choked on my water-filled throat.

And then I passed out.

EPILOGUE
IVY

One of the most embarrassing things about having more than two parents is the way they hover over you in an ER room, squeezing in between cabinets and models of the insides of a human body, and knocking into machines meant to measure my pulse. For the second time in ten minutes, Dad jostled my IV, causing the machine to beep, and he jumped, tripping over a sleepy Autumn and practically falling into her lap.

"Ow," said Autumn, lifting her foot out of her shoe to rub her toes.

"Sorry, sport," said Dad, rubbing her hair.

"Okay, guys..." I shut my eyes tight as the beep, beep, beep began to bore its way into my throbbing skull. "I'm okay. You don't need to hover. I didn't even need to get checked out." Sighing, I opened one eye and then the other to find Calder squeezed practically against the doorway and staring at the floor, his arms crossed tight. He was in a pair of sweats the firefighters had given him in the school parking lot after seeing his pants missing—and probably getting a very wrong idea considering we were both dragging Ember out. My own mushy wet dress was over in the garbage after I'd swapped it for a hospital gown. "It's Ember you should be worried about."

Noelle exchanged a look with Dad, and Mom averted her gaze

noticeably, probably at a loss as to what to do, so she settled for squeezing Autumn to her side. Autumn looked annoyed but let it happen.

"She's still unconscious," said Noelle quietly. "I'll go back. I just wanted to be sure... you're okay."

"I am," I said, clamping my lips shut at the knock at the door and the nurse's entry. She made a joke about the pesky machine being a diva calling for attention and then turned around, looking out over the group huddled around my bed.

"Immediate family only," she said. "Sorry, but we need some space in here." Her eyes landed on Calder specifically.

He nodded and I opened my mouth to say something, but Dad clamped a hand down on my shoulder, sending me a silent look. As if he knew Calder was somehow partially responsible for this mess. Like he could have possibly known. I wondered what any police or EMT technicians had told him.

Calder left with the nurse and I felt my throat constrict. Something tugged at me as he disappeared around the corner, like he'd carved a piece of my heart out and taken it along in his pocket.

I laughed then unexpectedly. I'd never have pictured myself understanding what those kinds of poetic hyperboles meant. But I felt it now and I...

"What's so funny?" asked Mom, all sense of humor totally lost on her.

I shook my head, ignoring the pounding. "Nothing," I said. "Just... Wow. What a dance."

"Your friends were in the waiting room," said Dad. "But I sent them home. They were all soaked, too, and I thought there was no sense in them catching pneumonia. But you're supposed to text them you're okay."

Letting out a heavy breath, I glanced at the trash can that carried my sopping dress. "I left my phone somewhere at the gym."

"Of course," said Dad. He dug into his pocket and brought out his. "You can use mine."

I shook my head. Unless I could use those subconscious-mind-reading powers on myself, I wasn't about to pull their numbers out of thin air. Updates would have to wait.

Noelle gripped the edge of my bed tightly, her knuckles turning an alarmingly vampire-like shade of white. "Ivy, Ember's unconscious, but you can tell me—what happened?" Her voice became strained on the last word, anger furrowing her brow.

Dad shot her a look, but she shot him one right back.

My fingers were still cold even as I took them out from underneath the warmed blanket and rested them on my dad's arm. Let her be mad. He had no idea of the depths to which I deserved it.

"We fell during the stampede out," I said, remembering what Calder and I had quickly thought to say to excuse it all.

Noelle glared, a vein pulsing on her forehead. "The policeman in the waiting room waiting to speak more with that *boy*"—she practically spat over her shoulder at the door through which Calder had exited—"said that you were found coming out of the pool, where an *explosion* had occurred, fighting with some other teenagers and that boy was *missing his pants* as you dragged *my* unconscious daughter—"

"Noelle, that's enough," barked Dad.

Noelle bit her bottom lip.

"It wasn't like that," I said. "Calder really did just lose his pants during the chaos. They were ripped and soaked and soot-filled—"

"Even his underpants?" asked Noelle, whipping on me.

Remind me never to get on her bad side again. My mouth twisting grimly, I wondered if it was really all over—if there was no more danger of me getting on her bad side.

"He didn't... do anything like that," I said, conviction pouring into my voice. "She fell into the pool and we dragged her out. That was all."

Noelle's flailing arm slammed into the anatomy model behind her as she gestured wildly. She ignored the crashing sound it made as it tumbled into pre-designed pieces under my bed. "Then why were those other teens attacking you?"

"They weren't teens," I spat. "They're older... They crashed the party with Ember and... Dean."

Noelle's face pinched. "And where is Dean, by the way? And Journey, for that matter? Her mom is worried sick—"

"Check Dean's house," I said. Dad slipped his phone into his pocket and grabbed hold of my hand. "I heard she and Devam stayed behind there instead of going to the dance."

Noelle looked at me quizzically but shook her head as her phone buzzed in her purse. She fished it out and her face soured. "Tom landed at the airport." She exchanged a look with Dad, and he just nodded.

He leaned over to whisper into my ear. "Ember's dad."

Wow. It must have been serious for him to consider coming. Dad had told me he saw Ember all of once a year.

"I need to call Lacey," Noelle said, and it took me a moment to deduce that was Journey's mother. She paused in her typing and stared down at me. "We are *not* done talking about this, young lady." She exchanged a look with my mom and dad, as if daring either to challenge her on that. No one spoke, so she moved toward the door.

"I'll be there in a minute," said Dad, but Noelle didn't respond.

The door shut and I was left with just the original members of my family. No step-family. No supernatural pseudo-boyfriends. Just Mom, Dad, Autumn, and me.

But it was just an illusion. Things could never go back to how they used to be.

"Your date wouldn't go home," said Dad and he exchanged a questioning look with Mom, who just nodded. Autumn was practically asleep against her side.

Puzzled, I considered that we'd just seen Calder a minute ago, so obviously he hadn't gone home—

Oh, Orin.

Dad looked down at me, resolved. "I insisted he call his parents, but then he told me something very interesting—he lived alone. And he owns the bookstore you work at."

I shrugged.

"You didn't tell us you were bringing an *adult* to the dance—" said Mom.

"He's just a friend," I said, all thoughts of how cute he was—if aggravating—somehow buried now deep down inside me.

"Sport, I don't *care* if you think he's just a friend, an adult has no business going to a dance with you—"

"I'm almost eighteen."

"But you're *not*." Dad squeezed my hand. "And just because *you* claim you're not interested in him doesn't mean *he's* not interested in you."

I removed my hand from Dad's, feeling the loss of warmth along with it. "It's not like that." I stared at the back of the door.

Dad sighed and Mom clucked her tongue. "We'll discuss this later."

Apparently, I was about to discuss everything under the sun later. Great.

A moment later, there was a knock on the door and the ER doctor walked in, a small laptop in hand. "Everything looks good for Ivy," he said.

Dad's face tensed. "What about Ember? My other daughter?"

The doctor stared down at him and nodded, striking the keyboard. "She's stable. We're confident it's just a mild shock—no signs of concussion. We think she'll wake soon."

Mom and Dad both let out a sigh of relief. I clutched the warm blanket, feeling the iciness of my palm war against the heat, letting go when I saw the sizzle of steam.

A little squeak made me notice that one of Autumn's eyes was opened, her attention drawn to the sight of my hand.

A chill ran through me.

"For Ivy," continued the doctor, oblivious, "just rest and plenty of fluids. I'll have the nurse send you home with care for bruises, but it should be pretty straightforward. If there are problems, follow through with her primary care physician. And if there's any sign of fever or weakness, make a trip back here." Mom and Dad nodded, but my mind was drifting. I hadn't wanted to be checked out by a doctor at all. I'd felt fine. Cold and clammy and bruised, but fine. "Let me work on getting you discharged."

He left and Mom and Dad started talking to one another in

hushed voices. Autumn stared at me wide-eyed now, but I just looked away.

Mom stood. "You're coming home with me," she said, all pretense of me getting to stay at Dad's for an odd Saturday out the window. "Your father is going to stay with Noelle and Ember and they'll call us at the first sign of news."

Dad helped me sit up, as if I were helpless, when the most I felt was achy. "I'll call you if there's any *bad* news," he said. "I'll text with good. I think you all need your rest." He turned around to give Autumn a hug and a kiss and then leaned down to kiss me on my forehead. "Rest up," he said. "And then we'll discuss the proper consequences for what happened here tonight."

I went silent. As far as he knew, I'd just gotten caught up in the same mess everyone else had and had *saved* Ember, but okay. I supposed there was still the older dance date—older than him, actually, older than dirt, probably, but he had no idea—and the half-naked boy who'd been naked on the wrong half.

A nurse knocked and entered and offered me a sweat suit that would make me look every bit as dorky as Calder. I nodded and Mom and the nurse helped me into it—again, I wasn't an infant, but I wasn't about to argue about it—and then the nurse insisted I get into the wheelchair to leave.

We moved through the somber hallways of the ER, seeming to draw the eyes of everyone. I saw Dad walk into a darkened examination room and I turned to look inside as we passed.

A brightly glowing pair of blue eyes looked out at me.

"Wait!" I said as we made our way through the doors to the waiting room and the patient loading zone.

The nurse stilled and Mom practically ran into her. "Ivy, we don't want to crowd Ember," she said quietly. "Let's go. We'll visit her tomorrow."

The nurse kept pushing, but my throat went dry at the thought. Who was in there with her? Dean? If not him, then... What had happened to him?

Though weakened, two of Dean's vampire puppets had tried to stop us at the fire exit. A vampire man had launched at Calder and tried to wrestle Ember away, but then there'd been a shriek behind us. "The prince!" one of them had called.

In the chaos of the struggle against the guy, Calder had knocked into the fire exit to find police officers and firefighters on the other side. They stormed in to break them up even as Ember had started weighing down on me. Calder had swooped in to keep us both from toppling over and then police officers had ripped him away, calling over EMTs to tend to her.

Then they'd swarmed me and when I'd kept shouting, "She's my sister! My sister!" they'd asked if I'd wanted to ride with her and I'd said 'yes,' but I'd gone drowsy in the back of the ambulance and when we'd arrived and I'd stumbled out to find my dad waiting, he'd insisted I get looked at, even though I'd told him I was fine.

As we kept making our way to the exit, we passed Calder speaking to two police officers quietly in one corner of the waiting room, his arms clutched tightly across his body, his stance one of confidence and calm. His eyes locked with mine briefly and he nodded. A jolt ran through me at his gaze.

"He called us," said Mom as we went through the automatic doors. "That blond boy. Told us you and Ember had been in an accident and were on your way to the ER." She hugged me to her chest as the nurse stopped before the final set of doors. "Oh, sweetie, you don't know how panicked I was—"

"Super panicked," said Autumn glumly. "She shook me awake and wouldn't tell me *anything*." She seemed annoyed more than anything.

"I didn't *know* anything." She stepped back and wiped her face. Then her expression changed, grew more serious. "No," she said to the nurse. "Don't let that boy—that man—near my daughter. I'll go get the car." She stepped through the second set of automatic doors, leaving us in the entryway, a blast of warm air biting through the chill that leaked in from outside.

I turned to find Orin strolling toward me, his hands in his pockets. "It's okay," I said to the nurse after Mom left. "He's my boss."

The nurse's lips pinched. "I'm sorry, honey, but you're a minor, so I have to abide by your guardian's request."

I sighed. Orin was the least of my parents' concern, but they'd gotten snagged on the wrong part of this, as usual.

So much for my bookstore job, but considering I'd completed the ceremony to become the champion of water, I supposed I wouldn't have much need to spend time in neutral territory regardless.

Besides, it had to be over, right? No more need for protection. Dean was... He looked dead. Dead again. Maybe the vampires had taken him or—

"What a night, yeah?" said Orin after the first set of automatic doors opened. He sounded thrilled and he let out a burst of throaty laughter.

"Sir, I'm sorry, but I'll have to ask you to wait in the waiting room until these young ladies have left."

Orin rocked back on his heels, tossing his hair back.

The nurse seemed to flush at his gaze and cleared her throat. "She's a minor, so I have to abide by—"

"You've done your job," said Orin. "Now stay out of it."

The nurse went unnaturally still then, crossing her palms in front of her abdomen and stepping to the wall.

A wave of nausea hit me. Did Orin—did "bloom"—have extra powers too?

Autumn jumped up and down in front of the nurse, waving a hand, but the nurse didn't move. "Whoa! How did you do that?"

"Autumn, that's not funny. Come here." I jumped out of the unnecessary wheelchair to grab her by the shoulders. I glowered at Orin and bobbed my chin toward Autumn. "Why did you do that? In front of—"

"Thought we should talk." He nodded toward the front doors as a car pulled up.

Mom was going to kill me. And maybe him. But I didn't want her to know more on top of it all—

It didn't take long for her to storm back into the room. "I thought I told you to keep him away—"

"Ms. Sheppard, please." Orin stepped forward and grabbed her hand in his. "I'm a friend. I'd appreciate if you treated me like one."

Mom's scrunched-up features seemed to melt and she looked *happy*—happier than I'd seen her in ages. "Of course! Orin!" She leaned forward to hug him and I jumped back, dragging Autumn with me. Autumn was laughing. "Thank you so much for taking care of my daughter," said Mom.

I turned around to try to find Calder, but he was out of sight of the door. Still, I sent silent vibes his way, trying to let him know something was... off. I knew he didn't need anything else arousing suspicions with the police, but...

Orin held a hand out to the nurse. "You're dismissed," he said, and she took the wheelchair and went back inside the hospital.

"Take your younger daughter to the car," he said to Mom, and she stepped forward to grab Autumn's hand. I let her take it, as much to get Autumn out of here as anything else, though I felt sick to watch her go.

Orin chuckled as the automatic door shut behind them. "You don't have to look so scared. I just wanted to talk."

"Okay," I said, clenching my right hand into a fist. "I'm listening."

Orin stroked his chin as he stared down at my hand. "Harming the observer is a war-losing penalty."

"The war is over," I spat.

He shook his head, smirking. "Oh, I'm sorry to say it's just begun."

"But I—" I swallowed. "We got Ember away from him and he sunk to the bottom of the pool."

"And was promptly rescued by fire personnel and then shook off all the damage and dried himself off. He collected himself and came to check on his champion."

My eyes darted around me, looking for signs of his vampire entourage. Surely he hadn't come alone.

"I convinced both families to lay off for the night," he said.

"And just let their princes come here without incident. You're welcome."

He sounded rather sure of himself at that last line.

Something felt off. Too calm. Too collected. "Who damaged the substation that night last week?" I asked. "Calder said it was the bloodsuckers, so they could take advantage of chaos and the darkness—"

"It was me," said Orin, as casually as if telling me I'd forgotten my wallet in the break room.

"Why?"

"Why do you think?" He chortled. "Maybe I'm tired of being referee and all this whinging. Maybe I want this cursed war to *start* so it can finally be over."

"What...? But you... You're supposed to be neutral!"

"I am," said Orin, walking backward. "I don't care which side wins, as long as there's a winner. Soon."

He jutted his chin toward me as the automatic doors to the parking lot opened behind him. "So I'll see you around, all right? If not at the bookstore, then just... around."

His words left me cold and unsteady on my feet. Mom's car waited patiently in front of the doors. I didn't even flinch as the other set of doors opened behind me.

"You okay?"

Calder.

"No," I said, clenching my fist hard. "I don't... I don't think I ever will be."

He swooped me into his arms and planted a kiss on my forehead. "I'm sorry," he said.

"*They* will be," I muttered, my hand going numb as I felt the blazing cold fill my fingers.

An emboldened merman. The daring girl who agreed to be his champion. The upcoming battle that threatens to change everything they believe in.

Ivy Sheppard never wanted the ability to turn into a mermaid—
though her wicked ice powers are nothing to sneeze at. Now her
step-sister is her enemy, the fairy she once trusted may not be the
ally she hoped for, and her new boyfriend wants her to transfer
schools to avoid the vampires taking over Union High. Between
dodging parents' concerns, pretending she can stand to even look
at the step-sister who sided with the bloodsuckers, and still aiming
to end it all without violence, Ivy is in over her head. Unfortu-
nately, these ancient enemies are itching to get the conflict started
and Ivy may have no choice but to become the warrior the merfolk
need her to be.

The second book in the Blood, Bloom, & Water series starts the
war between fangs and fins in earnest as the merfolk plan their
assault to bring down the unnatural undead vampires once and
for all.

Available Now

ABOUT THE AUTHOR

Amy McNulty is an editor and author of books that run the gamut from YA speculative fiction to contemporary romance. A lifelong fiction fanatic, she fangirls over books, anime, manga, comics, movies, games, and TV shows from her home state of Wisconsin. When not editing her clients' novels, she's busy fulfilling her dream by crafting fantastical worlds of her own.

Sign up for Amy's newsletter to receive news and exclusive information about her current and upcoming projects. Get a free YA romantic sci-fi novelette when you do!

LOOK FOR MORE YA SPECULATIVE
FICTION READS FROM SNOWY WINGS
PUBLISHING

DECEPTION SO DEADLY
CLARA KENSIE

Winner of Romance Writers of America's 2015 RITA© Award for Best First Book

RUN. It's all sixteen-year-old Tessa Carson has ever known. Hunted by a telepathic killer, Tessa and her family have fled home after home, hiding behind aliases to survive. Her scars are more than just physical, and as the only one in her family without a psychic ability, she lives a life of secrets, lies, and fear.

After the Carsons flee to a new hideout and take on new identities yet again, Tessa meets confident, carefree Tristan Walker. Their attraction burns fierce, but she runs from him too, knowing their love can never be true when she can't even tell him her real name.

But Tristan has secrets as well—secrets that will either save Tessa, or destroy her. The only way Tessa can save her family—and uncover the real reason they've been hunted all these years—is to forget everything she's learned from a lifetime of running away, and run straight into danger head-on.

Book One in the YA paranormal thriller Deception So series, Deception So Deadly was originally published as the Run to You serial parts 1 – 3, and is the winner of the prestigious RITA© Award for Best First Book.

"A dark, suspenseful, and romantic ride!" - USA Today

"The perfect blend of mystery, romance, paranormal thrills, and danger." - Mundie Moms

"A well-written YA paranormal read, with welcome dashes of thrills and plot twists, Kensie has written a gripping and engaging series that features great family dynamics and the enormity of first love." - RT Book Reviews

"A thrilling story, packed with twists, secrets, and swoon-worthy romance. I couldn't read it fast enough!" -Erica O'Rourke, author of the Torn trilogy (Kensington) and the Dissonance series (S&S BFYR)

PHOENIX DESCENDING
DOROTHY DREYER

Who must she become in order to survive?

Since the outbreak of the phoenix fever in Drothidia, Tori Kagari has already lost one family member to the fatal disease. Now, with the fever threatening to wipe out her entire family, she must go against everything she believes in order to save them—even if that means making a deal with the enemy.

When Tori agrees to join forces with the unscrupulous Khadulians, she must take on a false identity in order to infiltrate the queendom of Avarell and fulfill her part of the bargain, all while under the watchful eye of the unforgiving Queen's Guard. But time is running out, and every lie, theft, and abduction she is forced to carry out may not be enough to free her family or herself from death.

READ MORE FROM AMY MCNULTY

THE NEVER VEIL SERIES

"The story is fun and engaging, featuring a female protagonist who will resonate with young teens." -School Library Journal

"...A whirlwind of time-bending adventures that immerse readers in a maelstrom of plot twists and allusions to "Beauty and the Beast" and other fairy tale love stories, while Noll's understanding of gender-based social and cultural dynamics develops." -Publishers Weekly

Nobody's Goddess (Book One in The Never Veil Series), winner of The Romance Reviews Summer 2016 Readers' Choice Award for Young Adult Romance:

In a village of masked men, each man is compelled to love only one woman and to follow the commands of his "goddess" without question. A woman may reject the only man who will love her if she pleases, but she will be alone forever. A man must stay masked until his goddess returns his love—and if she can't or won't, he remains masked forever.

Seventeen-year-old Noll's childhood friends have paired off and her closest companion, Jurij, found his goddess in Noll's own sister. Desperate to find a way to break this ancient spell, Noll instead discovers why no man has ever chosen her. She is in fact the goddess of the mysterious lord of the village, a man who refuses to let Noll have her right as a woman to spurn him.

Thus begins a dangerous game between the choice of woman and the magic of man. The stakes are no less than freedom and happiness, life and death—and neither Noll nor the veiled lord is willing to lose.

The complete The Never Veil Series is out now and is free on Kindle Unlimited! Buy in digital form on Amazon or purchase the paperbacks at the retailer of your choice.

FALL FAR FROM THE TREE DUOLOGY

Terror. Callousness. Denial. Rebellion. How the four teenage children of leaders in the duchy and the neighboring empire of Hanaobi choose to adapt to their nefarious parents' whims is a matter of survival.

Rohesia, daughter of the duke, spends her days hunting "outsiders," fugitives who've snuck onto her father's island duchy. That she lives when even children who resemble her are subject to death hardens her heart to tackle the task.

Fastello is the son of the "king" of the raiders who steal from the rich and share with the poor. When aristocrats die in the raids, Fastello questions what his peoples' increasingly wicked methods of survival have cost them.

An orphan raised by a convent of mothers, Cateline can think of no higher aim in life than to serve her religion, even if it means turning a blind eye to the suffering of other orphans under the mothers' care.

Kojiro, new heir to the Hanaobi empire, must avenge his people against the "barbarians" who live in the duchy, terrified the empress, his own mother, might rather see him die than succeed.

When the paths of these four young adults cross, they must rely on one another for survival—but the love of even a malevolent guardian is hard to leave behind.

The complete Fall Far from the Tree duology is out now and is available widely in e-book and paperback.

BALLAD OF THE BEANSTALK

A LIbrary Journal Self-e Selection.

As her fingers move across the strings of her family's heirloom harp, sixteen-year-old Clarion can forget. She doesn't dwell on the recent passing of her beloved father or the fact that her mother has just sold everything they owned, including that very same instrument that gives Clarion life. She doesn't think about how her friends treat her like a feeble, brittle thing to be protected. She doesn't worry about how to tell the elegant Elena, her best friend and first love, that she doesn't want to be her sweetheart anymore. She becomes the melody and loses herself in the song.

When Mack, a lord's dashing young son, rides into town so his father and Elena's can arrange a marriage between the two youth, Clarion finds herself falling in love with a boy for the first time. Drawn to Clarion's music, Mack puts Clarion and Elena's relationship to the test, but he soon vanishes by climbing up a giant beanstalk that only Clarion has seen. When even the town witch won't help, Clarion is determined to rescue Mack herself and prove once and for all that she doesn't need protecting. But while she fancied herself a savior, she couldn't have imagined the enormous world of danger that awaits her in the kingdom of the clouds.

A prequel to the fairy tale *Jack and the Beanstalk* that reveals the true story behind the magical singing harp.

Ballad of the Beanstalk is available now in e-book, paperback, and audiobook.

www.ingramcontent.com/pod-product-compliance
Lightning Source LLC
Chambersburg PA
CBHW030606170726
48283CB00002B/484